The Presence of Evil

The fictional works of J.T. Patten do not constitute an official release of the Central Intelligence Agency (CIA), National Security Agency (NSA), or Department of Defense (DOD) information. All statements of fact, opinion, or analysis expressed are those of the author and do not reflect the official positions or views of the CIA or any other US Government agency. Nothing in the contents should be construed as asserting or implying US Government authentication of information or CIA, NSA, or DOD endorsement of the author's views. This material has been reviewed for classification.

The Presence of Evil

A Task Force Orange Novel

J.T. Patten

LYRICAL UNDERGROUND
Kensington Publishing Corp.
www.kensingtonbooks.com

To the extent that the image or images on the cover of this book depict a person or persons, such person or persons are merely models, and are not intended to portray any character or characters featured in the book.

LYRICAL UNDERGROUND BOOKS are published by

Kensington Publishing Corp.
119 West 40th Street
New York, NY 10018

Copyright © 2019 by J.T. Patten

All rights reserved. No part of this book may be reproduced in any form or by any means without the prior written consent of the Publisher, excepting brief quotes used in reviews.

All Kensington titles, imprints, and distributed lines are available at special quantity discounts for bulk purchases for sales promotion, premiums, fund-raising, educational, or institutional use.

Special book excerpts or customized printings can also be created to fit specific needs. For details, write or phone the office of the Kensington Sales Manager: Kensington Publishing Corp., 119 West 40th Street, New York, NY 10018. Attn. Sales Department. Phone: 1-800-221-2647.

Lyrical Press and Lyrical Press logo Reg. U.S. Pat. & TM Off.

First Electronic Edition: August 2019
eISBN-13: 978-1-5161-0863-3
eISBN-10: 1-5161-0863-9

First Print Edition: August 2019
ISBN-13: 978-1-5161-0877-0
ISBN-10: 1-5161-0877-9

Printed in the United States of America

To the shadow soldiers, who carry the burdens of war back home.

The world is better with you in it.

Suicide Hotline and National Suicide Prevention Lifeline at

1-800-273-8255,

text TALK to 741741

Part I

"The Talmud says, 'If someone comes to kill you, get up early to kill him first.'"

—Amihai Ayalon, former head of Israeli Security Service ("Shin Bet")

Prelude

Chicago, Illinois

Know your enemy as you know yourself, Gebran Daouk mused as he strolled past O'Hare Airport's TSA security. He followed the black nylon rope twisting through the international terminal's queue mixed with other faceless travelers and immigrants. His clothes, expression, and body mannerisms mirrored the types of features that didn't warrant comment or question or an eye of scrutiny. At least that's what his Hezbollah handler had taught him during the past month's preparation.

In similar consideration, Gebran wore his headphones around his neck. Not over or in his ears. He wanted to be respectful and attentive to anyone who may ask him questions or give instructions to arriving international travelers. He remained to himself, kept his head low but not too low, and prepared in anticipation to hand over his authentic South American citizenship credentials to the customs officer.

Gebran spread his sweaty hands wide, wiping them against his pants as he neared the customs officer's desk.

Paranoia dripped from his scalp and down his temple.

Pendejo. He cursed himself for his idiotic fear. *Rouh ntek,* he added in Lebanese Arabic profanity.

"Passport, please." The name Lindquist was etched into the man's badge plate.

Gebran immediately obliged and handed over his documents.

The middle-aged customs officer smiled, straightening as he examined the passbook and paperwork. "Venezuela, huh? D'you speak English?"

"Yes, sir, but it can always be improved." Gebran softened his face and wiped his palms again against his legs.

"Sounds pretty good to me. Now, let's see here. Gebran Dao-uk. Da-ouk," he pronounced. "Did I say that right? I've not heard that name before."

"Just Daouk. It's Lebanese."

"Oh, Lebanon." Agent Lindquist tilted his head and zeroed in on Gebran's eyes. "That's interesting. I was a Marine." He sneered, and his smile faded like the memory of the 241 Americans killed at the Beirut barracks in 1983. "Never been to Lebanon before, though. I heard there's a few hundred Lebanese expats in Venezuela these days. What a mess that place is now. Bet you're glad to be *here*."

Daouk broke eye contact, looking to the left and right, readjusting his posture, and lifting his toes from the sweaty slides. "I am. Very much. Thank you."

"Student visa it says. J-1." Lindquist raised his eyebrows as if the statement was a question.

"Yes. That is correct." Gebran fluttered his zip-up hoodie for more airflow.

"It does get hot in here." The agent looked down again at the passport and flipped through the pages. "Where will you be going to school?"

Gebran leaned in. "It says right here." And stretched across, pointing.

Agent Lindquist leaned back in his chair with the passport reeled in. He extended his arm Heisman-trophy style, pushing the Lebanese expat away. "Please remain standing on the line."

"Sorry. University of Chicago."

The agent pursed his lips. "You must be pretty smart."

"Thank y—"

"So, what will you be doing at U of C, Mister Da-ouk," he interrupted.

"Radiation Safety Officer. Institute for Molecular Engineering."

"Impressive. Your mom must be proud." The officer stamped the passport with a glare of forced approval.

Hezbollah is proud, Gebran thought, relieved to have passed Lindquist's three-minute interrogation. Just as they said it would happen.

He was in the United States and mere feet from the exit.

"Hey," Lindquist called from behind.

Gebran kept walking. Eyes forward.

"HEY!"

A TSA guard posted in front of Gebran frowned, dropped his clipboard on the desk, and hustled toward him. The security man's brow folded and nostrils widened, his pace quickened.

Gebran's hands gushed with perspiration, his mouth instantly dry.

"Sir," the officer commanded, reaching his hand out to Gebran's shoulder and giving it a firm squeeze. He forced Gebran to turn backward.

All disembarking passenger eyes around bored into Gebran with curiosity and scorn.

As Gebran was forced around, the seated customs agent had his arm raised, passport in hand. "You'll need this again, unless you don't plan on going back home."

Gebran's chest fell when he saw what he had left behind.

He vomited on the pavement as soon as he left the airport terminal building.

Just paces behind, the Hezbollah intelligence officers operating under Venezuela's diplomatic cover were unimpressed as they tailed him to the taxi stand. Gebran Daouk was still a work in process.

* * * *

In America's defense, on Nonimmigrant Visa Application Form DS-160 and during the US Embassy visa interview of Gebran a year prior, there were indeed questions as to whether he *sought* to engage in or whether he *had ever* engaged in terrorist activities, espionage, sabotage, or genocide. He replied no, thinking honesty would not behoove his true intentions and family history. And technically, there was never a question that specifically asked Gebran Daouk if he planned to steal fissile material as leverage to gain a seat at the Hezbollah leadership table.

Still, he would have denied it.

Nine months after arrival and assimilation, Gebran hefted nearly twenty pounds of radioactive nuclide materials over a large plastic-lined metal container marked *Radioactive Waste: Store for Decay.*

It was time. His gut churned from a spike of adrenaline.

A small specimen beagle, roused by the pouring movement, yelped incessantly as it spun around in its cage, hitting its worn and wounded head on the glass with every spin. A monkey still lay on its side, eyes a solid state of red, body shaking. Rats in the next cage palpitated at maximum heart rate within their overcrowded containment glass.

Gebran struggled to focus and poured the microfine particulate matter, "death dust," like sifted mustard powder, into the collection bin. From it, a yellowish haze hovered in the air for a moment before the overhead toxin vacuum lines sucked the nuclear cloud from the restricted work lab. The molecular blend he developed reduced the high radioactivity to a one-day half-life, accelerating the rate at which atoms of the deadly material would disintegrate after exposure to oxygen. Reducing the half-life was a project concession to balance higher lethality of the dust named after the archangel of death, Azrael, with a lower risk longevity—killing and disorienting quickly, but not immediately, then becoming relatively inert.

Gebran's program advisor, Dr. Niels Planck, peered at his prized student through the fume hood's plated lens and nodded with cautious approval. There was no turning back now. Even if the two men decided not to transport the material labeled as waste, they would face federal legal charges. Both scientists had knowingly changed the receipt and disposal logs, and Dr. Planck had signed off on the most recent radioactive material inventory. He was a puppy in Gebran's hands. Played like a naïve teeny-bopper being told she was pretty. But in spy games the professor had been spotted, assessed, developed, exploited. Completely unwitting. Just as naïve.

Gebran's safety suit was suffocating. His breathing was labored. He spied to his left through the three-inch protective glass into the university's outermost lab. The stainless-steel door latch was still locked and the room empty. Cameras were already removed, boxed up, and stacked. Next week the research lab and all the stored data would be secured for good, as funding from the Army Chemical Corps toxicology program had been killed in budget cuts. And the Research, Innovation, and National Laboratories arm of the university saw no need to further seed financing for radioactive material use in warfare.

Everything had to go. Including Gebran and Dr. Planck and the contaminated animals. The animals would be euthanized in the moments to come. The scientists were headed to Syria. Or so Dr. Planck was told. The ruse Gebran told his supervisor appealed to moral convictions of ousting opportunistic Islamic State foreign fighters without endangering American soldiers' lives. Azrael could be used in a surgical strike against the jihadis without spreading to civilians or lingering in the air, requiring long-term cleanup.

Gebran slid behind Dr. Planck and deftly snatched the twelve-inch thermocouple probe from the heating table. He nestled the rounded industrial protection head nicely in his gloved palm with the menacing pointed length outward.

"I'm sorry, Professor. Azrael will not be going to Syria," the young Hezbollah agent confessed, putting a soft hand on the professor's shoulder and violently thrusting the steel rod like firing race car pistons into his mentor's vitals.

Planck's knees buckled from the pain. He struggled to move, but Gebran was holding too tight. The young student continuously punched the probe into his professor.

Satisfied, Daouk released his hold of Dr. Planck. Instead of falling to the floor, the professor slowly turned around to face his assassin. The doctor looked to Gebran, eyes wide as if he saw it all so clearly, before his lids shut and jaw fell open and his limp body folded to the ground.

Allahu Akbar, Gebran invoked to himself with a smile of accomplishment as he watched his mentor in final death throes. The budding Party of God member cast an eye to the wall clock. *Alhamdulillah.* He was to meet his handlers in two hours but planned to arrive empty-handed. *Shahid Jaddi will be so proud. May God rest his soul.* "Blessings to Hezbollah," he praised. *I am ready to retake my family's seat at the table.*

Gebran, however, did not see things as clearly as his professor in those dying minutes. Little did Daouk know, the Party and its Iranian affiliates still considered Gebran to be a work in progress. He was a loser like Jaddi and would never take that chair. His future rested solely upon the delivery of the WMD.

Gebran scooped a handful of the Azrael powder and let the fine particle cloud fall over the animal cages. He watched for a moment as the dust enveloped the animals in a foggy haze of yellow. Their unnerving screams and gasps for breath allowed the particulate angel of death safe passage to fly into their respiratory and pulmonary functions, destroying everything organic within its contact.

Chapter 1

South Carolina

H Canyon, Savannah River Nuclear Reprocessing Facility

There is a moment of silence that exists when you are about to kill a man. Drake Woolf didn't experience that quiet or the whisper of silent judgment before dealing death. In fact, he heard three distinct competing voices, and that sound was deafening in his mind. It was a trifecta of agitating inquiries and orders assaulting his consciousness as the creeping Iraqi target entered his scoped night vision view.

Among the voices, Drake's tongue clicked three times, a tic that had followed him since early childhood. Often the muted sound was a subconscious signal that his body was switching to full operational autopilot like a virtual private network tunnel shielding itself from every unwanted viral thought assaulting his connection. Depending on the situation, it could be in an isolated triad or could continue in a sequential pattern until he could control his wits.

Woolf's Armalite .300 Winchester Magnum rifle rested securely atop a Leatherback bulletproof rucksack. He pulled the buttstock tighter to his shoulder, feeling the stiffness in his body from the latest of battle wounds that had decimated his flesh. Drake willed his body to stay motionless despite the discomfort. The ground was hard; the air was East Coast–heavy but still.

He focused on the distance, target movement, his non-optimal elevation, and the fact that his head was a circus show of sounds that he rucked in his fractured mind. Focus be damned, he had trigger-time work to do and difficult conditions weren't an impediment.

His obsessive-compulsive disorder required him to recheck his range—yet again—and while he was going over the ballistic data in his head, his concentration was shattered by the newest surge of voices.

"Do you have a shot?" squawked Sean Havens, the team leader of Task Force Orange, hoping for a positive sitrep as they prepared to take out the last of the Iraqi Special Operations assaulters that had been wreaking havoc on America for the past weeks.

"Roger. I've got the shot," a chill Drake confirmed, his boss's voice resonating through an encrypted bone-conduction headset.

Kill him, Drake, ordered the neuropsychic voice that medicine still failed to subdue in Drake Woolf's diseased brain. *Kill them before they get away. Don't screw it up. You screw everything up.*

All of you shut the fuck up, Drake's inner voice of reason cursed as he fought to maintain target viability and presence of mind.

He filled his lungs and pushed the voices, both real and imagined, to the far corners of consciousness. Then, Drake slowly released his breath and eased his heart rate to rebalance mental equilibrium from the cognitive overload that was his minute-by-minute nightmare every damned moment of the day.

The Iraqi, an Iranian-run surrogate exported from Mosul, headed toward the ten-foot razor-wire-topped fence, came back into Drake's scoped view, the reticle moving in time with his heart.

Woolf steadied his eager anticipation of the kill shot.

Not yet. Wait.

Do it. Kill him now. You may need to take a second shot when you miss.

You're going to miss, the head voice taunted in the echo chamber of opinions.

Never. Drake pressed the trigger. The round was sent.

A metal mechanism clink, a subdued subsonic pop, and a dissipated flash of light emitted from the Holy Trinity of discreet ops pipe hitting: the rifle, its sound suppressor, and flash hide.

The Iraqi Special Operations Forces, or ISOF, soldier tumbled forward like a stack of toy blocks, followed by a full face-plant before reaching the fence line.

Drake chambered another round and trained the rifle on the next scampering man, a blur in his view, but Woolf knew the Iraqi was headed in only one direction—in retreat from the dead body that just flopped to the ground.

Drake pressed again.

The second man fell to eat the earth in a heavy thump.

A third ISOF assaulter, also a long way from home, was in full sprint desperate to flee from his falling comrades.

Drake delivered his final judgment in the form of 180 grains of metal a couple hundred yards out.

The Iraqi operator had to have known how this would go down, and such was likely his last thought before all streams of consciousness evaporated like the exploding pink mist from his bullet-ruptured head.

"All secure," Drake announced to his team. Woolf scanned the fallen bodies again for good measure.

Shit. The second Iraqi was fumbling with his chest. Woolf suspected he had popped the man's chest cavity but perhaps spared the heart. The Iraqi was a goner, but why let Murphy's Law have a say in the final verdict. Last thing they needed was a man screaming like a dying rabbit in the quiet of the night.

Drake's weapon coughed out a final message in the international language of assaulters: "You're dead, shithead. Stay down."

The ISOF operator's wounded body hiccupped on impact, and he became motionless upon receiving the deadly news from Drake in a ripping translation that ended his traitorous life.

"Belay last. Enemy suppressed. Targets all down. Had to send a security round. You're clear to approach," Drake confirmed on the closed-circuit channel before Havens could radio in whether a fourth bogie had appeared. "Now maybe we can finally call it quits before the FBI gets a lock on us," he muttered to himself.

Unless there's someone else we trained who's waiting to kill us.

You did what had to be done, the voice of Drake's deceased father chimed in to the chorus of voices refilling the Man from Orange's head. *Can't talk now, Pop.* And with that, Drake Woolf popped four lithium, the last of the mania-reduction pills, to quell the voices in his head and relax his OCD tendencies. He prepared to move his shit to cover the rest of his domestic killing squad from a tree line as they collected the dead bodies for disposal.

While grabbing his kit, he checked the status of his earlier launch of an autopilot drone feed. Drake examined the real-time video confirming no additional movements from the facility or fence line. Once the team was safe and sound, he could get to his other electronics gear, and Drake would see if the cell phone signals on the Iraqi target list died like their owners. Maybe then the killing spree that had gone on for weeks would stop. But with the Iranian Republican Guards Corps General Shirazian, a Qods Force spy runner on the lam, and new intelligence coming in from the NSA to the team, Woolf knew hunting season remained open and the bag limit endless. Especially since Drake's task force was sanctioned and fully funded, and there was literally no stopping it now from hunt-and-destroy missions across the fifty states. Even if someone wanted to, they would have to find the team first.

That would be no easy feat.

FBI Special Agent Tresa Halliday was learning that challenge the hard way, ever since she was tasked as a counterintelligence ghost to hunt these military lawbreakers down. Fortunately, she was over five hundred miles from their whereabouts and not the wiser of their mission or all of their names, save for the name of Warren Drake Woolf. And that was because she had hunted the hunter and nearly snared him on a couple occasions. It was inconvenient for Woolf because, as dangerous as she was, somehow Tresa Halliday had found a small opening in Drake's humanity. Like the persistent voices in his head, he couldn't shake her from his mind.

He knew a life no different, and he sure as shit was no redeeming Ernest Hemingway character. He had no drive for honor, self-interest, or sense of purpose. War weariness, however, he had plenty of. But routine held him hostage to continuously going through the motions on the gerbil wheel of combat life.

Drake simply existed in the morass of black operations. And technically, as a US citizen identity, Warren Drake Woolf existed no more. He was fully buried in black.

Chapter 2

Woolf's main job was technical intelligence, specifically SIGINT, but shooting was second nature. His Ranger tab, if he wore anything standard issue, would show that he had earned the ability to kill silently. His body count proved it.

Intel was Ops and Ops was Intel. He was the wish-list vision of special operations leadership who wanted a shooter to be a Harvard grad who could win a bar fight. They'd have to settle for MIT distance learning Computer Science classes with Drake.

Operating on US soil, however, was still new, and it came with its own challenges, such as not getting caught and landing on death row. Hence, Drake Woolf's new uniform was whatever he needed to wear to get the job done and disavow himself from the buried-in-black unit. It was similar to when he formally worked for the Intelligence Support Activity. Orange. At least before it was decommissioned by President Ross and tucked under yet another highly classified Special Access Program and code-named ICEPICK. Even on the black books, Task Force Orange no longer existed.

Drake lifted his mini-binoculars for a moment while he packed things up. He was curious as to what was taking the big man, Lars, so long, despite the fact that the Scandinavian was an overweight retiree.

Ex-Chicago detective Lars Bjorklund was the third man on Project ICEPICK's disavowed domestic assault team's forward element. As the subject matter expert in forensics and how not to get caught by authorities, he had the dirty work of cleanups, cover-ups, and discreet logistical planning. The role served him well as a former dirty cop. He was also the brother-in-law to Sean Havens, making him both kin and in constant danger, which was okay for the recent retiree who found a renewed sense of purpose with the crew doing "God's work" to keep America safe. Or so they told themselves as they broke the US Constitution and most laws known to man, with the exception of kinky stuff.

* * * *

Lars tried to key the fist microphone confirming his readiness to body snatch the dead Iraqis while he fought to keep from busting his ass down the hill. As his over three hundred pounds jiggled with every jarring step, his wired earpiece flopped freely over his shoulder while a small backpack and large canister with hose and nozzle bounced from side to shoulder. The big Swede tried to control his descent, but his aged knees weren't having it.

Should have kept my ass in Scottsdale, he thought as his foot clipped a rock, sending him ass over teakettle.

He came to a rolling halt at the bottom of the hill, right next to the bodies.

"Lars, Lars, what the hell?" a tiny voice yelled.

Lars grabbed his earphone and shoved it into his ear. He was breathing heavy from the fall, and when he finally caught his breath said, "You are going to have to bring the truck to me."

Fortunately for the team, the three Iraqis had chosen a part of the fence line along a wooded service road that was obscured from guard towers securing the K Area Material Storage facility that housed excess plutonium.

"Did you just bust your ass?" Havens demanded, his laughter pouring through the earpiece.

"Got it all on camera," Woolf said a moment later. "Got a good shot of his ass crack too."

Lars grunted to his feet, tugging at his pants before raising his hand high, middle finger extended. He wasn't sure exactly where Drake was but knew the man saw him from his overwatch position.

Lars ran his hands over the first dead Iraqi, cataloguing what he found in the man's pockets aloud. "Got a cheap-ass Hi-Point 9 mil, some bolt cutters, burner phone, Chicom grenades." Each item went into a bag, just like it had when he was a cop in Chicago.

Out of all the stuff he pulled, oddly enough it was the wallet that gave Lars pause.

"What the hell?" he muttered.

"Whatcha got, Lars?"

"This shitbag brought his fake DL, credit card, and room key," he said.

"So, what? He's a dumbass, what can I tell you?" Havens replied.

Something wasn't right. While Lars wasn't an experienced operator, he had done his time on the streets and knew when something didn't smell right.

No way in hell a guy breaks into a nuclear materials management facility with a ghetto blaster and a wallet full of ID.

There was something tugging at his mind that he couldn't place. Something about the scene just wasn't right.

An op like this required more sophisticated gear than what the first dead man possessed. Having attacked and been attacked by jihadist killers in the past weeks, he expected his adversaries to have better gear. He brushed the thought aside and concentrated on using the UV light to scan the ground for exposed blood.

When he found a puddle, Lars sprayed the area with a chemical foam designed to break down the blood proteins after the bodies were removed. There would still be minute traces, but the FBI forensics were going to have to bring their A game to find it.

But if Special Agent Halliday learned of it, she'd be back on their scent, and Sean would definitely not get a chance to put her in another sleeper hold.

The longer Lars worked the cleanup area, the stronger the feeling in his gut grew. It wasn't so much what he was seeing, but what he *wasn't* seeing that had him on edge. Finally, he gave up and pressed the mic.

"Alpha-3 to…"—he fumbled with the protocol—"to…you guys, over."

"Whatcha got, Alpha-3?" Havens responded, his Chicago accent coming through. "I'm about two hundred meters out."

There was a brief pause. "Something isn't right here," Lars started. "If our intel said these guys were targeting building 105-K, that plutonium would be sealed in a welded container. And then nested in larger containers."

"What are you thinking?" Havens asked, probing for more.

"I don't know," Lars said, standing straight and panning the light across the scene. "Where's their semi truck, and big-ass army of mercenary goons, and blow torches, not to mention a lifting hoist? This asshole tried to knock off a DOE nuke site with a hundred-dollar pistol and a pair of Harbor Freight bolt cutters. It's like amateur hour."

"Just tag 'em and bag 'em. We will figure the rest out on the road."

"Copy that," Lars said, unrolling the black heavy vinyl body bag and stuffing the first dead terrorist inside.

He laid a second bag beside his dead compatriot and restarted his pat down. There was no wallet on this one, but there was a mobile device in the jeans back pocket. "They aren't even giving you guys 5.11 tactical digs. Iranian sanctions must be working somewhat," Lars muttered to himself.

Bjorklund pulled the dead man over and began searching inner front pockets and a small pouch with a grenade, as well. It was dark but close enough to the fence perimeter's security lighting that he could see a shadowy sphere rocking to a standstill on the ground. *Two grenades.* The second had rolled out, and it took Lars a moment to realize the safety pin was likely removed and the spoon released to initiate the fuse assembly.

FUCK.

Detective Bjorklund had seen enough action movies in his day to know that he had likely already lost two to three seconds of his now-fleeting final moments of life. He couldn't escape the roughly five-meter fatality radius, and Sean was driving inwards of twenty meters of the explosive device.

Lars tried to wave off Sean while rolling the dead Iraqi back over the M67 fragmentation grenade. Lars fumbled his grip in both fear and frenzy, and lost his balance, falling closer to the device.

A deep boom sounded. White sparks spit from the ground like a fountain, and a bright flash ruptured the night sky.

* * * *

Sean braked the Ford Transit hard and moved to shield himself, arm across his forehead. In the blink of an eye, however, he had watched his brother-in-law tossed over like a rag doll surrounded by the exploding light, and a large chunk of the big Swede separated and sailed through the air.

As if on cue from the booby trap's detonation, the woods came alive, spitting fire at Sean Havens's vehicle.

Chapter 3

A quarter mile away but still on the Savannah River Site, Iranian General Shirazian stood at the bank's edge listening to the unfolding firefight across the man-made cooling pond. He turned with a continuous nod of approval to the man standing at his side, Waleed El Aissami—Hezbollah's South American External Security leader.

"You see, Waleed, as I told you earlier, it is not the FBI following our soldiers. They would never come with so few men. This is something new. Something we have never seen from the Americans," he said in Lebanese Arabic. "And now it will be no more."

The staccato salvo ensued as a dramatic backdrop to the conversation.

"General, I do not understand why you baited them here?"

"Is it not a distant location from our planned Chicago attack? Does it still not convince America that their nuclear facilities will remain in constant attack?" the general tossed back.

"But with respect, you have come here at great personal risk. Brought me here at great risk. This should be handled by your operational leader, Mohsen. Surely, we are not here to gloat."

"Mohsen was a fool. He named South Carolina in our communications, and they tracked us here, as I suspected. The news media will be in a frenzy, adding to American fears and creating new costs to secure nuclear facilities being targeted by terrorists around the country. What you and your Unit 910 men will do next will maximize fear with reality. No more idle threats. Attacks on their homeland will create fear. This is why I have brought you. Fear wins half the battles. Fear keeps us strong. Fear creates economic drain. We will kill many but not for killing's sake. We are killing and instilling fear, so we do not risk our own safety to kill more. This is your future in South America."

The Hezbollah foreign special activities leader gave a polite nod to what he already knew, but he still was curious where his lower-level contact was. "And where is Mohsen now?"

"With God." The Iranian replied with no emotion and deflected. "It is the will of my leadership to have only myself or the Modarris contact the young Chicago scientist, Gebran Daouk, at this point. Because of your cover through the Venezuelan embassy in Chicago, we want no exposure that can link this operation to your Tarik El Aissami or Nassereddine's drug networks in America. Venezuela has enough problems as does our country. The Modarris can work with the gang, but we will not discuss your narcotics and other business arrangements. Similarly, we will no longer communicate openly. When possible, use a messenger. Designate only one or two of your soldiers to maintain communication through encrypted messaging to you."

"I will spread the word, as best possible."

"Please..." General Shirazian stretched his hand outward to the water. "The phone we gave you. Throw it."

Between sonic report cracks sounded a splash, and the two men turned their backs on the firefight opposite the water. Four Iranian-trained Lebanese guards with Venezuelan diplomatic passports tucked in their jackets stood waiting to escort their protectees.

Almost in an afterthought, the general addressed a guard in Farsi, "Do not let these Iraqi dogs cross the waters. Their services are no longer required. And wherever they came from, Baghdad, Basrah, Mosul, have our contacts pay a tribute to their families through your Unit 3800. We have completed the first phase. We will rejoin in Chicago tomorrow with the Modarris. The American president Ross will feel the bite back of his sanctions and withdrawal from our Plan of Action nuclear agreement."

The shooting unexpectedly stopped.

No one in the party moved or said a word.

General Shirazian broke the silence after nearly a minute when a scream echoed over the water from the woods. His voice cracked. "We must all go, now. Quickly. Something is wrong."

Chapter 4

Bullets snapped over Drake's head as he struggled to move parallel to the shooters. Their haphazard shooting was a jihadi spray-and-pray technique, which further pissed him off since the damned Deltas and Special Forces had worked tirelessly for years in Iraq to train the operators properly.

He maneuvered closer but didn't have a shot in the wooded cover and didn't want to give away his position. Suppressive fire wouldn't do much good now that Lars was dead. The barrage of bullets at Havens in the truck was another shock to the senses. Running to Sean would be suicide in the cone of fire. But Drake was no longer the indecisive, scared teen frozen in a Tunisian kitchen while his parents were gunned down nearly a lifetime ago. No, he was selected for the task force because he was an effective and remorseless killing machine.

His tongue clicked, but Drake was already game on. He dropped his rifle and swung the Leatherback over his head and tightened the two soft armor panels tight against front and back.

He snapped his Griptilian open, leading the charge with its steel blade. Woolf estimated three, maybe four, shooters from his vantage. They were spaced four to five feet of each other from what he could judge by the flashes, and they were just inside of the overgrowth before the service road.

The ambush assaulters must have approached from the southwest, which was out of his initial view and the drone's flight pattern.

Drake cut into the trees to come up from behind. Salvos like this didn't last long without returning fire, so Drake hurried along before they moved from their current position toward Havens.

He moved from cover to cover behind his attackers, careful to avoid sudden movement that could catch the eye of one of the assaulters.

Drake made his approach from their rear, knowing better than to try to slice their carotid artery. That shit was for the movies. To kill a man with full assurance you had to drive the knife into the base of the skull severing the spinal cord and brain stem.

Drake made do with his position and stabbed straight into the Iraqi's neck just to the side of the larynx.

He yanked the knife sideways and away; the knife's upper serrated edge ruptured the carotid and jugular blood bank line. Ripping the blade from the neck, Drake pulled the knife away, his legs already charging for the next man.

The second operator saw the blurred shape and turned.

Drake plunged the knife into the man's arm, felt the blade grind against the bone, and knew he'd missed the artery.

Shit.

The man spun, and Drake tore the blade free, the handle slick with blood. The Iraqi swung the rifle toward his face, but Woolf had already slipped low, spearing the ISOF soldier deep in the chest.

The man swung back, but Drake stayed low. He retracted and then repunched the knife up and under the ribs to the liver and made a carving sweep.

Feel it.

Drake hit another area, stabbing the metal into the leg crook of the man's groin.

Again, the Man from Orange was on the move.

The third Iraqi had heard the commotion and charged Woolf. Drake launched for a front strike to the throat but missed as the man deflected the attack.

The knife sank from high to low into the man's breast meat. The Iraqi screamed but had the presence of mind and quick reaction speed to hammer Drake in the head with a flying elbow.

Woolf was dazed and breathless. He stumbled backward, stopped by a tree trunk, the knife still stuck in the Iraqi's chest.

The Iraqi wasted no time and was upon Drake, who was shaking off the dizzying sparkles. The man claw-gripped Drake's shoulders, bringing him in close.

Woolf felt the man's balance shift. The Iraqi's weapon dangled from a sling harness and pressed between both fighters. Drake head-butted his opponent, smashing his skull into the man's nose and mouth. Woolf seized the swinging submachine gun, twisted it into the man, and squeezed the trigger.

Nothing.

Shit! Didn't we teach you Iraqis anything?

The Iraqi pulled a side arm and fired from the hip while Drake thrust the submachine gun up and into his foe's face with a sickening crunch as the handgun popped twice.

Drake's ballistic protection took the rounds, but bullet momentum and impact solidly punched the wind out of Woolf like a direct mule kick, knocking him back and dropping him to his knees. His lungs depleted and gasping for air, he willed his tingling legs to shoot him forward. His foe moving in, Drake took hold of his knife from the man's chest and backhanded it out and into the Iraqi's neck, wrenching it around and out until they both fell into foliage and onto the hard ground.

Catching a few quick breaths, his head still shocked from lack of oxygen, Drake knew that a fourth man would have engaged, so he pushed off backward out of the brush area and into the access road in a stumbling run toward Sean Havens or whatever was left of him.

Please, no. Please, no.

Chapter 5

Drake ran through the gun smoke that crept from the tree line and hung over Sean Havens's van. The Ford Transit was riddled with holes, and his feet crunched over the broken glass from obliterated windows. "Sean," his voice croaked upon seeing unmistakable blood spatter on the seat, visible even under heavy shadow and the darkness of the night. The smoke stuck to the back of his throat, choking him.

Drake expected to see Havens slumped in a bloody mess but was panicked to find no one.

"Sean!" he called again.

"Hey," a familiar voice grunted from the rear.

Drake swiveled, expecting to see Sean with his usual smirk as he came up from behind.

Sean wasn't there.

"Over here," Havens redirected, his voice strained and low to the ground.

"Oh, fuck." Drake's eyes followed a blood smear to a shadowed heap that was Havens lying on the ground. He was in bad shape. "How bad?"

"Swiss cheese bad."

Woolf dropped to his knees, squishing in a small puddle of blood. Havens was the closest Drake had come to having a friend in years. He clawed at Havens's clothes, running his hand over and in his shirt. It was dark and Sean's body was soaked with blood, making it hard to get a visual, but his fingertips felt no initial holes.

"That tickles."

"Still with the jokes?"

"Drake, I'm pretty sure we'll be surrounded by security guards shortly. You can massage me later. My hand and foot are the most jacked up. I think I'm okay beyond that."

"Okay. Should take ten to fifteen minutes before local authorities can get out here and through the checkpoints. They'll come from the north and east gates. I'm thinking we head to our entry point before the Allendale gate."

"Dude, I don't need a map. And we don't need another situation like Georgetown. We need to *go*."

"Yeah." Drake grabbed Havens under the arms to give him leverage up. "I don't know what to say about Lars. I fucked up, Sean." Emotion stole his voice for a moment. "I thought the guy was down."

"It's not on you," Sean assuaged. His voice also strained with emotion, and physical pain, to boot. "He was a trained cop, and I put him to the task. This is all on me."

"I'll go back and try to get him when you're in the truck."

"Torch him. We need to scram."

"What?"

"I can't help you carry him. And I won't just leave him. He wanted to be cremated anyway with no frills. There's a gas can in a metal box in the rear. Hopefully if it was shot up there's enough left. Road flares are in the box across from it. Light up the van, then give Lars a Valhalla Viking send-off. We're not going to be able to get him in and get away. He would see that as a waste. Just do it."

"You're serious."

"Do it. Really, we have to. AO is still hot, and this is as good of a setting as he'd ever want. He wanted to die a hero," Sean lied. "I'll head for your vehicle. I'm not going fast, so I won't be leaving without you, but you need to hurry. Just put it behind you right now."

Drake understood the sense of urgency and their dire situation. He didn't need to be told twice, despite his qualms.

In the quiet of their surroundings, Drake heard the distant turn of an engine from behind and through the woods. Giving a second of thought to the map he memorized the day before coming on-site, Woolf knew it was coming from a service road beyond the water.

Drake redirected the drone with his wrist monitor as he grabbed stuff from the van with a free hand. Rotating the drone and expanding the map, Drake spotted the dark object, tapped it on the screen and sent the drone after it.

* * * *

It wasn't okay burning Lars like that. It was unconscionable to leave him behind. The image of Lars in the explosion was seared into Sean's mind, and it constantly looped in his mind. The ancillary thought of Havens's daughter being fatherless was his sole justification for right or wrong. He refused to take a chance on being busted.

As he hopped down the dirt road, the emerging firelight from Lars reached out to Sean in the shadows. Havens's chest heaved in silent agony. He squeezed his bullet-broken wrist to minimize the flopping compound fracture and the pain it caused, but at least he was still alive.

Havens had dashed out of the van as the melee started, but not before one of the first fire bursts sniped his right wrist from the wheel, passing to his left shoulder. His ankle was tagged as soon as his foot dropped to the ground. As he rolled out and low to the ground, another had ripped through his bicep. All the while, the only thing he could think of was how he would tell his daughter, Maggie, that Uncle Lars was the latest victim of Sean Havens's curse. Aside from his daughter, there was no family left in their world. At least no one who hadn't asked him to stay far away.

* * * *

Drake's American Eagle drone followed an autonomous mission plan program. Its carbon fiber frame cut through the night air guided by a locked object tracker. With a FLIR multispectral zoom camera streaming real-time HD in night vision, the UAS buzzed along at thirty knots. Without an explosive payload, all the drone could do for the next two miles was intelligence collection. But in the first minute, it had everything Drake needed.

Havens stepped on a road divot and tumbled over. Like a hawk snatching a rabbit, Drake was already running up from behind and Ranger-rolled Sean, scooping him up in a fluid fireman's carry as he sprinted to the Jeep Cherokee still ten yards ahead.

"Fuck, Havens, I must have missed one. You're completely soaked with blood."

At the forefront of Drake's mind in caring for Sean were bleed out and shock. Both of which would be tough to prevent while hightailing it out of there with no medevac to call in.

"You still with me buddy?"

"Yeah," Sean grunted as he bounced along. "Wrist is the bad one. It's bleeding pretty good. Too dark to tell about the ankle. Round's still in there." Havens grimaced again. "Same with one in my upper shoulder."

Drake's SUV was nestled near the tree line, but at a slight road bend that blocked it from view of the responding vehicles.

"Okay, man." Woolf loaded Sean into the passenger seat and sloughed off his jacket and the pack. He tore a sleeve off his shirt and yanked the straps off the Leatherback to use as a tourniquet. "Make a fist with your left hand and raise it to your armpit."

With his fist between his arm and his side, Drake leaned into Sean's right arm, putting pressure indirectly to the brachial artery while he wrapped Havens's broken and bleeding wrist. "You sure you're breathing okay?"

More perimeter alarms sounded in the night, and headlights snaked toward them from as far as Drake could see.

Sean grunted.

"Okay, buddy. Hang in there. I'm getting us out."

Keeping the headlights off, Drake exfiltrated the SRS K Area along Four Mile Creek, slowing only on the other side of the woods to redirect the UAS.

Havens slipped in and out of lucidity as they drove.

Red-and-blue lights flashed as responders approached on the narrow access road. It was hardly the time for chicken, and without headlights on, any armed security responder would surely stop them if a collision didn't happen first. Drake slowed and pulled over to the right.

"What are you doing?" Sean mumbled. "This is not getting us out."

"I'll tell you if it works. Glad you're still alive."

Woolf returned the manual UAS control to his mobile device. Redirecting it yet again, he lowered its altitude and sent it toward the oncoming vehicle. Device in hand, Drake returned to the road and punched it.

"Fuck me," Sean exclaimed with a hint of lift in his voice. "If I don't die in the next minute, I'll die in the next two."

Drake watched the road and red dot of the UAS with one flitting eye as the oncoming car sped toward the drone and its camera. "Three, two, one, action." Woolf activated the blinding lumen bulbs on the UAS.

The oncoming emergency response vehicle veered quickly to the left, going off-road and onto the reed-filled mud flats.

The plan would have been a bigger success had there not been another vehicle following close behind the lead. The drone flew straight into the second emergency vehicle's windshield—an unexpected bird strike. Drake flashed on his own headlights and flipped the brights, praying the startled driver would regain control and get the hell out of the way.

Instead, the vehicle swerved toward Drake and Sean, out of control.

Chapter 6

Drake gunned the gas toward the oncoming headlights.

"What the hell are you doing?" Havens lurched back in his seat, staring death in the eyes.

"Assault driving."

"That's not a thing!" Sean gripped the seat belt strap with his good hand. "Oh, shit. This is gonna hurt."

Drake spun his wheel to the right then quickly back left, hitting the brake and sending their ride's rear outward.

The oncoming vehicle nearly sideswiped Drake's SUV but caught the back bumper, spinning their SUV back inward.

Woolf cranked the wheel opposite and stomped the gas again, controlling the spinout, fishtailing like a breeched marlin with Sean flopping side to side.

The emergency response vehicle spun off the road.

While Woolf would never wish ill will to any innocent victim resulting from the task force's actions, he checked his side and rearview mirrors to ensure he was no longer being pursued. The welfare of the innocent was a secondary thought. Most vehicles had airbags, he convinced himself. His only concern was getting Havens to medical care ASAP.

Of course, there was also the flashing red and white lights of the gate that they were closing in on, which was their next hurdle.

Drake drove the Jeep steering along the straightaway with his wrists as he changed the band on his Sentry phone to dial an open line.

"Nine-one-one," the operator answered. "What is your emergency?"

"Ma'am, this is the Radiological Control Group calling from the Savannah River Site," Drake lied. "We've had an accident and need to ensure roads are blocked coming and going from the north, west, and east entrance. There is some confusion about a breach, but we had a Red Team exercise go bad. I need you to alert all nearby hospitals to expect incoming paramedic busses. Hazmat is en route. Please contact local authorities and direct them to our website for the SRS Operational Radiological Emergency Response Plan. I'm running back to check wounded." He hung up.

Havens laughed then coughed and grimaced from the injuries.

Woolf caught Sean's face of pain, and in the fleeting light of passing streetlamps he saw blood coming from Havens's lips. He placed his hand on Sean's leg. "I'm getting you to the contingency site. We'll get you all patched up." He hoped. "Hang on, pal."

* * * *

The task force was nascent. Drake didn't know exactly how many months behind the scenes the small unit had been in the making, despite the recent weeks of operations. Drake Woolf had been operating on the fly in response to a direct threat that had killed dozens of military personnel. The same affiliates who had just ambushed them at the storage site.

The enemy were comprised of Iraqis formerly trained by Deltas and other government agencies, who had been retaliated against by their own people for aiding the Americans. Driven by vengeance and manipulation by local agents of the Iranian Revolutionary Guards Corps—Qods Force— these "Mohawks" and Iraqi Special Operations Forces had hunted down their trainers and coalition partners. Fortunately, Drake, his spymaster boss, Sean Havens, and ex-cop, Lars Bjorklund had managed to take out the known threat. They used Drake's expertise in signals intelligence and direct action to drive the rooting out while being supported logistically and technologically from the NSA by an ex-Brit program director, Sebastian, and two analysts. One witting to the program, one unwitting.

About the only thing the task force had really planned was this mission to thwart an unknown attack in South Carolina by the remaining Iraqi hunter killers. Within the plan was identifying in the logistics layout a local area surgeon who was a prior Special Forces medic turned spook. Now, that former 18-Delta medical sergeant ran an urgent care clinic, which would suit their needs perfectly, and since he was a trusted agent, the team wouldn't have to worry about a physician's mandate to report the gunshot wounds.

That would bring questions, and questions would bring more cops, and more cops would bring the Feds, and that would put Special Agent

Tresa Halliday back on their ass. And for as much as Drake knew, the FBI counterterrorism agent was a danger to their mission. He hadn't had a crush on a female like this since his teens, and that was nearly twenty years ago.

"Open the gate," the Allendale south gate security captain ordered the low-wage contract watch officer. "Just got a call from a Department of Energy security team lead. They had an accident doing a Red Team exercise by K Area." He figured that must be them coming in now. "Said they got a man hurt pretty bad. Must be what all that radio chatter's about."

"Red Team. Shit. Hope they didn't breach our sector."

The security captain put down his sleeve of Hostess donut gems and headed to the back of the little shanty. "I'm going to kill the camera and check the feeds, so our asses are covered just in case."

"And that's why they pay you the big bucks, Dale." The watch officer reached across the desk and swiped a snack.

With gates open wide and tire shredders down, Drake Woolf ignored the ten-mile-an-hour speed zone by the guard shack and shot through the checkpoint, fishtailing as he turned onto the main road and flew past state and local police with a hand wave out the window.

Chapter 7

   Tresa Halliday looked straight ahead into the mirror, thinking how much she hated Washington, DC. Above the bottles of spirits, she could see a cute guy's reflection three barstools over. He had dark hair that faded into a closely shaven beard. His cheekbones and jawline were pronounced. She liked his flannel shirt, which Halliday didn't see enough of in the National Capital Region. The handsome man, maybe late twenties, hopefully early to mid-thirties, was the only thing in this Georgetown Irish pub that reminded her of home, despite the hipster bend to rugged northern Wisconsin or Yooper manhood. Although, Wisconsin wasn't really home; Cicero, Illinois, was. But not many guys wore flannels in Cicero, either, unless they were Latino gang cholos, and she hadn't lived there since she was a child. Once they fled.
   "Same?" the bartender responded to her push of the empty pint.
   "Yeah. Harp. Another Jameson, too. And hey"—she leaned in over the bar rail—"get whatever the guy in the flannel is drinking and give him a Jameson too."
   The bartender turned and nodded. "Going in, huh?"
   "Girl's gotta sometimes strap on a pair if that itch is gonna get scratched."
   He smiled. "I'm guessing you don't need to try too hard. Coming up. Harp, two Jamesons, and a Michelob Ultra with a lemon." He winked and shrugged his shoulder.
   "He's drinking a Michelob Ultra with a lemon?" She looked back up into the mirror to check. "Pussy," she accused. "Guess that makes me a lesbo tonight. I could put the softie under the table in fifteen minutes."
   The bartender just laughed as he cleaned another glass.

The round would make six beers and three shots since she bellied up, and that wasn't too long ago. Just short of six feet tall in bare feet, Halliday could put any woman away in a drinking contest, and most men. Except, of course, those who gave her a run for her money in the northern Midwest. And forget about the Indian reservations in the upper lakes chains. Those day drinkers were pros, even as they moved from bar to bar on snowmobiles, or sleds, as they called them.

It had been only days since she lost the trail of Drake Woolf and his band of merry men. Woolf had saved her life; his partner had put her in a sleeper hold, knocking Halliday out until she awoke receiving accolades from responding police for saving the secretary of state. Her boss, head of FBI Counterintelligence, Earl Johnson, had encouraged her to just roll with it and get back on the scent to put an end to these rogue operators who were in blatant violation of the law.

"Hi, I thought I should probably do the shot with you, right?" the man from the mirror said, almost shoulder to shoulder.

Tresa turned her head and attention to the conquest target. God, she hoped it would be a conquest. It had been so long, she might call it a hundred-year pilgrimage. "Hey, yeah. I'm Tresa." She extended her hand right into his hand holding an overfilled shot. "Sorry."

"No, it's cool." He swapped hands and looked around for a napkin to wipe his hands.

You could use your pants, sport.

"Thanks for the drink and shot. I don't usually do shots, but cheers, Theresa."

Tresa, but whatever. "Cheers." They clinked and swallowed. "Whoo. And you are?"

"I am damned glad to meet you. Mind if I get my beer?"

Avoided the name. Whatever. As he grabbed his beer and barstool, Tresa did a quick mental inventory of her undergarments. Sports bra and a gray cotton pair of Jockey hip-huggers. Tough. He was getting laid. He won't care. Legs might be a bit rough, and the…well, best get him a few more drinks.

"'Scuse me, can I squeeze in here a bit?" he who remained nameless, holding a beer and a chair, asked the conjoined couple sitting closest to Tresa.

The conquest stood about six feet. *That will be fine,* she thought. His voice was a bit higher-pitched than she would have liked. His frame a little wirier than he looked in the bar's mirror. His face, still perfect. Exactly her type. He could have been related to Drake Woolf. She smiled as she sighed. But he wasn't Drake Woolf, and it pissed her off that that sucked.

When Earl Johnson phoned her in the next moment, she had mixed emotions about picking up. If Earl was calling this late, it meant the task force had been spotted. Game over for boot-knocking.

"Excuse me." She shrunk to her prospect, feeling both embarrassed and annoyed. His dark eyes were gorgeous. Teeth looked clean. Yes, still very doable. "Hey, boss," Tresa answered. *Don't go away,* she mouthed, feeling a little tipsy. More than she initially thought. She gave a light parting brush of her hand on his shoulder, feminine when she wanted to be.

"Apologies. It sounds like I've caught you at an inopportune time, SA Halliday."

"It would have been worse in an hour or two. Can you hear me? It's a little loud in my quiet Quantico apartment," she joked. "Neighbors are loud. I think they're agents from Alabama."

"I can barely hear you. Will you please step out of the bar? If you want a bar with some actual character, consider McClellan's. I suppose you prefer the type with hockey and cheesesteaks though. No matter."

Tresa took a deep breath and chose not to ask how he knew her whereabouts aside from the obvious. Plain and simple, Earl just knew things. "Yes, hang on a sec. I'll go outside." She held up a finger to the nameless man sitting on his stool like an anxious puppy. *My boss,* she mouthed. "Be right back," she enunciated again, pointing to the door.

The stool puppy nodded, implicitly assured that he may get a treat later.

A few short weaves around patrons and Halliday was in the cool air of old Georgetown. "Sorry. So what's up? Usually it's me calling you late in the night."

"Indeed. I think you may want to go for a ride."

You have no idea how close I was to getting one. "Ride to where?"

"We think the task force was just in South Carolina. You can fly out of Reagan. Bureau plane. Go to the private executive aircraft entrance. Do you know where it is?"

"Yes, I…" She decided against more smartass comments with Earl. He already considered her a second-class citizen. "I'll need to Uber it. I've got a few under my belt tonight."

"I'll have an agent waiting for you in Georgia. The incident happened in a nuclear waste repository just over the state border. Seven bodies."

"Shit."

"From the information we received, I suspect one may be from the task force."

Halliday's chest tightened. "Oh, wow. Which one? I mean how can you tell?"

"I'll let you tell me once you get there. Again, my apologies, but thought you'd like to be tapped for this trip. I'm running interference for the moment. You're the lead for now, but I'm releasing the site to the local office after you get a head start on the scene."

"Okay. Thanks, Earl. You owe me some sex, though." She cringed as soon as the words passed her lips.

"I don't even know what that is."

"Earl, did you just make a joke?"

"Happy hunting, Agent Halliday."

Two girls walked around Tresa to enter the pub. "Hey, if I give you guys twenty bucks for the effort, will you pay the bartender here sixty for my tab? I gotta go."

"Sure," one responded eagerly, with hand held out.

"Thanks," said Halliday, trying to get one last peek through the door. "And, hey, there's a pretty cute guy at the bar sitting near an open stool. Dark hair, trim beard, flannel. If you're into the lumberjack thing."

The second girl's face wrinkled. "Is his name Dan? That's my boyfriend." Her head cocked, her eyes squinted.

Tresa handed over the cash and turned to the street. "Of course, he's your boyfriend." She cringed then chastised herself despite knowing a plastic spoon threesome with Ben & Jerry's Oatmeal Cookie Chunk ice cream was the outcome she'd really end up choosing if a one-night stand was truly on the table. Even if she was originally from that one part of town in Cicero where girls rarely, if ever, said no.

Chapter 8

Drake's mouth clicked. He fidgeted his hands on the wheel. It wasn't the first time he had transported a casualty, but it was admittedly the first colleague he'd truly bonded with in past years. The thought of losing him rattled Woolf.

Drake glanced over at Havens again. He was in bad shape. Sean's breathing looked shallow from what Woolf could tell by the low-light chest movement and Havens's slipping lucidity.

Twelve more miles. Tension pneumothorax. We'll need a fourteen-gauge needle initial pneumo treatment to let air out. Occlusive dressing. That just buys time. Maybe they can do a thoracotomy. Then need to get you to a thoracic surgeon for exploratory surgery. Sebastian will need to evac us to...

He's going to die. You have no one left. They're all gone. You let everyone die.

"No, I don't!" Drake yelled. He slapped the wheel and stomped the floor in a fit of rage.

"Dude! What the hell?" Havens was startled, wide-eyed. He leaned away, a little freaked by the tantrum.

"Fuck!" Drake wiped his face as if his hands could reset his mind. The lithium wasn't working even with a megadose. Doctors were never an option. "Sorry, man. Just trying to decide if I need to let some pressure out of your chest."

"For what?" Havens wiped his lip and saw the blood in the glow of the dash electronics. "Damn, *you* got me good."

"Me? What are you talking about?"

"Bit my lip when you lifted me over your shoulder. Cut the shit out of the inside. Might need a stitch there, too."

"Are you serious?" Drake broke a smile. "I thought you took one to the chest that I missed." He let his head fall back on the headrest in relief.

"Drake, how are the meds holding out?"

"I think I'm doing better."

Sean stiffened and changed the topic. "I saw you put something on Lars's body from your pocket."

"You were supposed to be hopping away."

"I wasn't."

"I had a quarter in my pocket. Thought it was right."

"Lars wouldn't have known what the tradition meant, but he would have been honored if he did," Havens acknowledged, recalling the practice when soldiers put a quarter on the grave of a fallen comrade they had been present with at time of death.

"He was a good man. He deserved better than how I left him."

"You did what I asked. I'm the one who left him."

After a long silence, Drake cleared his throat. "I know we talked some time back about stuff, but not sure if I mentioned that I lost my dad when I was pretty young. They got my mom, too. I was a pretty messed-up kid afterward. Some wounds never heal, especially family."

"How did it happen? I remember bits and pieces from what I heard before I knew you."

"You probably know, Dad was CIA. We were in Tunisia. They first came in and killed my mom. Dad and I were in the kitchen. He tried to get me out. I froze. Total choke."

"How old?"

"Thirteen, fourteen. Dad would've died anyway, even if I had left when he told me. I just know he went out and got killed not knowing if his sacrifice was worth it."

"How'd you make it out?"

"No clue. I blacked out. I killed a couple with the ice pick my dad was using. Can't remember any of that part unless it comes back in my dreams. Then I got shot. Shrinks said I blocked a lot out."

"You killed armed men with an ice pick? Holy shit, you must have." Havens paused in a moment of thought. "OT knew. That's why this group is Project ICEPICK? Ho-ly shit."

Drake deflected Sean's realization. "My dad was a good dad. OT was not."

"OT took you in then?" Sean asked, referring to Robert O'Toole, a renowned special operator and intel czar who had just recently met an untimely end amidst the recent attacks. Although, OT's demise was strongly personal.

"Yeah. Him and my aunt. My aunt was great. More of a mom than my real mom was. Like cookies, and caring, and shit like that. She was crypto with NSA. But she couldn't really dictate how my uncle should be a dad. OT, as you can imagine, had a unique way of parenting. More like how you beat a pit bull into becoming a ring dog."

"I would imagine he was pretty tough."

"You have *no* idea."

"Siblings?"

"Older brother. They thought he was involved with my folks' murder. Dexter was his name. Dex was a lot older. Always on the streets, always getting in trouble."

"Yeah, so why did the Agency want him as an asset?"

Drake whipped his head at Sean's fucked-up remark. "Asset to what? What are you talking about?"

"His work." Sean shrugged. "With the Agency." He winced from the shrug that sent a jolt of pain throughout his arm.

"What are you talking about?"

Sean tensed.

"Dude. What in the *fuck* are you saying?"

"Drake, I'm sorry, I thought you knew. From what I remember hearing about the Woolfs, your dad was Alex Woolf, right?"

"Yes," Drake confirmed, hanging on every word.

"Yeah, he got your brother in, and then your brother changed his name."

"In to what?"

"As an access agent that became a full-on operations asset. He's not a CIA officer. He's a deep black NOC. Completely flying in the wind save for his handler and only a few others in Langley. He's as native as native gets."

"How do you know this?"

"Like all things Langley. You're standing with someone or sitting in a room, and someone assumes you're read in. I heard a lot about Alex Woolf over the years, but only once did I hear about his son who was an asset and another one, you, who was military. That's all. I just kept my mouth shut, since I knew it wasn't anything I was probably supposed to know. But I really don't know anything more."

So, it's true.

Chapter 9

Special Agent Halliday crunched on a second handful of Breathsavers as she exited the Savannah field office's Chevy Suburban SUV. Special Agent David Scullen, her local point of contact, met her around the side of the car. "You doing a little better?"

"Yeah. I'm good. Another cup of coffee and I'll float away."

As they approached the gaggles of local and state law enforcement, Halliday saw them muddled about the rather unusual crime scene with a lot of posed photographs being taken that didn't appear to be for forensic work.

The area was awash in lights, both vehicle headlamps and the spots from type one and two fire engines. The charred van in the center of all the fanfare dripped with fire-fighting water. White cloth covers dotted the area where bodies remained.

"David," Tresa spoke softly to her Savannah counterpart, "would you mind talking to the locals? Since I'm just observing for another case, may be best if you be the face of your office."

"I'd sure appreciate it, Agent Halliday," he said with a slight Southern twang. She figured he was from Arkansas, probably assigned to this sleepy area by a bad luck of the draw. Unless, of course, he was looking for a place to hide and raise a family. Maybe it was genius.

"Probably should have discussed it on the ride in. I just figured you were, uh, tired," he joshed, giving her a friendly elbow to the side.

She gave him back a friendly poke to the arm with the back of her balled hand. "Stop. But thanks."

"All right, everyone," Special Agent Scullen called to the masses, clapping his hands. "Could y'all gather 'round for a quick minute and squeeze in here. I'd appreciate knowin' what y'all have seen, learned, and figured out so far, so I can tell my bosses."

The law enforcement bubbas slowly sauntered over.

David added, "I'm just here to support you, if you have any needs or if we can bring some resources to the party." Agent Scullen gave Halliday a wink. "Scoot, missy," he whispered. "Just bought you some time to sniff around alone for a bit."

Only in the past weeks had Tresa experienced the teaming and warmth of the greater Bureau. She realized that she had either not seen it, gotten in with a bad lot, or maybe it was there all along and she had been the one to shun it. No, the harassment had been real. Threats had been real. The thumb in the ass was damned real. She was just seeing another side now, and it made her proud. Because it enabled her to do the job. A job that she really wanted to do well.

Tresa sauntered out to the side of the nearing responders. She remained casual, not wanting to encroach on turf or stick out as taking any liberties. The ground was soaked, which told her the fire response teams were less concerned about evidence than dousing what appeared to be an enflamed vehicle. She knew the make and model was the same as the task force's. They'd been here all right. But the burning question that was at the forefront of her mind and a fist-sized lump in her chest was whether one of the bodies was Warren Drake Woolf.

Halliday worked her way around, starting in the tree line. Flashlight in her left hand, she lifted the first sheet, holding her breath. The dead Middle Easterner had clearly been killed up close and personal judging by his bloodied and swollen face. The next two nearly made her gag. In her heart of hearts, she knew Drake Woolf was alive, because she'd never met anyone else who could kill like this. As much as it sickened her, her heart glowed with a twisted sense of relief even though there were four more covered bodies.

It was the body of the big man that gave her more pause than she would have expected. Tresa didn't know his name, but by the rough size and her memory of him exiting such a vehicle in Georgetown, Tresa was nearly certain the crispy corpse was the same fellow she had seen with Havens. Seeing his burnt remains twisted her convictions. Certainly, what he and the team were doing was illegal, and they had knocked her out as part of their escape—also illegal. But they had loaded her SUV with their weapons and let the FBI take credit for thwarting an attack. More than part of her respected their work and their mission. It was evident that the big man had lost his life stopping these terrorists from entering the secured facility, to protect America. To keep Americans safe. She was hunting the hunters. The good guys.

"Pretty slick," Scullen admired, behind her.

Tresa turned to see the other special agent pulling on something attached to the burned van wreckage.

"Paste on," the state police officer replied.

Halliday walked over to the half circle of men.

Scullen pulled a smoked white laminate off the van. "I used to see this in Mexico along the border. Auto thieves would put different-colored skins on cars they stole so a vehicle description wouldn't match."

Tresa squeezed in to inspect the finding. "It's black underneath. Damn."

"Black or blue. Looks to me like a midnight blue. Light has to catch it just right out here."

FBI intersection camera surveillance had lost the van days ago. The task force had simply changed the color of the Transit. "Son of a bitch."

Scullen trained his attention on Tresa. "Whatcha pinballin' up in that head of yours? Bad guy car or other bad guy car?"

"Looks to me like the guys had a disagreement. Maybe one group was stealing nuclear waste material and the buyer took them out. Could be an ambush from either vantage. Middle Easterners, but with no terror event, I think I have all I need. Doesn't really match the attacks that we've seen across the country in past days." Tresa shrugged, feigning closure.

"Uh-huh," Scullen drew out. He leaned in to Halliday out of earshot of the others and whispered to her, "If I wasn't standing in mud, I'd say my boots were in bullshit."

Ignoring her fellow agent, Tresa addressed whom she believed to be a facility security lead. "Sir, did your gate guards report a vehicle leaving the premises?"

"They did," he confirmed matter-of-factly, offering no more.

"But they didn't stop it?"

"Uh, no, ma'am. They did not."

"And is there anything you can share about that encounter? Did they ram a gate? Shoot at the gate guards? Do you have any identifiers on the suspects or vehicle?"

"That is still being determined. It appears there was some confusion." The site officer stuffed his hands in his pockets, licked his lips, and acknowledged his peers who had now heard the story for the second time. The music didn't sound any better. "Apparently, the guards were informed to let the vehicle pass, due to an emergency."

"Do you have video surveillance?"

"Uh, no, ma'am. We don't have that either."

"Do you not keep video footage of the gate?"

"Uh, yes, ma'am. We do." He coughed. "It was turned off."

"I see."

"But they did say there were two men, one reclined in the passenger seat. It was moving out pretty good. Black Jeep Cherokee."

"Could it have been blue like this one?"

The man leaned in a bit to inspect the color of the Ford. "I'd say that's fair."

"And would it be fair to notify authorities of a dark-colored Jeep Cherokee within"—she checked her watch—"a couple hundred miles? With a focus on thirty miles of nearby hospitals, clinics, veterinary hospitals?" She scrunched her face, looking for a little help from the boys playing law enforcement.

One officer in a tan uniform patted another officer in a black uniform, or as the theme of the evening went, "potentially dark blue" uniform, and suggested, "Can you get on that, please, Wendell?" He snickered. Perhaps because the other officer's real name was Joe.

"Thank you," Halliday acknowledged, not realizing they had little intention of doing anything. "My bet is on a small clinic that you wouldn't expect to have lights on at this hour. And I'd like to do it before they see us coming."

Chapter 10

"Toto, I don't think we're in Kansas anymore," Sean mumbled as the young hood rats approached the vehicle just outside the clinic in what might be considered by some an "up and coming" neighborhood. Even if up and coming meant leveling the area in five years.

"Roll down your window, Sean. Tell them it's past curfew and they have midterms to study for." Drake panned left to right and back again in a much more crowded back parking lot than they had expected.

"Dude, don't make me laugh." Sean flipped his head toward Drake's window. A hooded figure approached in the darkness. "He's on your side, Drake. I'd like a Whopper, onion rings, and a shake."

Woolf rolled down the window to a black Ruger 9mm pointing at his head.

"Get the fuck out the car," the man ordered, his voice deep and slow.

"Can't," Drake replied. "Need Doc Wentworth. This guy's got a compression wrap on that's tying him to the seat. If he moves, he dies."

"I don't give a fuck if he dies. If you don't move, you both die. Ain't no Doc Wentworth here. Get out the car, man."

Others circled the Cherokee, their hoods cloaking faces in a rather symbolic death ritual.

Havens leaned toward the window with a grunt. "Hey, pal, no disrespect, but go inside and get Patches right the fuck now."

The thug leaned his head in the car for a better look.

Drake grabbed the gangster's dangling chain and twisted it in the blink of an eye around his right hand while poking the man's throat with a blade.

The man didn't flinch. "How you know Patches?" he asked, still making eye contact with Sean.

"We worked together." Havens's voice was tempered. "Get us in, and I need you guys to lose this car. Get us another one as fast as you can. Patches will pay you five grand. Tell him Fritter is here. He's not expecting us, but we called to make a reservation a couple days ago in case we needed him. Now we need him."

"He's got one of my homies in dere now. You wait," the street soldier warned.

Havens turned to Drake. "Bro, get ready to throw this truck into reverse, and kill this motherfucker right now."

Drake's tongue clicked three times. He revved the engine and honked the horn with his elbow giving all quite a jolt of surprise.

"Wait, wait!" the thug yelled.

Havens caught movement to his right just past the hood of the SUV. The hooded knights west of Martin Luther King Jr Blvd in Savannah's more impoverished of neighborhoods parted. Another large figure emerged from the darkness, carrying a red aluminum baseball bat.

"Malcolm!" the new player on the scene shouted. "If I tell you and your boys to stay outside, that doesn't mean shaking down my other clients. Get the fuck away from that car."

"He stuck, Patches," a noticeably taller hood informed the former Special Forces medic. "White boy's in dere holdin' his head and won't let 'im go."

A few others tried not to laugh.

The former 18-Delta special forces medical sergeant, who retired as Sergeant Major Augustus "Doc" Wentworth, approached the passenger-side door to see who was next in the reputed safe-zone charitable clinic. "Shit. Back away, boys. Go inside and get your guy then get out of here and go home. No more shoot-ups tonight. Feel me?"

Out of the grumbling and shuffling rang out a few faint yes-sirs.

"You goddamned right, 'Yes, sir.'"

He opened Havens's door to assess the initial damage. "You all right, man?"

"Yeah, good to see you, Doc. Hey, can we keep one or two of those guys who may want to earn a little side cash taking this Jeep up to Augusta? We need to ditch it but need to give ourselves some air gap."

"Y'ain't gonna get none of my boys killed, are you?" Patches asked, his concern genuine.

"No. I don't care if they take side streets or the highway. I just figure someone will be trying to surveil the vehicle. Maybe you have someone with a clean record? I can give you a title."

"Shit, you at Victory and Burroughs, my man." Patches laughed. "Hey, Chicklet," he called out. "You with your brother?"

"Yes, sir, Patches."

"Boy, why you got that boy out here so late? You ain't got school tomorrow?"

"We ain't got no school tomorrow, Patches," a higher-pitched voice replied. "It supposed to snow real bad." The young man laughed.

"Don't you pull that shit with me, child. You sixteen yet, Nibbles?"

"No, sir, Patches."

"Okay, perfect. You driving."

"How much you got for these boys?"

Drake replied, "I've got five K we can give 'em. If you need more, can you spot 'em and add it to the invoice?"

"I ain't no ATM," Patches rebuked. "'Sides, that's too much for these boys. You give 'em that much, they'll buy dope to sell."

"Hells yeah," a voice in the crowd confirmed.

"Shut up, Darrius." Patches called back to the teens, "You boys get two hundred each. Rest of you all get a hundred to keep your mouth shut." Patches peered across Sean, ducking into the car. "Malcolm, you get five, since it's your crew. You make sure that lil' kid get to school at least three times a week, you feel me?"

Malcom was still held by Drake, knife pressed to the skin. "That's coo', Patches, and you get this white boy from stickin' me no mo in my throat?"

"Fritter, have your boy let him go, and let's get you inside. What's your name, buddy?" he asked Drake.

"Mr. White'll be just fine, Sergeant Major."

"Ummm, hmm. Get your shit that you need outta that car after you help me inside. Goddamned spooks in Savannah keepin' me up now. You know I charge double for overtime. I ain't no CIA SAD anymore takin' a government paycheck. I'm runnin' a social hospital, I am. Can't tell from out here, but behind these walls is state of the art."

"Yeah, Patches," a thug chimed in, "you all Mayo Clinic patchin' up these foos everyday an' shit."

"Mayonnaise Clinic with these whitey," a voice joked from the back with a laugh.

"Oren, get. And don't be usin' those words round me, hear?"

"Sorry, Patches."

"These boys are good kids. Almost all of them have righteous African and sub-Saharan African ancestry here. More than anywhere else. Got no jobs though, and crime's going up. If you all have some folks lookin' for you, they ain't coming in here."

Havens gritted as Doc lifted him from the car with two armfuls but not even a hint of effort on the older soldier's face. "That's why we came to you, old buddy."

"Shiiit. You came to me 'cause I know what I'm doin' and Uncle Sam knows I ain't askin' no questions. And don't say it's because you saved me. I knew that sumbitch had a gun."

Havens just laughed, and Drake followed along wondering just how many shit holes Sean Havens had actually been in over the years.

Chapter 11

"Special Agent Halliday, looks like we may have gotten lucky."

"How's that?" Halliday asked while staring at a map on her mobile device.

"We were able to get a couple pictures from signal cameras. Looks like they headed down Route 17 over the river toward Savannah."

"How long ago?" Tresa spread her fingers on the screen over Savannah then closed them to see how far they may have gotten without a stop.

"That was over four hours ago."

"Four hours." She huffed at the futility. "Anywhere after that?"

"Can't say. We reached out to Georgia State Police. Once they crossed the state line, we don't have that access."

"Of course not," she mumbled to herself. "Which is exactly why they did it." *Those assholes.* "Okay, let me see if we can get someone on our end to check camera feeds." She manipulated the map some more. *Where are you guys going now?* Halliday thought they would cross the border if they were pursuing another terror suspect or evading. Clearly, from the past weeks and what she knew of Warren Drake Woolf, they were based out of the National Capital Region. *You drove here, probably so you could bring your weapons, which means you need to also drive them back northeast, so where are you headed? Unless you stopped for medical help in Savannah.* "Trooper? When you reach out to Georgia, find out where gunshot victims tend to go in the city if they don't want police to find them. See if any of those doctors or clinic owners are affiliated with the government, military, mafia, military contractors, anything like that."

Just within earshot of Halliday, and knowingly so, an officer snickered. "If Tommy Lee Jones looked like that in *The Fugitive*, I'd do him."

"Maybe she'd like the man with the wooden arm," a trooper added.

"Oh, yeah. She looks like she could use a wooden arm. Maybe she'd lighten up." He turned to Tresa. "Hey, Mrs. Fed, anything else you need us to do? Get you coffee, donuts? I can't imagine any one of these ragheads is hoping you catch whoever shot them. Personally, I hope you give 'em a medal."

Halliday strolled over to the officer as slowly and delicately as it was possible for the confident Amazonian to do. "Can I see your car keys?"

"They're in my car," he sneered.

She leaned in and breathed into his ear. "Can you show me which one is your car and take me to it?"

He nervously looked around at his peers. "Sure, I'll show you my riiide."

"I was hoping you'd say that." She smiled. Tresa reached up and lightly touched his arm.

"You go, buddy, I'll let your wife know you'll be late," an officer called out, which was met with a raised arm wave.

The two walked about fifteen yards from the others, and Halliday stopped abruptly. "You know, when you take a sheep away from the flock, a wolf pack makes easy prey of it."

"It sure does." He salivated, testosterone surging.

"Shut up," she barked, stepping into him. She gave him a slight push. His demeanor melted in an instant.

"But," she interjected, and poked her finger into his chest, "if you take a wolf away from its pack and a badass cougar sees that lowly dog removed from strength in numbers, that long-fanged pussy will just tear the shit out of that little yelping ground bitch," she spat, stepping into the officer again as he retreated another step back. "So, find your own way back into whatever town you came from, bitch," she warned, turning away, "or I'll have you arrested for obstructing a federal agent. Tell my partner I'm headed to Savannah. Have him text me any clinics. And, officer"—she turned—"I'll tell Tommy Jones you said hi. I could tell right away that you liked boys. You just kinda carry yourself that way."

Chapter 12

Drake Woolf was still pacing when Patches exited his clinical chamber to the waiting area, which was more like a college student's living room filled with mismatched, donated, and scrounged furniture.

"I thought you'd be crashed out after cleaning up," the medic mulled aloud to Drake. "I know I slept like a log after an extraction. Truck, helo, shit, I could have dozed on a horse. I needed my downtime to shake it all off."

"Yeah, I'm not tired. I prefer to stay busy. Thanks for letting me shower off and giving me a taste of thug life," Drake jested, looking down at the black sweats, and raised his hands to show the full splendor of the black hoodie that Patches also provided.

Patches sat on the armrest of a heavily worn leather or pleather overstuffed sofa. "Glad they fit. I keep plenty of spares. I'm sorry I kicked you out of the room. I know you were trying to help your friend. I just needed to focus on him and not you. Your hands calm down?"

"Yeah. Just wearing down the edge. So, how's Sean?"

"He needs to get to a hospital. GSWs are patched. They'll hold. I've got him on an antibiotic drip right now and some fluids. But that wrist is bad. He's going to need a specialist. The break is angulated, there's a lot of small fragments, and he'll need more sophisticated fracture fixation. Pins at best. Probably plates and screws. Surgical drains. At best, three months of healing and therapy just to get functionality. Could be a year for maximum improvement."

Drake squinted at Patches then laughed out loud.

"Guess he's not as good of a buddy as I thought."

Drake shook his head. "Sorry. I figured about the wrist. I'm still laughing at how you completely switched your speech from street to head of Johns Hopkins surgery."

Patches gave a knowing nod and smiled. "Hearts and minds, brother. Man needs to blend in to his surroundings. I don't even know the real me anymore," he admitted with a light chuckle that reflected more the comedy of life than real humor.

Woolf gave a knowing huff. "Ain't that the truth."

The two men sat in silence for a moment, both reflecting on the long roads each had traveled in their military careers. "I'll make a call," Drake suggested. "Need to confirm that I can still get a private jet in the area. We're on our heels a bit."

"Need to bring in a commercial jet or military? I'm guessing spooky either way."

"Gulfstream V. Executive jet. Can go to airport or a base. We had a couple of the airports earmarked as a contingency."

"Gulfstream V. The old 'prisoner rendition transport,'" Patches confirmed. "You all have CAC cards? Base access?"

"We can have our guy call it in."

"I'll get you guys to Hunter Army Base. I still do some basic-level trauma response training over there. You have 'em come in there. I'm guessing you boys need to lay real low, if I know Havens any."

"Thanks."

Patches got up and started heading back to check on Havens. He turned back to Drake, as if in an afterthought. "Mind if I ask you something?"

Drake shrugged. "Can't promise an answer."

"Fair enough." The seasoned military man gave pause, appearing to Drake that he was contemplating whether he should leave it alone or still pursue the question. "I wanna go back to you in there." Patches cast an eye to the care room. "I seen that kind of twitchy decompression. Add to it the long stares. An air of detachment but almost manic at the thought of losing maybe one of the few people you're close to. Like a thin piece of string that could break and drop you at any moment. I know you got it bad. You doing anything for it?" Before Drake could reply, he added, "And I know why you're not sleepin' either. Guessing it's the ghosts."

"I need to make that call. Can I go in there and get his phone?" Drake walked to the room, stepping to the side of the former operator.

Patches leapt up, sidestepped, and blocked Drake's path. "Nothing to be ashamed of. You getting help or taking anything for it?"

"No snowflake here, Doc. You won't get me to take a hug or cry about all the people I regret killing, if that's what you're getting at. Because I don't. And plenty of guys out there and throughout history have seen or done worse than me. Just part of the job. And anything else you may have thought you were seeing, well…" Drake stared past Patches into the care room, looking at nothing but high-end equipment and bright lights. "Anyway, nothing you can help with. I'm holding my own just fine."

"You so sure about that? Killing quiets things until it don't."

Drake took a step in to the man. "We're paying you to patch physical trauma. If you want to win my heart and mind, please back the fuck up so I can make my call. There's nothing to see here."

Kill him, Drake. He's going to turn you in. Kill him while you have time.

Drake watched the medic-turned-physician's heart beating within a large neck vein. It pulsed and protruded like a fat nightcrawler after a spring rain. Woolf's eyes slid to the man's larynx. Crushing the trachea wouldn't be a problem with a fast punch through the lean man's thyroid cartilage. At the very least, Drake could dislocate the larynx from the trachea.

Go see your friend, Drake. Cool it down. You're safe. You're protected. Trust him. "Okay, Dad," Drake muttered to himself before blinking twice. His eyes met Patches's. The man had slowly stepped back a pace. "Can I go see Sean?"

Patches tightened his lip, sporting a look of concern that was not lost on Drake. The man knew he was a fucking embattled head case.

Drake's eyes softened. A good man was standing in front of him. The kind that would have been nice to have had around in the early years. Woolf relented. "If you had something like Tegretol or something close to it, that would help. But that's about it."

"I know you don't have seizures if you were with a unit, so it's either migraines or bipolar." Patches looked to the low ceiling and bright can lights and then at Drake. "It's not migraines."

"Helps stabilize the mood. Takes away the edge."

Patches pursed his lips. "Or manic episodes like in there. Okay. Just happens I may have some Depakote. Could be expired. Guy down the street had epilepsy but no insurance. Was stabbed to death before I could give it to him." Patches inhaled deeply. "Go check on Sean and make your call. I'll see if I can find it. But the pills can only take you half the distance, my brother. The rest you'll need to open yourself up to receiving from others."

* * * *

"Knock, knock," Drake announced before stepping through the curtain.

"Hey, man," Sean forced. Pain was written across his face. "You get any sleep?"

"Yeah, a few winks," Drake lied as he assessed his team leader's condition. "I feel pretty good."

"Bullshit."

"True," Drake affirmed, his voice monotone and distant. He hadn't known Sean long but hated seeing him in this condition. Sometimes combat wounds were worse than seeing a buddy who died in the field. Dead guys, if you didn't see them pass, could look fake. Depending on the wounds, they could look like a surreal soulless physical casing. But seeing a wounded pal was a reminder of vulnerability. That even though men were warriors, they were still mortal men. Depending on how well you knew a guy, you could almost see through to the younger version when they were a kid. It was in their eyes. Maybe the fear. Maybe the pain, but something always seemed different in a time out of war when it didn't make sense and didn't seem to matter. A wounded buddy who died, however, could have a rallying effect. Payback drove a team back into action. But for some reason, seeing Sean bandaged up with the dried blood soiling his clothes and skin touched Drake in the *feels*. He fought back the emotions rising to the surface signaling to Woolf that he had few friends, fewer loved ones, and a dad who would never be coming back. Havens was the closest thing he had felt to having a dad again, and losing him would have caused Woolf to completely check out.

"You in there, Woolf?"

"Huh?" He blinked. "Yeah. Just glad to see you made it."

"Me, too," Havens joked before recoiling from a new source of discomfort. "Can you make the call to Sebastian for me? I'm going to be toast for a while." He elevated his hand slightly. "Not sure if they can even save this. I may be out of the game for good. You may as well start taking over now."

"I can't do this alone, Sean. We're done. The task force is done. My uncle's dead, Lars is fucking dead, we took out the Mohawks, ISOF. It's game over. Fuck it. Patches said we can bug out from the base. He'll get us there, we fly you back home, get you fixed up, and I don't know, let's just go fishing or something after they save your hand. We did our job. Shit, we've done our share of the job for years. And with that Fed on our asses, we're going to be in prison as our reward." Drake's tongue started clicking. He was shuffling his shoulders, and his eyes started to blink as he looked around the room.

He stopped when he saw Sean looking at his restless hand movements.

"Okay, Drake," Havens appeased, "let's call Sebastian and get *you* home."

Chapter 13

Tresa Halliday pulled in to the deserted urban parking lot that screamed danger. She double-checked the address on her navigation unit, but her eyes lifted to the movement of shadows that emerged from the darkness toward her SUV. Halliday unholstered her Glock and kept it at the ready across her lap.

"This is called over your head, girl," she chastised herself and the growing ego that recently drove a number of her bad decisions.

A dark hooded figure tapped a finger on the glass.

Tresa reached to the window button on her left armrest and lowered the glass while raising the weapon. Her finger toying the side of the trigger in gentle taps.

The shadow man laughed. "Bitch, you the second white person threating me tonight. I'ma hasta call five-oh. This neighborhood's going to shit."

A chorus of laughter erupted in the silence between night and first light.

"I need to see—"

"Bitch, Patches ain't here."

Patches. The medic. Bingo. "You said there was another white guy. Were there two of them?"

"I didn't say shit."

"You said—"

"Bitch, the only thing I *said* is this message: 'It's over.' The man who I didn't see and who was never here, axed me to just say they're done and it's over. Now get your white ass out of my muthafuckin' hood before I break my promise. You feel me?"

While Halliday had been feeling her oats over the past week, there was a time and place for playing it tough. It was best for her to get the hell out of this neighborhood and figure out what to do next. Drake Woolf wasn't here. Her hunch had been right, but she was too late. The ghosts had vanished again, and now they were apparently done. Just when she was getting started.

Then again, she had found them more than once on a hunch.

Halliday rolled up her window, said nothing more, backed up, and bugged out. As she drove, keeping her head on a swivel, she called the dedicated Bureau line for field support.

After some cursory introductions and validations, she asked, "Can you tag my vehicle and direct me to the nearest airfield?"

"That's easy, Agent Halliday. Hold on."

Tresa drove slowly in the decrepit neighborhoods, still very mindful of her surroundings as she waited.

"I assume you mean commercial? Or do you want military?"

"Which is closest?"

"Hunter Army Base is about the—"

"Yes! Get me there."

Tresa fumbled for a moment to get all the bells and whistles of the emergency lights going. Flashing blues and whites, she gunned the SUV while taking the live voice directions until she hit the checkpoint.

A military guard stepped out of his well-lit shack, raised a hand and stepped forward.

"Federal agent! FBI," she announced with badge and identification available for access. "Raise the gate!"

"Ma'am, I'm going to need to see your identification a little closer," he rebuffed while sauntering over.

"Soldier, I'm—"

"Ma'am, there's nobody here being pursued. Think maybe you made a wrong turn." He stepped back. "This a Tahoe? Slick."

Far up and to the left of her windshield, small lights rose in the darkness. Her hunch was right. And she was certain she was being stalled. That or everyone in this general area of the country was a backwoods moron. "How can I find out where that airplane is going?"

The soldier squinted. "Not usually any planes taking off this time of night. You can come back tomorrow and ask someone in the office."

"I doubt I'll get any answers tomorrow either."

"Probably not." He smiled and handed her back her identification.

Dammit. She slapped the wheel while putting the Tahoe in reverse. Halliday was not happy this was dying down. She was having the best time in her whole career. Yet, she needed answers more now than ever before. Earl owed her some answers as to exactly who and what she was chasing but getting blocked all along the way.

* * * *

Patches sat parked in the shadows of the military base with his headlights off, engine killed. This was typical Havens, from the commercial jet coming in here to someone pissed off coming after him. He'd just wait this one out here for a while. Patches reclined his seat back, crossed his arms and closed his eyes. "Fritter," he reminisced aloud with a chuckle, "you are one special dude."

Chapter 14

Tresa Halliday called Earl. It was late. Or early. But technically, he hadn't told his newest ghost that she shouldn't call at all hours of the night. At least not in the past forty-eight hours he hadn't. And since this threat was a matter of national security, why let it wait until morning?

"I found a mess, Earl," she blurted as soon as he greeted her. "You were right. One of their guys is dead. Burned beyond identification most likely, as if he even has an identity. The other casualties are more of the same. Middle Eastern–looking terrorists. I tracked Woolf and his partner down to a down-low clinic and received a message, 'It's over.'" Tresa's voice dropped with the last remark.

"You sound disappointed."

"I am." Her nostrils flared. "We still need to hunt them down, right? I mean, they can't just fucking call time-out."

"Tresa, you've worked tirelessly for weeks. Get a hotel; get some sleep. Sleep for a couple days. Have a nice meal. Let's figure out our plan after you've rested."

"You haven't answered my question."

"I didn't realize I had to," he responded firmly but softly. "You've done well. Very well. Good night, Special Agent Halliday, you've earned it. Let's talk in a couple days if nothing has materialized on your end. And I'd prefer that it didn't. I need some time to think. Agents react. The ones on my team spend equal time contemplating as they do in movement. I need to work this puzzle a bit," Earl Johnson quipped before hanging up.

Tresa dialed again.

"I wasn't disconnected by a technical glitch," he asserted in place of hello.

"They fled in a small jet from a military base, Earl. They had access to a military base. You owe me some answers, sir."

"Because you called me sir, let's have lunch tomorrow." And with that, Earl hung up a second time.

* * * *

Drake kept a concerned eye on Havens throughout the whole flight.

Sean slept fitfully with an IV bag rigged to keep fluids and antibiotics flowing. High-altitude flights were not optimal post-trauma given his sedation and the risk of pulmonary embolism with free-wheeling clots. Still, the risk of death was better than sticking around and getting an assured death penalty.

As the Gulfstream landed, Drake saw from his window two awaiting vehicles, an SUV and a high-topped van. The van he knew would take Sean away to a secured and black medical facility, where the quality of care would be top-notch. The SUV would be a ride with Sebastian. As the remaining team member, it would be up to Drake to brief the program director on ICEPICK, code name for their Task Force Orange unit of one, and the shit show op that wiped out two of three members in a trap. FUBAR to the max.

Medics were the first to board, whisking Sean off and into the van like precious cargo. Drake, on the other hand, disembarked to a waiting Sebastian, who simply outstretched a hand holding a mobile device.

"You okay, kid?" Sebastian coaxed with fewer words than Drake expected.

"I'm the better of the crew. Happy to hot wash it with you, whenever you want to discuss."

"I need you to make a call first. Just hit send once you get in that black beast. Come get me when you're finished."

"I don't understand."

"I didn't ask you to understand, Woolf. I was fucking explicit in my directive. Dial so I can get you secured and me back home so the wife quits texting me. Tech company owners don't leave their homes in the wee hours."

"Understood." Drake hit send as he entered the vehicle and shut the door, all the while wondering if the SUV would be detonated with the signal or if a Predator would send a screamer in to blow the shit out of him.

"War?" an unfamiliar voice addressed him by an abbreviated name he hadn't heard for decades.

Drake held his breath in trepidation.

"Warren. It's me. It's been so long," the voice confessed in a sound that became more familiar as memories flooded in.

"It can't be you." Drake flopped back against the leather-trimmed seat more scared than he'd been in his lifetime. His breath quickened and chest rose and fell with each word he anticipated hearing from the undead brother who had consumed his life in search. "My brother would have found me a lifetime ago."

"Little brother, it is me," Dexter Woolf assured again, after over twenty years of absolutely no communication with his kin. "I don't have long, but wanted you to hear it from me. Our uncle was responsible for the death of our parents. I was the one who put an end to it."

Drake's mind reeled. Words could not form. His tongue clicked.

"You're still clicking," the voice said, bemused. "I've missed it."

"Why are you calling me now? After all these years, why the hell now? It seems like everyone else knows something about you except me, and I was the one looking for you all over the world."

"Sebastian will fill you in. I can't over this line. He'll tell you more about what's coming. But someday we'll be together again. Soon."

"Would you have reached out if you hadn't killed Bob?"

"I don't know. It all came together recently. I hadn't planned on coming back to the States."

"You're here?" Drake looked around reflexively.

"Dad was getting out. He had me take a different path. Uncle Bob didn't know Dad was getting out because of his condition. Uncle Bob thought Mom was forcing him out."

"What condition?" Drake asked unconvinced.

"Like you."

"What's that supposed to mean?"

"Voices. He had the voices, too. That's why I was taking over. I won't be in touch much, but I'll be there where you're going and will help where I can. Save this number, little brother, so you can answer it if I call. I will never have it on for longer than a couple minutes unless there's a problem. If I need to reach you, I'll leave you a disappearing text or encrypted voice mail on WhatsApp. Use this number if you need to get a message to me, but I'll never answer it." And with that, the line fell silent and disconnected.

Chapter 15

As Drake sat in disbelief, a light rapping echoed through the tinted glass.

When Woolf opened the door, a sympathetic look was on Sebastian's face in the dim glow of the interior dome light. "Can we go?" he asked Drake.

"Yeah."

It didn't take but a few minutes before Woolf broke the silence. "He said you have some more details for me."

"I do. But I suspect you can figure it out."

"CIA?"

"Nay. Not directly." Sebastian cocked his head. "Your brother started as an access agent. He's what you Americans term as an *executive* agent now. Placement, access, he kills, sabotages, and helps Central Intelligence recruit. Your father trained him, had him go through Field Tradecraft Certification, which is unprecedented for this type of situation. Certainly would be where I come from, but that's my opinion."

"How long have you known?" Drake asked flatly as he still processed a conversation that he had longed for his whole adult life and didn't happen at all how he had fantasized.

"Not long. I knew of the code name only so we could white-list it at NSA, but never knew the man or the history. He came looking for you. He found me."

"How'd he find you?"

"Your uncle's files. Which as you can imagine troubled me greatly, but not of your concern. It's been remedied."

"How did he come to you? I'm guessing not at the front door."

"Let's say it was quite the surprise and something I'd rather not discuss. Short-lived incident. Comes with the life."

"Did he really kill OT?"

"No question."

"You know this or he said this?"

"Both. I suspect he did it for personal reasons and to protect you. But he left the surveillance video that caught part of him in the act. Probably to reinforce his cover. To finish a job. Beyond that, I can't say. He's in neck-deep. Bugger me if I've ever heard someone so long mixing with those sorts. Some question, and I'm just saying this in full transparency, right?"

Drake absorbed the news.

"They say he could be working for them now. Turned. Native. A sympathizer."

"It's a lot to take in."

"Did he tell you about Chicago?" Sebastian asked.

Drake shook his head in the darkness of the SUV. "No."

"He wants to help you take down the next wave. Hezbollah has acquired radioactive materials and plans to use them in the city. We have verified this from sources and technology. I know Sean's down, but the task force was meant to be one man from the start. You'll have support. I surmise your brother will remain close. Comment?"

Drake gave a weak laugh. "No. But what else do I have?"

Sebastian turned his head to the rear. "You have a country…and you have a team."

"I'll settle for a car. And a new persona package."

"Right. I'll drop you at the shop where you will stay for the time being. Proper accommodations have been completed to the level of a warrior's appropriate comfort. Shitter, shower, and a blanket. Documents to your identity are in the vault. As for another automobile, consider yourself in isolation. I'll have the team bring you food when they arrive at 1300 hours."

"What team exactly is this?"

"Your new team, mate. Remember, I'm just a program manager. I handle administration, and you handle the dirty work. I'm an old man. I need my sleep. You'll meet the crew tomorrow after some rest, Ibuprofen, water to hydrate, and fresh clothes. You'll be right-ways in no time."

Part II

"We must take the battle to the enemy, disrupt his plans and confront the worst threats before they emerge. In the world we have entered, the only path to safety is the path of action. And this nation will act."

—President George W. Bush, June 1, 2002

Chapter 16

Iran's Major General Qasem Soleimani's outburst was unprecedented. Relaxing in the family sitting area when his phone rang, it was his aftermath of shouts that awoke his napping granddaughter from his arms.

She was crying, he was frustrated, and he chose to hang up the call and tend to baby Anya after only replying, "I will advise Department 9000, and it will be done. Unit 400 operations in America will cease with my call to Major General Abdollahi."

The call was unexpected from the commander of the Iranian Republican Guards Corps Major General Mohammad Ali Jafari. Jafari reported to Iran's supreme leader, as did Soleimani.

Soleimani called most IRGC and Qods Force shots, but he still reported, if in dotted line, only to Jafari. It was a dose of cold water reminder thrown at Soleimani that a pecking order remained. Jafari's unusual call was short. Americans had just announced a discovery of new material support ties between Hezbollah, Iran, and Syria, and had linked them to Venezuela. Soleimani received in those moments from his superior subsequent stand-down orders while details of the crackdown remained unclear. The international investigation could take months if not years, but under the renewed scrutiny, a terror attack on US soil would most certainly bring a fury of reprisals. The Iranian regime wanted no loose ends that could be discovered about the Qods Force–driven operations in America. Iran didn't need to give the Zionists any further excuse for direct retaliation, and the Soviets had weighed in heavily as well with a very clear message to the IRGC about containing their forays to their own immediate region and to reduce the footprint in Syria. Venezuela, specifically, was already a shit show and certainly didn't need American boots on the ground there, too, sniffing around Iranian investments. Tehran's *birun marzi*, meaning "outside the borders" group, also known as Department 9000, would handle the matter with the assistance of Unit 400 assassins. Whether it was tacit or explicit, the supreme leader called the stand-down, and sanitization, in favor of global political pressure.

"Shhh," he hushed, continuously walking and bouncing the baby to calm both of them down.

His wife rushed into the room with a cacophony of questions.

"Shhh," he said again, this time to his wife, waving his hand down. "It's all okay," he assured her quietly in Farsi.

His wife reached out her arms to take the baby. "If you have work, I will take her."

The Iranian Qods Force leader blocked her attempts with his shoulder. "She's asleep. I have this little blessing now. Work can wait. What's done is done." The close-cropped silver hair and beard of the Revolutionary Guard commander darkened as he moved to the shadowed corner of the room where he sat on a long white sofa. "Come. Sit with me." He beckoned to his wife, patting a cushion.

His wife of over thirty years nestled closely to her beloveds. With her left hand, she stroked her granddaughter's head. With her right, she scratched her husband's.

"That is what I needed." He tilted his head back and closed his eyes. "I am a blessed man."

"You have few wants. I think you are tired."

He smiled. Eyes still closed. "I am not tired. I am weary."

"Weary of us?" she joked and rested her head on his shoulder. The olive-green uniform had softened with age, as had her husband.

"I could never be weary of you and my precious little one." He confirmed that which she didn't need reassurance of. "I'm tired and weary of the work."

"Syria?"

His eyes opened, and he turned to her. "We cannot speak of this. Ever."

"Qasem. Am I not to know my husband? My husband's work? The world around us? The world views of our country? I'm an educated woman." She tapped her husband's head and tried to pull it back again. "And I know my love."

"It's best that we do not speak. There are rules. Not just to keep secrets, but to keep you safe."

"I don't need to know details. I don't want to know details. I only want to know what is troubling you."

The most powerful shadow warrior in the Middle East sighed and straightened, careful not to move too much and wake his granddaughter. He winced while adjusting. A quick pinch from his lower back pain and the tightness he felt in his prostate made him shift back to his former position. "There was a plan made. At great lengths. The Zionist regime and their American friends have made a discovery. It is unflattering to our country. And to my commanders. The Americans are threatening more sanctions. The Russians have made demands of us, as well. Once I stopped my personal control of our interventions—"

"You can't control everything," she dismissed his justification. "We can't even control our own children." She referenced their eldest daughter living in Malaysia, who had chosen a different path in life.

"It is simpler on the battlefield."

"The battlefield is for young men, now."

"Battlefields are changing now. Men are changing. I have to stop our plan. It was in my grasp," he ranted, squeezing his fist tight.

She reached to his arm, giving it a rub and pushing his hand down. "I don't know much of war planning, but this I know, my husband. Every mother in this land talks of the honor of martyrdom." She stood and took the sleeping baby from her husband.

He remained quiet and listening, which was truer to his nature.

"But in our hearts," she continued, "we want our children to be happy. Have opportunity. Stay with us in our lands. Be married. Have children. To celebrate life together. And to never worry about missiles. Bombs coming to our homes at night." She headed toward the hallway, leaving him to his thoughts.

"It will not happen," he tried to assure her.

"If it does, the people will rise up." She turned back to him. "They continue to take to the streets. They want freedom. Opportunities. Can you protect the children if this happens?"

"It is because of children that I am willing to stop this."

"Then you know what you have to do. Simple." She smiled.

It may be harder to stop than we think, he fretted to himself.

His orders were to obliterate the mission and all evidence. And that included everyone. Even if he had one in a noose.

Chapter 17

Drake Woolf popped two of Patches's prescription pills and put his head down on the cot in the darkness of a nondescript outbuilding located within the premises of the Department of the Interior's Geological Survey structure, simply known as the TFO "shop." Within an hour of staring at the ceiling, fighting fatigue, Drake succumbed to his exhaustion and closed his eyes.

As he drifted into slumber, a vivid event unfolded in the night terrors he sought to avoid by shunning sleep until his body could no longer resist.

The mission in his mind was going wrong. Drake had a lock on the terrorist "crow's" position by creating a signal triangulation. But the children were on the bus. It didn't make sense because the man he was hunting was driving in the North African Sahara Desert. The UAS Predator feed on his display showed a white SUV. No, that was the screen display showing white within the black video. But the kids. They were there too. But not. They were in color. Drake's brother Dexter was young again. A teen. Just as he had remembered him from back in Tunisia. Dex had a yellow-and-gray Walkman headset over his ears. Their parents were now in the car. The Predator was armed. The feed split and depicted a text prompt with the writing "SELECT TARGET." He had to choose. His body was in the back with his brother now, but also in the back of the bus with the children. The selector was on a handheld. He had to choose. The rush of terror and emptiness surrounded him. He had to choose. Dad looked back. So did Mom. A little girl smiled at Drake. She handed him a petaled white flower with pink ribbon around the stem. He took it and thanked her. A little boy, wearing traditional Iraqi clothes, handed him a small box, which Drake opened. The boy danced with excitement. In the small container was a phone.

"Push it," the young boy coaxed, pointing to the Send button. "Push it," he repeated, reaching over and pointing to the button. Drake looked at the small girl. "Push it," she insisted. The kids on the bus chimed in. "Push it. Push it. Push it."

"No. We can't push it. It's too dangerous," Drake replied. He searched his harness and kit for candy to hand out just as they had in the early days of the desert wars. His pockets were empty.

"Push it, Daddy," the little girl said. The straight-haired, emaciated Iraqi's face changed to have curly brown hair silhouetting brown eyes and cherub cheeks. She had a blue Band-Aid on her forehead. Special Agent Halliday was sitting in a lounge chair by the pool. She wore a yellow flowing dress and had a cocktail with an umbrella. Her dress was like the one Drake's mother wore on the last day of her life. "Drake!" Halliday screamed. "What did you do? Emma!" Emma. Drake was glad they chose that name.

Emma pushed the button, and the Woolf family SUV exploded in a ball of fire. The touch pad flashed ARMED, and the white cross hairs showed the house with the pool explode with Woolf back in an operational position. The house erupted, and the flash from within the bus engulfed the children. Their faces flickered in front of his eyes. Faces of the dead he had seen in combat. The evil men he'd killed over a lifetime of professional soldiering taunted him. They were alive. They were shooting at him from all directions. He could see their faces, but they were dead. He had seen their gruesome death looks, and as his mind displayed them, their bullet-riddled, burnt, broken and torn faces showed of his parents, his brother, former teammates, his uncle, and his aunt. Drake reached into his harness, seeking magazines to reload. There was only candy.

"You okay?" a voice asked from behind. It was Sean Havens and Lars. Drake thought he had awoken but was still trapped in his dream. Havens fired a sidearm into Drake's stomach. Lars wielded a heavy axe to Woolf's head. Drake didn't feel the pain but felt his head falling to the ground, a witness to the surroundings of war's hell before him. And the screaming got louder until his severed head turned to the noise, and he awoke as the falling sensation started again with the report of AK rounds snapping off in the distance exchanged for a succession of beeps, and a loud click, and his name.

"Warren. Safe place. Safe place. You're okay, lad."

Sebastian is in the room. "Am I awake? Is this real?"

The dark voice roused in his head. So much for the pills. *They've come to kill you, Drake. You slept, you idiot. You fucking fell asleep!*

Sebastian responded with his deep Scottish accent. "I'm behind you. You are in a safe place, Warren Woolf. Safe place. Nothing can harm you. Picture show's over. They're not real. Nothing's real, boy. Plays on the mind. I used to drink myself to lights-out just to make the pains go away to the corners. You're among friends. You're in the team building in McLean. Lying on a camp bed. You came back last night from a bit of a mess. You spoke to your brother. Havens is doing well. Can you hear me?"

Drake slowly unfolded from a twisted and tight sweaty body position. On his back, his arms flapped out limp and splayed over the cot edges. "Fuuuck." He rolled over, tightening his body like an armadillo. "Get out," he groaned.

"Team's out front of the building. I'll buy you twenty minutes to shower. It's past 1300. We'll come back in at 1330. Collect yourself. You've got the bollocks. Drive it through. You're strong enough. Game face on, and you be ready. If I tell you to take the ball and run, you do it. If I tell you to live another day, I expect you to." Sebastian gave Woolf a pat on the shoulder and rubbed it to the blade and back. "You'll be okay. Just getting the war trash out. It's been our way since the dawn of man. What hasn't taken our flesh and bone has a claw on our soul. Shower up. Ready in twenty."

"I can't."

"Soggy pudding. Listen to me, boy." Sebastian's grip tightened. The man put a finger into a pressure point that Drake never knew existed. "You're no more off your tits than any other special service soldier. I've seen war, and there is more war to come. I've also seen me, like you, fall into self-loathing. I protect my men, but I'm not a babysitter. We Charlie Mike up. Continue the Mission."

"It's done, Sebastian. I can't. I can't keep doing this." Drake squeezed himself tighter.

"Of course you can. You survived the hard stuff. On with the easy stuff."

"I don't want to anymore," Drake argued, his voice muffled.

"Look. If you're going to off yourself, do it before I get back. Get cracking and do something about it. No one forced you to do this job despite what your shrink may be telling you. Normal men can't go into battle and watch their friends, enemies, and innocents die. All-action, full ops tempo, never ending persistent threats? You eat if for breakfast because you're an alpha. Embrace it. Taste it. Let it take you over. You're a killer of men. And a bloody good one. That's why you've done it for years. No one has you on a leash, man. Submit to yourself and banish the tears and teddy bear holding. If you can't…get the fuck out of *my* shop."

Sebastian slapped Drake on the shoulder. "And if you choose to blow your brains out, don't make a mess. I'd prefer you hang yourself from a rafter in the rear. Plenty of paracord in the boxes."

Chapter 18

Drake took two more pills when Sebastian left. Sure as shit, twenty minutes later Drake could hear voices again. They weren't in his head, they were in the building.

Woolf finished toweling off and threw on the same shirt, albeit inside out as if that would help the dried-in white salt sweat and stench. He didn't want to keep a team of his peer operators waiting any longer, and wondered if he may recognize any of them. Without knowing the mission, Drake suspected the usual type of crew. Tier One. A spook. Probably everyone was off the books.

Now that he was more than technically a ghost, Sebastian would have hopefully thought about how to make introductions and assure full backstopping.

But as Drake rounded the rough drywalled corner, he wouldn't have been more surprised to see dogs sitting around the team table playing poker and sipping 7-Eleven Slurpees from a straw. There were just three of them. Sebastian. A woman, Middle Eastern from what he could tell, wearing a headscarf. And across from her, another Middle…no, it was a Sikh. Indian.

What the fuck? is what played in his mind. And for the first time, his head voices were silent. Maybe the shock, maybe the extra dose of meds. *This is a deep cover black ops team?* Drake thought.

No way. This was fucking international night at the community center minus cultural hors d'oeuvres. *Total joke. A Scot, a Persian, and an Indian walk into Danny's Palm Bar and Grill in San Diego…*

The woman before Drake had a reddish iced drink in a large clear Starbucks cup. Her turban-wearing cohort had what looked to be a milkshake or frozen coffee drink in a similar plastic container. Sebastian sat with a shit-eating grin on his face. The Scot-born Brit had a small white Starbucks cup with the writing "Chai Skim" in one hand and his other outstretched, presenting the sorry sight sitting in all its shitty splendor.

"Good. No mess," Sebastian said to Drake. "That means we're carrying on like soldiers." Sebastian spoke the words to Drake with a voice of venom, followed by a nod and stiff lower lip over a jutting chin. "I'd like to introduce you to the task force, D."

D? Drake questioned to himself, realizing Sebastian had not yet established an alias for Drake. Nor had Drake looked at the new cover docs. Amateur hour. Himself included.

The Sikh stood, taking his drink with him as if the Arab sitting to his right was going to steal a sip. He was tall. Maybe six foot six. Well groomed. His shoulders were wide. He could have been a football player, but his gut said pizza and potato chips. His eyelids or lashes were so dark that Drake squinted as the guy approached to see if they had makeup. "I'm Mojo," he introduced with no discernable accent. Mojo extended a large hand and executed an anaconda-crushing handshake that surprised Woolf.

Mojo leaned in, causing Drake to pull back. The younger man mouthed, "I knew your uncle," and beamed a friendly smile and a wink. Mojo motioned back toward the, for lack of better words, open-concept kitchen or break room table behind them against an exterior wall. "We didn't know what you wanted, so we brought you a black coffee. I think it is the Sumatra blend." He turned to the woman. "Did you get Sumatra or Colombia Medium?"

"Sumatra." She visibly cringed. Her response was sharp. Her accent and enunciation, just in a word and from what he heard in the background before was now in context of the Iranians Drake had been dealing with in the field, indicated she was Persian. Drake assessed her as Mojo rambled on about the other coffee being a vanilla latte, and that they had cream and sugar. The guy sounded more like a surfer or skater dude than he appeared outwardly. He was a fucking tool, but Drake suspected he was brilliant. It looked to Woolf like the Persian would agree with the tool judgment based on how her appearance of discomfort and agitation grew the longer the guy spoke.

The Persian cast an eye to Sebastian.

Yep. She was about to explode. But was she uncomfortable for Drake, or herself? It was clear that this chick had some serious fire inside. Then again, most Persians and other Middle Eastern women Drake had met over the years all had the capacity for some serious nuclear unleashing when provoked.

The woman pushed her chair back. Drake wondered what her hair looked like under the scarf. Short or long. Probably long. She definitely wore eye makeup, with the fashion trend that made her look catlike. Her nose was longer than average. Roman. She was tall, too. Not like Halliday, but probably five foot six or seven. Thin. Not unattractive by any means. Conservative in dress.

She approached Drake, leaving *her* drink behind. Keeping hands at the side, she said, taking a sharp breath, "Mena. Foreign affairs analyst, senior analyst team chief for the DIA before leading a section within the Agency's Persia House. I've degrees from Georgetown's terrorism and nuclear proliferation studies, American University in political science, and Princeton international relations. I've studied at the National Defense University for my master's in strategic intelligence, as well." She extended her hand after the biographical sketch.

Drake took her long fingers in firmly. "Thanks for the resume. Any sports?"

She stammered as if being told she left out a letter during the national spelling bee championship. "I don't understand."

"Exactly." *You're a fucking tool, too.*

Tool, tool, and a go-take-the-hill-at-any-cost asshole. Drake shrugged to Sebastian. "What gives, Chief?"

"Can you sit with us a moment?" Sebastian motioned toward the back counter. "Take a coffee and just listen, if you will."

Drake headed for the joe. "I'm listening," he called back.

"We can wait another minute. The discussion requires full attention—of the *team*."

Woolf gave his senior the appropriate level of respect, grabbing the closest coffee cup, and quickly took his seat. This was going to be good. Drake didn't have to like his situation, but his career was honed within the time-honored traditions of respecting superior officers, or at least the appearance when situations suited. His uncle, OT, had quite literally beat that into Drake.

"Let me start by saying Mojo is read in to this effort since day one. He has primarily worked with NSA Special Source Operations in the Enviro Analysis branch. With your approval, I would like to add Mena. She is an authority on our situation, and I feel she could help you. She has met your other two colleagues and assisted in some of the initial analysis and planning."

Ah, the one that almost got us killed. Check. Drake brushed his palms together in agitation but said nothing. He expected his head voices to be screaming in protest, but they remained silent. "Fine. I'm listening," he defended sharply, not meaning to snap so aggressively. "Sorry. First coffee."

"Okay, great. Our situation is this. We've attained message traffic that coincides with reports of stolen radiological agents from the University of Chicago. What news media has not been privy to, nor uncovered at this juncture, is the dreadful nature of the radiological agent."

"Let me guess. It's the most powerful weapon ever developed that will wipe out the entire Eastern Seaboard if we don't stop it within the next twenty-four hours."

The table glared at Drake.

"I'll shut up." Drake took a large pull of his coffee. He was off. More hostile and argumentative than normal. He didn't mean to try to pick a fight.

"D. It is indeed weaponized. Quite deadly, but it has what the experts call a short half-life. Or duration to cause affliction."

"Got it."

"The person of interest is a Venezuelan student, who has not yet been located. We assume by his prior communications that he has been using another device for communications. From the social linkages and background information we have received through the NCTC, his extended family had mid-level leadership positions within Hezbollah."

"Was he recruited back in?"

"We're still developing this," Sebastian elaborated. "However, what we do know is that his grandfather was suspected of being a double agent in Lebanon working for the Israelis. He martyred himself in an explosion that killed a number of Israeli soldiers. Intelligence reports, going back some time now, asserted he may have been trying to reclaim honor and clear the family name. The family moved to Venezuela before that time. We have no intelligence on the suspect's family in Venezuela due to a lack of collection priorities and frankly the black box to operate there in past years. In his last known activities, we find no physical training evidence, no communications seeking advice or target talk. No weapons training. No unusual financial patterns. No pretext to travel. Essentially, his affairs are in order with no plane tickets or luggage purchase. He is today's young terrorist. Lazy and entitled."

A question formed on Woolf's lips.

Mojo jumped in. "You want to know what *we've* been looking at to find this out. We have a system that is, as I am sure you are aware, capable of passive and active SIGINT collection systems interception. VoIP traffic is processed through TURMOIL's HAMMERCHANT module, and digital telephony through CONVEYANCE. Those systems are interconnected through a number of databases for mission system interfaces and data repositories. In particular…"

"Stop. Mojo, right?" Drake continued with affirmation. "I know how the NSA components, selectors, cross-feeding databases, and programs work."

"Right." Mojo started again, his words working as rapidly as his hand movements, which looked like they were signing for the deaf at an Eminem concert. "Basically, once we knew where his location typically was, we triangulated other communication devices in and around that same, well, more precise location, like, exactly where that fucker was at all times. Right? Call chaining and data diodes between high and low sides of a network. We use CRAYONBAD Co-Traveler Analytics to develop more targets that are unknown associates who may be traveling with or meeting our known target. Then I do a little magic with Thunderbunny, Wireshark, and Splunk."

Mena closed her eyes and took a deep breath with her palms on the table and fingers spread out in silent screams.

Mojo continued his rambling, "…and then overlaid it with other communications of interest and those actors around the world, ya know some Low-Level Voice Intercept teams humping Wolfhounds, got the King Air suckers, do a lil' Splunk data sorting, then…"

The Persian's eyes shot open. "Goddammit, Manmeet, just tell him we think he was talking to Hezbollah in South America, people at the Venezuelan embassy, and those people are talking to the Iranians, for God's sake," Mena blurted.

"Jeezus," Mojo responded, then shut his Admiral Analyst mouth feed.

Drake softened with a grin, turning his own hand up from the table to a thumbs-up to Mena. "Any target identified yet?"

Sebastian pursed his lips and shook his head no. "The United States is a target-rich environment. It could be anywhere. We have some good intel but don't want to exclude anything. Still chatter on the lower East Coast, but nothing in the past twenty-four hours. Some still in Chicago, but that has also reduced in frequency and endpoints." He shrugged.

Mojo stole the floor while Sebastian's remarks set in. "There's the most likely connection there, especially with the theft. I've just last night put in the prospects for lat and long location data, GCID to compute date, time, locations, and movements. Collectively based on functional relevance. Also tabbing closeness for frequent power-downs and handset swapping. But you know, prior, terrorists have been technically challenged getting WMD in-country. Whether you Americans, well *we,* have just beaten the odds or whether WMD acquisition has been out of their reach short of a few scenarios…"

Sebastian raised his hand and put a finger on his lips. "Shhh."

Mena added her two cents while Mojo was silenced. "Any attack could cause mass disruption and anxiety. The compounds stolen are likely not at a size or complexity to reach catastrophic threshold, to your earlier remark."

"I was kidding before, but tell that to the family of the first person who dies, to the news media that overreacts, or to the market crash," Drake tossed out. "Just for starters."

"True," she conceded, "but from a national threat standpoint, this isn't a high priority given the safety mechanisms the administration has in place. Most powerful radionuclides can be detected with radiation systems at ports of entry and exit or international borders. Our hypothesis is that this may remain in Chicago. I have my own belief that—"

Mojo jumped in, "Our fear is of an indiscriminate, relative mass-casualty violent event. Like face-peeling shit on CNN. You know. Like fucking babies dead in the street like our own version of Syria." Mojo tilted his head, bulged his eyes and stuck out his tongue.

"God, Mojo." Mena choked in disgust. "As I was starting to say, I believe that—"

Sebastian interrupted, "Mena"—he smiled politely—"I know what you're going to say, and let's stick to facts."

Mena's dark eyebrows pointed down her beaklike nose to tightening lips. "It's important to mention the—"

Sebastian double-tapped her with a shooting look that killed whatever she was going to say.

"Okay. Who do we need kill to stop this? The student?" Drake pressed to Sebastian. "And aside from the theft of radioactive material in Chicago, I'm assuming you have tied the Iranians that we've been hunting to this and to the Venezuelan consulates in the US from the drone footage I saved from our last pursuit…" He shot a look to Sebastian. "I'm assuming they aren't read in to that, so I'll leave that alone. But bottom line, if you are bringing it to me, it means the WMD factors for homeland don't matter. You know the people, they have the material, the money doesn't matter so fuck following it, and you've got the SIGINT to get all the data and knowledge and orders with all the lines of communication that you can eat. But since you don't know what infrastructure they are going to attack, you need someone dead fast. And going through the motions of calling the FBI to do legal wire taps will be too late for a year-long approach. Am I right? You just want the Chicago players taken out."

Mena shot a cross look to Woolf as if she just heard Celine Dion was leaving Las Vegas and girls' weekend was canceled. "What are you saying? You have no idea what they are capable of. Sebastian. Tell him. This isn't about killing. I can't believe—"

"Let me stop you there, sister. This isn't coffee shop poetry night." Woolf's hand was raised and jutting out in full Heisman-trophy extension. His rear communication knife hand was locked and loaded for the next point. "What do you do in the absence of knowledge when a major threat persists?"

Flummoxed, Mena answered as if it was an academic question. She started with the intelligence cycle. "First you do your collection, your—"

"No." Drake paused for a second before the onslaught of head voices slowed his ability to articulate himself without interruption. Still they were silent, but his frustration was growing. "Mena, this isn't a policy issue. It's counterterrorism. The strategic intel phase is done when you walk into this shop. This is targeting. Tactical. Kinetic response. We kill who we can in war. If you're here in this building, and you want to be part of what we do, you need to come to the realization that I am only here to hunt down and kill whatever is out there in the forest." He paused for emphasis. "Nonviolent war is diplomacy. I'm no diplomat. I just want this done."

Mena remained blank.

Drake figured she was thinking of a rebuttal, so best end this now. "Let me say this another way from a seasoned intelligence community voice. When people come to me, they either ask me to develop the whole target package from scratch or they give me one. I would expect you to have a target. I need to know everything about him. This unit is about signals and HUMINT. So, the bottom line is, just tell me where he lives, who he calls. Does he email, text, Snapchat, Skype, WhatsApp? Tell me about Chicago. Who would handle administration, logistics, security for a cell? Is an emir involved? We need signatures of their movements and communications. Their pattern of life. Target package. BBC. Whatever you want to call it. Red bull's-eye to snuff. AFO reconnaissance and surveillance clock has counted down to zero. You've given Sebastian an intelligence picture. From there, he committed me as the resource to confirm battlespace conditions with steel and gunpowder. Off the books threat elimination."

Mena looked down.

Mojo's face showed a good poker hand. Maybe even a smile. If he worked with OT, he was waist-deep in the dark mire. Drake left him alone. The guy was a dork and annoying, but he was analyst as fuck. He could stay.

"Sebastian?"

"Yes. That is an accurate view. And Mr. Singh here has much of what you require of our Lebanese target and his Venezuelan compatriots. But Ms. Shabpareh…" Sebastian reached over and touched her hand, which she retracted. "Drake raises a good point. While I know you can appreciate the notion of this being a gray-zone conflict, and that the aggressors are more than willing to accept terror, covert action, and subversion, it may come down to elimination and not just collection." He guided a stern look of disappointment to her. "I thought you understood this."

"Sebastian, you said that I would be accompanying a SIGINT specialist to Chicago to help identify and assess—"

"Hold the fuck up. No. No, no, no, no, no. No!" Drake slapped the table. "No fucking way!"

Mena postured. "I can assure you—"

Drake popped up from his chair and lurched with both hands coming down heavy before him. *Let's see what this bitch is made of.* The inner voice was Drake.

Mena was a statue. Not even a blink.

Mojo reacted with a shout and dropped his coffee, which exploded on the table, sending ice sliding across.

"Assure me what?" *Fucking kill this cold bitch.* Again. Drake. "You're…a goddamned virgin…telling me how to write a sex scene!" Woolf screamed.

"Dude, *I'm* not a virgin," Mojo muttered, still twitchy from being startled.

He was met with eyes of rage building in the Man from Orange.

"Just sayin'." Mojo shriveled.

Drake refocused his aggression toward the Persian idealist. "When our boots hit the ground as we're chasing Elvis, it won't be long before the first explosions or gunfire go off. I won't be able to drag you as we go room to room trying to remember names and faces committed to memory as we assess our shoot don't shoot options. There's no time for questions. No time to think. No time to question orders. You pull the trigger and you kill what's in front of you most of the time." He stopped. "Take off your headscarf."

Her mouth opened in shock at the mere suggestion. Mena glanced at Sebastian and then to Mojo.

Sebastian looked like he was holding in a smile, and then his hand passed over his mouth.

Mojo looked like he had just swallowed a cockroach.

"Don't look at them." Drake sizzled. "Look at me. This isn't an HR complaint you get to make and a call for witnesses."

"You have no right," she accused, visibly offended and wallowing in her own growing anger.

"You have your rights and values. My rights and values are the mission. This isn't about your ability to keep secrets by being here. It's about breaking laws to keep the rule of law."

"This"—she pointed to her head—"is about my religion."

"If you work with me, you better be fucking ready to break covenants with God every damned day. If you can't take off a *hat*, you're going to shit your pants the first time we kick in a door and violate hundreds of civil rights protections and global human rights laws. Take it off, lady, or get the fuck out."

Mena arose. Her breathing noticeably accelerated. She headed for the door without a sound. Then, "I'm not leaving because of what you said. You're a stupid man playing vulgar games," she hissed just over her breath.

"Sorry, lady, hated to tell you for the first time that people don't really fight terrorists from the cubicles," Drake called out. "They fucking shoot 'em in the head. They send targeting coordinates and blow them off the road. And during weddings. They slit their throats in the dead of the night. And they sure as all fuck don't wear a headscarf on the streets of Chicago when they're discreetly hunting down dudes looking to blow up the city and themselves just so they can get laid in heaven!" Drake taunted mercilessly. He was being cruel now but couldn't stop.

Mena whipped around and stormed toward the men. Her hands and arms were a flurry of movement around her head. As she navigated around the table, she removed the dark fabric from her head and tossed it to the ground. Her jet-black hair dropped, draping eyes of hellfire.

Fuck. Wonder Woman's coming at me.

In a flash, she dodged around Mojo and beelined to Woolf. Upon entering Drake's personal space, she roared, "I've dealt with this bullshit—"

The Man from Orange grabbed her outstretched arms above the elbow, jerking Mena over the chairs and onto the table. His face was expressionless as he tossed her down onto the coffees, her legs flopping akimbo.

"Fuuuck," Mojo muttered as more coffee exploded everywhere.

Mena was enraged and grunted as she flung her legs up toward Drake's head.

He rocked his neck back just in time and pushed her arm closer to him up and away.

Her flailing legs flopped down hard away from him, crashing down on the table.

Mena flung her free right arm back toward Drake's groin.

"Ameri-Do-Te" Mojo chuckled, his eyes wide at the spectacle.

Drake countered, pivoting his hips inward, slid his grip down to her wrist and gave it an inward twist. She was wily and agile for a bookworm who carried her diplomas in her purse. Surprisingly strong and had fire. Maybe she had taken a Tae Kwon Do class as a college elective or kickboxing when her Pilates class was canceled; Drake brooded in the moment but could not afford to let his guard down for even a moment.

She bent her elbow in and flopped onto her stomach, guided by the extreme joint pain and physical pressure of the fulcrum lock.

Drake's hand was now on Mena's, locking it askew. She kicked at the table, grumbling.

Sebastian slammed his hand on the table. "Warren Woolf! That will be all for now."

The MI6 man still looked more amused than agitated despite just outing Drake.

The Man from Orange jerked his head up, sending a flaming look to Sebastian. "If that's how the British do OPSEC, no wonder you get owned."

Sebastian winced at his revealing mistake caused by the heat of the moment. To Drake, Sebastian was trying to draw out the alpha in all of the team members. Or at least Drake and Mena. This wasn't a meeting. This was selection. Staged. Exactly who was being selected was the bigger question.

Drake scanned the people in the room. There was absolutely nothing stopping him from killing every one of them and then just stepping away from it all. He contemplated that for a moment. The head voices were saying nothing. The delusions were all aligned and in favor of him wiping out the room. Even the sounds of his father were quieted. Maybe all it took to quiet the voices was to fully succumb to their desires.

Drake leaned in to Mena's ear. "I have nothing against you, miss. You're not trained, and you *will* die in the field. That could get *me* killed in the field. And if *we* die, *more* people will die."

Drake released her arm and stepped back. "You don't get to come for a ride-along, because people discriminate against you because you're Muslim, or a woman, or some other human resources social bullshit," he lectured. Calm now. The rage was at a simmer. He couldn't believe how calm the voices were. The meds might be working. He never attributed the growing uncontrollable rage to them.

"Harsh," Mojo quipped, amused.

"You either, dude," Drake snapped, pissed at the glib remark. "Have you ever seen combat? Have you ever been in a fucking war zone?"

Mojo shook his head, flummoxed. "I mean. I…"

"You what?" Drake stepped toward Mojo, who scooted his chair back, ready to make a break for it. "What the fuck have you done?"

"I…nothing really. I can shoot."

"Shoot? You've killed someone?" Drake stopped. His brows raised and head tilted, waiting for the answer of the century.

"Not. Not a real—"

"A paper target? A zombie. Don't you dare fucking say a video game. Don't you fucking say that for one second."

Mojo's head cowed, looking up over dropped shoulders to the alpha before him. "Bro, I never said I wanted to go. I'm cool just doing my thing." He glanced to Sebastian, who was busy wiping coffee splatter off his suit jacket. "Dude, get the fuck away from me. You made your point. We're just here to help."

Drake ran his trembling fingers through his still-damp hair. He walked around Mojo, who swiveled slowly, unaware of what this nutjob would do next.

The headscarf lay on the ground in a delicate little heap. It was a religious adornment that triggered a recollection to Woolf of a lover's teddy tossed on the bedroom floor. A sight he hadn't seen for nearly a decade. Even then, it had only lasted a week. Drake picked up the hijab, sorting the fringed ends and letting them drop as he gingerly held the middle of the fabric to let the cloth flatten. He folded the ends up, squaring the satin hijab shawl, and placed it on a dry spot on the table before turning his back to the team, never making eye contact.

Without a word, Drake Woolf walked out the door.

Chapter 19

Mena first looked at Sebastian. With a slow nod, she chased after Drake. Sebastian shouted for her to just let him go. This Drake heard as he was taking his last step down from the stairs, and the door opened and then slammed against the brick wall.

The shout and slam startled Drake from his circling thoughts. He winced because the loud slam surprised him so badly, causing an instant, indescribable rush of fear that washed over him. His eyes were already pooled with remorse and self-doubt, and he turned away to hide his vulnerability. "You don't want round two, lady," he said without turning back.

"Things got out of hand." She quick-stepped down the concrete. "I want to talk."

"There's nothing to discuss." Drake cut the corner, evading her. "We're done. I'm not apologizing."

"Then I'm going on my own."

"Good luck with that."

Drake had no car, no home, no family or friends, so as he walked off, he realized he really had no place to go. It didn't matter. He just needed an escape. For the first time in his life, Drake wished the voices were there to drown her out.

"I know General Shirazian and have studied General Soleimani's strategies and movements. I know what they can do."

Drake quickened his steps. *Of course you do. Another analyst who thinks they can profile from CNN reports and* Time *magazine articles.*

"He's going to use children. That's what he does."

Drake stopped. Maybe it was the dream he had.

"Young boys and girls."
Now you've got my attention.
This Mena knew.
She was in.

Chapter 20

The Chicago Lawndale Christian Church of God "community outreach" bus revved in the weed-filled, deserted parking lot. Oswald Robinson adjusted his tie impatiently in the driver's mirror. He flipped his eyes up to the mirror and counted the children behind him. His girlfriend, Shawnay, caught his glance. She smiled, exposing her meth-mouthed cavern of decay that was chomping on a piece of gum before swatting the boy to her right. Girl had switched to other junk, but there was no saving those rotting choppers.

"Quit yo fidgetin', Dantrell." Shawnay threatened across the aisle, "I'll smack your ass you do it again."

"Keep your hand off me, bitch! You ain't my mamma," the young boy reminded.

"No, I ain't no *whore* like your mamma." Shawnay stood up and hammered down on the boy.

He ducked into the green pleather seat. The blow glanced off his shoulder. His head popped up with a gapped grin of a nine-year-old. "Missed, bitch." The grin quickly faded as Dantrell saw a different open palm swinging down. The force and pain of the sting dropped the young boy from his seat to the filthy, gum-stuck floor.

"You mind your mouth, boy," Oswald shouted, towering from above. His hand cocked back for round two.

Shawnay started to pile on additional scolding to the boy when she, too, was met with a sharp slap, sending her purple gum flying out of her mouth and onto the floor. Her body collapsed into the green seat as she cursed. Her own hand went to her stinging cheek as she looked at the small boy still doing the same.

"You can just shut the fuck up, too." Oswald gave a smile and a nod to the other kids as he walked back to the front. "Zarielle, Kayjon bothering you?"

"No, Mr. Oz. He just talkin' some shit. But he aight," confirmed the eight-year-old girl with her hair in looped braids and pink ribbons.

Her seatmate, Kayjon, shrunk down in the seat, leery of a whack.

Oz leaned over the seat and pulled at Zarielle's shirt sleeve to cover a burn across her wrist. "Cover that up, girl. You playin' too hard in the school yard. White folk don't wanna buy candy from no skeezer with cuts an' shit."

Two more boys entered the bus. Each held large cardboard boxes with smaller boxes within, visible from the opened top flaps.

"Got the candy, Oz," confirmed one older boy, maybe eleven years old. He wore a maroon Lawndale Athletics football jersey with gold piping and letters.

The boy behind him, approximately the same age, announced, "Yo, Oz, Two-bags is outside. He wanna talk."

"Two-bags, huh?" Oswald's face dropped as if it was met with one of his own jaw-rattling slaps. "He say what he want? He didn't say nothin' about the money, huh?"

"No, Oz. He just say to get muthafuckin' Oz ass out there and shit. But he don't seem pissed or nothin'. He just bein' all Two-bags."

Oz ducked to spy through the bus windows.

The white BMW 7 Series with white rims was sure enough there, its luxury a contrast to the deteriorated backdrop of shuttered, condemned, or abandoned buildings. Full block-out tinted windows were rolled up save for the passenger side that was cracked about four inches down.

Vagrants and junkies kept their distance and their eyes straight ahead and away from the car. Nobody was up for getting near Two-bags now that he was calling the shots in Lawndale. He had piled plenty of bodies to climb to the top.

"All right. All right. All good. We all good." Oz rubbed his ear. "Okay. Y'all just be chill. I'll be back, and then we head out and make some money. Hear me? We runnin' late, so we just do Oak Park neighborhoods. Make our dime there on the west side. Aight?"

Any kid paying attention just shrugged and kept their trap shut.

Oswald exited the yellow-orange bus with blue-and-white lettering over old-school script. The candy-man readjusted his tie again as he swaggered over to the neighborhood tough's car.

Two-bags ran everything now like his Chicago mafioso predecessors ran the city in the thirties. As a street-gangster leader, he took profits from the candy gangs like Oswald's, as well as running drugs and weapons in this part of Lawndale and its touchpoint neighborhoods. In a matter of two short years, he had united the local gangs: Four Corner Hustlers, New Breeds, Black Souls, and Gangster Disciples to off-seat the Vice Lords, and established the Lawndale Legends. To that end, he was king of these blighted streets.

As Oz approached the big boss, he wondered who would come to his own funeral if Two-bags and his crew opened up on him in the next seconds.

The windows lowered further. The driver two-hand-steadied a large silver pistol pointed right at Oswald.

"Hey, hey. N-no need to put th-that squeezer up in my grill, you know what I'm s-sayin'," Oswald stammered with a broken voice.

Two-bags blew out a haze of smoke from behind the driver.

"There he is. That's the man, Two-bags. Good morning to you, sir. Good morning. Hallowed ground I'm walking on heeya." Oswald gave a slight bow.

Two-bags extended a fist bump from the window to Oswald. "Oz the Wizard." He laughed. "The candy-man can, right?"

"Ha-ha," Oz chuckled nervously. "That's right. The Wizard making candy magic for you. Fixin' to make more here in a few. Got a new crew today and have three more runnin' later. Here to make you some Benjamins with the young Gs while I learn them respect."

"Shiit. You think I give a fuck about your chocolate bar hustle?"

Oz still couldn't see Two-bags's face in the shadow and smoke.

"Yeah, man. I know you makin' the *large* coin. Cuz you the man's man. I know you got your fingers in a lot. A lot!"

"Shut the fuck up."

"Okay. Okay. Shuttin' up. All shut."

"How many busses you got?"

"Busses? I got one. I make a drop. Come back, get my next load. Drop them. Get the next."

"You got four crews? How many dat?"

"Well, they don't always show, know what I'm sayin'. Sometimes more, sometimes less."

Another silver handgun emerged from the window. This time through the smoke and on the ring-adorned hand of Two-bags. "How many?"

"I get about eighty kids on a good day. Can get about a hundred if cops do a sweep an' push the young-uns from the corners."

The gun retracted and was replaced by another of Two-bags's ring-adorned hands. A diamond and gold watch or bracelet dangled behind three stacks of outstretched cash. "Buy me three more busses. Get them from churches. Give them this cash and say Two-bags wants them to get a new bus and give theirs to you. Have them ask their congregation who can drive a bus on a day I say."

"Ho, ho. Two-bags. You too generous. That's a big operation. I can't—"

"It's for another job. All you need to do is get the busses. Park them here in this lot. Make sure no one fucks with them. Get security. I want a hundred kids ready to go this Sunday."

"Sunday? This comin' up Sunday? That's St. Patrick's Day. No one's gonna be around to want candy with all the parades and parties. Why you want—"

The gun re-emerged. "Take the motherfucking money. Do what I fuckin' say, and you get paid. Feel me? You gotta be point man. Can't miss a beat, and you can't be off your square. I got bi'ness meetings an' shit. People tryin' to get the ups on me when I all motherfuckin' generous an' shit."

Oswald looked around the area and took the cash, stuffing it into his suit jacket pockets. "I gotchu. All good. Two ears for listening. One mouth for talking. And I'm shuttin' the talker." Oz stretched his neck and chin to show his closed lips.

"And this." Two-bags held out a ZTE prepaid flip phone. "I will call you. If there are problems, you call me. But we ain't gonna has no problems. Or you gots the problem. This is a direct line to me, and I'll kill you, your family, and all those kids if you lose this phone or make any calls with it to anyone but me. But you ain't gonna call me, because no problems."

Oz took the phone. "See," he insisted. "Still not talkin'. But I do hear you loud and clear." Oz pulled a finger across his lips like a zipper and dialed Two-bags's number.

When it rang, Two-bags's eyes about popped out from his head. "Is you a dumb motherfucker or what?"

"Just showin' you it works. And I ain't sayin' nothin'. All good with a roger 10-4, good buddy."

The slight geolocation device separation as Two-bags handed the phone to Oz was captured by the NSA satellite relay through Co-Traveler Analytics. The 4G LTE Tracfone data set had been last tracked in Caracas a week ago until it was turned on again this very morning upon leaving the Consulate General of Venezuela in Chicago's Civic Opera building. The raw data was sent as an alert to Mojo Singh's desk, among others in the building, but only Mojo would actually look through it proactively and set the attributes on his monitoring sessions.

Chapter 21

Mena spoke softly as she neared Drake, explaining in detail what she believed Chicago was up against. "The generals have used children for war. My brothers were taken in the war when I was young. They were ten and twelve. My father, before he passed, said General Shirazian gave thousands of boys keys around their necks to sweep minefields. The boys thought they had keys to heaven. They rushed the Iraqis. The ones who didn't explode."

Drake turned to Mena, his face softened only slightly with details he had only heard anecdotally over the years.

"The Iraqis panicked and didn't shoot at the children. They were overtaken by small waves of Iranian soldiers who followed closely behind."

"That was about thirty years ago. Isn't that a specific tactic to clear the minefields? It would never fly now, even with the current regime."

"He was a young commander. The world does not know what he did to the Kurds and to ethnic groups in Iran, Azerbaijan, Afghanistan, even to the north, with the same approach of using children in battle."

"Turkmenistan," Drake noted more to himself than to Mena.

Mena nodded. "Gas disputes. The general sent children over the border on bicycles with grenades. There were second waves of attacks much greater that were hidden by the confusion of the children."

Drake shook his head. "I'm sorry to hear this, but I can't see this happening in Chicago. I mean, where are they going to convince kids to be suicide bombers without that raising some serious red flags to local police?" He wrestled with the concept. "Is this what you were trying to say in there?"

"I've been trying to warn the intelligence community for years about General Shirazian. Even in my position, no one wants to listen to me."

"I can't help you. It's farfetched, likely biased from your own experiences, and you're not qualified to work in the field. Are you?" He didn't wait for a response. "Did I miss something, or did you at least go through FTC?" he asked, referencing the abbreviation for the down and dirty basic spook course.

"No. But I know I can help. I can stay out of your way. I can work with Mojo, who's going to stay back at the Fort in Maryland. I can get things set up. Hotels, buy you things. I'll be just support."

You're a liability. And why would Sebastian add you to a quick and dirty kill mission?

His mouth clicked once, but he caught the next and forced his tongue into his teeth. Drake processed what little he could ascertain about Mena. True, she had to have been extensively vetted. She would have been subjected to a full-scope polygraph that combines counterintelligence and lifestyle. She's obviously over thirty years old if she was born in Iran during the war. So, to have come from Iran, become a US citizen, work across DOD and the CIA, and to be pulled in by Sebastian, she was probably a valuable analyst. To somebody.

Shit. What to do?

"Hello? Are you going to say something?" she asked impatiently.

"I'm thinking. I prefer to think than talk."

"Well, it's not like you have a panel of experts in your head, so why don't you tell me what you're thinking?"

Drake glared. "You'd be surprised. My experts just aren't saying anything right now."

"Look. Warren, right?"

"You need to seriously forget that you ever heard that name. I mean gravely serious, as in if you ever utter that word, I will be there."

His warning meant nothing in the moment. Mena was fixated on expressing her point. "I just want to be in a position to make a difference. I need to be where I can do something and not just get cut off or ignored. I don't have family anymore, I'm not married, and I can't talk to my cousins or aunts and uncles because of my job. I won't get in your way. If I get killed, it's not like anyone will notice anyway."

Drake took in a chest full of her sob story and breathed out the residual thoughts of potential bullshit. *Guess that makes us both fodder to take this guy out.*

"I'll talk to Sebastian. We'll head out tomorrow."

"Thank you, I'll pack my things tonight."

He guided her back to the building with a light hand to her back. "No, you won't."

"Why not?" She stopped, ready for another fight.

"You want to play with the big boys, you're with the big boys. Welcome to pre-op isolation." Drake extended his hand. "Give me your phone. Find a place on the floor to set up your cot for a few winks. But get ready. You're in for a night of tradecraft 101."

Chapter 22

Special Agent Tresa Halliday had expected her boss to meet her at a casual diner or coffee shop somewhere close to headquarters. When she received the text directing her to a DC location called La Chaumiere, on M Street just off Pennsylvania Avenue, her gut nagged, *Girl, you're way underdressed.*

The inside of the restaurant, however, was cozier than she had expected. The floor had a rustic tile, and although white tablecloths looked fancy, the chairs looked like they could have been in a Wisconsin family restaurant, and certainly the burgundy leather- or pleather-covered booth backs would fit in to the Midwest or any other decent Greek family diner. She kind of liked it and assumed this was what "French country" may mean.

And then she saw Earl Johnson. *The* grand poohbah of the FBI's counterintelligence function. He was dressed in his usual style, which Tresa considered conservative high-brow slob. Pretentious in attitude, polyester in reality. The other patrons were more sharply dressed. She suspected Earl wished he were one of them. He probably thought he was smarter than them all, but she figured he lacked the upper-crust pedigree.

As she approached, he didn't stand. He simply motioned with a hand for her to take the seat across from him.

"Sir," she acknowledged before taking a seat.

"Sparkling or still?" he asked.

When she didn't answer and was looking around confused, he repeated, "Water. Tap or with bubbles."

"Yes, sir. I know what it means. I was looking around to see if they had iced tea. *Still* iced tea," she joked, but the levity fell just as her napkin slid off her lap, too. "So, do all the CI agents get to come here?"

Earl lifted his chin and straightened his glasses. He looked as though he had lost even more weight in the past week, and the guy didn't have much to spare with his tall and gaunt frame. "I take my new ghosts here. It's as close as we can get to the original."

"Original what?"

"La Niçoise. An old Georgetown classic. It's where Angleton frequented in his day, boozing it up with Beltway contacts and who knows whom else."

"He worked for our group?" she teased, knowing who he was talking about but wanting to jack with all that was holy to grumpy old Earl.

She evoked exactly what she hoped. Earl looked at her sideways with raised eyebrows. "James Jesus."

"James Jesus who?" Halliday could hardly keep a smile from cracking.

Earl Johnson folded his hands on the table's edge and, looking down, shot his head slightly in what could only be interpreted by Tresa as disapproval.

"Uh, is he still or sparkling?"

This time, the levity found that miniscule warm spot in Earl's heart, and he softened like a parent accepting a weed from a toddler who was calling it a flower. He took in a deep breath. "For counterintelligence agents, he is the Godfather." Earl nodded again in deference to only himself. "Albeit he had his flaws in both ways, mindset and...assessment of character." Earl paused as if satisfied with his answer. "He was brilliant, but he alienated many. I fear I share some of those same traits." He looked up to Halliday.

She shrugged. "I got nothing."

Confused, he continued. "Angleton believed that secret elements of the government, in his case, intelligence, never had to comply *with* the government. And that is flawed. Deeply flawed." Earl took a sip of his sparkling water then poured some more. The label read Topo Chico, which Tresa was pretty sure wasn't French. The server came around and Earl dismissed her as soon as she entered their airspace.

"Excuse me, miss," Tresa called back to the woman. "I would like something. Iced tea, please." Tresa turned to Earl. "Continue." *Dick*.

Earl lowered his shoulders and moved slightly forward to Halliday. "He, Angleton, believed and often acted like he could disobey the rules. And that his job demanded it. Follow?"

She didn't and said as much. "You want me to start breaking rules to catch these guys?" Tresa asked, also lowering her volume.

Earl pushed back into his chair. "No." He looked around at the people turning toward him. He leaned in. "Not us. Them. They are breaking the rules. They know that our enemies think we have certain limits on our own soil, and we do; well, we're supposed to."

"Well, correct me if I'm wrong, but isn't that the whole reason we're trying to go after them?" She raised her no-shit hands.

He huffed.

"What? Can't you tell me who *they* are?"

Earl motioned for her to come closer. "ISA," he said with a lowered head. "Orange. They were a special mission unit. The president, for all practical purposes, disbanded them. But that was a cover. They kept a small contingency. Our man. A handful of others. They are chartered to do preemptive strikes against threats within the country. They have a charter to kill."

"And Woolf and his crew have that charter, which allows them to fly out of bases, disappear, get all kinds of gear and gadgets." She nodded. "And they are so deep no one knows how to find them."

"Or wants to find them," he added.

She squinted, uncomfortable about the next question. "Can we eat? I'm starving."

Ignoring her, he leaned in again. "We need to penetrate them. Which leads me to another lesson about Angleton." He didn't wait for her approval to go on about the legendary spymaster. "Angleton didn't think very highly of women. He thought they caused problems instead of solving them. I know you are a dedicated problem solver. That's why I need you to penetrate them." His look was matter of fact. And he didn't appear willing to debate the topic. End of discussion.

"I don't even know where they are. And if I did, then what?"

Earl's hand drifted to his silverware. He tapped the knife with his finger and stared into her eyes. His brows furrowed over the glasses' frames. "In counterintelligence and counterespionage, if you can no longer frustrate your enemy, eliminate your enemy. Their recklessness killed our director. I want them dead. And I want you to start by following one Sebastian Francis Haggerty. But caution. He is not a man to be trifled with. Hell, he may actually be following me. Something I still have to determine."

"And is Sebastian a big secret, too, that I'll find out about in a week from now? Whenever you feel I'm *fit* to know?"

"Not at all. British MI6 who worked for years with the SAS Increment hunter killer teams. You think Drake Woolf is a threat, this man is the definition of ungentlemanly warfare. But for now, he runs ICEPICK, the TFO program, while covered by his contracts at NSA. He will keep an arm's length for sure. He won't go on missions; he won't sit from day to day with his analysts. He will remain having fancy lunches with the intelligence community's directors and deputies."

"So, it seems pretty stupid to follow him. Why not just trace his phone? See where he banks, and ask your contacts who the guy's closest community allies are. In the meanwhile, I'll try to figure where they are headed next and try to get close. Unless, of course, one of them just calls me up and asks me out on a date."

Johnson sipped from his glass again and swished the water in his mouth. "They have a cassoulet that you may enjoy. You probably call it a Swanson pot pie where you come from."

"Thanks," she said, getting up with a loud screech. "They probably call it that where you come from, too. You just eat it with a box of wine with a cork on the side. I've got work to do, Deputy Director…Johnson. If you'll excuse me, I think I'm getting my period," she announced.

Halliday walked away as Earl Johnson ping-ponged his head to see who among the crowd was looking at him.

Chapter 23

Gebran Daouk had been in lockdown, hiding for a week. Things were not going according to his initial plan, to say the least. The Hezbollah scientist and heavyweight wannabe peered through a crack opening of the shaded third-story apartment window. It was a sunny day in Chicago, and while the weather outside looked cool by the dress of passersby, it was stifling in the cramped apartment.

"Did they call yet?" Gebran asked the two men relaxed on a tattered sofa in an adjoining room. One played a video game, thumbing a wireless Xbox controller. The other man was slumped into the worn cushions, feet on a scratched second-hand coffee table, spooning dry cereal from a bowl.

"It's only been two days," the gamer replied. "They won't call anyway. You're lucky they haven't killed you for making such a request and not telling them where you hid the material," he reminded the younger man in the tongue of Lebanese Arabic. "But don't worry, they'll have you in a palace sitting on a throne in no time. Or a bullet once they find your bomb materials."

The two men laughed. Gebran did not.

"You're a bastard, boy. And you'll never be given a commander position if you haven't fought in Syria or Palestine. And they won't call. New protocol, Gebran. You would know this if *you* were in charge. The master planner of Archangel has no wings without the Azrael bomb."

Gebran was furious. "I've told you who my grandfather was. Don't mock me. You idiots should be working for me. And it's not a bomb." Gebran needed the WMD for his own leverage, but he hadn't expected such delays. They should be speaking to him about the plans so he could optimize the attack. Some other idiot committed to going to prayers all day could kill themselves as a martyr. At least that was his long-held opinion. He was a leadership legacy, or so he told himself, and intended to stake his claim.

"Would we still be idiots if we were working for you or bigger idiots?" asked the other Lebanese man on the couch while crunching loudly on his cereal.

His buddy guffawed. "We could be your *Despicable Me* yellow minions, Doctor." He laughed again. "It's on my phone. I can stream it. We should watch again."

"That's it. I'm leaving," Gebran announced as he turned for the door.

Even with the noise of the *Fortnite* game, Gebran heard the slide clicks of actual guns and knew they were once again pointed at his back.

"Go ahead. Shoot me. Kill me. They will kill you and your families."

"I think they would promote us."

"Nasrallah would have your heads. My grandfather was close with Mustafa Badr al-Din, head of External Operations. My grandfather even helped appoint Talal Hamiya of the Overseas Unit. He had a seat at the table."

"Sit down, Gebran. Here is your only seat. Don't be this way. We are all tired of being here. But this is what we are told. And like good soldiers, we do as we are told and take our orders. How can you be a leader if you can't be a soldier first? Come play. I'll give you a new skin for your man and show you how to be a good soldier."

Gebran stood in the hallway, slowly beating his head against the wall. "The Americans will be looking for the materials, too. They have ways to find these materials with sensors. The longer they wait, the more chance of discovery."

"Then tell us where you hid it. We can help secure your bomb-not-bomb. We have two more men down the street sitting in their apartments, bored as well. Come sit." He beckoned. "The only people happy about this are our neighbors who are happy to help the Party. Even the Pakistanis love us here. I'll call to them for more food."

"You miss my point. This is the first time anyone has gotten this level of purity for a radioactive weapon. It's the work of legends. We can find our own target. I can deploy it for optimal impact. So why do we need to sit locked in discomfort while the others are free and in luxury? They will claim the credit."

"Credit goes to God. You would know this if you were a *true* Party leader. Perhaps your grandfather forgot to tell you of this important lesson."

"Yes, but they will remember us so we can move up ranks," Gebran preached. "We are the new leaders of tomorrow. We have the teeth of the tiger to do such acts. Don't you see?"

"We should wait," the gamer instructed, his weapon tucked away and controller back in his hand. "They will call when they are ready to call."

"One more day. We wait one more day. And then we live properly until the Americans' St. Patrick's Day parade. And then we will take our place within Hezbollah."

The gamer turned. "Keep quiet, Gebran, and know your place."

"You don't know what I know. The power is in my hands. They will know soon enough."

"Shut up, Gebran," the two Archangel guards said in unison.

When the phone rang, no one breathed.

Chapter 24

Until recently, there was only one person alive in this world who knew that the elder son, Dexter Woolf, existed, and that was his former CIA handler, Tom Mendle, a former friend of the asset's spooky father. An only slightly larger handful of people within the American intelligence community knew Dexter not by his actual name but by his declared identity, Daniel Waters, which Dexter had earned after completing five years of service within the French Foreign Legion. Technically, it was five years and roughly seventy days, the days consisting of brutal interrogation when he was initially taken into custody with a throng of Tunisian fanatics that the Legion intercepted in the desert, courtesy of an anonymous call by Tom Mendle.

It had been the plan all along between Dexter's father, Alex Woolf, and Tom Mendle to turn the adventure-seeking wayward but willing son into a CIA asset. Both senior intelligence officers knew that a covered identity and even the role of a Non-Official Cover officer had loopholes in true anonymity and secret-keeping firewalls. But to be taken in by the Foreign Legion under its rule of *anonymat* whereby one's old identity was set aside during their initial year of Foreign Legion service, and given that he became associated with his parent's killer during the execution of the transformation, which was not part of the strategy, Tom had to make a stressful judgment call and hope Dexter could survive a series of interrogations instead of the traditional screening process. Per the cover plan, Dexter did not leverage the reverting-rectification, "military regularization of the situation," to reassume his former name and instead assumed a declared identity and nationality of another French-speaking country in Africa where records were often lost or could be encouraged with a small sum of money to be completely destroyed. Even now, Dexter's surviving brother, Drake, had no idea of this history.

In addition to the new name, Dexter benefited from the Legion's regiment training and direct combat experience as an alternative to being a vetted spook going to the CIA's Farm training for Field Tradecraft Certification. He was off the grid, which made his next foray into the world of Muslim extremism that much easier, and in a few more years, this Legionnaire with American heritage but a foreign passport was welcomed in as Daniyal bin Alfaransia and soon took on the esteemed advisory role as the Modarris, or Teacher.

* * * *

It was fifteen minutes after evening sunset Maghrib prayers at Chicago's Masjid Darul-Qur'an mosque in the northern part of the city. Dexter Woolf, the Modarris, walked accompanied by four security guards through the West Ridge Nature Preserve in the West Edgewood neighborhood to a predetermined coordinate at the Rosehill Cemetery.

The vast property's description was on point, with majestic old trees, large statues, monuments and a grand mausoleum. Even at dusk, Dexter could appreciate the beautifully serene place, although his eyes still watered and blurred from the fumes of hot peppers he had been boiling for hours alone in a safe house before the evening atonement. Fortunately, the cough from the harsh fumes had subsided and not interrupted the prayer.

A guard, Khalil, tapped Dexter's elbow with his mobile device. "We are here, Modarris." He motioned to a small open structure a few meters from his extended finger. "But the structure does not look large enough for a meeting. Have you received any new notification?"

Dexter turned to face the men. "I will go and see. Stay here. Keep watchful."

"I don't trust the Persians," declared another Venezuelan-passport-holding Lebanese guard named Zander. "I will go with you, Modarris."

"Praise God for giving me such loyal men. I am blessed. But all of you men are far too important to the great event. I am but a pawn. You have learned all I can teach, praise be unto him. I have faith that all will be well, *inshallah.*"

Dexter approached the structure with confidence, gently pushing the worn wood door to the side, and entered.

Two shadowed figures stood in the relative darkness.

"General Shirazian," Dexter said with a slight head bow.

"Daniyal," the IRGC officer greeted in return. "Go first, and then we will talk."

The man next to Shirazian handed Dexter an object, heavy enough that the Modarris's hands dropped some. Dexter peeked his head from the stone tomb and signaled to his men outside. "I have something to show you. Come, you will be pleased. It is safe."

As they hurried to their instructor, Dexter charged the small Daewoo suppressed submachine gun screened under concealment by the wall.

Khalil heard the mechanic click first and stopped in his tracks.

Before he could respond or warn his brethren, the K7 emerged in Dexter's hand.

The Modarris thumbed the fire selector to a 3-round burst with a swift motion, curled his finger to the trigger, and pressed as three of the four men loomed nearer. As their bodies shuddered in the shaky jig of the death dance, Dexter released the trigger for but a second, switched to automatic, swung the weapon across his body, and emptied the thirty-round 9mm magazine behind him into the Iranian-filled crypt.

He spared Shirazian, who yelped then held up palms.

"What have you done?" the general asked, lowering his hands, pressing them to his cheeks, and assimilating the surprise attack.

"It is nothing personal. Orders."

"Orders? Orders from who? The only one who could have…" Shirazian's voice trailed off. He knew and hung his head. "The supreme leader is fearful that if we carry out the attack, Americans will retaliate. He's lost his teeth. We will look weak."

"It is not my decision to make," Dexter offered. "Even if we simply stole the materials, the Americans would spend more resources looking to recover the WMD and protect the future. However, I can assure you there will be an attack. This simply allows for assurances, General."

"Deniability," Shirazian suggested.

"Indeed. You will be hailed as a martyr. Your country will bury you with honors. Your family taken care of."

Shirazian raised his chin. "May I stand like a man?" he asked, rising to his feet, not waiting for permission.

"Go with God."

Flashes of light from the tomb ignited the darkness.

Chapter 25

It had been a long day by the time Oswald and Shawnay returned from their day using underage and underprivileged street kids to pawn stolen candy off to white suburbanites under the auspices of charity support.

A candy crew working a twelve- to fourteen-hour day could gross $6,250 a day, and Oz always had at least two crews working each day to pull in about $12,500. That meant each kid could get paid fifty dollars per day and get beaten but not shot, while Oz and "his bitch" took home two grand less gas, and over five thousand went into the hands of Two-bags, the leader of the Lawndale Legends, or L2, as Two-bags and his people called themselves.

Like the kids, Oz could take an occasional beating and avoided getting shot day by day, and the relatively legal enterprise brought in a nice daily dollar for L2. Plus, Two-bags liked the idea of being able to recruit top hustlers for the street corners to sling rock that had learned basic salesmanship with the candy crews. The cost—he'd just give Oz another bag of dope.

Oswald and Shawnay collapsed on their third-floor apartment's couch in exhaustion. They had two bags full of McDonald's French fries and chicken nuggets, two two-liter bottles of cola from the corner store where they bought their menthol smokes, and had their fix of heroin for the night. With a thousand-dollar-a-week habit for both functioning addicts, the racket that supported them when all street taxes, neighborhood fees, turf protection, and "vehicle parking charges" was done left them very little. This made the opportunity Two-bags presented all that much more lucrative.

A loud pounding at the door startled both junkies just as they started to cook up their junk.

"Get the door," Oz ordered.

"Fuck you. It's my turn first."

"Bitch, if it's the po-lice, you ain't getting your turn."

"Well if it's the po-lice, you best take care o' them so I get my turn." She reached into the couch cushion and pulled a small Raven Arms .25 semi-auto and handed it over to her man, who laughed at the purse pistol.

The sound at the door persisted.

"I'm coming," he announced, slipping the gun into his back pant pocket. "Man, fuck that," he walked back to the couch, sunk his hand deep into the other side behind two filthy pillows and retrieved a Smith & Wesson .38 revolver. "That's my strap."

"Puleeze, you thinkin' you all Dirty Harry and shit."

He pointed the gun at Shawnay. "Make my day, bitch."

She laughed. "Get the door."

"Who there?" Oz asked, his ear to the door.

"Two-bags sent us. He gots stuff for you."

Oz cautiously opened the door. In the dim hallway, at first count, were five teens carrying large cardboard boxes.

"Two-bags said this is fo' the kids an' shit on the busses. He say, tell Oz not to fuck it up. Says it's from the Chavez *chamos*."

"What is it?" Oz asked.

"We ain't told to look in the boxes, motherfucker, we told to deliver the boxes."

"Is it the police?" Shawnay yelled. The television volume was up loud, and she chose not to turn around in the fifteen feet or so that she was sitting from the door.

"Naw, bitch, Two-bags makin' us a delivery," he called back.

"Pizza?" The voice carried into the entryway.

"Shut up, bitch," he called out.

"I'm starting then."

"Oz, take these boxes and don't get them lifted or lost. Two-bags'll fuck you up."

Another gang member taunted, "Fuck that, Two-bags gonna kill your ass and your bitch if you fuck this up." He jumped past his boy and sucker-punched Oz, knocking him down. "That's a fuckin' warning shot from Two-bags."

As the thugs left, Oz shook off the haze of the punch and started dragging boxes into the other room.

Shawnay's heroin hit was already flooding her brain with dopamine in the short time Oz was at the door. She was stuffing her face with fries and nuggets under the rush of euphoria.

Oz eyed the fix and took a quick look in the boxes, ripping away the packing tape. "What the fuck?" He pulled out green T-shirts, orange beards, and little green bowler hats and laughed. He put an orange beard with the elastic strap over his head and set a Kelly-green cap on his balding crown. "Where's my Lucky Charms, bitch," he mocked before toasting up his own fix and slipping away into the short-lived sensation of warmth, safety, and the casting away of everyday street blight.

Chapter 26

The Man from Orange, Drake Woolf, was the first to arrive in Chicago. Mena was to follow shortly after on yet another private solo flight that Sebastian had arranged—however it was that the ICEPICK program director did what he did.

Drake was the only one on the plane save for the pilot and copilot. His thoughts were focused and the voices still calm. All mental directives must have known that Drake was on a righteous mission, and the alpha part of him was leading the charge. Then again, taking four of the behavior-stabilizing pills that morning may have helped, too.

Mojo, for his part, gave Drake new toys. The first was a Molar Mic personal communication system. The Molar Mic was a DOD and In-Q-Tel introduction of a wireless audio interface embedded with a tiny microphone for talking and a speaker-transducer for hearing in a compact mouthpiece that snapped around Woolf's back teeth and passed sound through the jawbone while eliminating external noise from traditional commo. Plus, it was invisible to anyone looking at Drake, or Mena, who had one too. The second gadget Mojo provided was an augmented mobile handheld device that the Sikh had called Pitbull. Not a dog, Drake had been told, but rather the rapper Mr. Worldwide, which was evidently part of this electronic's capability. The handheld was a functioning cell, interface to the Molar Mic, and had both software and satellite power for IMSI detection. According to Mojo, Drake would be able to also execute from the screen display a man-in-the-middle attack to interrupt targeted devices using FuzzBunch-EternalBlue-DoublePulsar exploit chains, making it a slave to a designated phone tower or Wi-Fi, and had the capability of active or passive listening surveillance mode. The capabilities also included the functionality of a system called Marlin, which could steal calls made on satellite phone networks like ISatPhone, Immarsat, and Thuraya. It was slightly thicker than a normal iPhone 6s Plus with the added satellite, memory, and extended-use battery. Mena had rolled her eyes with the tech gadgetry, but Drake couldn't wait to play with it and had to keep taking it away from Mojo, who wanted to share and discuss every bell and whistle ad nauseum. It sure beat the hell out of lugging a laptop, antennae, and other accessories.

The topic of Mena had been glossed over regarding the event in the breakroom. In a side conversation, Sebastian had raised the question as to whether Drake had fears that Mena was a mole. Quite simply Woolf stated, "If I take her in the field, I'll know within a day or two if she is a mole, and if she is, I'll kill her on the spot. You can come get her." Sebastian was calmer about the outburst and literal assault than Drake would have imagined from anyone, much less a supervisor. Again, in the back of Drake's mind, he couldn't help thinking the dialogue and escalation seemed in hindsight a bit provoked if not staged. Although the fact that Drake was having more than average difficulty keeping his temper with the new meds prevented himself from raising the issue to the boss.

After a short taxi ride upon landing, a white utility van picked Drake up from the tarmac of the Wheeling, Illinois, Chicago Executive Airport. The driver opened the back doors for the Man from Orange, who was simply a discreet personnel pickup. No name, no details, no question short of an exchange of confirming reference numbers to validate the package and carrier.

"There, as you can see, is a shopping cart in the back, a plastic bag, and a jug full of piss, just like they told me."

"Thank you. Might need to top it off, myself."

"I'm not here to judge or ask questions, brother."

Drake stepped into the open back of the van with a gray duffel, wearing khakis and an embroidered navy polo with the lettering: IBM Q-Radar Analytics.

An hour later, the van backed into a narrow alleyway just north of Chicago's Little India on Devon Avenue. Drake seated his Molar Mic and slowly opened the door, searching for people, cameras, or anything out of the ordinary.

Clear. "Neptune 1 to Ocean 1. Over," Drake called once he opened the channel on his device.

Mojo answered from a small Operational Control Element area within Fort Meade, home of the National Security Agency. Ideally, they would move over to the safe house shop in the next month once it was fully equipped and enabled. Apparently, within all the meetings Sebastian had with Foggy Bottom play makers, he would start collecting approvals for electronics and piping without telling anyone exactly where it was going and how it was to be set up. How that happened was above the team's pay grade. Until then, the op was blocked on a schedule of internal Cyber Threat Operations rooms within the Fort for the next week by Sebastian as *Electrical / Mechanical Training Session.* "Ocean 1 to Neptune 1. Perfect timing. Over."

"Sitrep on Starfish 1?" Drake asked, regarding Mena and the situation report of her whereabouts.

"Starfish 1 still heading to AO, over."

"You're sounding like a pro already, Ocean 1. Bravo Zulu."

"Tango Mike, Neptune. I played a lot of *Call of Duty.* I can totally see you turned on your handheld now. You are good to go. Oh, and no hits on that number you had me enter into the cell phone coverage matrix. It's turned on a couple times since I logged it."

"Where?"

"Chicago. Not far from where you are."

Drake's hands got clammy. The thought that his brother was within mere miles of him and yet they still were not together was an emotional hurdle that Drake could not fully process.

Mojo adjusted one of the multiple screens on the desk. It was a DARPA advanced radio-frequency software called RadioMap and wireless and cellular mapping capability, called WALDO, that indicated Drake's signal power in the selected channel and would soon include Mena's. Mojo was nearly finished adding all of the various suspect devices that involved the scientist, Hezbollah affiliates, or any Iranians they had been monitoring, in addition to the special request number that Dexter had given his brother, Drake. The spectrum would help eliminate battlespace noise within the city of Chicago and that could be fed back to Drake's tactical Pitbull sensor, which operated like a mini-Harris Stingray or Hailstorm catcher. Should new cross-linked devices appear on Mojo's screen, he would have situational awareness of multiple emissions in the electronics picture overlaid to a street map that included a 3D building view. The system gave the team an edge to equalize an otherwise environmental nightmare of hunting men and watching their back in a megacity. It was a system of systems that looked like a spider web of relationships and linkages.

"Roger that, Ocean. Neptune out."

Drake readjusted his bulletproof ballistic base-layer compression vest. He yanked the bent and rusted shopping cart from the van, pushed the duffel down in the large basket, then tossed the plastic bag of aluminum on top. He tore the Hefty and let the crushed cans fill the spaces. Finally, he took a deep breath and opened the jug, pouring the urine content in and over his oversized jeans, on the pre-soiled jacket, and over the tops of the oversized shoes that he had just spent the last twenty minutes beating on to look just right. From a few of the beer cans, he poured the little remaining fluids down his neck and shirt.

With a slap on the back of the van, the dirtied faux-beard homeless man emerged from the shadows, muttering to himself and making a drunken beeline to the first trash can and an address etched in his mind to go check out while his newbie partner did her thing.

* * * *

The reality of the situation and her world sank in for Mena as soon as she approached the Gulfstream G280. A pilot dressed in khakis and a white button-down oxford with a fleece vest stood at the foot of the descending stairs, gawking at the approaching spectacle, and shook his head as if in disbelief. He offered a simple, "Ma'am," and turned away.

She'd been treated this way on more than one occasion, especially when adorned in full battle rattle Islam garb. Mena mounted the midsized business aircraft to find no one else on board. The cabin was vast, offering comfortable gray leather seats, and to her surprise, beds. As she stood trying to figure out where to sit, the pilot closed up.

"Excuse me, ma'am, do you speak English?" He was curt and sounded annoyed.

Mena nodded as Sebastian had instructed. So far, everything was perfect. If intolerance and social isolation was considered good.

"I'm going to need you to stow your bags in this cavity." He lifted one of the seats. "It's easy to lift and close, so you can retrieve what you need when you're airborne. The head...I mean the washroom, is aft...back to the left. We'll be in Chicago shortly. No snack or drink service, so hopefully you brought something on your own."

Mena nodded again. She saw an open cooler full of waters as she entered the plane and a wicker basket of snacks and fruit. Evidently, they were not for burka-clad passengers. So much for a State Department–contracted charter flight for United Nations dignitaries. Mena placed her personal bag into the compartment and then the Vera Bradley flowered bag that held Drake's tools that he asked her to transport to their destination.

When the pilot was behind a closed cockpit door, Mena unzipped the bag and moved the cloth items aside to reveal the black metal pieces that Drake had already shown her in the "shop," as he called it.

The disassembled British Sten Mk2 integrally "silenced" submachine gun and thin magazines spelled death even as pieces. She was resolved to it and tucked it back away. Mena had gotten her wish and quite literally all the baggage that came with it.

Mena buckled in, fighting with the black bulky full-body cloak chador, and yanked off the long capelike veil, *khimer*, that covered her hair, neck and shoulders. Under it was a smaller headscarf that she pulled behind her ears to get more air. She was hot, frustrated, and tired. The team had rehearsed all night with an overwhelming number of tasks to be memorized and "not fucked up," as Drake had so delicately encouraged, certainly didn't reduce her stress. Mena thought back to Iran. It was a lot less long ago than she had shared with Drake. That knuckle-dragger didn't have the need to know about her covered status. Clearly Sebastian didn't think so either. As a former Mojahedin-e Khalq, or MEK, the CIA had recruited "Mena" from her hometown of Natanz, in the Iranian Isfahan Province where the central facility for uranium enrichment was located. Her contact, another Iranian working on behalf of a CIA case officer, then handed her off to the Israeli *Hatzomet* who in turn passed her off to the *Kidon*, the Mossad's tip-of-the-spear assassins chartered with killing Iranian nuclear scientists. She was eighteen at the time and agreed to the service for education and citizenship. By the time she was twenty-two and going to school in America, she had seven kills to her name. It had been over a decade since she had killed a man once becoming a legitimate US intelligence officer.

Still, she feared for what Woolf would do to her if he knew of her primary mission. That thought scared her more than the act itself.

The jet exploded from the runway, airborne faster than she had ever experienced on a plane before. Her nerves were fried. There were no cabin indicator lights to signify when it could be a good time to unbuckle and vomit.

How do I serve two masters?

Chapter 27

Saad, the Archangel cell's chief security man and only part-time gamer, stepped out of the steaming apartment bathroom, a towel around his waist and another drying his damp hair. "We need to wash these," he called to Youssef and Gebran. "They smell."

Youssef was on the sofa playing his first-person shooter video games, but replied, "You use too many towels. If you had just one, you could reuse it more."

"They all stink. We should ask someone down the hall to wash them for us today," Saad babbled while walking into the living room still sniffing the mildewed cloth. "Gebran, does your towel smell?"

No answer.

"Hey, anointed one. Now that you got a private call from the Modarris, does your towel smell like mold or esteemed ass? Or do you make a chemist's potion to make the smells go?"

No answer.

"He's not in his room?" Youssef got up from the couch, looking around the room as if a kitten or puppy had to be asleep in hiding.

Saad darted into the scientist's assigned bedroom then popped back into the hall. "No, I last saw him in the kitchen." Youssef hurdled an end table and disappeared into the adjoining room. He called back, "Not here either."

Both men then sped to the entry door, which had an unlocked deadbolt. They looked at each other in horror.

He was gone.

* * * *

For the first time in weeks, Gebran was free. He sucked through his nose the fresh air and cultural scents from the surrounding restaurants and hot-food carts.

Gebran sported jeans, a sweatshirt, a winter knit skullcap, and his favorite white Oakley wraparound sunglasses, which was fortunately one of the items he didn't have to leave behind in his old personal apartment before Archangel started. He knew that he was a wanted man in Chicago, but it was more important to him that he exercise his right to freedom and desire to move the radioactive material for the Modarris now that proper assurances had been solidified for Gebran's future. He walked with purpose to make quick distance between himself and the apartment.

As he made his getaway, Gebran swerved to avoid a foul-smelling vagrant foraging cans from the trash and then scurried past Devon Avenue's Southeast Asian and Middle Eastern shoppers. Cutting through the pedestrian traffic, he scanned for a cab before realizing he had no cash. Reluctant to go on his mobile device for longer than was required to send the Modarris a confirmation message, an Uber ride was his best bet if his credit cards weren't now frozen by the FBI. And if they *were* tracking him, he'd be at the hide site in no time and could turn off the phone as soon as the WMD compounds were moved. Then Gebran himself would be moved to a location for greater discussions with Hezbollah leadership about the attack plans. He had shared a great deal with the Modarris in private where the others couldn't hear him speak. Mostly the compound properties, first order effects, time between symptoms to death, etcetera.

Out of his purview, the homeless man spun, searching around, crazed and speaking to himself.

A half-dressed Saad with Youssef turned onto the street at a fast gait. Saad turned to the left at an intersection while Youssef, his hand glued to his forehead, took the right, looking frantically for the man they were charged with babysitting.

A white Honda Accord pulled to the curb, the Uber sign displayed on a rear window. Gebran Daouk had fled his captors and just skirted past one of the most deadly men in the business, who sought to kill him.

* * * *

"What just happened?" The voice of Mojo startled Drake. "Did he just go right past you?"

Woolf didn't care who saw him talking to no one. Such was unfortunately commonplace of the streets' homeless but suited his cover for action. He spun, looking for anything out of the ordinary. "I didn't see anything." He paused. "Hold one. Got something."

"Doubt it. The scientist that Chicago's looking for just went past you and got in a car. He's heading south."

"I've got two other guys. They look like they just lost something important, but from the way they look, I don't think they're law enforcement or security. Belay that. Two concealed carries. They must be looking for the guy who bailed."

"Nope, not seeing them on my radar. The mark is still headed south."

"One of the guys near me is taking out a device. He's talking. Maybe just short of fifty yards from me. Can you pull up some signals and sort?"

"Yes! Just saw it go on. It's linked to…whoa."

Chapter 28

Drake backed up toward the alley to avoid too much attention. "What's whoa? I need to make a decision."

"Hang on. I'm adding a social network filter on this and linking to another database," Mojo responded. His typing was coming through Drake's jawbone conductor.

"Dude, hurry."

"Dude, shut up." Mojo read through the names listed in a complex web of names and numbers and sublinks. "There's a bunch of thugs, then it goes up a layer to links I have across South America. Venezuela, Tri-Border, it goes to Lebanon. Shit, to Syria. Palestine. Let me scale back again, yeah, Ghazi Nasr Al-Din, a Venezuelan diplomat with Syrian ties, Walid Garcia, a drug kingpin. The list goes on. Yeah, holy crap. The hit goes back up to a phone we tied to Cilia Flores. Chick recently busted for corruption and drugs in the Ven. Tarik El Aissami. Boom. He's a Venezuelan leadership guy tied to Hezbollah. There's other phone connections to financial network, criminal terror ties. This reads like a sanction list. Let me pin this guy to my map. Can't let him get away."

"Listen. That's all fine, but the fight is here. Where's the scientist going?"

"No clue, brah."

"Go back and see where you got a signal hit of the scientist's phone and when the credit card was charged using the device. Within the time of pickup. Maybe five minutes, see what signal was in immediate proximity to him when he got in the Uber. The driver would have to validate the pickup using his mobile, and *that* would coincide with the cellular transmission that sent the credit card payment."

"Damn, bro. Nice. Give me a bit." Mojo retained everything Drake had said and walked the data through the pattern. "I'm tracking." Mojo added a few more filters to the signals that displayed at the snapshot in time. "Wow, okay. Got it. Yep, simultaneous transmission. Same rate of speed. That's some slick shit."

"Track it to see where he's going and pin the drop point. I'm sure it won't be right where he's going, but that gives us a radius of a mile to work with. Probably less than a block, if my guess is on point."

"I'm on it, man."

"I'll see if I can follow these guys to wherever their lair is. I'll need Starfish to meet me before I can go say hello."

"Roger that. Starfish 1 is on the ground en route to AO. I'll direct to your location."

"That won't work. Starfish'll have too much luggage. Have Starfish drop everything but the fancy bag at hotel first, and I'll improvise until then."

"Coolio." Mojo thumbed an old MP3 player that was NSA approved for use on premises. He selected his Johnny Cash playlist and fired up the "Folsom Prison Blues" and sang aloud. "I hear the train a comin'…"

* * * *

Saad and Youssef had been with the Party long enough to know that an admission of neglect securing an operational cell could get them killed; however, a cover up or running would not only get them eventually killed but would endanger their immediate families, as well.

The news they shared with the Venezuelan Hezbollah touchpoint traveled quickly through the ranks outside of those who were otherwise operationally silent to the Qods Force handlers.

Senior Commander Majid Alawi, formerly of the Iranian Ministry of Intelligence and Security, presently of the IRGC Qods Force Unit 400, bypassed his boss, Major General Hamed Abdollahi, and went straight to Major General Soleimani. Alawi traveled from the Unit 400 Golzar Tower in northern Tehran past Harvi Square to the Qods Force headquarters, ironically located in the former US Embassy. A fact that still tickled Alawi to this day, as he approached.

After multiple waves and handshakes, the intelligence operative Alawi was escorted by two guards and given entrée to the modestly appointed chambers. "Qasem, my brother, pardon my intrusion, but I wish to discuss something with you in private."

"Come in." Soleimani rose from his chair and greeted the Persian spook with a hug and kisses on the cheek. "It is so good to see you. Please…" He directed Alawi to a leather chair to the side where they could both sit as equal men.

"Thank you. Forgive me for cutting to business and not exchanging pleasantries. I hope the children are well."

Major General waved it off as nothing. "They are fine. Please. Something is on your mind." He motioned for the man only a few years his junior to continue.

"You have no doubt heard news of the scientist's escape."

Soleimani again nodded, his face expressionless.

"He is no matter," Alawi dismissed. "We have the material and can transport it to a safe location. We will pay our American partners for their troubles, as I know they remain valuable to our Hezbollah associates in the region."

Soleimani reached out, putting his hand on Majid's arm. "What is your question?"

The balding man shifted uncomfortably in his chair. "It is about the Modarris. Not so much a question, rather a concern."

Chapter 29

Sean Havens readjusted on his recovery bed, mustering enough mobility to reach for a peanut butter and banana smoothie that was left for him on the roller cart while he slept.

He was stiff from yet another early morning orthopedic operation, which had him out for three hours and groggy in bed for another three. Now, he was just bored and decided to catch up on years of missed sleep since he would hallucinate either way.

Havens answered the knock on his room's door with a cheerful, "Come on in, it's open."

A guard's head popped in. "Mr. Havens, Special Agent Halliday is here at your request. You sure this is a good idea?"

"Thanks, Mitch. Yeah, it'll be fine. She and I go way back. Justice won't know anything more about this place after she leaves than they did before. Did you get what I asked?"

"Yes, sir, it's in the fridge. I can bring it in if you'd like."

"Please. Thanks, pal."

The ex-CIA guard nodded, opening the door for the tall blondish-haired Amazon standing in wait. She cautiously stepped into the room.

"Hey, you came," Sean beamed. "No candies or flowers?"

"You've got about thirty seconds to talk before I arrest you."

"I think I would have gotten you a panda. Do you like pandas?"

"Talk."

"Pull up a seat," Sean offered, nodding to a chair at his side.

"I'll stand. I'm not staying, and I'm trying to think of how quickly I can just arrest you."

"Don't do that. I just told my pal out in the hall that we go way back. It would be really embarrassing if this place got raided. I'm afraid I'll have to snap my fingers and have him take you out of here." Sean snapped.

Mitch reentered the room, carrying a six-pack of Wisconsin's Spotted Cow lager. "Where do you want it?"

His reentry gave Halliday a start.

"Good timing. It's for Special Agent Halliday. You can give it to her. That'll be fine. Thanks again."

Tresa accepted the bottles with a glare of impatience.

"I thought we would start with a peace offering. I'm sorry about Georgetown. I was out of line. Thought you might like a little taste of home." Sean grinned and reached his hand out. "I'd shake your hand but figured we should start with a beer."

Tresa pulled out a bottle from the pack on her lap and bypassed Sean's hand, opening the top on the metal hinge of the hospital bed.

"Nice," he conceded, taking the bottle. "Packers fan?"

She affirmed with a nod then used the same leverage to open her own beer.

"Where'd you get these? I didn't think New Glarus distributed out East."

"I have access to transportation. Don't worry. Didn't cost tax payers anything, but that six-pack did just cost me about five thousand dollars."

Tresa was looking Havens up and down. "How many times were you shot?"

"More than I wanted." He lifted his right hand, which was bandaged like a big Q-tip. "The ankle's going to be okay. But this guy is definitely going to set off a metal detector. Body shot was a graze and a through and through. Can't remember the other one with all these meds."

"Should you be drinking?" she asked, then drank about half her bottle in a swallow.

"Look at you." He admired her rawness and instantly liked her. Still, her masculinity under her beauty gave him pause and he eyed her throat for an Adam's apple.

Havens's smile was contagious, and she too cracked a smile. "No," he said, "I probably shouldn't have more than two or three, but the doctors come in and leave early then come back and leave really late. Day jobs and all. I never had a chance to ask them about beer, but I have a feeling you may finish them before I get my second."

"Why am I here?" She circled her head to the room. "Is this a CIA safe house out here?"

"Nope. Completely commercial private medical facility located in a very large house. Now who their main customers are, I have no idea," he confessed sarcastically. "I'm paying in cash."

"Like your friend Patches?"

"Nice. Score two for the Bureau. You must have been closer than we thought."

"And I saw that your reckless antics killed your big partner?"

Sean's jovial face turned solemn. "He was my brother-in-law. Former police. Chicago."

"Wow. Some family he must have been to just leave him burning in the dirt like he was just one of the dead terrorists." She finished her beer and pulled out another.

Sean drank his without a word, set the bottle between his legs, and reached out to her for another.

"Yeah," he finally said. "It was real shitty."

"Sean. It is Sean, right?"

"I gave you my true name in the message. All cards are on the table."

"You're wanting immunity, I take it?" She handed him the bottle, from which he took a long pull. The beer dripped a bit, and he wiped it with his bandaged hand.

"Bet you wish you had one of these." He waved.

"I can still get a handcuff around your wrist."

Havens smiled. "Bet you'd like Drake to handcuff you?"

This time it was Halliday who broke eye contact.

"No, ma'am, I'm not looking for immunity. We're looking for a partner. And we need you fast so we avoid another 9/11 terror event."

Chapter 30

While the Uber driver navigated the southwest Chicago streets, Gebran fantasized about his future life as an anointed Hezbollah leader. He would have power and influence. He could travel throughout South America with a security team and have respect. No one would ever make disparaging remarks about his family's trustworthiness. He would be unstoppable and renowned throughout the global Party's ranks.

They drove past the Cook County Department of Corrections on West 26th Street, and Gebran instinctively shrunk lower on his seat as if the perimeter was under heightened surveillance. They continued on to California Avenue, and the area's poverty and destitute lives became increasingly visible. The corners were chock-full of kids and adults loitering with blank faces as potential drug-buying clients drove by. It was the same as Venezuela. A group like Hezbollah could provide these people with medicine, protection, and other services. Whether they followed the laws of God or not, substance abuse and other earthly debauchery would have to go. Hezbollah would never stoop so low as involving itself with drugs. Or so he naïvely thought.

As they neared the self-storage facility, Gebran had the driver pull past and up a block where the budding Hezbollah soldier intended to get out. Curbside, however, Gebran received menacing looks from locals who swaggered up to the vehicle.

"Go," Gebran instructed the driver. "Go back around. Just drop me back at the storage building." Trepidation rattled his voice.

As they circled the block, Gebran viewed a large auto repair lot. Yellow school busses lined the fence, and gooseflesh popped along his arms. He was so close.

Once they neared the storage building, sets of eyes peered through cracks from behind a brown sheet metal fence.

* * * *

"Neptune 1," Mojo called. "The subject has stopped south of the city's business district. I'm pulling up a satellite view." Mojo paused. "Ew. Shitty neighborhood. Yeah, he's in a serious red zone area that pops up with… damn. Major violent crimes. Shooting. Stabbing. Killing. Your kind of vacation spot."

"Sad but true," Drake agreed. "I never get to work in the posh places. Just tell me where I need to be."

Chapter 31

Contrary to what many believe about Iranian covert military activities, the specialized Qods Force is not an independent fighting force, but rather is a segment of IRGC elements and mercenaries that it has trained. In the case of dispatching two individuals to handle the US problem, both Eksandar Kordbacheh and Ghazi Farahmand were selected and thought to be reasonably capable.

The two men had served in the IRGC's 19th Fajr Brigade in Syria, proving themselves as formidable soldiers and resistance leaders before being transferred together to train foreign nationals at the main terrorist training camp in Iran, the Imam Ali Garrison, through the Qods Force training directorate 12000. From there, they requested a joint transfer to the Shahriar Garrison to train Afghan mercs who would be later deployed to Syria. At Shahriar, the duo trained surrogates on infantry skills in Kalashnikovs, mortars, tactical movements, and sniper skills.

To reward their efforts, they were granted the opportunity to work in Venezuela and the Tri-Border areas. A reward signed off on by Brigadier General Hossein, Qods Force deputy Brigadier General Ghanni, and finally Soleimani himself. Indeed, the South American post was taken quite seriously.

It was therefore with slight hesitation that Eksandar and Ghazi were tasked to travel to the United States last minute with orders to terminate members of the five-man Archangel cell. They were not clandestine assassins, but they knew the targets and had killed their share of men before. Most importantly, within twelve hours they could fly from Caracas to Colombia and then hop a direct to Chicago. Venezuelans at the Chicago embassy could provide the weapons upon the Qods arrival—courtesy of border transfers enabling arms transport through diplomatic pouch. The same method world intelligence agencies used as thoughtlessly as packing their toothbrushes and clean underwear.

Eksandar marveled from his passenger-side window as they drove toward the city skyscrapers. "Ghazi." He pointed from the back seat to the scene out the windshield. "Sears Tower."

The Venezuelan security diplomat in the passenger seat turned. "It's Willis. Wil-lis Tower now," he corrected in English, not knowing Farsi and having been told the Persians spoke limited Spanish.

"Who is Willis?" Sandar asked.

"A company. They do that in America. You know 'company'?"

Ghazi nodded. The word was basically the same in Farsi.

"One day it's one name, the next day it is bought and they name it another company name," the diplomat shared. After a few minutes and their turn off, he said, "There is the Trump tower."

"Ah, Donald Trump. Build a wall," Ghazi joked.

Sandar chuckled. "Do we tell them where we need to be?" he asked in Farsi, his mind now shifting to the task at hand.

Unsure of how the translations would go, Ghazi pulled a small piece of paper out and handed it up to the front. "You were told of our requirements?"

Both Venezuelans nodded. "Change. No Makarov. We give you Russian 9mm 'PYa' Grach. And silencers." The South American riding shotgun reached between his legs and raised a locked, zippered bag. "When we arrive, I will give. It is best I keep for now. Diplomatic security, you know."

Those driving along Chicago's Lake Shore Drive wouldn't have known that behind the black SUV's smoked mirrors, the lethally trained soldiers inside protected by immunity were having a hearty laugh at the operational convenience of American liberties with or without physical barriers.

Chapter 32

Drake was cautious not to make his pursuit of Gebran or the two Hezbollah cell members look like—a pursuit. He was an ambling homeless man with nowhere to be and no rush to do it in, even if he was trying to prevent a disaster from occurring.

"Ocean, I need you to do the best you can to keep eyes on these guys. I'm not going to make it around the corner without raising suspicion. Do you still have the view up to see if they're going back to the target building?"

"Neptune, it's just me. I've got screens, but it's taking me a bit to make sure that's where they're headed. I could use a drone right now. I'm not prepared to grab camera feeds or anything to enhance the ops spectrum."

"Do the best you can, buddy. This is the Olympics even if we're the Jamaican bobsled team." Drake couldn't believe he just made a sports reference, and shifted thoughts to Sean Havens. After so long working alone, he missed having the older spook and sports enthusiast by his side.

"They're heading back into the building, Neptune. I'm getting a couple more hits on their phone. They called another number, and it's tied to more known bad dudes."

"Ocean, there's a mob brewing in the alleyway. I need to get in a side door." Drake's mouth clicked in anticipation of an escalating scene mobilizing potential combatants.

Ocean laughed. "Dude, this is Chicago. There's no mob."

Drake whispered, trying to be careful of alerting the men as he mounted the stairs. "Wait, what time is it?"

"Oh, fuck, dude. Yeah, you have a healthy bunch of people. It's prayer time. Let me just…a mosque. Hmm, thought I checked this," Mojo said to himself. "I thought it was a parking garage. The mosque's about a half block from you. It's behind the main drag. The entrance is in a direct line to the street you're on."

"I'm about to have my own Mogadishu Mile, aren't I?"

"Not if you're quiet." Mojo typed away on another keyboard. "It's Sunni. Not like these Hezbollah dudes are card-carrying members, so probably no threat of anyone calling them up to help. Just…be invisible."

"Gee. Thanks." *We'll see.* Drake ambled around the corner and opened the stairwell door. No one walking in parallel paid much attention to the bum heading into a low-income apartment complex. Woolf climbed deserted stairs and wider than expected muggy landings to the third floor. Still trying his best to be silent, Drake heard muffled shouting a few doors down.

"Ocean. How many cellular signals are you getting from the apartment?"

"Can't really tell. There's a pretty dense view of the complex. I can't really make out different floors in the building. I'm showing on my screen well over a dozen conflicting cell phone identifiers near the numbers we tagged." Mojo poured a handful of Mike and Ike candies into his palm as he worked the problem of sorting bad guys from good guys amidst the cell phone signals emanating from the target area.

"Filter it," Drake whispered, but the sound came through loud and clear with the Molar Mic. "Take out all main carriers from the spectrum like Verizon, Sprint. The biggies. Our bad guys won't be filling out a two-year contract."

"Okay. Give me a sec. All right, that cut the population in half. I can see signals from MetroPCS, Cricket, but the lines are still connected through the carriers, who are using AT&T or T-Mobile networks, so I really can't tell. And dude, that area you're in for a square mile is full of Middle Easterners and Southeast Asians. A lot have prepaid phones. Culturally, us sorting this way isn't going to work. My parents use burners just so they can load prepaid minutes to call family in India." Mojo waited for Drake's response while sorting the candy. Greens from yellows and oranges and pinks.

"Shit. This whole thing isn't going to work. I figured I could take out two by surprise, but there could be half a dozen armed men in there. How far out is Starfish?"

"She's about…"

Drake heard two all-too-familiar mechanical clinks. "Shhh." Two more. *Suppressed shots.* Woolf flipped his mind from Mojo to full battle mode. Residents wouldn't have thought much about the sound, but a trained operator knew it like an old-school ringtone. He was just feet from the apartment entrance and heard footfalls coming toward the door. The language had shifted from Arabic to Persian. *Iranians. Someone's pissed about the fuckup.*

We can take them, Drake. The inner voice was confident but not disparaging or hostile. New? The mental voices had been silent with the new meds and Drake's self-prescribed dosage. OCD also moderated. *There can't be more than a couple. We were ready to take down two. They killed the Lebanese men you're following. You know they did. Let's go.*

There's another way, Drake offered as a suggestion to himself.

Drake dropped to the ground on his back. "Mojo, I'm going to be busy. Out for a while."

The door handle turned, and he could hear the door mechanism unlatch.

Drake quickly unzipped his pants, exposing that which he would not normally pull out on a mission.

As the men walked out, Drake prayed that he wouldn't get stage fright, and like a baby on a changing table, he started the waterworks with an arch of urine streaming like a fountain. Woolf slurred his words as he sprayed the hallway.

The Qods Force assassins giggled like elementary school boys when they saw the spectacle.

The bum was blocking their exit.

Drake assumed they would wait a moment to finish laughing and pointing and readying themselves to jump over the unexpected sight before them. But when the pissing stopped, they scolded Drake. Their voices turned menacing.

Drake lolled his head around, getting a good look at the two Iranians and their position. Their weapons were not in hand, but if they were assassins, most assuredly they were trained men and would still get the drop on him. Until he could get them close, he didn't have a chance.

One Persian prodded the other to get going. The man closest to Woolf moved his hand back toward his side. Drake was unsure if the Qods soldier was contemplating putting a bullet in his head.

Desperate times call for desperate measures. Woolf slid his hand down toward his crotch and started to laugh a drunken man's cackle.

Fearing the bum was going to start jacking off in front of them, Eksandar and Ghazi turned to the wall, lifting their hands as they tried to slide past the wall.

Drake quickly pulled from his pants pocket a half foot of scrap steel that he scrounged on the street. With a rapid outward sweep, he caught the first man under the kneecap. Drake flipped his legs up, pushing with his hands on the ground to thrust a solid kick to the point man's face. Spinning on his lower shoulders, Drake whirled and exploded a flurry of kicks into the second man, then swept the guy's legs out from under using a rigid arm.

Unfortunately, the more Drake moved, the further his pants moved up his legs and bound his knees.

Before Drake could get up, the first man had enough presence of mind to pull a firearm and direct it to the raging vagrant on the ground.

Drake identified the immediate threat and shot a frontward donkey kick with both feet. The impact sent the weapon into the wall, and it dropped within reach of Woolf.

The Man from Orange grabbed what by the touch could have been a suppressed SIG Sauer or Makarov service-type pistol. He raised it not knowing the caliber nor caring, but the weight told this experienced shooter that there was at least a ten-round magazine. Four shots had been fired by someone in the apartment, so worst case there were three bullets for each dude. Drake squeezed off three rounds in rapid succession. Killing the man or not mattered little at that point.

"Ghazi!" Sandar shouted as his friend collapsed.

Drake swung his arm backward, his head following the turn to see the second Qod scrambling. Woolf popped off three more. Two in the man's chest and one in the bean. No doubt about the life expectancy of this one as the money shot painted the wall with a horror-show spurt of red.

Turning his attention, Drake's first adversary was on hands and knees. Drake cranked back his leg and launched it into the man's neck, seeking the jawbone as target. The Iranian's head snapped back and flopped to the side. Arms and legs folded to the floor.

Exhausted, Drake lay on the ground panting, then realized his junk was still flying free. Woolf pulled up his pants, got himself situated, and started rummaging through the men's pockets, stuffing whatever they had into his own.

"Dude?"

Drake spun to the noise, forgetting the internally integrated commo system for a moment. "Shit, I forgot you were there."

"Dude, you okay? I heard a ton of grunting and voices."

Drake also noticed heads peering out of the hallway doors.

"I'm okay. I've got company so need to do a quick site ex, to see if I can grab any intel." Drake collected himself and entered the apartment, unsure of what he may find, and he sure as hell didn't want to be surprised. The fact that no one else had poured out in the melee was a good first sign.

The room was as he suspected.

Drake may have been in America, but the way that tangos lived in a safe house the world over was all the same. It was as though they were single college kids minus the beer cans. And of course, instead of being passed out like collegiates, these two Hezbollah jamokes had been stone-cold executed.

Drake did a quick toss of the place, finding phones and passports but not much more. There were pistols on each man, which told him they weren't expecting to die. Now, why Hezbollah was being killed by Qods before an operation was very odd. Even if he thought they could be executed to remove loose ends, the IRGC Qods Force didn't work that way. They built trust and networks. Hezbollah assets weren't smoked, especially if they were low enough in the ranks where they ran headfirst into battle or suicide missions. Drake was examining the passports, both Venezuelan, when he heard loud voices from outside in the hallway.

Woolf closed his eyes, placing the language that resonated like his own tongue, but to label it for a second threw him off. Being home, CONUS, and in combat with Middle Easterners was throwing off reality despite dealing with it the past weeks. Still, as a balding heavyset man wearing a wife-beater tank top and baggy traditional Southeast Asian pants screamed at him in Urdu, Drake pulled one of the firearms and double-tapped him. Another man charged in wearing pretty much the same thing but hefted a steel cleaver. Drake popped him twice, as well.

Drake heard sirens from the windows behind. The high-pitched emergency noise still sounded a ways off, but first responders were no doubt coming toward his position.

More male voices were gathering in the hallway. Some shouting. They were drawing near his position. To go back into one of the adjoining rooms would leave him trapped. There was one way out. Through the front. He was back in the sandbox. Drake's mouth clicked as his eyes and mind processed combatants pouring through the narrow door.

The Man from Orange raised two handguns and started firing at the residents. They dropped easily. One after another. Head shots. Chest shots. Drake threw elbows and shoved falling men off as he fought to get out of the hallway and into the apartment.

The men tried to grab him, but Woolf kept firing. As his arm was pushed down, he still pulled the trigger, popping people in the hips, thighs, ankles, and feet until they fell away. Drake dropped empty firearms when he could no longer shoot them or bash the people in the head. He looked back for a moment down the darkened hall to see children yanked back into door openings. Women shrieking, as they too entered the corridor to see what the ruckus was about.

Amongst the clamor, Mojo's voice found its way to Drake's attention. "Dude, what the fuck is going on?" Mojo shouted.

"I'm clearing a path!" Drake shouted automatically in Urdu to Ocean 1.

"What?"

Drake pulled open the stairway door to find two thirty-something men, lightly bearded wearing sweaters and pocketed sweatpants. They looked more like college grad students and stood in the landing on their way up to his location. Drake paused, unsure of their intent.

"Are the other two Archangel dudes here?" Drake asked Mojo as he raised his weapon. He had lost count of the rounds, which didn't matter since he never knew how many he started with. It was better to raise a weapon and not pull the trigger than wait and die with a pistol tucked in your pants.

The other two members of the Hezbollah cell, too, went for weapons, shocked to see a bearded homeless man drawing down on them. This they hadn't counted on after being called over to help hunt for Gebran the scientist.

"Never mind." Drake got off one shot before hearing the gut-dropping empty click. It bought him a moment as the bullet found one of the Hezbollah soldier's arms, causing him to drop his weapon. Not a bad result for what was supposed to be a head shot.

The other man aimed and fired.

Drake heard the combo crack and whiz, not sure which came first, but it just missed his head. As the shooter kept pulling the trigger in a one-handed grip, the bullets rose higher. This Woolf could only tell by the firing succession through recoil.

Woolf launched low, kung-fu-poster style, down a dozen stairs. He was off his mark and needed to make a hasty transition to land on both feet, letting his body ride the momentum. He threw a shoulder into the second Hezbo soldier, crushing him into the wall, then pulled back just enough to come back with an elbow to the man's breastbone.

The first man was fumbling for his weapon on the ground. Drake stomped the man's lower back and refocused back on the next. Another gunshot fired, and Woolf felt the side punch of the bullet.

"Motherfucker!" Woolf gritted, struggling to catch his already winded breath. Drake head-butted the man and thrust his hand to the man's open throat and squeezed.

The man was trained and swung up and over, hammering Drake's arm down and breaking the lock. From the corner of his eye, he saw the other guy crouched and ready to fire. Woolf man-handled his standing adversary with all his strength and leverage, yanking him backward into the partner. The bullet cracked, and Drake saw the sparks hitting the metal stair rails.

Gotta end this fast. Drake's strength was failing, and he was feeling light-headed from lack of oxygen. He bent and threw wild and loose punches. The metal bar in his back pocket slipped some, triggering a final option in Drake's mind.

From decades ago, he envisioned his father in that scorching kitchen of Tunisia holding the metal ice pick. "Drake, when you do this, don't use one hand like me. Use both hands around and interlock the fingers." Drake had done that to try to kill the men who attacked his family. Drake reached back now and grabbed the steel in his palm. Dad was right, but in the years of military training learning the art of ungentlemanly warfare, Drake had learned new tricks. He slammed the steel down into the side of his adversary's neck. He hammered it back and forth to the neck, to the temple, and when that man went limp, he went for the struggling man below.

The sirens had multiplied, and now shouting was coming from the stairwell below. Drake shoved the bloodied metal bar up the back of his body armor plate and flopped to the ground face down. Hoping both guys he just fought were finally goners.

"Up here," a voice called out. Police radio calls joined in to the climbing ruckus sounds. "One man down! Make that two. Oh shit. Three. What the fuck?"

Drake felt a hand tugging on his shoulder.

"Joe, don't touch that junkie without gloves. You'll get the hiv."

"Shit, you're right. God, it smells like shit in here." The officer pulled Woolf over, and Drake prayed he wouldn't notice the body plate or the fake beard.

"Aggghh!" Drake's eyes popped open.

"Holy shit!" The officer jumped back and stumbled off the first stair.

"Fucker's alive!" his partner yelled, catching and stopping his partner from a fall.

Drake wrapped his arms around himself. He slurred, "Don't hurt me, don't hurt me."

"Buddy." The officer snapped his fingers in front of Drake's wild eyes. "Hey, are you in there? What happened?"

"Up here," another other officer called back to those climbing up from behind. "Holy crap. This looks like a fucking gang hit. What happened up here?" The voice faded as the CPD officer took in the rest of the massacre.

"Hey, Mahoney, forget the bum. We'll take him and get him cleaned up and see if he can talk. You see if you can help up here at this fucking mess. Detective Neil and I will call a bus and have the techs check out these other guys."

"Thanks, Daniels. I appreciate you pros giving us first look."

"Hey, consider us helping a friend." The detective smiled.

Chapter 33

Drake tried to brush off the detective who was grabbing fistfuls of his clothes. Drake flopped around, protecting his Teflon secret and playing the ruse through as long as it could take him out of the long arms of the law.

Detective Daniels leaned in. "I'm supposed to say 'Old Yeller was a cougar.'"

Drake's eyes nearly popped from his head, and he stopped struggling.

"Are you okay?" Detective Neil asked with a nod. "Can you get the fuck outta here?"

Drake turned back to Daniels, still not saying a word.

"We're going to put you in a car. We need to move quick. Anything we need to know or that you need to do? God, you smell like piss."

"Bag." Woolf croaked. "I have something downstairs with the cans." He coughed. "I need a duffel bag that's under cans in the cart."

Daniels glanced back to his partner. "Go check it out. Throw it in the trunk." The detective pulled at Woolf. "Let's go, soldier. Sean Havens just called in another chit. This one better not get me shot."

* * * *

Within the rows of storage containers in the Self-Stor facility, Gebran unlocked the vault where he had stashed the vehicle and compounds just days before. He lifted the rolling overhead door and let out a breath of relief at seeing the van still there.

Entering the facility, he headed straight to the passenger-side door to access the glove box. Within it was a white handheld radiation detector that he snatched and powered up.

Gebran toggled the menu settings to display the dose rate and history in the same view as current radiological levels.

In the back of the vehicle were two storage containers with yellow block lettering. One was full of the radioactive powder and the other full of radioactive waste materials such as gloves, wipes, throwaway compounds, as well as two stolen radioactive cobalt 60 seeds that had been written off as packed and transported. Signed off by Dr. Planck.

Gebran scanned the van and the area with the device. The difference in radioactivity was significantly lower than it was days prior, which meant the container was holding fine and residual contaminants outside of the boxes had lost their effective life due to exposure with open air. The readings calmed Gebran, knowing any government air sniffers wouldn't be able to locate the stolen materials.

"You're an ambitious man," a voice suggested from behind.

Gebran dropped the device, rattled by the sound. The radiation detector shattered its plastic frame on the concrete floor on impact. A shard shot across the ground and was stopped under the foot of Dexter Woolf, the Modarris.

"Foolish, but...ambitious," Dexter said.

"Your voice. You're the Modarris. But you're American?" Gebran's voice was more breath than sound.

"Are you going somewhere?" Dexter put down a large brown-and-gold Louis Vuitton duffel that made a solid thud when it hit the floor.

"No, Modarris. How did you find me?"

"Have you communicated with anyone else?"

"No, Modarris. My guards wouldn't allow me to use a phone."

"This is not the location you provided me with earlier."

"I'm sorry, Modarris. I needed to be sure that your assurances would be true. I needed leverage if I—"

"It is not yours to leverage."

"I'm sorry, I just wanted to have Hezbollah's word that I would be promoted to a leader."

"Where? Where do you want to lead?"

"I don't know." He paused. "America? I could develop cells and plans."

"You're a wanted murderer in America. Too dangerous. You would expose any activities. This is your own burden, as we never wanted you to harm your professor. Where else could you be of value?"

"I could go home to Venezuela and plan activities in South America."

"Same scenario. Your country, as corrupt as it may be, will just welcome you back after stealing radioactive material and killing someone while on a visa? You would be extradited. Perhaps denied a return. You would be hunted even in your own country to gain favor with the Americans and Venezuela's own neighbors."

"Then Lebanon."

"Where you have never been and know no one?"

"I have family. My grandfather was legendary." Gebran raised his chin with pride.

"Yes, he was. But you are not. The Party men in Lebanon are war-hardened. They have fought the Israelis, fought in Syria. How do you expect to lead such men?"

"I'm sure I—"

"You have already made your contribution, and you too shall be a legend." Dexter Woolf slid a boxy integrally suppressed Maxim 9mm handgun from behind his back and fired its subsonic ammo twice.

Gebran stood in shock. He saw the weapon but heard about as much sound as a nail gun would make.

He dropped his eyes to his belly and fell to his knees at the sight, not understanding what had just happened or why. He clutched his leaking stomach and fell back in initial faint from the sight of his own blood. The dark wetness slowly creeped from under his back as he stared at the fluorescent light above. "You promised," he groaned.

The Modarris gave Daouk a swift kick to the temple, silencing the egotistical young scientist. Dexter then weighted his foot on Gebran's neck, shifting weight forward and collapsing the throat to ensure the deed was done.

He reholstered his weapon within the small of his back and thumb-flipped his mobile device screen to the Telegram app. Dexter sent an unencrypted message through an unencrypted network connection, as ordered, to Major General Soleimani, confirming that Gebran Daouk had been found and terminated. However, he added that Daouk had been interrogated prior to his demise, and the information gleaned indicated the Venezuelan had sold the materials to an unknown buyer. If the international community ever investigated Iran's involvement, Soleimani and Gebran had just broadcast their efforts as evidence that IRGC attempted to thwart any hostile acts against America. At the very least, NSA would collect the info within its secret data coffers.

His next text was a closed communication using Signal, an Edward Snowden–endorsed private messenger mobile application, through a VPN network tunnel to Drake Woolf to share the location of the storage unit.

Dexter heard the footfall from behind, and the baseball bat smashed his ribs as he turned. A metal pipe hammered down in a glancing blow to his head, swirling him into the blackness.

Chapter 34

Mena's role, aside from being a weapon mule, was to contact the Chicago-based Venezuelan embassy in person and say that she was there to meet the Modarris. Once she had made the inquiry, she contacted Mojo, who started monitoring new embassy communication instances and their links that may have gone active upon Mena's message. After thirty minutes of waiting on a small sofa in the embassy waiting area, a receptionist came back out to inform Mena that, regrettably, there was no one there by that name.

Mojo's display lit up like a Christmas tree as Waleed El Aissami started to panic and General Shirazian was not to be contacted directly by phone.

Chapter 35

"Ocean, this is Neptune, do you copy?" Drake murmured under his breath.

He contemplated in the moment maintaining radio silence without knowing who these guys were. It went a long way that they mentioned Havens's name, which even folks in the community wouldn't drop. The way they swept in at the scene to bug him out was classic Havens. Still, he was out of his element and didn't want to announce his broadcasting before the detectives came inside the unmarked Ford Explorer shorty squad car.

Drake heard a radio call and knew it would be for more "busses" to transport dead and wounded. He tried to drown it out when they entered the vehicle.

"Guys, I just wanted to thank you for coming and getting me. When did you talk to Havens?"

"He pinged us earlier today saying we may need to help one of his people out. Few hours later, we heard it was 'go time,' so we busted our ass to get to you," Daniels said.

Neil added, "No questions asked. Sound like you got blindsided in there by a couple guys. You lucked out. Some of those places could empty out and give a guy a lot of trouble. Let's just pull out of the area, and we can talk."

Drake said nothing and contemplated for a moment just what had happened. He had target objectives, but the people he had also killed or injured trying to get out were likely US citizens. He wasn't in a war zone, and most of those people responding could have been innocents just helping a neighbor. Even if they had differing beliefs, he was on their turf. America. He murdered them.

Woolf let his head flop back as he recited in his head the Oath of Enlistment's first affirmation, "...to support and defend the Constitution of the United States against all enemies, foreign and domestic." Maybe they were enemies and maybe he was obeying orders of the President of the United States, but this was not constitutional, nor did it adhere to the regulations and the Uniform Code of Military Justice. Once again, he had just become black with rage and survival instinct.

Drake, they deserved it. The dark voice didn't miss a beat. *As soon as the radio call comes in that there are multiple deaths, they'll have to bring you in. You'll bring the whole op and task force down.*

Another radio call.

Drake tried to jump the gun again over the dispatcher and responding remarks. "Hey. Is there a convenience store or something around here where I can get a Gatorade or something?"

"Yeah, we can pull into one just around the block," Daniels replied. "I'll go over to that one on Clark."

Neil gave an approving nod. The detective turned his head for a moment, listening to the calls. "How many guys were in that building?"

"A lot. I came across a crime scene that was pretty disturbing. National security situation. Seems they beat me to the punch then came at me when I tried to get away. I'm just surveillance. If you can't tell by the smell."

"Trust me," Neil assured, "we know."

And there it came. As they stopped at a traffic light, over the radio more calls started coming about the missing homeless man who according to witnesses had killed unarmed men.

Both detectives turned around.

Drake shrugged while looking at his mobile phone and the street map. "I think some of the locals thought I was stealing things from the pockets of the fallen. I was checking to see if they had weapons that could fall into the wrong hands." Drake pointed toward the front of the car. "Is this the place?"

"Yeah," Daniels replied, slowly indicating to Woolf that he was processing the load of crap he was being fed.

"I'll jump out and grab something," Neil offered. "Then I think we need to have a chat. What flavor?"

"Anything. Mind if I get out too? I need to get a phone out of my duffel and send something to Havens." *I could also use my meds.*

Both detectives looked at one another and gave a shrug of indifference in the moment. They needed time to get their heads around what Havens had just dumped on them.

"You go get the drinks. I'll have a Gatorade Ice, too," Daniels suggested.

"Got it. I'll see if they have anything for this guy to eat in there, too."

Daniels recalled a time when they interviewed Havens as a suspect after the apparent murder of his family. Things didn't add up with Sean at the time either. In truth, it had become a bloody shit show, but Havens had saved lives. A friend of Havens was a guy they'd give a chance, but the line only went so far. Daniels and Neil were vets, but they were also good cops. "I'll get him his stuff."

Woolf watched Detective Neil enter the small convenience store, and swiveled his head checking out any visible cameras or pedestrians. It was a good spot.

Daniels exited the car, heading for the trunk.

"Ocean, do you have my location?"

"Yeah, good to hear from you. I wasn't—"

Drake cut Mojo short. "Ocean, I need a ride out of here. Get me an Uber, or whatever. Hopefully, you have a PCard or something. Or see if you can see a cab on the opposite side of the street as me. I need to move quick. Just tell me where I need to go. You've got four or five minutes max."

Daniels came around to Drake's side and opened the door, holding the duffel.

"Let me get out for a sec, my calf is seizing up like a bitch."

As Woolf exited the car, he awkwardly maneuvered around Daniels and snatched the detective's handgun from a shoulder holster.

Chapter 36

"Open the box, man. I'm not calling Two-bags until we make sure we got the stuff," snapped a thug who had just knocked out the bearded man in the storage unit.

"Motherfucker, don't you see that triangles picture on that thing? It's got those nuclear bomb Hiroshima don't-open-this-shit logos on it. Like the shit'll melt your face off. He has the same thing in his bag. Shit'll fuck you up and blow up the whole hood."

"Then you call Two-bags."

Dexter Woolf roused, his head splitting in pain and eyes feeling like they would pop out of his head. The pain in his side indicated the likelihood of broken ribs. He lay on the floor and watched mice run around across oil-pooled concrete, heading for the corners of the garage. The good news was neither his hands nor feet were bound. He reached back to feel his head. It was swollen, but his hand was dry. No split skull or skin from the best he could tell.

One of the Lawndale Legends gang members, Antoine, caught Dexter's movement from the corner of the open van door. He reached out and gave his buddy Sketchers a tug of the shirt.

"Why you pullin' on my—"

Antoine jerked his head in the direction of Dexter. "Osama bin Muthafucka's awake."

Sketchers hopped out from the back. "Don't get up, man, or we'll pop you again across the skull."

"Fuckin' bang your building-blowing-up ass but good."

Dexter spoke to them with no foreign accent, which surprised the thugs based on how the Modarris was dressed. "You're making a mistake. We had a deal with Two-bags."

"Deal changed, camel man. He only dealing with the embassy dudes. He don't know you for shit and don't like no terrorists. America, motherfucker." The hood laughed.

From the outside of Dexter's pant pocket, he probed a finger to his mobile device's power button and pressed it on.

* * * *

"You do not want to be doing that, brother," offered Detective Daniels, knowing what had just happened even before Drake spun the officer and gave him a push toward the backseat entry. Drake pressed the barrel into the detective's back between the bulletproof vest and pants belt.

"I need you to get into the car. Trust me, man, you don't want any of what I'm doing to get on you."

"Look, brother, whatever it is, if Havens said you need help, we're here to get you out of any jam."

"Please, get in."

"I know you're not going to shoot me. I was a soldier, too. Did the whole—" Daniels started to turn when the gun fired.

Chapter 37

When Sean Havens checked in with Sebastian about Drake, he found it suspicious the way their program director had mentioned Dexter Woolf's involvement. Not enough time had passed in the last days where an unknown community asset would be relied upon, especially after what little relationship Drake had over the years with the older brother. What Drake had confided to Sean in the past week raised the small hairs on the shadow master's neck. He needed to check it out.

Unfortunately, Sean was less than mobile, and the one person who could find things out wasn't exactly speaking to him. Still he had tried hoping that another chit he was calling in would be received in the spirit of national security if friendship was out the door.

Havens checked his mobile device app to see if he had received a response yet. Still nothing.

A light rap on the door signaled Mitch's warning before coming in to Havens's recovery room within the safe house, which was really a small mansion on loan to the CIA or anyone else who knew the code word for "don't ask, don't tell" services that were paid for from an unnamed trust of a former OSS member's estate. "Sean, there's a call coming in for you on the line over there." Mitch crossed the room to grab and relay the dated handset to his recuperating guest.

Sean's "what gives" gesture received the same body language response from the house security guard, Mitch. Neither had a clue how a call would have found its way in.

"Hello?" Sean answered, his face wrinkled with puzzlement.

"I'm still not talking to you, but clearly you've gotten someone else in a jam. What's your question?"

It was "X." After a long history with the techno intel whiz, Sean and his former colleague had a falling out. Mostly because Havens had fucked over his pal, which X was still getting over with no fingernails and three missing teeth.

"Thank you, Mitch," Sean dismissed in the polite language of *piss off for now.* "Sorry. I'd ask how you got this number, but that just validates why I need to chat with you. How are you?"

"I'm connected to the system. Just tell me what you need. Don't pretend to care, or you would have reached out before you needed something else. That's just who you are." X's voice was tired. Indifferent. Clearly, he was still broken and would be for years to come. He may never get over it, but at least X was working. For whom was an age-old riddle.

"Point taken and deserved. A name. Dexter Woolf. Covered agent or asset. Maybe a NOC. Just don't know. He works as a double in the Middle East. Don't know code name or his handler. Assume CIA. His father was Alex Woolf. Former case officer. Now deceased. Guy's brother is—"

"Birddog," X tossed out flatly. "I know the guy. Well…knew him."

"Knew it. What did you think of him?"

"Does it matter? Thought you wanted something on the brother."

"Yeah, I was just curious though."

"Curiosities are not priority intel requirements. There's nothing on Dexter Woolf, and Drake Woolf is dead. Right Sean?" he asked after a slight pause.

"Did you check on Dexter?"

"I just said there's nothing. Take this name down. Tom Mendle."

"Hang on. I need to find—"

"Get out of the bed, Havens, and maybe you'll find one. It's on the right-hand side of the room on that bookshelf."

Sean looked around the room to see where a camera feed could possibly be for X to hack into.

"It's in the smoke detector. That's why you don't see a red or green light. We use them so we can hard wire the pinhole cameras. The safe house you're in isn't just for our own guys. I'll respond to your message post with the number of Mendle. Encrypted."

"Do you have an address? What if I need to find him?"

"He's on his property. I just checked. Don't call me again, Havens. And for what it's worth, Sean, no one from his old unit really believes Birddog is dead. So, cover your tracks even if Orange and Woolf don't exist anymore. One last thing."

"Yeah."

"I'm glad Maggie is well and doing great in school. She's going to be a great hacker."

The line was dead before Sean could respond or ask about his own daughter, who had been tucked away at an NSA National Center of Academic Excellence in Cyber Operations university with a new identity and an internship at the Fort. Not even Sebastian knew.

Regarding X, his old friend was right. Havens never checked back on his pal after the Vineyard. As always, Sean got caught up in his own family or work crises and never looked backward to those he left behind. Sean Havens had failed his wife, his daughter, Lars, and his friends on multiple occasions. He eyed the wooden cane left at the other side of the room.

Team meant getting his ass out of the bed.

And finding out what Tom Mendle knew.

* * * *

Adding insult to injury, Drake cold-clocked Detective Daniels with the firearm and shoved the policeman into the back seat. While Woolf would have loved to keep the weapon, Daniels and Neil had helped him. The last thing they needed to get busted for was a missing pistol. He tossed the weapon into the footwell and made off in a sprint down the side street and toward a visible alleyway. He knew Daniels would have a small tear and burn from the bullet direction and had seen the bullet hole remnant in the hard-plastic seat back of the car.

"You still with me, Ocean?"

"Dude." Mojo gave a long pause. "What are you doing? I'm not good with this. I'm hearing everything and, man, I'm fucking sick to my stomach. I did not sign up for this. Dude, you crossed a line."

"I need a lift, Ocean," Drake said, his fist balling up tightly around the duffel strap. "Everyone wants a white-hat hero, but the job takes a monster. Suck it up and find me a ride."

"I've got nothing. I can't get a payment through this fast. We're not set up for that."

"Fuck it." Drake ducked into the alley, changing his flee abruptly to a casual walk. There was no one around nor visible from his brief scan of the overshadowing buildings. Woolf yanked off his wig and beard, and quickly shed his jacket. From the bag he pulled a thin wool pullover, a ball cap with *Tabasco* stitched across, aviator glasses, a protein bar, and a sports drink. He tossed everything into two separate dumpsters save for the wig and beard that he stuffed into the top opening of a restaurant's grease disposal. No need for a duffel when it was supposed to be holding weapons by now.

Coming out the opposite end of the alley, Drake spied a gray Honda Accord parked along the curb. The car had a driver, its engine running. Windows were down. Again, Woolf gave a security scan of his surroundings. No one appeared to be paying much attention. No cameras were visible. While he no longer looked the part of the homeless, he didn't want to expose himself in near true form, which would be an inconvenience for the next five to ten years of his life if he even lived that long.

The dark voice interrupted his plan. *You'll have to kill him. They'll find you with a description.*

I know, Drake replied as he rolled the gummy latex adhesive off his upper lip and cheek. *Shit. I pitched the pills.*

Drake's OCD and necessity for meds didn't trump his need for moving out of the area quick. He pulled the hat down and made his approach.

Chapter 38

Tom Mendle threw the last of the filleted fish skeletons into the fire pit. He wiped the blood and scales off his hands and knife using a wadded oil-stained rag that had been lying on his tackle box. Tom smiled at his wife, who sat on a chair quietly reading. He then walked down to the river's edge and dipped his hands and the cutting board into the cold water.

"Don't fall in," his wife called out, never raising her nose from a book.

He dried his palms on his pant legs and walked back to the fire, where he pulled the pot of coffee off the fire rack. He poured a cup for himself and poured a cup for his wife, who sat bundled in a blanket, a hard-cover mystery in hand. Their house was only thirty, maybe forty feet away up the hill, but this was their daily routine while enjoying retirement.

"We're out of creamer," she informed with a smile. "You going up to the house to get some?"

He gave his wife a sideways glance. "If you'd drink it black, you wouldn't have that problem," he replied with an equal smirk.

"I would drink it black if my loving husband didn't insist on buying the cheapest coffee in the store and then burning it on the fire while he pretended to be a settler back in the day before electric coffee pots." Her smile grew, and she cast an eye to her steaming mug. "And it smells like fish now."

His phone rang in his deep barn-jacket pocket.

"One of the kids?" she asked with concern.

"How the hell should I know? It's still in my pocket." He looked at the number then waved her off and started walking up the hill.

She called out, "You better not go into the study and start working for them again. You're retired. And getting my creamer, right?"

Tom Mendle could almost feel his testosterone rising once he saw the No Caller ID display across his device. He answered with a smile, hoping someone was calling about something that was security related. The kind of people who drank their coffee black.

"Y'ello!" he answered.

"Tom Mendle?"

"Yes, sir," the seventy-two-year-old man responded as he opened the screen door, kicked off his boots, and headed for the den with a slight skip in his step.

"I know this isn't a secure line, but hoped I could still ask you about someone from your past. A Dexter Woolf."

Mendle stopped in his tracks. His joy deflated in a word. "You did say Dexter?"

"Yes."

Tom Mendle backed to the hallway wall and slid down onto the hardwood floor. His knees raising to the chest. The pain in his legs was shooting, but Tom couldn't stand. He ran his free hand to his head and under his MacDill Bay Palms golf hat.

Sean waited for a reply that never came. "Sir, are you—"

"Just tell me what that son of a bitch's done now."

Chapter 39

Drake stepped from the curb down to the street level and approached the car from behind.

Pull him from the car.

I can't escalate things more to draw attention to myself.

You've ruined things again. You're locked up for good now. Dead man.

Drake's nostrils filled from a sweet smell lingering in the air as he came up to the driver's-side door. The window drew down a few inches to let a plume of smoke out, then went back up again. Drake could hear the music and recognized it from his childhood. Dexter used to play the same song repeatedly. David Bowie's "Rebel Rebel." The window came down again. Lower this time as the driver's hand reached out and tapped the ash of a joint to the ground. The man was singing along and drew another lungful.

"CPD. Hands on the wheel."

Startled, the long-haired man dropped the joint and fumbled for it at his feet.

Drake reached back, opened the driver's-side rear door, and got in behind what could have passed for a younger forty-fifty-something Jerry Garcia in a Hawaiian shirt. "Drive."

The man stopped fishing on the ground, gave a few stomps with his feet, and turned. "You're not a cop."

"Drive! Keep your eyes forward."

The driver started to laugh. "Dude." He looked into the rearview mirror at Drake, with round spectacles and friendly eyes. "Twenty dollars and I'll take you wherever, but you're not taking my car. And you're not a cop."

Drake smacked the man on the side of the head. "Drive. I don't want your car. And I'm not going to hurt you. But I need you to go, now."

"Dude, you hurt me," he accused, holding his head. "No way."

Drake smacked the guy again. Not so hard this time. "Please."

"Stop, I'll go." The man put the car in reverse, cranked the wheel hard, popped it in drive and exited the parallel park job in the blink of an eye. He turned the music off.

"You can keep it on."

"You like Bowie?" Garcia strained to turn.

"Eyes on the road. Yes. I like Bowie. What's your name?"

"Walter. Did you steal something?"

"No."

"You did something, because you haven't told me where you're going."

"Ocean, this is Neptune. You copy?" Drake held up a finger for Walter to hang on, then waved him forward to ensure he didn't stop driving.

"Fuck," cursed Walter, looking back again in the mirror. "You *are* a cop. Am I busted?"

"I'm here, Neptune. Just glad you didn't kill anyone else. That was a cop you shot. Cruisers are being dispatched to your area. I can't hear what's being said since we're not monitoring their radios, but there's a lot of cars going really fast to your area."

Drake saw the vehicles rushing to his right as they crossed the intersection. He keyed his mobile device, honing in on the number that Dexter had given him. It was still live but had moved a few blocks away then lost signal. Drake's signal app, however, showed a message was waiting. "Walter, need you to take the next right on Ashland."

"Where are we going?"

"Lawndale. South."

"You're not serious. Fuck that." Walter swerved to the outside lane. Police cars screamed by. He made a fast turn to the right.

"Hey, we're going to Lawndale. I don't give a fuck what you think about it." Drake raised his hand, causing Walter to flinch.

"Chill. I'm going, but I'm not taking Ashland. We'll get into Cubs traffic. I'm taking Lawrence."

Mojo spoke up again. "We've got a problem, Neptune. Starfish moved ahead to her objective and thinks she may have a tail from the Venezuelan embassy. You need to help her out."

"Okay. We'll figure it out. Tell her cavalry's coming, and I'll try to figure out how to patch her in. I'm halfway through my battery, so may need to power you off more."

"You'd be doing me a favor, man."

"Yeah. I know," Drake said with true, heartfelt regret. The voices disagreed and were getting louder. While the meds wearing off allowed the voices to come back, the enhanced aggression and insatiable rage remained escalated and very difficult for Drake to tone down. He wanted to call Havens. The closest thing he had to a friend or shrink. Seemed now that all Havens could do for him was provide the "phone a friend" detectives, one of whom he just shot. Drake rationalized it was to help keep Daniels from being accused of aiding and abetting a murderer. The reality was, Drake didn't care and would have just as soon gone for the belly, but for the life of him, he didn't know why.

Chapter 40

Tom Mendle sure as hell hadn't expected to hear the name Dexter Woolf, much less any other Woolf, that day or for the rest of his life. "I don't believe I got your name," he replied to Sean while still folded on the floor.

"Sean Havens. I used to work with our Uncle Sam."

"I know your name from the halls. Figured if you've come across the Woolfs, you have a need to know. And since they're all dead, or supposed to be, probably safe to chat a bit. What do you need?"

"Is Dexter one of us?"

"I figured he was alive. Sure wished he was dead."

"I don't really know that I can confirm that. Ends are pretty loose."

"Well, I can tell you this: His father, whom I enjoyed a close friendship with, had a bit of a dark side. Mind you, the dad could control it. At least when he wasn't operating in austere conditions. Think that's why he was looking to get out of the business. From what I can tell, the oldest boy, Dexter, did as well, but he was wanting to get into the business. Alex had blessed it. Not sure why, other than maybe he didn't know what else to do with the boy. Some of it was probably influenced by Alex's friend, and later brother-in-law, Bob O'Toole. I'm sure you know of him."

"I do."

"Heard he was dead. Not surprised. Live by the sword, die by the sword. Anyway, I suspect the rest of that darkness kinda came from their own insides. Think they had some mental challenges. I know the youngest did. Warren was his name. Went by Drake. Great kid. But think his world kinda went upside down. And I don't just mean the death of his parents. His uncle was downright brutal with the boy. Thought about taking OT out myself a few times. In the early days, he'd beat Drake to a pulp trying to toughen him up. Killed the kid's emotions. His nerves are like dead ends. I used to spend time with him to give him a more balanced male figure, but he stopped coming around, and then I heard he passed. Probably for the better. He was broken beyond repair. Probably would've hurt someone in time. Meaning, a noncombatant. So, you tracking all this?"

"I'm following."

"Okay. So, stop me if you heard enough. I'm just giving you all I know so I don't have to do this again. Ever. The oldest boy got himself into some jams and absolutely hated his younger brother. I mean hate, as in wanted to do him harm. So much so, they kicked him out of the house. Now, depending on who you asked, that opinion could differ. Alex was afraid Dex may hurt Drake, the mom thought Dex was jealous that the dad was always protecting the runt. At any rate, Alex thought maybe the kid needed some adventure and freedoms. I think since Dexter never got as much attention from his dad as he did his mom, he jumped at the chance. Now, at the time, I was only working for State. I don't know the ins and outs. And really, I didn't know about his potential Agency ties until almost the deaths of the parents. Turns out that ole OT had his fingers in things, as always, and came up with a pretty elaborate plan. I ended up with the Agency, and in short order, they had me as his primary contact and helping put some things together. Have to say we put Dex in a pretty bad spot, too."

"He was a case officer?"

"That's where I'll need to be careful here in what I can say. The way they ran him was through his layering, and a little stint with the Foreign Legion. It made things a little hairy. Let's just say he wasn't on the list for the company Christmas party."

"He ever ask about his brother?"

Tom's wife entered the house with a scoffing expression. Her face squished together seeing her husband sitting on the ground. "Who are you talking to? Why are you sitting there?"

Tom said nothing. He stood and entered the study, closing the door from behind.

"Are you having a heart attack? Dammit, Thomas, you promised," she bitched, muffled, slapping the door.

"It's about the Woolfs. FBI!" he lied. "Sorry. Wife doesn't want me working anymore. She sure won't want to hear about Drake Woolf, but she'll stop now. She could never understand why I wanted to spend more time with him than even my own boys, much less my daughters. But anyhow. To answer your question, and I'll be frank, the only time I ever heard him ask about his little brother was inquiring if the boy inherited all the family money. When I told him his brother had gone into the military and had been searching feverously for him, he laughed. Not a ha-ha laugh; it was dark. Like catch me if you can. And here all the while, I knew where he was but couldn't say a word. Really ate at me, but I thought it was best for Drake, even knowing he was chasing the world for a ghost."

"I get it. You couldn't."

"But it wasn't right." Tom stared at a small picture on the back of a cluttered credenza. It was a shot of him with Drake holding up a stringer of smallmouth bass. "Drake really missed his brother and truly thought his brother cared for him. He had no sense of the contempt and hate his brother had for him. I think if he'd known, he might have thrown in the towel. Once, I saw how ragged he'd get from the deployments. Boy, they just kept stringing him on deployment after deployment. I tried to get him over to SAD just so I could keep a closer eye on him. But he wanted to go back. All the while, he'd try to get deployed to the far corners of the sandbox and Africa, searching for that damned brother of his. But it kept him going. So, I kept quiet."

The news was a tough pill to swallow for Havens. The background explained a lot about both brothers. "So, when did you last talk to Dexter?"

"Years. He broke off ties to the Agency. Disappeared. He became that Modarris persona. Completely off the reservation."

"Pulled a Colonel Kurtz, huh?"

Tom laughed. "Brando, right? *Apocalypse Now*? Haven't seen that movie in years."

"Thoughts on how far native he was?"

"I wish. No, one thing about Dexter Woolf is, he's not crazy. He's evil. And we tried taking him out once or twice."

"Assassinating him?"

"He made the targeting list. Went native, as you say. Training people to fight against us. He was a legitimate target. Couple drone strikes on his position and his collaborators. ISIS. Hezbollah. Qods Force. He's gotten in with some pretty scary folks. Last strike they thought they got him. The Modarris, that is. No one at Langley knew of him as Dexter Woolf."

"But you don't believe he died?"

"No, sir." Tom paused and spoke again but quieter this time. "I heard an argument one time. I was on the seventh floor of the building. You know what I'm talking about, right?" He referenced the executive levels of Langley.

"I do."

"Okay, well, I wasn't a bigwig and had only been up there a couple times. But after the strike, few months later, we were around the table talking about Iran and Hezbollah, and up come the name of Modarris. Before I could say he was dead, someone said a group had him as their asset. A group I hadn't even heard of before. But evidently now he had a family, and they thought he had settled down and gotten right about the mission. He'd hooked up with an intelligence entity that was very hush-hush and far-reaching. I just tried to break eye contact and started doodling on my notepad."

"But you don't know the name anymore?"

"I do. But I'm not saying it."

"The Pond?"

Tom Mendle took off his hat and watched out the window as his wife walked down the hill toward the fire, carrying a white porcelain cup of what must have been creamer. "Mr. Havens, I hope I've been of help to you. Sorry I can't help more," he lied.

"So, it was the Pond? And he really hasn't been working for the Agency?"

There was no response. "Hello?" Havens asked again. He checked his phone screen. Mendle was no longer on the line.

What he couldn't see was Tom Mendle fully embracing his retirement and forgetting names that were better off never said or remembered and asking forgiveness in a short prayer to his longtime friend and CIA colleague, Alex Woolf. He left the house toward the river for another cup of coffee. With cream. Tom knew there would be more calls to come.

Chapter 41

"Ocean, this is Neptune, patch me in to Starfish. I must be doing something wrong."

"Roger that, Neptune. Let me connect the channels. Nope. She had her channel locked. Must have flipped it off so you didn't hear her dropping the kids off at the pool."

"Knock it off."

"Didn't think you'd like poop jokes. You are live in three, two, one. Starfish, this is Ocean connecting you to Neptune. How copy?"

"Starfish here." She sounded out of breath. "I'm fine, but I'm being followed."

"Neptune here. Good copy both. Give me your sitrep, Starfish."

There was a delay in Starfish's response, causing Drake to wince, assuming she was turning around to see who was trailing her. "Keep it discreet, Starfish. We don't want to let them know you're a pro."

Walter blazed up another joint. He turned the fan on high, causing the smoke to blow into the rear seats.

"Walter. Enough with the weed already."

Walter's eyes appeared in the mirror. "Dude, I'm not smoking it. You smell like major piss. I'm just freshening the air."

"Who's that?" Mena asked.

"My GSA Uber driver," Drake replied. "What makes you think you're being followed?"

"I saw two men come to the reception area as I was leaving. I could see in the glass door's reflection that the receptionist was pointing to me. I took the elevator down, asked the door security where the nearest

Starbucks was, and when the men got out of the elevator, they zeroed in on me right away."

"Okay, so two," Drake confirmed.

"I think more. There was a black SUV with embassy plates turning from a side street. The passenger gave a nod to one of the men exiting the building. Not subtle, but I'm kind of worried."

"Ocean, what is Starfish's location now?"

"She is headed east on Washington Street toward Franklin. Washington is a one-way."

"I have no idea where Washington or Franklin is." Drake tried zooming in on the map view of his device.

"Washington and Franklin?" Walter asked. "You need to get someone else?"

Drake's jaw hung slack. "Do you mind?" *I can't believe I'm asking this.*

"I'm having fun now that I don't think you're going to kill or arrest me."

"Okay. Starfish, we're heading your way. Here's what I need you to do. You're going to do some light evasion. I need you to cross the street and head back to where you came from. Anyone following you on foot will still try to hold back and look discreet. The SUV won't be able to turn around." Drake leaned forward to Walter. "Where is the easiest and fastest way to pick someone up if we time it just right so we don't stop and wait?"

"Hmm."

"Walter. Please."

"You're not going to arrest me, right?"

"Walter!"

"I want immunity if you're a cop."

Drake reached over and grabbed Walter's forearm. "Walter, we don't have time for this shit."

"You have blood on your hand. Where's your microphone. Is it in your shirt?"

Drake gave Walter a gentle smack on the head.

"Neptune. Where am I going? The men are crossing," Mena said, anxiety growing in her voice.

"Walter, I'll give you two hundred dollars cash. Give me a good pickup point. Please."

"Wacker and Monroe. Have the person go on the east side of Wacker, cross halfway on Monroe."

"East side of Wacker, cross halfway on Monroe," he repeated back. "Thank you. Did you get that, Starfish?"

"Yes. Heading there now," she replied.

"Are you a spy?" Walter turned off Lake Shore Drive onto Lower Wacker. The bright sky disappeared as they drove under the city. "Like CIA or something?"

"Starfish? Starfish." Drake fiddled with his Molar Mic using his tongue and checking mobile device connection.

Walter turned his head. "Oh, you probably lost connection. Can't get anything down here."

Drake's concern for reaching Mena switched to himself when he saw the barricades and police cars all around him.

Chapter 42

Walter, what did you just do?
They were waiting for you. It's a setup.
"Yeah, you're not a cop. I see you freaking out back there."
"What are they doing?" Drake's eyes ping-ponged to the left and right.
"Getting ready for tomorrow, duh... You're not from around here, are you?"
"No."
"The river over there"—Walter pointed to the small view of the waterway—"it gets turned green. Columbus is the only main entrance tomorrow for floats and busses. There's a big parade by Millennium Park. St. Paddy's Day. This is an underground start from this side to the staging area."
"Big parade?"
"It's huge. This whole weekend, everyone's going to be wasted. Some of these guys had to police the South Side Irish Parade already in Beverly. They're going to be wiped. Can you imagine trying to control like a hundred thousand people wasted before nine a.m.?"
The revelation hit Woolf. "How much longer before we get to the intersection?"
"Right where you can see the sunlight coming in."
Walter changed lanes to take a ramp awash in the day's light.
Drake saw bars adding on his connectivity. "Starfish, what's your location?"
"I'm at the intersection. Light just turned green. I'm walking to the halfway point. Where are you?"

As soon as the car emerged from the underground roadway, Drake saw Mena to his left crossing toward their vehicle.

Drake flung the car door open and beckoned the Middle Eastern woman wearing a headscarf into the car.

Woolf scooted over to the right and scanned the pedestrians. He saw the top of a black SUV over other parked cars to the side of the road. Two men were quickly turning to the walkway. One started fingering his device then lifted it to his ear as he watched the gray Honda accelerate through the green light.

Looking back, Woolf saw the SUV pull out from the curbside.

"Ocean. Do you have locks on the devices of the pursuers?"

"Sure do. Have exactly four. Also have a strong signal from the SUV. It's sending a locator transmission back to the embassy. I'll send you the transmission signature so you can add it to your own device."

"Shut them down," Drake ordered his tech. "I need their signals jammed or disconnected."

"Dude! Awesome. Coming right up." Mojo got to work typing on all keyboards like a church organist on speed playing Bach's "Toccata and Fugue in D minor."

"Do I smell marijuana or cat pee?" Mena sniffed the air, following the scent to the front.

Walter waved back. "Guilty. He's guilty too. But you're right. It does smell like cat piss. Hey, is that a disguise? You guys are CIA, aren't you? My dad's friend from college was CIA. I had a sweatshirt with the logo. Hey, where are we going now? Lawndale or are we good? I can drop you off just up here."

Mena raised a hand to Drake with a quizzical expression.

"That's Walter. He's stoned," Drake relayed as if this was all part of the original plan. "Walter, keep going to Lawndale."

Mena's face remained rankled. "You smell horrible."

"That's what I've been saying the whole ride," Walter insisted. "You're Starfish?"

"And we'll be changing to alternate call signs next time," Drake announced to the team.

Chapter 43

"Looks like you was at the wrong place, wrong time," Two-bags taunted with a smug laugh.

He was flanked by two gang members looking to fully play the part for the cinema screen. Shades, hoodies, leathers, baggy pants, and pistols held at their sides. Fingers on triggers like first day civilians at a gun range, which made the Modarris a bit nervous.

Dexter Woolf remained cross-legged on the floor. His head still splitting with pain.

The two thugs that had thumped him stood behind their captive. "He shot the guy we saw go into the storage unit. But we did just like you said. Called you up and let no one leave."

Dexter's head hung low. "I told them they were making a mistake."

Two-bags nodded to the thugs in front of him. One gave Dexter a hard kick to the side, crumpling him. Two-bags laughed again. "So why didn't you do something about it?"

"I wanted to see you. But didn't want to call." Dexter groaned. "They're listening."

"Er'ybody's listening. But that's why we use throwaways. You ain't telling me shit. An' Feds can't get warrants fast enough to tap us. They get their paper, and we done sittin' back get sucked off by shorties two years later." He laughed. Two-bags sent another visual message to his crew, and they gave Dexter another boot. "Don't you stick your nose in my business. Fuckin' terrorists running around blowing shit up. That'll get po-lice on my ass in no time."

Dexter was crumpled again. He coughed. "You have no idea." The Modarris raised his head and sent visual daggers to the gang leader. "And if one of these monkeys kicks me again, they'll be dead. I'm the one who will be getting you your money, or you will not be getting money any longer—or product."

"Ha! You ain't doin' shit. Man supposed to be ringing me up is some teacher or shit. The fuckin' ragheads' main man. You don't look like anyone's main man. You some wannabe Arab poser wearin' that shit. Goddam pajama party or some shit."

Dexter watched Two-bags nod to the man on his rear right. At the count of two, Dexter leaned to his left, pulled a belt knife from its concealed sheath. The Modarris turned in to the right, shoving the knife straight up into the thug's upper groin and slicing down to sever the femoral artery. He spun under the man's leg and tumbled him into his crony, buying enough time to stand and grab the second thug as hostage, holding the bloodied knife at the man's throat.

Neither of Two-bags's security guards leveled their weapons. Instead, they gawked at the bleeding-out street hustler writhing in a pool of blood where the docile Middle Easterner once sat.

"I *am* the teacher. Any questions?"

"I think that might do it," Two-bags conceded, not making eye contact as he, too, was transfixed by the man on the ground reaching and begging for help.

"Might?" Dexter shoved the knife into his hostage's throat. As he twisted the blade, he yanked the man backward, sending him to the grave, as well. "How about now?" Dexter asked, taking a step forward. "I am here to teach you about war and sowing chaos. And I have less than a day to do it."

Chapter 44

Mena's eyes were fixated on Drake's erratic hand movements. Stained a dark red with cuts and bruises across his knuckles, they danced on his lap as though he were signing to a deaf person. He was visibly deep in thought, staring beyond anything she could see outside the windows. Drake was saying nothing, but his lips were moving. Every now and then his eyebrows would lift or he would make a brief facial expression.

"Are you sure you're okay?" she asked gently, touching his thigh in case he couldn't hear her.

He blinked and turned to her. "What?" Drake's eyes dropped, trailing her hand as it pulled away from his leg.

"I was just seeing how you were. You look really tired."

He smiled without looking at her. "Yeah." Drake tapped on his mobile device, pulling up the tracking app. Dexter's phone was still off. Drake fiddled with the app's features and noticed, however, that Gebran's device was on but hadn't moved in a while.

"Ocean, can you hear me?"

"Yeah, are we changing call signs?"

"Not today. I'm hoping this is over soon. One of the lines we were following went dead. Our original is still live. Did you notice anything in particular about where they went stationary, who they linked to, or anything else?"

"They were practically on top of each other."

Meaning Dexter was with the scientist.

Mojo continued, "Other proximate devices, and I mean like same location too, have been in the range where there were criminal reports in the last week. But those phones must be throwaways judging by carrier and registrations. Just burners."

And they're interacting with local thugs or criminal leaders. Marriage of convenience, community of purpose. "Can I load one of the code packets on my device into the phone that was turned off so I can hack in and look around?"

"Dude, you can totally power it on, load the exploit, and see the activity. The exploits are designed to override frequency, power, modulation, and slave it for interoperability if you want. Same types that you would find with Kali Linux and the NSA ones you've used in the field. Shouldn't take too long."

"Walter, how much further?"

"We are just about in shitville now. You can tell me where you need to go or I can put it on my iPhone. But don't take my phone away after." Walter stretched an arm and readjusted his back. "I'm getting hungry. You guys in a rush?"

* * * *

"For the last time, Sean, you're not going to Chicago." Sebastian gripped the steering wheel tighter. "I came to get you so you could recover in your own home, not get in the way of the team."

"Chicago's my home. Lars and I were living out of an extended stay. I've got nothing left keeping me in DC, and most of my personal items are in storage."

"You know what I'm saying, mate. You'll not be gimping around making things worse."

"Sebastian, you're asking Drake to do something completely unrealistic. That girl may be bright, but she's not going to be effective in the field for him, and as slick as Mojo may be with stuff at the Fort, he can't juggle everything by himself for tactical support."

"The Iranians are on it. He's got a team of their top soldiers going in to take out their cells."

"*He's* as in Drake's working with the Iranians?" Havens shook his head in disbelief. "There's no way. What'd I miss?"

"A phone was delivered to the State Department early this morning by an Iraqi diplomat. There was a voice message from General Soleimani. Apparently *he*, Soleimani, used to do this in the Gulf Wars with Petraeus when the IRGC wanted to disavow involvement that could be perceived as being driven by their hand."

"We know they were involved in the attacks by the Mohawks over the past month."

"Indeed. This, however, may be different. He claims that the theft of the radioactive material was done by an overly ambitious lone wolf inspired by Hezbollah. NSA has corroborated communications data and voice from Tehran frantically trying to get their arms around the situation and sending in a kill team."

"Bullshit."

"It's not bullshit. One of their generals was found dead in Chicago along with what we assume to be his associates. Lebanese and Iranians with Venezuelan passports look to have had a shootout with each other. We don't have much of the details though. They may be covering up that aspect so this WMD threat isn't tied to the other domestic attacks. That or the new sanctions or someone up top got wind of the looming attack and decided it would have too dire of consequences. I just don't know."

"Does Drake know this, or was it Drake?"

"He wasn't in that location according to our tracker." Sebastian expelled a breath of air. "Sean. President Ross will need to know about this operation. With the Iranians involved, it complicates who I'll be able to say is driving the mission. Since it isn't sanctioned, it would help if we are in a position to say two rogue brothers have a hand in it. The narrative is too perfect. It fits."

Tell the story. Make the story fit. "This brings me back to a place I thought would never come back. I'm not putting our own guy out to burn."

"We have to let him go. He's bad news. It's a matter of time before he offs himself, regardless of whether he survives any next missions. He's already dead. There is no blowback to anyone or any program."

"What's that supposed to *exactly* mean?"

"He's sick."

"Who isn't after doing all this shit."

Sebastian dismissed the remark. "I was able to get a security team over to Bob O'Toole's file safe."

"What?"

"Drake's brother, Dexter, came to my home. Bob had mentioned him to me once. Casual remark about running assets, but he said that if anything ever happened to OT, he had a file on that boy."

"Did he?"

"Nothing I could find."

"So, what's the big deal?"

"I found medical files on Drake. He can't stay with this unit. Regardless of Chicago. Goddamned psychomotor agitation, it said. As a bloody child.

Prone to violence, it said later. And that the bastard enjoys his manic symptoms and states. They damned well diagnosed him with a diminished capacity for trust and collaboration. Did you hear me? Diminished capacity for trust and collaboration, and he was selected for a tier-one unit, much less basic infantry training. Be real, man." Sebastian took a hand off the wheel, holding it up to stop Sean from commenting next. "I sent Mena to terminate Dexter Woolf, if she has the opportunity to seize. I know Drake won't. In light of these files, if she has the opportunity, I strongly advise putting Drake down, too."

"Back up. That Iranian wallflower?"

Sebastian gave Havens a knowing glance.

"Shit."

"Your reaction to Drake? If you didn't hear me, I'd like to take the opportunity to take care of Woolf, too. Mojo contacted me. Warren Woolf murdered multiple American citizens this morning and a police officer. That won't do. Technically, as I stated, he's already dead. It could allow us greater security for the task force to continue on. You could handpick. We still have full funding. This capability can't be risked with someone's mental health that has been clearly covered up for the entirety of his career. And likely worsened. You yourself saw it. Can you put your life in the hands of a man like that?"

"I heard you. I'm just mixed. Not about offing him. That's ridiculous. But honestly, if I rationalized things, I'm at both ends of the spectrum. Frankly, we're all crazy like that. Brain chemicals simmering in constant fear and guard, desensitized and obsessive. Drake's scales may be tipped a little more in one direction, but I'll tell you this much, he's absolutely not a person I feel I can count on if I trust my head. If I trust my gut, he may just be the only person in the world I would trust and the one person who will always get the job done."

"Lad, then I agree. I think you're as mad as Woolf. That doesn't change the fact that he committed atrocities. Crimes against US citizens. It's tantamount to terrorism. He needs to be put down. I don't want this on my hands as a program director."

"Then let me take over. Let me run Task Force Orange." *I'll be Nick Fury without the eyepatch.*

Chapter 45

"Walter, we need to put distance between us and the SUV following us. Turn right up here at the next light," Drake suggested, following his digital map. He turned around to look out the back window. "Hang a right at the next street. Then make a quick left to the first street or side street. I need you to accelerate when you do that. Understand?"

"Just like *Person of Interest*. This is so cool. I got it." Walter punched the gas pedal.

Mena turned around as well. "Are they following?"

"I think so. They were a few cars back, so I couldn't see the license plate."

"Dude," Mojo interjected, "why don't you ask me? I assumed you knew. I have them still pulled up."

"Sorry, man. I'm still a little out of it. I appreciate it. Are we gaining distance?"

"It's cool, brah," Mojo eased. "Draw them to the right, and then make two quick lefts. If you get good enough space, it should buy you time to get where you're going and ditch the car."

"Right." Drake turned again, looking for the tail.

"Right?" Walter swerved.

"Yes, but I didn't mean you," Drake corrected. "Too many people talking. Walter. Take two quick lefts next. Give me a minute, Ocean, I need to do something. Walter, real quick, hand me your license."

"What?" Walter looked back in the mirror.

"Quick."

Walter struggled to pull his wallet from his rear pocket while belted in and driving a surveillance detection route for the first time in his life. He started to hand it back. "Why do you—"

Drake snatched it from his hands, opened it and pulled out the man's driver's license. Woolf snapped a picture of it, then compared it to what he had up on his mobile device. Handing it back, Drake threatened, "I know where you live, where your son and daughter go to college, their names, and from the social media profiles that I just snapped, I have friends and other family, too."

"What a dick." Walter shook his head in disappointment. "You didn't need to do that. I wasn't going to say anything." He shook his head again. "That's not right. I don't care who you work for. You're not a good person." Walter looked into the mirror, setting eyes on Mena. "You guys aren't good people. You're evil."

"Pull over to the side, Walter. Please."

Walter pulled the car up to the curb and watched a few hundreds fall out of Drake's hands onto the front seat. As he looked back to his passenger, whoever he really was, Drake hammered him with a fist to the temple, knocking Walter out, much to the shock and astonishment of Mena.

"He's right, I'm not a good person. Let's go."

Chapter 46

The two dead gang members lay dead on the floor, their blood pooling and spreading across the grimy auto garage floor.

"I don't know if you all just bury your homies in the sand, but you can see I got a problem now," said Two-bags.

"Then that's your second lesson. Body disposal. Who do you have, how fast can they get here, and what do you do with bodies to make sure they aren't discovered or are discovered later? I suggest chopping them up and making sure they can't be identified."

"Motherfucker, you don't know Chicago. We punch up on a nigga like a mothafuckin' balla pro. We pole that bitch and leave their shit in the street. Fuckin' po-lice deals with that shit. But this. Man, this is our crew. They mammas need to have a funeral, proper like."

"Not my problem. What is my problem is tomorrow. How many busses do you have?"

"I got four."

"Okay. Perfect. Gather up your drivers by ten a.m. tomorrow. I'll need you to take me to the busses tonight. I'll drive the van."

"Hol' up, hol' up for one minute. I know your people said I'm to help you out an' do what you say, but tell me the part where you helpin' me with my issue an' how I'm gonna take more space in this area an' sell more product. How 'bout you start by teachin' me that shit before I go helpin' yuz. I'm the Sheck Wes mo'fuckin' Green Goblin here. No frontin'. Feel me?"

"I understand you need to take out rival gangs, correct?"

"Correct."

"What do you think is going to happen when a dirty bomb goes off during a parade and then another one goes off later when you drive busses full of panicking people to an FBI emergency trauma and disaster aid area at the Soldier Field and McCormick Place parking lot?"

"You gonna smoke a lot of people. But that don't help me. You killin' a bunch of drunk white people is all."

"And where are the police going to be?"

"All at the place where the bomb's going off," Two-bags's soldier answered. He fist-bumped the crew chum to his right. "I got that answer all *Jeopardy* like. Alex, I take bomb those motherfuckers for $400."

"Top quality talent you attract here," Dexter remarked. "And where are any other police and emergency response people going to be going? You two, shut up."

Two-bags drew an ear-to-ear grin. He nodded. "They gonna be headin' to the lake, too."

"And who's going to be able to respond to your outside areas if you start throwing Molotov cocktails and start other neighborhoods on fire, and you start looting your competitors' areas and start more looting? And when you drive through and kill your competition while they're carrying shoes and televisions?"

"All right. All right. While the cat's away the mice shall play. And the Lawndale Legends make their claim." Two-bags raised his fists to his lieutenants. They pounded to the thought of a major victory dance.

"Now where do you guys hang out or headquarter so you can prepare your army for tomorrow night?"

The gang members said nothing but looked to their leader. He looked down to his shoes and pursed his lips. "We sometimes use the Lawndale Theatre. I own it now. Of course, through other ownership structure," he bragged. "But that shit's mine. Private property. Boarded up windows an er'ythin'." Two-bags gave a laugh, and the others chimed in.

"And you've got the costumes for the kids? The kids have to look like they're dressed like a community group that's part of the parade."

"Those munchkin midgets'll be running around like Lucky Charms. An' that means, you need to pay ole Two-bags here some more Benjamins for lost revenue if you blowin' their shit up, too."

Chapter 47

Drake hurried Mena along the sidewalk adjacent to their destination, according to the readout.

"Was that really necessary?" she asked, still incredulous.

Drake looked back to see if the SUV had found their location. They were clear. "Listen. I didn't ask you to come here. I didn't ask to be here. But I came to help, and this is what I do. Where I come from on the other end of the world, that guy would have been expendable. He's lucky he'll wake up at all. We're all expendable. Sooner you learn that, the better off you'll be. We're just fodder."

"You're crazy."

Drake snapped and literally spun his hands and arms outward to stop from attacking his teammate. He gritted his teeth and leaned in as she backed up. "You're goddamned right I am. I can hardly hold it together. I've got shit in my head screaming to kill you and another bunch of voices telling me to sit with you, have a cup of coffee, and see what you think of this whole mess we're into. But if I stop, then my body shuts down. And not only do I hear more things but I start thinking shit. Shit that I've done. Shit that I did today. Shit that I've done all my life. And the only guy who could have ever helped me is dead, and the only other guy is lying in a hospital or something in DC. And the fucking guy who evidently knows what's going on is a fucking ghost from my past playing some fucking game like I'm supposed to follow bread crumbs, and I don't know if he's helping me or setting me up to kill me."

"We'd better go." Mena stomped off ahead.

"Well you wanted to hear it."

"No, we'd better go. Look what's coming."

* * * *

Blocks away, Special Agent Tresa Halliday bypassed the visitor processing at the Chicago FBI Field Offices on Roosevelt Road with a series of ID flashes and waves. The new building was considered Fort Apache centered in one of the city's less affluent areas, thereby constraining many Bureau employees to the secure confines, which raised productivity since no one was stepping out for coffees, long lunches, and early evening "source" meetings in the city's financial district Loop, as they once had before relocating to the new facility.

Waiting for her local contact to come down and greet her at the entrance, she used the hallway restroom and peeked into an arrest artifact room just across the hall. Tresa examined the glass cases of weapons and mug shot faces of arrest over the Chicago field office's years. Many of the white-collar crime and syndicate arrests involved her father's outfit in the Chicago mafia. With the exception of her boss, Earl Johnson, no one would know her witness protection name nor her family's unflattering history.

"Theresa?"

Halliday turned to find a smaller man, perhaps fifty or so. He looked fit even in his slacks and shirt sleeves. His facial features were chiseled. Dark-haired although balding in the front and top with equally pitch eyes from what she could see in the dimly lit corridor.

"Tresa. Yes, I am." She extended a hand. "Jay?"

"You got it. Sheesh. It's like a Tinder date meeting, or what." He laughed.

Halliday took no offense. She could tell the agent was a straight-shooting Chicagoan and saw the humor and awkwardness in the way they met. Tresa immediately liked him. She laughed, lifting a hand to her mouth.

"What? I… Sorry, maybe I shouldn't have said that," Jay apologized.

She was still laughing and waved a hand. "I was going to ask if you were going to swipe right or left, but I couldn't remember which, and just ate it. Sorry."

"At least you didn't say I lied about my height on the application."

She chuckled again. "Where can we talk?"

"Let's just grab a meeting room in here. It's kinda big, but we can just pull up a chair and talk. Sometimes they have meetings in the morning and leave food and drinks around. Need a water or anything? Coffee?"

"Water would be fine."

Jay handed her a plastic bottle from a table just outside the room entrance and once inside pulled two chairs around in the area of about a half dozen table rows and about sixty or seventy chairs. He leaned in, squinting as if wrapping his head around her presence. "You came from headquarters because you have some questions about suspicious Iranian activities here in the city? I mean you coulda just called, right? Why the trip?"

She nodded in understanding. "True. But I've been tracking some related things, and it seemed best to do in person. I don't know if I mentioned, I'm National Security Branch, CT-2."

"Yeah. Counterterrorism domestic disrupt and dismantle, blah, blah. I mean no offense, but you know, we're kinda different here than headquarters people. We've got our own CT-2 folks. I mean, to be honest, I kinda like us sticking to our stuff and, you know, you guys do your thing. I mean we'll help, but I'm not sure what you really need." Jay leaned back like he had said his piece and gotten his angst off his chest. "We can do the 'I'll show you mine, you show me yours' thing, but I'd rather just see how we can help you and not get HQ all in our shorts."

"Okay, I get it. But it's because of the NSB aspect that I want to lay low. As soon as I say WMD and counterproliferation, which as you know falls under an NSB counterintelligence directorate and big bureaucratic Joint Terrorism Task Forces, people start getting all squirmy." Tresa raised an eyebrow and took another pull of the water, hoping he'd buy the line of shit. "Oh, by the way. Tony at Quantico said you were just up there for a training and did some boundary waters fishing before that. Catch anything?"

"I did," he responded. And seemed more interested.

Halliday gulped the rest of the water, wishing it was a beer with this guy. "I've pulled some monster pikes out of Lake Agnes and Boulder River. Plenty of northern just short of forty inches."

"I've had good luck years back around Gabbro and Crooked," he shared.

She could tell that he was now giving her the up and down look but from a different lens. "No shit. Steel leaders?"

"And heavy tackle helps the fight. That's where I know your name. You worked Indian Country."

"I did." Halliday hoped that was where it would end and wished her name was not coming up in the Chicago field office where there were no Indians or tribal jurisdiction issues.

"Shit. Okay, so you're not HQ exactly."

"Not in the least. I'm a Cicero girl a way long time back. Grew up in Wisconsin though."

"Okay. Now you're talking my language, Halliday."

"Tresa."

He pointed a finger at her. "Tresa. Got it. So, Iranians. Well you know we're all still looking for that student who swiped the radioactive material from the university. But he's linked to Hezbollah. I mean, I know in the Middle East they're tied, but it's a stretch for Chicago. Then, we just busted two Iranian spies here checking out the Jewish sites and people funding that other group. Can't remember the acronym."

"MEK? M-E-K."

"That's the one." He snapped his fingers up in the air as he reclined back on the ergonomic chair. "Can't remember all these characters." Jay leaned forward. "But the real shit came down in the last days. North side. In a cemetery, a meet and greet went bad. I think they were Venezuelan from the passports, but one of our intel guys said he confirmed Iranians, too. I'm like Iranians and Venezuelans? Talk about two messed-up places to come from. And then it ties in with the scientist kid. Right?"

Halliday was about to make a comment, but Jay started up again. If there's one thing Halliday learned about interviewing and interrogation, it's if someone is singing, let them finish.

"Here's the other shoe that dropped today. Before you got here, and shit. This. Was. Bad," he emphasized with arms outstretched. "Crazy shootout back up north. Indian and Pakistani area. Complete bloodbath. Knives. Shooting. A lot of people were killed or injured. We're still trying to sort that out. But I don't think they're Iranians. I mean, does that help?"

"Big time." She leaned over the narrow table toward Jay and lowered her voice. "So, let me ask you this. And you may not know, but was there anything that seemed professional about those hits or attacks. Or something out of the ordinary outside of the acts themselves?"

"Mmmm. Nah. I don't think so, but I can ask." Jay looked up to the ceiling, searching in earnest for a nugget. "I wasn't at either one, and CPD is taking care of most of it at this point. I'll check with a couple guys."

"I'd appreciate it."

"Sure." He crooked his head a bit in what appeared to be an afterthought. "So, there was this one thing."

She leaned in to imply it could be their little secret now that the whole HQ thing was behind them.

"One of the detectives I mentioned earlier, responding to the Devon Avenue attack, got himself shot by a bum they picked up at the scene. I mean, they were helping this bum who was wrong-place wrong-time attacked while he was, I don't know, maybe looking to steal something or maybe he was drunk or looking for a place to crash. And he gets ahold of a gun and shoots this detective. I mean, that's pretty fuckin' weird, but he ain't Iranian. He was just some stinky like white bum guy."

Woolf.

"But like I always say, 'Welcome to Chicago, where the weird just gets weirder.'"

Chapter 48

Drake expected to see that it was the black SUV tail rolling up on them based on Mena's concern and wide-eyed panic. Instead, just out of his periphery came a small band of street hoods strutting toward their position.

Drake counted five.

If they were strapped, he couldn't take them all. Normally, he'd have little fear of being approached by gang members during the day. No one wanted trouble, and no one wanted to get busted. But this neighborhood was almost completely boarded up. There was no police presence, and there sure as hell wasn't going to be anyone saying something to investigators of a crime scene about a white dude and Muslim woman getting rolled in this neck of the woods. Snitches in ditches ruled a place like this.

"Ocean, we've got a small contingency coming up on us. Any police in the area you can see? I don't see a way out of this confrontation."

Mena turned to see another young tough coming from an alleyway toward them. He lifted his oversized sweatshirt to brandish a pistol handle tucked in front of his pants.

"Ocean. Fast," Mena added. She drew closer to Drake despite his rancid street smell.

Mojo expanded his map view, selecting the population of mobile devices that were sending signals closest to Drake and Mena. His fingers rattled the keyboards, only pausing to reach out to touchscreen monitors. He selected radials then restarted typing.

Attack, Drake. Violence of action. Take the initiative first. You've got the element of surprise on your side. "Anything, Ocean? I hear you fucking Googling or something. I don't need you to send me a PDF of survival."

"Neptune and Starfish. Pick up the pace to your target. Don't look back. Airwave support coming in hot!"

A phone started ringing from behind Woolf as he quick-stepped down the street with his colleague, as instructed. Then another ring. And another varied ring tone. Within a second, all the hoods who were coming toward Drake and Mena were answering their phones.

Drake heard Mojo's voice through the commo. "This is a Drug Enforcement Area. Lay your weapons down. Hands and face to the ground. There is an armed drone over your head."

Drake couldn't hear what happened next, but the thugs started bending over. Some dropped their devices, shouting about how hot the phones just got. Others grabbed their ears cursing. One of the devices on the street burst into flames.

"Tango Mike, Ocean. Not sure what you did, but it's working."

"Hashtag Jack Ryan that, bitches!" Mojo replied. "Sonic bomb with high-decibel bursts and max load on battery beyond recommended levels. Analyst as fuck! Yeah, baby."

Drake heard a loud bang then cursing over his audio.

"Ocean, you okay?"

"Spilled my Coke. Shit."

"Hoo-ah, for the support team."

"Dude. Not cool."

* * * *

Within minutes, Drake and Mena arrived at the site of the scientist's prior signal. Still in the clear, Drake lifted the orange metal door.

Mena wrapped her arms around herself but said nothing when they saw the lifeless body on the floor.

Drake was hit hard by a flashback sight and smell. With the vivid mental scent recall came the sights and sounds of war from when he last experienced the same odor. It didn't take a decomposing body to have the crackle of gunfire snap in his ears with the background sound of technical trucks crunching the hard, unpaved ground. Shouts and screams came next.

He broke out in a sweat, and his mouth dried.

In his vision emerged Walid, his Lebanese asset in Saida, who was found just like the body before him. As a result, Drake had to hide out in the Mieh Mieh refugee camp with no food or water for days before he was able to make his entrance to the Ain al-Hilweh camp on the hunt for Ali al-Hamad. He learned through street talk that Hezbollah had killed Walid's wife and children in recent days. Their sacrifice, while not intentional, gave Woolf cover for action.

Adel's face came into Drake's mind's eye. The four-year-old was so pleased to receive the gift of a yo-yo. So simple, but it brought such a smile. The kid was gone. He never asked to be martyred for a US mission.

"Drake."

Woolf slowly came back to reality.

"Drake. We need to shut this door or just leave. Do you want to check the body?" Mena touched Woolf's arm gently as he was locked again into the stare. His mouth moved, but he was inaudible. "Drake?"

"Turn on that light over there." Drake nodded. He checked his six and gave a short peek to the left and right. They were still clear, so he lowered the door behind them and took a seat on the floor.

"Are you okay, Drake? Anything I can do?"

Drake stretched out on the ground, his head resting on a folded arm. "I'm tired," he admitted. His voice was soft and flat. "This is a dead end. I don't know what to do next. I'm tired of running. Tired of chasing. It just never ends. Find one bad guy, up pops another. And for every bad guy that I find, I lose more friends. It's just not worth it."

Mena moved closer to him and sat cross-legged. "Ocean, we need a minute. We're turning the comms off." Mena deactivated the communications link. "Turn yours off, too, Neptune."

"I'm fine. I don't feel like messing with it."

She persisted. "You should really turn it off. I can see on my monitor your battery is only at a twenty-five percent capacity or so."

He looked at her hard. She was fixated on him and his device while a dead guy was lying in the pool right next to her, to which she paid no mind as if it were her uncle Faisal or something taking a nap. She had a Persian accent, but her nuances and phrases didn't match. She was a devout Muslim but made absolutely no religious references nor common, everyday blessings and traditional remarks. Westernized, maybe. Assimilated, possibly. Full of shit, most likely. *Trap.* "Mena, why are you here? And who are you really?"

Chapter 49

Two-bags, like most successful street kids who rose to the top, managed his crews by fear. While it may not yield long-term loyalty outside of self-preservation, it created responsiveness. Within minutes of his lieutenant's calls and demands, items that the Modarris had requested started rolling in.

"Where I should put this, Two-bags?" asked a hood carrying two bags of CG Industries ammonium nitrate pellets. He was trailed by four other young men, each carrying one or two bags of the high-density agricultural grade prill.

Dexter Woolf pointed the men toward the large red cannisters of diesel fuel.

Next came two younger boys, each carrying a can of aluminum. "Hey, Two-bags, that mo'fucker, Mr. Jenkins, he didn't give us our change back. He said we were going to get in trouble with this shit. We told 'im they was for you, and he said you could come down and get it at his store."

The Modarris cast a dark eye to the gang leader.

"Y'all don't be lookin' at me an' shit." Two-bags nodded to two larger men in his crew. "Go get my money and make sure Mr. Jenkins shut the fuck up."

"You gonna hurt Mr. Jenkins?" a boy asked. "He wearin' his veteran hat today."

"Naw, little man. We just gonna remind him ain't no room for old Marines stickin' their noses in shit. This is my hood. You feel me?"

The two boys nodded.

"Yous go get some other kids and go get your leppa'con outfits from Oz and his bitch. Make sure you have the hats and shirts and everyone gets those lil' orange beards. Just bring the boxes here now."

"Even the girls wear beards?"

"Slap that little motherfucker."

The closest thug to the kids obeyed his boss without question and swatted the designee hard in the ear.

"Yes, the bitches. And you best not be late. Go get Dantrell and Kayjon, too. And you have them text me if that junky fucker gives you any shit."

"Yes, Two-bags," they confirmed in unison.

Dexter watched the two boys leave the building. It was the same the world over. Africa. Middle East. Asia. He thought of his own two sons and hoped they and their mother were still safe.

Chapter 50

"I've already told you who I am. I'm not the one who should be questioned here," Mena deflected. "I thought we were past this."

"Either someone beat the shit out of you for years when you were a kid, or you've had some training. When I blew my top in the shop, you hardly flinched. And when I had you on the table, you didn't look back to Sebastian for help. You stared me dead in the eye. When I let you go, you didn't freak out on Sebastian or bail out of the building. You came after me. And then here in the street, you stood close to me but didn't grab my arm in a freak-out way or do any other things some academic analyst would do. Scared, maybe. Untrained and unused to stressful situations, I don't think so. So just level with me."

"You should check the body."

"No, Mena. I think *you* should check the body. The dead guy didn't shock you. Surprised you to see? Maybe. Even a bit of self-reflection on your face, maybe, too. It's not the first dead body you've seen either." Drake stood and walked up to the body of Gebran Daouk. He looked at Mena squarely and gave the corpse an unexpected kick to the ribs, never breaking eye contact with her.

The brutal act caused Mena to flinch slightly at the sight. She looked back up at Drake. It was well-played on his part. She didn't have time to think about a scream or other normal reaction that someone would have.

"I'm no spy. And I'm not a mole."

Part III

Terrorist attacks can shake the foundations of our biggest buildings, but they cannot touch the foundation of America. These acts shatter steel, but they cannot dent the steel of American resolve.

—President George W. Bush

Chapter 51

"I never said you were a mole, Mena." Drake bent down, stepping to the side of the congealed blood on the floor, and checked Daouk's pockets, only finding a phone. He paid Mena's defense no mind as he was having his own mental discussion with the advisory panel in his head.

Woolf found the phone was locked, placed it on the dead man's dry upper chest, and retrieved his own device, on which he thumbed a number of prompts and commands.

Daouk's screen lit up, then went dark, then on again. Drake thumbed away on his own device for a few moments more. The device of the Hezbollah wannabe stayed on and the Man from Orange smiled.

Woolf swiped across apps and opened others. From the corner of his eye, he spotted a white handheld device. It was cracked on the front, and the side was missing pieces of plastic. Even from the slight distance Drake could see the green edge of a circuitry board. "Mena, I know you're not a spy. I know you're not a mole. I have no idea if you can shoot, or if you even plan to kill me somehow. That's just how things have been for me lately, so it wouldn't surprise me. Truth is, you'd be doing me a favor, so right now I could really give two fucks."

Drake picked up the white device and tried unsuccessfully to turn it on. He continued with Mena as he fiddled with it. "Unfortunately, you all involved me in something, and I'd like to see it through; otherwise what the fuck use is all this training in me if I can't save some lives." Drake opened the back of the handheld, examined a single wire and a broken solder joint. He pushed the wire into the small metal loop lug, bent it with a fingernail and tried the device again. It powered up. He looked up at Mena with a smile of success. "The question I have is can I depend on you as a partner to have my back if you can even operate. Do I have that with you until we at least see my mission through?"

Mena nodded.

Drake handed her Gebran Daouk's phone. "If the screen goes off again, the password is Starfish. There's some interesting communications going on. This guy's opsec was for shit. See if you see anything different than I do." Drake turned his attention back to the Geiger counter and viewed the historic readings. "We're in over our heads."

Holding the phone and scrolling through message traffic, Mena kept her eyes on what she was reading. "What are you suggesting?"

"I've got a buddy at the FBI I think I need to say hello to. She's in the DC area, but she'll know who we can find to help us."

Chapter 52

Tresa Halliday was still chatting with Chicago agents Jay had introduced her to at the Roosevelt Avenue headquarters when her phone rang. The unknown caller on her display sent a wave of both dread and euphoria through her body like a poker-faced teacher returning a graded paper. She knew in her gut that it was Drake. Although the possibility of it being Havens clouded the moment, and before she knew it, the men were looking at her and the phone had rung five times.

"Excuse me." She broke away, accepting the call and stepping out of the room to a wide and bright hallway. "Hello?"

"Special Agent Halliday, it's me. I need your help."

"Is this who I think it is?"

"Yes."

"Why are you calling me?"

"Needing help didn't clarify?"

Halliday rolled her eyes. "What help do you need?"

"I found the scientist. The one who stole the radioactive stuff."

"Where is he? Is he alive?" she asked, excited, then covered the mouthpiece as people passed by.

"No. He's on the floor here, dead, and there are no radioactive materials. I'm in a storage warehouse on the west side of Chicago. Big enough to park a vehicle, and from the way his body looked when I arrived, I suspect someone drove off with the goods after taking him out. There's a handheld radiation detector that was broken on the floor, so I am also assuming he may have been testing levels. Don't know if that's for leaks, quality, or what. Surprising that no one took the detector unless it slid under the vehicle. Thought maybe you should call someone here in Chicago. This is going to be bad if someone doesn't prepare for it or help stop it."

"Drake, I'm here in Chicago now."

Woolf's shoulders dropped limp and jaw slackened. "You are?" was the best he could come up with.

"Yeah. Your buddy sent me. He sends his regards."

"What buddy?"

"The one who had bullets taken out of him and has had surgery on his wrist and foot."

Dread passed over Drake, concerned that she had nabbed Havens and was on her way now to get Woolf. Instinctively, he hung up and grabbed Mena by the arm. "We need to go."

* * * *

"Shit." Halliday stomped the floor. "Shit!" She wondered why it was that for a man she knew less than a month or so, Drake was like an ex-husband that she still couldn't let go of but who still infuriated her every time they spoke.

Chapter 53

Drake hoisted the door, checking for anything threatening. It appeared clear.

"Ocean, are you still on?"

"Never left. Still don't have Starfish reconnected. You laid down some heavy shit, bro. I've got your back one hundred percent."

"Thanks, man."

"Things cool with you two? Not like I thought you were going to get a room or anything."

"That's exactly what we're doing. We know there's a strong probability that the attack is tomorrow. Seeing loose ends being tied up all around the city tells me things are in play. We need a safe place to just think."

Mojo gave a nod that no one saw. "Need me to find you a place?"

"No, I found a pay-by-the-hour motel on the way in. I'll have Mena grab us a room."

Mena could only hear one end of the conversation still, so her expression looked like she was confused. She reactivated her comms.

"We just have to figure out how to get to the hotel without getting mugged on the street or carjacking another civilian." Now on the open street, Drake turned in to the building as a nonthreatening pedestrian passed by the two of them paying no mind until getting a whiff of Woolf. "Guess I need a shower, too," he said as an aside to Mena. "Here's what I need you to do, Ocean. Pinpoint each location that we have not yet been to that has a crossing of communications. If there are signals coming from locations without multiple endpoint transmissions, I need you to search and see who the individual is who is registered to the phone or where it was purchased. Since most will be burners, see if there is any other cross-information you can pull from the database. We need to roll up the network quick and start with the outermost spots in the city and work our way in to the most centralized. That gives us a better chance of hitting a place that isn't having a party. My guess is the Archangel cell has been eliminated and the Iranians have taken over the job. Since they would only use a proxy, the new focus is probably on a criminal outfit. Make sense?"

Drake raised his eyes to Mena. "Docs that work for you, or do you have any other ideas?"

"Yes. Ocean 6," she confirmed, referring to Sebastian's temporary call sign, "had told me that there was another source we were getting intel from. Have we heard from him…or her?"

Drake tried to read Mena's face. Clearly Sebastian had told Mena about Dexter. The old man evidently made a habit of this, which did not please Woolf.

Her face was blank.

She knows, Drake. They are putting the pieces in place. Check, check, checkmate, Drake. You're the pawn. The warning would have rolled off Drake were it the dark voice's constant berating, but instead, it was the sound of his father. And that scared the living shit out of him.

"Nada," Mojo responded. "I haven't heard anything. One of the devices Ocean 6 was tracking was the person of interest."

This time it was Mena who cast a look of surprise.

Drake smiled inside. "I'm not sure we would consider him a source or an agent in place. *His* phone went dead. Ocean, make sure you include that device in your tracking and mapping."

"Roger that, Neptune."

"Anything else, Starfish?"

"No."

When Drake turned, Mena adjusted the shoulder straps of the light gray commercialized Leatherback backpack he had given her.

She had filled it with exactly what Drake said to put in. A book, a couple magazines, protein bars, some trail mix snacks, a couple bottles of water. And then she concealed in the middle inner pocket exactly what Sebastian had said to put in it.

"Okay, Ocean," Drake said. "We have a tentative plan and less than sixteen hours before something real bad happens in this city." It was at that moment that he knew he needed to call Halliday back. If she was in Chicago, she was potentially at risk, as well as potentially a million others. Yes, this was bigger than him. It was in the next moment that he saw the big black SUV racing toward them.

Chapter 54

Major General Qasem Soleimani hadn't expected to receive two harrowing calls that week. He listened attentively as Major General Hamed Abdollahi expressed concern on the phone as to the status and current whereabouts of his Unit 400 operatives.

"Qasem"—Abdollahi teed up before launching into his next point—"and what have the Venezuelans said?"

This was a very different question from the last, to which Soleimani could only respond that he had not yet heard of any news. What the Unit 400 commanding officer was now asking, Soleimani had received indirect word. He was compelled to share it. "My dear brother, their news is more dire, but we have not been able to confirm. The American news has reported multiple deaths in one of the more ethnically populated areas of Chicago."

"You made no mention of this when I first asked."

"I said I do not know. Even the news from the Venezuelan embassy does not tell me. At this point, what it tells me is they have completed their mission."

"Will you be at Golzar Tower tomorrow?"

"No, Hamed. Tomorrow, I have much to attend to. I go back to Syria in short order. But soon. Soon. I promise."

After hanging up, the Qods Force leader, Soleimani, checked another device after completing the requisite security protocols in three layers of authentication and cyber defense. He retrieved the latest unread message sent by the Modarris on an unencrypted account. It confirmed the wave-one elements were no longer a risk. It further confirmed Gebran Daouk had been eliminated. It finally confirmed that a Chicago gang was now in possession of the materials and high explosives. All of which meant the signal intercepts by the global Five Eyes alliance could add credence to the deniability of malicious intent by Iran. On the world's stage of scrutiny, there was evidence, even to the point of spilling their own blood, that the Persians tried to thwart an attack on the Americans. Everything was in order.

The supreme leader, Ali Khamenei, would be pleased. Hezbollah would be pleased when they received their monies for time and resources. Win. Win.

Still, the prior news from Senior Commander Majid Alawi about the Modarris was troubling. Soleimani crossed his office to open a large wall cabinet. From a closed box he retrieved a labeled plastic bag with a fish-eye camera. The bag was dated and labeled *Ain al-Hilweh, the Man from Orange.*

Chapter 55

"Start walking. Now. The embassy boys are coming back," Drake instructed as the SUV closed distance on their position. Woolf did a mental inventory on what he had or what he could MacGyver in a matter of seconds to stop whoever was rolling in heavy and hot.

"Drake," Mena said, forgetting to use a call sign, "what are you going to—"

Mojo interrupted, "Hey guys—"

"Not now, Ocean," Drake barked. "We have a situation."

"But—"

"Shut the fuck up!"

"Go, Mena!"

Woolf started off at quick clip in the direction of the barreling-down SUV. He had no illusion that if he jumped in its way it wouldn't mow him down.

There was a shopping cart turned on its side about fifteen feet away now, the SUV doing about sixty roughly forty feet away on the quiet and deserted street. As intelligent as Drake Woolf was, this was no time for mathematical story problems, so he busted ass to the cart, hoping to toss it into the street and buy Mena more time.

From the SUV's driver's-side window first came an elbow.

Shit, they're going to light me up. Drake turned to see how far Mena had gotten. She was out of sight, so must have turned at a street or found cover.

As the driver's-side arm unfolded from the window opening, Woolf panicked at the new thought that Mena may have been snatched by the two other Venezuelan street pavers.

Drake gave the cart a pull, hefting it up while trying to maintain some cover behind a parked car.

A white bandaged hand emerged from the SUV's window and waved. The driver popped his head.

Sean Havens was sporting aviators, a spiral-corded secret service style earpiece and a new close-cropped buzz cut. From the bandaged hand, he elevated a middle finger as he veered over, braking hard parallel to Woolf.

"S'up, dick. Where's Scheherazade running off to?"

Chapter 56

"Starfish, we've got a ride," Drake transmitted. "Sorry, Ocean, I'm guessing you were going to let me in on our new surprise teammate?"

"Trying to," Mojo responded, exasperated. "Sucks. I wanna be there, too."

Havens chimed in to the conversation on his wired earpiece comms, as Mena came into view. "We need you there, Ocean. You are the only reach back we've got who can give us near real-time situational awareness. Guys, we'll talk about this a little later, but while you've been doing a great job, our targeting approach is chasing tactical intel. You're connecting dots and making geo-links, but we're now at an intersection of two nation states, a terror group, and gang activity. Chasing phone numbers all around the town and killing whoever's holding one only gets us so far. We need to ask ourselves bigger questions, and we don't have much time. Make sense?"

Drake nodded. He was instantly relieved to have the coach walking back on the field to lead the team.

As Mena jumped in, Havens gave a concerned but quick sideways glance to Drake. He mouthed, "You okay?"

Drake nodded, filling his lungs with the scent of security one had when evac showed up on time.

Woolf was good about wearing the mask to hide the ghosts of war. Yet, in the mere weeks that Sean had known Drake, the weakness and wear of Woolf was becoming more evident. His veneer of invincibility was fading. Though a younger man, Drake Woolf was a combat warrior old-timer. His comrades had moved forward or fallen on the battle field or even to their own pills, bullets, and booze in the relative safety of their homes. He had avoided contact with newer soldiers in response and let relationships fall by the wayside after deployments. He appeared to prefer being alone, which was on the downward spiral of constant isolation. A guy like Woolf could never adjust to civilian life, as if he ever had in the first place. Havens wanted to get Drake into an emotional reset wound-healing program with a friend at All Secure Foundation, but the operational tempo had, as usual, fucked that up for the time being. He couldn't let it go though. Sean pressed Woolf again with a head tilt and eyebrows that raised above his shades.

Drake closed his eyes as they drove. The rumble of the SUV navigating potholes and otherwise bad street conditions and random debris on the street felt like a helo cutting the air chop. In his mind he could hear the beating of the rotor blades. Feel the pitch and sway of the Black Hawk, his legs weightless as they dangled out of open doors. He tasted the powdery grit of the desert caked on his teeth and felt the pit of his stomach wrestling with post-combat anxiety and excitement.

"Hey, you sure you're all right?" Havens pushed.

Drake shrugged and gave a slight head shake. No. "I think I'm just tired."

Sean pursed his lips. At least the dialogue had started again. "Okay. Let's get you cleaned up and see if we can get you some food and a little rest. Smells like a gang gave you a long golden shower. You smell like absolute shit, unless that's you, Mena." Havens cringed, realizing that as he talked to her in the car, he was still on closed and encrypted radio, but the bad tradecraft was still a huge snafu.

Mena just rolled her eyes. A gesture that was becoming as routine as a blink.

The crew was certainly different from what she was used to in Foggy Bottom. These knuckle-draggers were the complete antithesis of high-brow higher education intelligence professionals. She might have felt differently, however, knowing Havens's full background and the fact that doing overseas distance learning while killing bad guys, Drake had completed most graduate-level electrical engineering and computer science courses offered through MIT's open courseware.

"There's a hotel I found about two blocks away." Drake arched his back, trying to retrieve his device from his pant pocket.

"We've already got digs set up."

"Safe house?"

"FBI's pretty big to call it a safe house. We're assisting FBI Counterterrorism as Delta advisors. Your girlfriend's there, too." Havens relished the harassment and smiled a shit-eating grin.

Mena reached up to Drake and slapped him on the shoulder. "You've got a girlfriend? This I've got to see," she mused, sitting back and literally biting her lip and removing her headscarf.

Chapter 57

The Task Force Orange team disconnected and stowed their communication devices once inside the Bureau's entrance while waiting for Halliday.

Mojo was relieved to be able to cut off and focus on the data analysis.

The clicking of Sean's cane on the floor echoed within the high-ceilinged, wide, glass-enclosed space as he limped along.

"Explain to me…Gramps," Drake chided, "because I'm kinda uneasy about this. How is it that we go from being hunted by these guys"—he motioned toward the FBI crest on the wall—"to parking in the guest lot and just walking in the front door and announcing ourselves. I'm kinda expecting to be fully surrounded by a tactical team in seconds."

"I called her."

Drake's contorted expression showed his vexed state. "Dude, I've got bloodstains up to my elbows."

"Hmmm." Sean hobbled up to the thick-glass security desk. "Is there a bathroom?"

The middle-aged African American woman pointed to her right. "Just down that hall. It's a girls and guys, unisex."

Sean motioned to Drake, who was transfixed on Mena putting her long dark hair in a ponytail. She had a blue raid jacket with bold gold lettering that Havens had offered to her from a duffel in the trunk. Drake was to wait for his jacket until he cleaned up. Mena, however, looked the part. But she, too, was distracted, watching the television news broadcast in a wide-screen panel above the chairs in the waiting area.

In what appeared to be ongoing coverage, the display flashed news video and photos of the Devon Street area, then the detective's police car parked at the convenience store. A surveillance camera's footage looped twice, showing Drake in the vagrant's disguise, pushing a cart on the street, then another from a higher angle being escorted out of the flat by police.

Mena turned to Drake, her eyes wide and directed on the baggy pants he still wore.

Sean, too, noticed the concern she wore on her face and the coverage.

"Oh, boy," he breathed.

It was Drake who was the most unsettled, however, when the next violence-in-Chicago news item showed police gathered around Walter's gray vehicle. In the corner of the screen was a photo of Walter. His hair was shorter, he wore a shirt and tie in the photo. The broadcaster was saying something, but the volume was down. Her coverage segued to an on-scene reporter at a Chicago middle school where Walter had been a distinguished benefactor of a new science lab. The news bar at the bottom of the screen referenced him coming from a prominent family, and then cut over to a number of family photos.

"Gentlemen?" a male voice called to the rear after the clack of locks and squeak of a heavy hinged door.

The team turned, surprised that it wasn't Halliday.

"And lady," the fifty-something suited man added with no introduction. "If you will please come with me."

Sean took the first steps forward. "We were supposed to meet Special Agent Halliday. Is she coming down?"

"Things have changed. I'll need you to come with me."

"Like Custer to the Indians," Drake muttered.

Mena fell right in line, passing Havens.

"You're sure not worried," Woolf said as she passed.

The Persian analyst turned with a smile. She whispered back, "I'm not. I'm Agency, and I haven't killed anyone today. But you've already heard my résumé...and backstop."

This is a bad idea guys, Drake admitted to his voices before they chimed in. His mouth started to click, ready to respond with deadly force, if necessary. He had no intention of being detained.

Chapter 58

Jay brought Tresa another cup of coffee. "I was getting another, thought you may want one, too." He placed the blue cup embossed with a golden FBI logo on the side to the left of the stack of papers she was reviewing. "Sorry we don't have much more on the Venezuelan kid."

"I'm thinking the guys who are coming up may have some insights they can share. They may be a bit skittish, though."

"Usually we get more notice if the Deltas are coming to Chicago. Especially if they've got a spook from Langley." Jay sat down and fidgeted with a pen against his coffee cup. He gritted his teeth. "I spoke to the department SSA as he was leaving. Not many people here on a Saturday. We have to let the SAC know. I'm not going to blindside him if this turns out to be something. With everything going on in the city today, he should know there are some other resources here before he asks for them, and should know where the connections may be."

"Jay, you've been really great. Maybe we do this: let him know Earl Johnson at headquarters put this together, sending over a few of his task force liaisons. That way, we're all covered."

There was a knock on the closed office door before it opened with the salt-and-pepper-haired agent announcing the party's arrival. "Do you want me to put them in the conference room, Jay? One of the guys really smells like shit. They have a bag for his change of clothes. I can always take him to the locker room, and he can shower off. He's kind of a mess. Are they operating here in the city?"

Jay turned his head to Halliday. His brow dipped. "They weren't up north, were they?"

The agent at the door laughed.

"What?" Jay asked. His tone short and bothered. It appeared to Halliday that Jay's mind was churning. Maybe she hadn't played her card right in an attempt to get closer to Orange.

Before she could sway the conversation, the older agent raised hesitation. "I don't know about this bunch. There's a guy who looks like he just walked out of the hospital after getting hit by a bus." He stepped into the room and closed the door, lowering his voice. "A Middle Eastern woman who looks like she's going to college, and the smelly beat-up dude can hardly keep his eyes open. Probably undercover surveillance or something, but hardly anyone that had to fight their way out of a paper bag."

"Right," Halliday interjected seeing an opening. "These guys are techies. Total dorks. I think the one guy may be a raging alcoholic, but he's good at tracing and tracking. Why don't I go get them settled in and say we link up in an hour, unless you need to go home. I know it's getting late. I can ring you if there's anything that comes up. I mean, it's not like the city's going to go up in smoke tomorrow."

The agent at the door commented, "Yeah, I can get them into the conference room and take stinky downstairs on my way out. We've got a St. Paddy's Day party to go to tonight. Told my wife I'd be home about two hours ago."

"Okay, Eric. You have a good weekend." Jay leaned back on his chair, taking a loud slurp of his coffee. "Hot." He winced. Jay reached across to the files, slapping them in a rhythm on the table. Halliday watched his eyes. They were locked on the royal-blue folder, but he was seeing well past anything that was inside. That was the problem with running into a seasoned agent who had succeeded by trusting his instincts. It was apparent something wasn't passing Jay's smell test. He just hadn't caught a scent on the trail yet. Her cover story could get real thin real fast.

Chapter 59

"Go get your boss," Dexter Woolf demanded of the Lawndale Legends hovering about while the Modarris inspected the compounds and the large blue plastic vat. Dexter wiped his brow with unease.

In moments Two-bags strutted over, his entourage in tow. "What'chu want now, mister teacher?"

"I need you all to clear out. I have to assemble the detonator."

"Bullshit, not a chance. This is too high stakes. You a shady mo'fucker, an' I ain't e'en trustin' you." Two-bags folded his arms, outstretching his belly in contempt.

"If I've got all these distractions around me, it could cause a slipup. Do you want to run this neighborhood, or blow it up with you included?"

"I ain't getting all blowed up," said a lieutenant by Two-bags's side.

"I ain't gettin' all blowed up, neither, Two-bags," another insisted.

"Aight, we all clear out. But I'm keepin' two of those dumb muthafuckas back there just outside. And I'm tellin' them to put caps in your ass if you even pop your head out the door. I ain't seen no money yet, and I ain't gotten my goods yet from no one, so I'm trustin' our business. But I ain't havin' to trust you."

"Fine," Dexter appeased. "And please have one of your men find me a big stick or a broom handle before you go. Once I have this all mixed and wired, we can get it on the busses. I'm putting together two vats. Come back in an hour. We'll load this up before midnight and then get the rest of the chemicals and supplies over to your theater so you can get things ready for tomorrow night for your assault. We'll get working on that after the kids are on their way."

"Sounds like a plan, Osama." Two-bags outstretched his hand for a fist bump.

Not wanting to show disrespect or suspicion, Dexter obliged in what he assumed would be the first and last fist bump of his life.

Chapter 60

Sean Havens watched Tresa Halliday hurry past the open conference room, stop, and back up.

"This place is a maze," she said to Mena and Sean in small-talk but stayed in the doorway. "Did they take Drake downstairs?"

"Yeah, about five minutes ago. Something wrong?"

Tresa pulled fingers through her long brown-and-blond skunk-striped hair. Moving hands to hips and looking left and right down the empty halls, she looked perplexed.

Mena stood and outstretched her hand. "Hi. We haven't met. I'm Mena Shabpareh. White House Situation Room. Persia House. Central Intelligence Agency."

Tresa didn't move from her position but took Mena's hand, giving it a hard shake. "Cool." She turned to Havens, not giving Mena any additional attention. Halliday didn't do girls club. "I need to move you guys but can't let them take Drake back up here."

"Can you get me down to the locker area? I can run in, get Drake, and we can go wherever." Sean turned to Mena, trying to judge her body language. This was all getting too weird. "Halliday, what gives?"

"I may have overplayed my hand. I'm not exactly loved, and this place is hard to read. I think the guy I'm working with here suspects something's up. I'm counterintelligence, so that doesn't make sense to him why I've got a CIA chick and two Deltas with me and no protocol communications going to the boss."

"So basically, you kinda screwed up and have us in the middle of it. Maybe not even thinking about the fact that Drake and I are on security cameras here now, which was stupid on our part." Sean stood. "Look, this isn't exactly what we had discussed." He looked at his watch. "We don't have time to be room shuffling. We need to get Drake some food and rest, and need to figure our next steps. We're wasting time.

"More importantly, the field office here should be informed of everything at this point that we know about the suspects and links. I don't want to be the subject of scrutiny here, but there's a potential attack on the city that appears imminent at this point. I'd be less worried about hiding us in broom closets than telling whoever can help pitch in what they need to know."

Halliday nodded. "Yeah, makes sense. I'll get back to Jay. Let's go get Drake, though, and get out of here. I stay at a hotel every now and then not too far from here in Greektown. I'll use my credit card, get a couple adjoining rooms. He can rest, we can talk and plan."

"Sounds good, Special Agent Halliday," Mena confirmed. "We look forward to working with you and your team. This Jay, may I know his full name and level?"

Tresa gave her a hard look, but with a smile. "Just Tresa, Mena. You're trying too hard. You're in Chicago now." Halliday grabbed a remaining bag off the floor. "I'll get this. All on the same team." She winked.

Havens winked at her. "Don't you go trying too hard either, Halliday. I came to you because my hometown needed help. Not so you can snuggle with our outfit and roll us up after we save the free world as we know it," he said, overdramatizing their role, and outstretched his hand. "I'll take my own bags, thank you." Sean buzzed his lips, displaying his impatience. "I sure do love interagency task forces. Hamstrung already just finding a goddamned conference room."

Tresa dropped the bag on the floor and spun to the door. "Well, then I guess I won't need to share with you the Chicago office's gang findings."

Mena sped up and walked out with Halliday.

Chapter 61

The men's locker room could have been set in an upscale New York gym or even one of the snooty private golf clubs. Mahogany wood trim, shiny stainless-steel fixtures, and contemporary styling.

Drake peered around the walls of the locker room, feeling as fresh and revived as he could despite muscle aches, a bullet impact, some light abrasions, bruises, and old war wounds that persisted in discomfort.

Let's go, Drake. We need to bug out. Halliday is going to fuck you over. This is a trap. Havens should have known. He sold you out. Mena is just as you expected, a plant to watch your moves and take you out.

Drake squeezed his eyes shut trying to push the voice from his thoughts and senses. The Man from Orange was trying to hear if the voices he heard talking to one another in the private shower stalls were still talking to each other. While he couldn't see who was talking, it sounded like a couple young agents who had finished working out at the building's gym were planning their evening's social activities.

If there was one thing that Drake knew about men working the mission, they had trust in each other. And trust in their secured environment. Due to that level of trust, Drake hoped that they had left their weapons, IDs, and perhaps other items of use to Woolf unlocked.

Sure enough, there were weapons stashed on the top locker shelves. Drake grabbed a pair of green tactical pants from one locker. A quick check of the inner waistband size tag indicated a larger waist and slightly longer inseam, but with side adjustment straps, he could make it work. He checked their boots, but his own distinct Vasque Juxts were too perfect to dump, unlike his earlier pair of shoes for cover that nearly fell off in the skirmishes.

Woolf raced to put on the new clothes, stuffed a weapon in the nylon holster, and the other in his lower back. Both weapons were Glock 17s. He snatched the two 9mm standard capacity magazines. That gave him seventeen rounds each. Judging by the grip, sightings, and green receiver, the two dudes in the shower were SWAT. He liked these better than the FBI's formerly issued modified Springfield military 1911 .45 ACP. The Glock would give him no problems if he could put the rounds in the right place.

Drake pocketed the agent's neck strap credentials and badges, and stuffed his own rancid clothes in the trash. He grabbed the extra raid jacket Havens had given him, tucked it under his arm and walked out the door. How and where Havens snagged raid jackets before showing up to the field office was a mystery but not beyond Sean's prowess, especially if he had landed up at Fort Sheridan where the Bureau did some training.

The special agent escort was waiting near the elevator bank, having a heated discussion on the phone as Woolf stepped out. The agent gave a quick double-take then turned away, lowering his voice and raising his finger up to signify the universal hold one minute. It was evident to Woolf that it was a domestic issue by the tone, words, and apologies. Typical. Mission men and women blew commitments all the time. Not having his own family was the best thing Drake ever did, he thought. He would have destroyed that, too.

Drake raised his voice to the agent. "I'm just going to grab something from the car in the visitor lot. I'll be right back."

The agent turned and waved then went back to assuage the wife that he would still be back in plenty of time and able to stop at Mariano's along the way to pick up green cupcakes, only the chocolate ones, and the green cupcake cookies that were white but had the green icing, and swing by Red Box so the kids would have a movie and his wife could finish drying her nails, which he helped her realize would not be overly green with the goddamned white shirt underneath a Kelly-green vest and black tights.

The elevator opened and out poured Havens, Halliday, and Shabpareh. "Is he still in the locker room?" Tresa asked.

The agent shook his head no and pointed outward.

Halliday shrugged and lifted her hands for more clarification. "Where?"

Havens gimped to the locker room and did a quick about-face as soon as he heard "My pants were right here. Someone's messing with us."

The SWAT men were laughing, but in the next five minutes, it wouldn't be so funny. Havens knew what was happening. Drake Woolf was not exactly a team player and no doubt never received an interagency challenge coin in his life.

Drake exited the FBI Field Office, his mobile device map orienting him around the area, which was still in the same vicinity that he had been for the later part of the day. Still, he needed to find a place where no one would notice him, ask questions, or generally give two shits, while not being a hostile environment either as he thought about next steps. The Lagunitas Brewing Company was two blocks away. Preferable at this point, yet not an option. He expanded the map view and found gold.

Drake turned on Damen Avenue, walking with rapid purpose, and headed to the Jesse Brown VA Hospital. Sean Havens was good at diplomacy, thinking things out, and coming up with plans. But the fact of the matter was, Drake had targets and locations. That's what he was paid for. Time was ticking, and sitting in a chair around a table wasn't killing bad guys any faster, the voices had convinced him.

With a free hand, Drake reapplied the Molar Mic. "Ocean. Neptune here. Need you to message me the targeting map I asked for. Start where the most converged signals are coming from."

"Hey, Neptune." Mojo yawned, the fatigue fully setting in. "Yeah." He yawned again. "Knew the quiet wouldn't last long. Ocean 6 is here. He got me pizza. You're on speaker."

"Hey, boss."

"Lad, how you holding up? Did you link up with your friend?"

"Yeah, he found us just over an hour ago when he landed."

"No. I didn't make myself clear. Your other friend who paid me a visit and dialed you up."

"Ah, no. We had his device up for a bit then lost it. Ocean, did you get any other hits?"

"Yeah, he sent a message through an encrypted account. There were a lot of relays, but in the end, it was accessed in Tehran. They were taking responsibility for taking out the Hezbollah assets."

Sebastian added, "Mate, there's something afoot. General Soleimani had a more direct message relayed to the JSOC commanding general. He claims that Iran has nothing to do with what is going on and has sent men from their own special mission unit to help take out the threat, which corroborates the surveillance traffic we pulled electronically."

"So are they bullshitting, or did I just wipe out the rescue party? Can't say they announced themselves too well."

Drake walked up to the VA hospital that was devoid of any activity. He took a casual seat outside on a bench and continued his conversation.

"Reports we're getting on the high side indicate other Iranians have been taken out too. Is this your handiwork?"

"Sir, I can't make heads or tails of half the people coming at me, and don't have much time to check them out before I'm either running away or running to the next shit show. And as much as I'd like to give you a good sitrep and brief you on my full battle damage assessment, I'm kind of in the thick and ready to go dark. Can you put Ocean back on the line so I can get back to work?"

"Is it okay?" Drake could hear Mojo asking Sebastian in the background.

"Hey, Neptune, I'm sending you to an old auto shop where your Alpha One's signal burst for a bit and then went down again. It was in the same direct location of communications with Venezuelans from Caracas and their Chicago embassy. Not real good tradecraft, but maybe that's why Venezuela is so shitty, anyway."

"Make that signal Bravo One. I'll put both in my feed so it shows me current status and historical." A roaming security guard walked past Drake. Neither said a word, both just gave a slight hand lift hello under the light of the hospital entrance's glowing awning. Drake glanced in the direction from which the lackluster guard came. There was a small security service company's branded car curbside. The hazards on. A dome light still illuminated. Drake got up from the bench for a little recce.

"Roger that, Neptune. There is another one that's popped up from time to time. It's actually registered to a name. Oswald Robinson. Petty crime and narcotics record. But signals that just left the area of Alpha and Bravo are heading to him. You may be able to figure something out."

After a long pause of no response, Mojo spoke. "You there?"

Sebastian chimed in. "How copy, Neptune?"

Drake Woolf slipped into the idling vehicle, turned off the headlights and interior, headed west on Polk back into Lawndale. He knew Sean Havens would be steaming right now, but with the man limping around like a busted-up Avengers leader from S.H.I.E.L.D., just having him in the city gave Woolf the extra boost he needed.

Chapter 62

Oswald Robinson turned back to the young Zarielle, shooting her a terrifying glance before shutting and locking the door. Oz, as he was called on the streets, entered his apartment living room where his girlfriend Shawnay lay passed out on the couch, her fix lying on the beat-up table to her side.

Oz checked his pants fly, then pulled a chicken finger from the brown fast food bag also on the table along with Fritos lying about, catsup and hot sauce packets in small piles, and four full two-liter plastic bottles of RC cola. He walked to the window, sliding the moldy beige curtains to the side, and looked below in the small entry courtyard three floors down. Music was playing from the alcove entryway. A glass bottle broke, and laughing erupted.

Oswald raised the thin window and popped his head out. "Y'all shut the fuck up down there." He threw the last of his chicken finger at a kid smoking a joint against the wall.

"Whatchu throw at me, Oz?"

"Dinner, bitch. You better not be all fucked up in the morning. Twobags, he fuck you up if you ain't on the bus."

"I ain't wearing that leppa'con shit anyway."

"The fuck you say," Oz called down.

"Baby, shut the fuck up," Shawnay said, roused from her high. "Git me some French fries."

Oz pulled his head back in. "Bitch, shut the fuck up. I'm doin' bi'niss." He kicked at her, hitting the table and knocking the two liters over on end. "They's still fries in the bag, bitch. Put 'em in the oven you want 'em hot again."

"Baby, why you kickin' at me?" she slurred, rolling over to face the cushions.

"Pssht. Bitch." Oz peeked back out the window into the relative darkness below.

A glass bottle shattered against the brick wall, just missing his head.

"What the fuck!" he shouted. Oz ducked in and looked around the room for something to throw back that was of no value to him. He snatched one of Shawnay's high-heeled shoes from the floor, jettisoning it down to a small group of three to four laughing on a stair stoop.

They laughed even harder. One girl called up from the group. "I'd axe you to throw down another so I gots a pair, but I know that ho Shawnay took these from the trash. They Laquisha's ole shoe." She muttered, "Garbage pickin' bitch," to the others.

"Fuck you, bitch. I pulled them out myself. Perfectly good shoes so she don't need to be spendin' my money." Oz spit down below, losing sight of it as it fell.

Two pairs of two dark figures approached the hoods in the courtyard. Oz craned his neck, then leaned out the window more to see who was coming around.

The pleasantries they exchanged were just out of earshot to Oz, until one shouted up. "Oz, they comin' up. Best get that bitch of yours shit straight."

"Fuck," Oz cursed. He closed the window and started pushing on Shawnay. "Bitch, get the fuck up. Two-bags sent some homies up. Get your shit awake." He slapped her ass.

"Hey, baby, you come to be getting some of this?"

"Ain't want none of your nasty—"

Oz fell silent as the pounding interrupted his attempts to show anyone coming in that his shit was in tow.

"Hey, yo, comin' right away. Comin' now. Don't be beatin' the door in." Oz opened the door to see two teens waiting, another two holding back.

"What up, Oz," the smaller of the two boys greeted, his dark hoodie bobbing back.

"Hey, my young hustlers. What do I owe the pleasure?" he inquired nervously, his own junk having recently left his body, bringing him down.

"Two-bags want the boxes. Says we takin' them so you don't fuck it up."

Another boy spoke up, "Yeah, he don't want you tryin' to sell 'em and shit."

"Boy, shut the fuck up," Oz scolded. "How'm I supposed to make any money off a orange beard?"

From the shadows one of the punks stepped forward. His stainless-steel revolver emerged from between the other two boys in front. "Get us the boxes, bitch. And you ain't drivin' no busses tomorrow. Stay the fuck out, and shut the fuck up."

Oz backed up with a nervous laugh. "Hey, my little man. Okay, okay, no need to get impersonal here." Oz laughed again. "I need to roll the busses so I makes the dough. Surely, Two-bags knows that."

One of the boys reached into his pocket and outstretched a hand, which Oz accepted. The kid dropped a small yellow rubber-band-wrapped baggie. "Two-bags said you get this. He say if you stay away tomorrow, you get your bus back the next day. So go get the boxes. We gotta bring them back to the car shop before he move the busses."

A slap came from nowhere, hitting the boy from behind. "Shut the fuck up, Twon. You ain't supposed ta be sayin' none of that shit."

Chapter 63

Drake's map directed him through the dark zombieland neighborhood. Figures walked aimlessly around while others sat or stood from recessed alcoves, the only light emanating from glows of yellow-white flames or glowing embers burning at head level or sparking as they rolled across the ground.

Woolf couldn't see stop signs and really saw no reason to slow at street corners where wraiths of the night bent for a closer look at the driver in a white rent-a-cop sedan. He did jam on his brake as four figures crossed the street from nowhere carrying what Woolf assumed to be old television boxes given their size and his pre-judgment. Since televisions were flat now, maybe microwaves or boxes of clothes. They had to be kids, judging by their size, but their nighttime activities looked even more desperate and suspect than what he had seen across the globe.

"You have arrived," his phone announced, startling Drake. Clearly, Mojo had left some commercial features. His heartbeat was raised and his shallow breathing rose high in his chest. This was an unfamiliar environment to Woolf. A new battlefront. In the Middle East, at this time of the night, people scurried around like rats running in and out of the darkness. Here, there were ever-present eyes. It was more like his experiences in Somalia, but here, the buildings felt darker and more dangerous. Partly because he felt that most everyone in Somalia was out to kill him when he was operational. Here, it was a different vibe. He couldn't see the weapons. He didn't know the people. And he didn't know if he could intimidate the locals here at night to back down.

As Drake pulled in along the curb of South St. Louis Avenue, he could hear the crunching of broken glass under the tires. That sound wasn't nut shells. At that point, he also realized that with no backup and no one to stay by the car, it was a slim chance that it would be there when he came back. At the very least, he was certain that the glass would be broken across the seats.

Drake turned off the headlights and took a deep breath. To his left was 1809. It was exactly as it showed on the map. A large three-story building in 3D view with a narrow courtyard entryway that would have Woolf surrounded on all sides, and deep alcove entryways to conceal attackers. He had to assume that the first entry to his left would be the one. Then he only needed to climb the flights of stairs to get to his objective. Whatever that may be.

He took another breath, knowing it was time to move.

They're all combatants. Kill them all if they pose a threat. Kill every fucking one of them if they get in the way. Kill your way in. Kill your way out. No police will be coming. You get a free pass.

Drake's father started to chime in with usual warnings and encouragement to abandon going it alone and to forgo his hazardous approach to finding answers.

The Man from Orange was focused, though, and as he exited the car, navigated the broken sidewalk and turned into the low-fenced area past the high bushes and into whatever lay ahead, he feared nothing, because no one in this godforsaken neighborhood had killed as many men as he. And no one in this darkened labyrinth had as hard of a heart and black of a soul as Woolf, he thought as he brushed past person after person without even a word, not even a glance.

Yet from behind began a chorus of whistles and claps and shouts to warn—someone.

That all came to a screeching halt by the time he rounded the staircase on the second floor.

Chapter 64

"He's still not responding to voice comms or the mobile," Mena said to Havens.

"And Mojo?" Sean asked, then turned to Halliday, realizing he had just outed one of his crew again.

If she caught it, her poker face gave nothing.

"Do you have any clue where he would have gone?" SA Halliday posed to the group as they entered the gated parking garage to load up.

Mojo relayed to Sean, "His location display is turned off, not exactly sure how he found that feature, but whatever."

Mena put Mojo on her device's speaker as they slalomed between parking stalls and wide concrete supports. "But regardless of location display, do you know where he was heading? He's off on his own, and I'm sure he's going back to the target lists that you developed," Mena probed further. She turned back to see if Sean was able to keep up as she and Tresa speed-walked to one of the few SUVs in sight. He gave her a wave.

"I gave him an address of one of the targets. And since then, that immediate area lit up with signals."

"He's going to be doing the Mogadishu Mile in a few minutes," warned Sean. "Not the best area in town, and it's a nice night out. That's not good."

* * * *

As Drake bounded up the stairs, on the second-floor landing a fire door burst open. From a dim hallway light a dark man rushed at Woolf. "Who you, five-oh?" the big man asked, his hand hitting Drake's vested chest. The momentum, if not checked, could have sent Woolf through the wall.

Bad move.

Drake raised his left arm and spun inward, crashing his forearm down. He intended to punch the man's throat next, but the big man folded with the arm strike. Drake hammered the back of the big man's neck, sending him to the ground. Woolf stomped the man's lower back. A low-pitched snap and the feel through Drake's strike confirmed the dude would not be getting up on his own.

Another man who stood watching mustered enough courage to come at Drake next.

Drake saw the young African American man come at him. The guy wore a black ball cap, but Woolf's mind saw the yellow eyes of a Nigerian Boko Haram jihadist who tried to overrun the small military outpost he was stationed at nearly three years ago.

The Bokos were pouring in on the one-story barracks from every unblocked opening. Windows, doors, a hole in the wall made from a vehicle that broke through the dried clay blocks. They scurried in like insects, never looking back as their colleagues fell. Each one whacked out on anything ranging from cough syrup codeine to diazepam or tramadol or whatever they could get their hands on for a high.

Drake and two of his unit men just kept shooting, two in the chest, one in the head, as best they could. The hands grabbed at him.

Kill him, Drake. They're going to overrun the base.

Still transported mentally to a time back in Africa, Drake pulled the Glock from its holster, raised it up under the young Chicago man's chin and fired twice. As he fell, another coming up from behind reached for a weapon stuffed in the front of his pants. Drake outstretched his weapon to the next thug's forehead and double-tapped the trigger. In the flash of the discharge, Woolf saw the fear in the young boy's eyes, and the golden sticker under the kid's hat. A Wu-Tang Clan yellow logo on his black sweatshirt.

Shadows behind the falling young men fled for their lives.

Drake stood frozen. Half his mind was half a world away in Nigeria, the other half returning to present and looking at murder. His arm and weapon still raised. His breathing got faster, and he struggled to slow it down. Woolf tried to reorient himself between where he was and where he was supposed to be going, but the walls were spinning, his ears ringing from the shots. He looked down at the first man who came after him whose spine he had stomped on. The dark heap was whimpering with fluttering hands. Drake knew the man was in panic. His back was broken. Probably now paralyzed from the waist down.

Woolf eyed the pistol grip peeking from a dead man's waistband.

Put him down, Drake. He tried to kill you. He'll never walk again. Just do it. Quick.
Go, Drake. Stick to your objective. He can do you no harm.

Woolf pulled himself up the stairs, struggling to focus while clearing his mind from images of the present and past. They all had the same last looks before they died.

It was the same everywhere. People attacked their attackers. Whether defending their lands or their turfs. You couldn't blame them. Today, like every other day, Woolf was the invader. But unlike any other day, Woolf had continued to invade America.

Chapter 65

Drake opened the third-floor landing fire door. The sight before him was surreal. Two young girls, maybe five or six, were playing in the hallway, an apartment door cracked slightly ajar to cast some light in the blacked-out corridor. They were dancing to music, a tinny sound playing from a phone on the floor. Had they not heard the gunshots? What time was it?

"Are you the po-lice?" a little girl asked Drake, staring nearly three feet up at him without the slightest bit of fear.

Someone shut the door behind the girls, and the hall went completely dark.

Drake heard the scratching and click of a lock, keeping the kids and whoever was in the hall out. He couldn't even tell them to go hide inside.

Woolf then heard muffled shouts and noises from behind in the closed-off stairwell. They were shouts not of anger but of disbelief. Clearly, they were shocked by what they had seen of their crew or whomever they were or whatever they were called.

"Girls, I'm not the police. Can you call the police and get some help?"

"We don't need help," the little girl said in the dark, until her sister or friend lifted the phone and turned on the flashlight. She shone it in Drake's eyes. "Do you need help? Your coat says you're po-lice. FBI po-lice."

"Girls, you need to get away some place. Fast." *They're going to be expecting you, Drake. You lost the surprise. You're a dead man. Screw it. Screw this place. Just leave. They can't always put stuff on you.*

"We're playing," said one.

"Yeah, we're playing," repeated the other.

"Girls, you need to get into your apartment. It's not safe."

"We can't go." The girl moved the light around, trying to get a look at Drake's face. He tried to shield it with his hand. "Mama has a guest. We can't be inside when she has her guests."

"Stand back." Drake could see in the lighting where the door was. He edged the girls to the side and kicked in the door. "Get in!" he barked.

The girls screamed and ran in, yelling for their mama.

"Fuck!" Drake hated himself, if possible, more than ever. He raced down the hall, pulling his device with a free hand, trying to read apartment numbers. The magic one was 306. *There's 302 to the right, 303 to the left, 304 to the right, 305 to the left, 306 to the right.* "Of course."

Drake stuffed the phone back in his pants, withdrew the second Glock and readied himself for a solid breaching kick.

These were criminal groups. They weren't waging a war, technically. They couldn't be judged as war criminals, nor could they be treated as enemy combatants. However, the whole reason that Drake was here was because they were colluding with terrorists. Colluding with hostile nation states.

The dark voice prodded, *Get in there, Drake, if you're going to do it. You have no time left.*

Woolf fingered his sweaty hands in the pistol grips.

Warren. The name shocked Drake. He could see his father standing in the kitchen. Feel the Tunisian heat across his face. Sweating in that sticky kitchen. His dad never called him by his first name. *Warren,* he called again. *This isn't you.*

Drake huffed. *It's exactly who I am.* The Man from Orange took a glance down the long hallway, ignoring the small head peering from her apartment, and splintered the door frame, sending the door into a wall with a loud slam.

Chapter 66

Oz had the thin line of Two-bags's gratis heroin cut on the glass of his mobile phone. He had no interest in why the invisible supply chain no longer brought the high-quality white dope from Colombia through the Venezuelan Hezbollah partnership with the Sinaloa cartel. Nor did he care or worry about how it went up through Tucson to Chicago, where it further branched out to the Midwest. Even though Oz's preference was the Mexican black tar heroin produced with other synthetic drugs within Guerrero state and up along Sinaloa, Durango, and the Chihuahua states, he only cared how it felt when it entered his brain.

Involvement of Hezbollah to reclaim the Colombian connection was in full force, and they were courting gang leaders such as Two-bags, while at the same time increasing high levels of fentanyl-laced heroin to their competitors to hamstring the Mexicans. But this, too, was neither of interest nor mattered outside of his manageable candy-hustle business that Two-bags was sticking his fingers in.

All that mattered now was he had the next day off and a bag of party mix to celebrate with. Oz had no clue how much fentanyl was laced to make sure he never came back down.

"Hey, baby. You comin' down hard? I got a treat for you."

He passed the phone over to his girl just as the apartment door burst open.

"Oswald Robinson?" the man yelled.

Oz dropped the phone and raised his hands. Shawnay struggled to put her top back on while raising her hands up, out, to the sides in an effort to comply.

"She in there." Oz pointed down the hall.

"Who?" The white man spun to the short hallway. He carried two handguns and wore a face of blood spatter and fury.

"The girl. But I didn't touch her. We just has her locked up so she don't get in no trouble before she go to work for us in the morning."

The man looked confused. He blinked his eyes often. His mouth made a clicking sound.

"You can go check." Oz started to stand, but the man rushed up and shoved a foot into Oswald's chest, knocking him from the small kitchen chair onto the floor.

The man towered over Oz, both barrels pointed down at him but periodically swinging to the right at Shawnay.

"What girl?" he shouted again.

"Zarielle, her name Zarielle," said Shawnay as she readjusted her top. "We look after her. Like fosters."

The angry man's face continued its contortions, and he started shouting, using his pistols in the gestures.

"Who the fuck do you work for?" Drake kicked Oz in the side.

"You can't go hittin' him like that! I'll sue your motherfuckin' ass an' this whole city." Shawnay started to get up.

Drake backhanded her across the head with his pistol. "Don't you fucking move."

"Shawnay, shut the fuck up."

The man pointed his weapon back down at Oz. Oz's head was scrambling, and then he saw the yellow lettering on the blue jacket. FBI. *No, sir. Two-bags'll have me killed in a minute.* "I want my lawyer. I ain't sayin' shit."

The FBI agent hit Oz across the head with his weapon.

"You motherfuckin' crazy, cop?" Oz raised his hands to his bleeding head. He had had more than his unfair share of beatdowns by the cops over his lifetime. And one thing he had learned, FBI was going to go a lot better than a whisky smellin' red-faced CPD beat officer on a Saturday night. Oz rationalized that he probably wouldn't get any more lumps from this Fed. "Take me in. I don't know nothing. I want my—"

The white Fed turned again to Shawnay. "You! Face down on the couch. If you move, you're dead." When she didn't comply, the agent holstered his weapon, grabbed her by the hair and forced her face down into the seat cushions.

The man clicked his mouth three more times, tucked the second weapon away and reached down for Oz's shirt.

Oz expected to be lifted up; instead, he saw the fabric pulled over his chin then hard across his mouth, and then lifted again from the bottom over his eyes.

Oz expected to feel hard metal against his forehead. He heard the hiss of escaping air. Like from a pop bottle.

The fabric pulled across his lips. Oz opened his jaw to stop the cloth from pulling so tight. At that moment, the liquid started pouring in. Sweet at first, but then the drowning sensation sent him reeling in panic. He was back in the water. Six maybe seven years old. Down at the South Shore's Rainbow Beach Park with his cousins. The wave had knocked them all down. Oswald laughed at first, then sucked in a mouthful of water. He somersaulted underwater and saw his little sister and cousins doing the same. The water threw him down then pulled him up. They were tugged back into deeper water.

Oz choked on the sweet cola and could feel his eyes roll back.

He felt himself lifted back up. The chocking stopped.

Shawnay was screaming in the background.

The man yelled again. "Who do you work for? What do you know about a plan for an attack tomorrow in Chicago?"

Oswald felt his body fall backward again. His head hit the ground hard. The shirt tightened across his mouth once more, and before he knew it, his mouth had opened in reflex; then the soda cascaded into his throat again. His nose and up to his eyes burned from the carbonation pain entering his sinus cavity and down his choking throat.

I'll talk. I'll talk. But the words never came. Instead Oswald was drowning again. Reaching for his sister's hand. He saw her slide down the sand into deeper darkness as the bubbles spun around him.

Oz flew up again.

"Last time, who do you work for?"

Oz pushed his tongue against the wet shirt. He wanted to speak. He would tell them who he worked for. Then the FBI would have to stop. He didn't need to say more. Two-bags wouldn't know who dropped a name. Oz heard the hiss again.

Shawnay screamed, "No!"

The man shouted back at her. The sound was distant in Oz's head. "Fucker, you *will* talk, I guarantee. I'm not playing by the CIA enhanced interrogation manual here. We're in my territory now. My rules."

Oswald's head hit the floor.

It started again. It was the same feeling from Lake Michigan. He couldn't see, he couldn't breathe. He knew they were all going to die on that beautiful summer day. But Oz had lived. So had one of his cousins. He wanted to live. His body, once completely rigid, relaxed. *I'll tell you everything. I'll say all that I know. Let me live. I'll change.* As his body started to spasm, he felt as though he was out of his body until it lifted up again. He suffered a hard slap to the side of the head; then the covering came down and he could breathe. First, he saw the light. Then heard the clicking sound that the monster made. Shawnay's crying was muffled.

Then the loud voice again. "Now, tell me all!"

"Two-bags. I work for Two-bags. He runs Lawndale. He runs everything. Drugs, girls, he's got all the corners. He stays during the week in some rich suburbs, but he and his boys own places all around the area. I can show you. He just needed me for the busses and the kids. That's all."

"What busses and kids?"

"I drive them around selling candy. To the rich white folk. We make money off that, sayin' we a charity." Oz choked hard, and the man turned him to the side as he vomited.

"What does Two-bags want with the kids?"

"I don't know. I don't know."

The agent yanked the shirt back over Oz.

"No!" Oz screamed. "He's got some deal with the Arabs. But I don't know more. He had me hold some boxes. For the parade tomorrow. So the kids could get dressed up."

"Does he have a weapon? WMD?"

"What?" Oz's eyes were wide in terror. "I don't know what that is? No. Maybe. I don't know."

"Weapon of Mass Destruction. A bomb."

"I don't know. Really, I don't. He has four busses."

"Where are the busses?"

"They're moving them. I don't know. I swear. I don't fucking know. Please don't kill me. Please just take me in. I'll tell you. Put me in protective care. He's going to kill me. He'll kill me for sure."

The man let go of Oz, who flopped to the floor crying.

"You motherfucker!" Shawnay cried, dropping off the couch as the man stood and walked to the hallway. She rubbed Oz's face. "Baby, we gonna sue the whole city. They can't treat us like this."

"Neither of you move."

* * * *

Drake Woolf's hands were shaking. He had lost all control. He had what he needed, but still needed to check the room.

Woolf kicked an orange strip of fuzzy fabric that was stuck to the outside of his shoe as he unlocked the door. Uncooperating, he had to reach down to pull it off, tossing it down, where it landed on a child's green and gold necklace.

Drake listened at the door before opening it to find complete darkness. Drake felt to the side for a light switch, but flipping it up did nothing.

"Please don't," a small voice begged.

Drake pulled his mobile out and pressed it on. The phone shined enough light that he could see a young girl peering out from under the bed, her hand tethered by rope to a bed frame.

"I'm going to get you out of here. I promise."

"Are you a policeman?"

"I am today. Hang on."

Drake stormed out of the room to find Oz and his girlfriend sitting on the sofa. There was a flicker of red-and-blue lights on the ceiling inches from the window wall. New noises coming from the outside hall.

Oz stood. "It's not what it seems."

Drake grabbed Oz by the neck and fisted a handful of the candy gang leader's pants, then tossed him through the window glass.

"Freeze," a female voice shouted.

Before Woolf could turn, he heard three rounds go off in rapid succession. Then a heavy thud to the floor.

As he turned, he first saw Special Agent Tresa Halliday, her gun drawn and pointed away. Drake saw Shawnay lying to her side on the couch, eyes open, but dead. The left side of her head had a bullet entrance wound, the side of her staining with blood. On the ground, a Smith & Wesson revolver. Where that had come from Woolf hadn't a clue.

Relieved, he smiled. "I'm so glad—"

"Hands where I can see them. Warren Woolf, you're under arrest."

Chapter 67

"Slowly, get on the ground," Halliday ordered. "Fingers locked with hands behind the head."

Drake stood firm. "There's a little girl in that room who needs some help." Woolf nodded to his left.

Halliday turned for a moment to the dark hall and, returning attention to Drake, saw his gun leveled at her.

"We're not going to do this, Woolf. I'm here to help you guys, but this is not the way. I can't just stand by and—"

"Sure you can," Mena interrupted.

Drake saw Mena step from the shadows. She was wearing a raid jacket, but he could see she had Drake's bulletproof backpack on underneath. Mena had her own weapon leveled at Tresa's head.

"No, Mena." Drake lowered his weapon. "I'll give her the gun. She's right. And she's just doing her job."

Mena remained steadfast. "She's going to bring the task force down. You guys have already created a colossal constitutional and human rights travesty, and I want no part of that."

"A little too late for that now," Tresa added, not helping her own situation. "You were there when we called for backup, bitch. It's going to look odd to CPD when two nobodies try to leave and a special agent is down."

"No, it's Woolf's weapon. He keeps it in the vest as backup. But after I shoot you, we'll leave the weapon. This crime scene is a mess. And half of our people don't exist. I'm not worried. One phone call and I'll be out."

"Girls, both of you put the weapons down. We're all on the same side. I know who we need to go after next, and they're planning on using kids tomorrow in the parade. All we need to do is stop that, and we go home.

At this point, we can even turn that over to the FBI to handle. They're better equipped than we are."

"Iran's generals have used children historically, but as a first-wave attack. There will be a next wave to immediately follow," Mena cautioned.

Most people would be nearly inconsolable. Halliday, however, was pissed. Drake could see it in her eyes. "Fine, I'm putting my weapon away." As Tresa turned to holster her weapon, Drake could see her turning the barrel backward.

"You can't," he said as Mena started to lower her own weapon.

Drake fired twice at Halliday, sending her into the wall and down into a heap.

Chapter 68

Mena jumped back in surprise. "You shot her."

Drake holstered his weapon. "Shut up," was all he could say before dry heaving.

Mena rubbed the back of her neck and thought, *You kill all these men, and vomit now. She really was special to you.*

Mena stepped back to the open door. She extended her leg backward and closed the door quietly with her foot. *You can do this, Mena. You have to do this.*

Drake continued to gag and retch and dropped to the side of the couch, coughing. As he supported his weight with the coffee table, his hand rested on Oz's overturned phone.

Do it now while he's down, she coaxed herself. The reality of shooting someone she knew versus the scientists who were strangers made a world of difference. Mena swallowed hard, mustering courage.

When Drake stopped coughing, he said, "Let me see what I can get off this junkie's device before cops get here. You get the girl." He nodded. "She's gotta be scared shitless."

Mena gave a nod but didn't move.

Drake retrained his attention to the suspect's phone.

Mena leveled her weapon at Drake. *Low caliber. Two in the head. If Drake knows Sebastian put me up to this, I'm dead. It's not personal, Drake. It's survival, and you're just as evil as the men you hunt.* She took a step closer.

"Where's Havens?" he asked.

Mena held her breath, thinking Woolf was about to turn around. He was fast. She was overthinking this. Where would he move if he saw her?

He was wedged between the sofa and the table. "He's outside stalling the Chicago Police. Mojo called 911 and gave Sean the heads-up." Her hands were sweating. They always sweated before she shot the scientists. She waited too long then and was waiting too long now. *Pull the trigger.* "He told the police not to come up until his man came out."

"Smart. He's a thinker." Drake looked up.

"I really am sorry, Drake. Sebastian doesn't need you to save the day. He just needs it to look like you tried. We know the Iranians are involved, but we don't want them to stop the operation. They need to take full responsibility."

"You bitch," said Halliday.

Mena spun to the voice of Tresa.

Drake turned around, firing Shawnay's .38 into Mena, center mass in the chest.

Halliday fired two to her head.

* * * *

"You killed her!" Drake popped up and jumped the table over to Mena, who lay lifeless on the floor. He dropped to his knees, cradling her head.

"Well, no shit."

"I shot her vest like I shot you. She was just—" Drake dropped his head. "Fuck. This wasn't supposed to happen. You naïve girl, Mena."

Muffled voices slowly approached their position from beyond the door.

"CPD's coming down the hall." Tresa pushed herself up, still breathless from the bullet impacts to her body armor. "She was going to kill you."

"She should." Woolf pocketed Mena's weapon. "Dammit," he whispered and closed her dark, staring eyes.

Halliday half shrugged and hustled down the hall to check on the young girl.

Woolf continued to an audience of himself. "I'm a fucking sociopath." He raised his voice, walking to Halliday while checking his six for cops. "You know what I've done today. Tonight."

Halliday bit her lip and pulled her hair over an ear.

"Just take me in, SA Halliday. Fuck it. Take me in. They can lock me up, kill me. I fucking deserve it."

"She's gone."

"CPD! Coming in," Chicago's finest called out from the entryway to avoid friendly fire.

Chapter 69

The plainclothes cop was the first to come through the fractured door frame and witness the two dead women. Other officers were queued up behind him, struggling to get a view. "Agent Halliday?" the officer called out.

Woolf froze in the entryway of the master bedroom. He was in between roughly fifteen feet from the officers coming in and from a maintenance stairway in the bedroom's far end where Halliday had ducked out in search of the girl. Instinctively, Woolf reached to his sidearm.

Detective Neil saw the movement but was still sizing up the man in the dimly lit corridor.

Woolf's tongue clicked in its usual succession.

"You!"

No way Drake was shooting another cop today, but if there was one thing Drake Woolf knew about the city of Chicago, if by reputation only, he needed to run before he got himself shot.

"Freeze!" the detective yelled before firing.

In anticipation, Drake had jumped from view into the bedroom and leaped around a bed to get to the maintenance staircase opening.

The footfalls and shouts drew closer.

Fuck it. This is how it ends.

"Don't shoot!" someone yelled. "He's FBI."

"The fuck he is," the detective responded back.

As Drake jumped down the stairs, he could hear the detective trailing close behind. "There's no way that guy's FBI. I swear it's the same guy who shot Daniels."

Drake quick-footed each step and thought he heard down below Halliday yelling FBI. *What a shit show.*

* * * *

The two old men sprawled out drunk in the apartment stairwell posed no threat. For that reason, they had no idea what a woman with the FBI would want with them. They were just having a small party, laughing about old times.

"I told you, I don't care. Did you see a girl come down here?"

"Yeah, yeah. She ran out that way." One of the men pointed.

"No, she turned and went the other way," the other protested with a gentle and friendly push.

"Do you know her?"

"I know she one of Oz's candy kids is all."

"What are candy kids?" she asked.

"They go off to all the places around the area and sell candy. Jus' like I said."

"Underprivileged and underaged kids pulling a profit for adults." The bitter reality of the sweets they sold and for whom sunk in.

Drake jumped down the last steps to the main floor. There was a boiler room sign adjacent. Oswald must have also been the super in addition to his other money-making schemes. "CPD's on my ass. Move!"

In the light of a sole bulb above, Halliday hesitated.

Drake assumed she was struggling with the decision to bring him in or not. He wasn't privy to her orders of trying to infiltrate the task force by getting closer to Woolf.

The footfalls grew closer.

Halliday cast her eyes up then back down to Woolf. "Stay close to me." She shouted up the stairs, "FBI, don't shoot."

Chapter 70

Sean Havens was still trying to stay back and out of the fray of EMTs responding, officers taping off the area, and onlookers trying to get a look or share their opinion about the unwanted police presence notwithstanding the belief that cops threw Oz from a window.

CPD worked well with the FBI, but by all indications, this situation didn't have anything to do with current collaborations or information-sharing of the Chicago field office, which raised some questions at first. But within a few minutes of Sean doing everything he could to confuse those asking him questions, he had a number of the top responding brass standing around him laughing.

Halliday and Woolf slinked around the corner, screened by the darkness and high bushes around the decrepit building.

Havens had his bandaged hand and foot raised in the air. "The guy said, 'I knew the husband was that small, I wouldn't have taken a chance jumping out the window with a Doberman in the backyard.'"

The CPD District 10 cops busted out laughing.

"Hope she was worth it?"

"Who?" Havens asked straight-faced.

"The wife," a hefty officer asked, giving Havens a swipe on the arm.

"That's just it. The guy was doing the husband while the wife was at work."

The officers in the semicircle fell silent for just a moment, then erupted, slapping at Havens and each other and wiping tears from their eyes.

"What the hell?" Halliday asked rhetorically.

"I swear to God, he's one of the best intelligence pros I've worked with."

Sean caught their movement. "Hey, guys," he said to the officers, "I think they're waving you up." He pointed them in another direction.

"Where?" an officer asked.

Sean pointed. "Up at the window."

The men all turned around.

"Pretty sure I saw one of your blues giving you a wave to come up."

The men traipsed over the crumbled sidewalk through the courtyard.

"We need to move out?" Sean asked Halliday and Woolf. "Where's Mena? You guys all turned off your comms."

"She's dead, and if you didn't see him before, one of your detective pals is going to be coming around the corner after me."

Halliday tried to steer Drake toward the SUV, but he pulled back.

"Sean"—Tresa gestured with a thumb to Drake—"she was going to kill him."

Drake checked to see if the detective was nearing. "She had orders the whole time to take me out. Do you have the same orders, Havens?"

"No." Sean didn't beat around the bush with any sarcastic remarks. He exhaled. "Let's get out of here while we can. For now, CPD will think she's FBI. That gives us time to get ahold of Sebastian."

"And say what?" Drake grumbled as he fast-stepped around the SUV. "Sorry, boss, but the chick I thought you sent to help us didn't succeed in killing me, but what would you like us to do next?"

"We don't know that Sebastian did that." Sean smiled to other officers and gave a wave as he cautiously stepped in to drive.

"Oh, goddam," Drake said. "Tresa's on the hook for taking her out. We're in the black, but she's in the wind for a shooting with the Bureau. You can't just leave the scene, Tresa."

Sean wasn't taking any chances and started driving away. "Then we'll spin it that Mena was working with the Iranians. Like SA Halliday suggested. She was a mole."

"No," Drake protested again. "She wasn't a mole. She was an operator. She was doing her job. We're not going to defame her. I don't care if she tried to kill me. If there's going to be any spin, it was that she sacrificed herself. She did it for her adopted country."

"You're fucking crazier than I thought. You grew a conscience in the last minute?" Havens accused. "We're all fucked and all *way* outside the law."

Drake said nothing.

"I can't figure you out, Woolf." She blew out her cheeks and continued. "You kill a dozen people in a day and then want to give full honors to a person on your team that tries to kill you."

"She wasn't a traitor," Drake insisted again.

"Whatever."

Drake's tongue started to click.

"And what's with the cli—"

"Enough!" Havens shouted with enough volume to fill the SUV without turning heads outside. "Halliday, shut the fuck up. And Drake, she doesn't know the situation and isn't trying to be belligerent. So, both of you just chill the fuck down before I turn around, stop this car, and slap the shit out of you. I'm dealing with fucking children."

Though in the moment Sean didn't mean to make a joke out of the situation, the levity was welcome and the team settled down.

After a couple minutes of driving in silence, Drake reached over and put his hand on Tresa's leg.

"Knock it off. I'm serious." She laughed, keeping the new mood in the car light as they cooled off.

Drake turned to her with a look of pain.

Havens looked in the rearview mirror and just shook his head as the two behind him exchanged glances.

* * * *

In the glow of the console and spinning emergency lights, Tresa Halliday held her eyes on Drake and saw the man she had seen just weeks before. A kind and vulnerable man with a youthful sadness in his eyes. Which man Drake Woolf really was, she didn't know.

Earl Johnson wanted her to get close, though. Those were her orders. Would she be the next person to receive orders to just take out Woolf, she wondered. And if Mena really was acting on orders, she had just killed an intelligence community officer and as a sworn agent of the FBI. Not only was Halliday supposed to remain at the scene, she was supposed to turn in her weapon as soon as a superior arrived until they cleared her. But this was not her first use of deadly force. It could cost her her career. Then again, before she got this gig, her career *was* over. No, this was Earl Johnson's mess. He could clean it up. She was doing whatever was necessary just like he asked. And the guy sitting next to her was not only beyond the bad choices she usually made in men, he was unquestionably the most unstable and violent human being she had ever laid eyes on, on either side of the law. He scared the living shit out of her, but yet she could feel the intensity of his pain and what must be the deepest and darkest emptiness if he could do the things he did to people.

Halliday reached to put her hand on his. As she stared at him, she remained confused as to how the complex and violent warrior next to her could be shuddering with emotion, his face wet with tears.

She couldn't know that the voices in Drake Woolf's head were screaming to kill her.

Chapter 71

Earl Johnson sat at the dining room table, looking into his study and longing to sit in his espresso chair and finish the last chapters of *Moby Dick* with a glass in his palm of Taylor's Vintage Port 1985. It was Saturday night. Saturday nights, now that the kids were out of the house, meant his wife played bridge. She played bridge, and he was free to go out and see a movie, listen to chamber music in Georgetown, dine on Ethiopian food, and do whatever the hell else he wanted to do because it was *his* Saturday night.

"Dad, are you paying attention?" His son-in-law Darryl had both elbows on the table. His breath smelled like foul beer.

Earl watched Darryl hold in a burp then release it under his breath to the side. The smell still lingered. Corned beef. Earl squeezed his face, reacting to the repugnant smell. Darryl graduated from Yale, but he was pedestrian. He had all the advantages in life that could be afforded to him, and yet he still preferred to indulge in bad swill beer and tubed meats, taking in any and all Nats and Redskins games with the early start of full pregame intoxication. Worse, his wife, Earl's firstborn, Ellie, graduate of Georgetown Law, sat across from her father, wearing a green Notre Dame bucket hat with a button, *Screw You I'm Welsh*.

"Dad," Ellie barked, snapping her fingers in front of Earl. "You're not listening."

"I am listening. You came in wanting to talk. Your mother isn't here, and I don't very much feel like talking. You're both drunk, smell like a two-bit commercial tavern, and are interrupting my quiet evening. It isn't enough I have to still slave to pay off your education while you spend your earnings frivolously, that on the free nights I have you insist on sponging off that, as well."

"It's an opportunity, Earl," Darryl said, getting up from the chair, sliding it across the floor.

Earl leaned over to examine the floor, fully expecting to see a blemish on the hardwood. "You should have waited for your mother."

"We wanted you to hear and be excited for us. We got the call tonight while we were out. Darryl has been waiting for an opportunity like this to really skyrocket his career."

Earl slammed his hand on the table. "He works for one of the most prestigious private equity firms in Washington and is taking a year off to write a finance book from a beach in Australia!"

"When else will he be able to do it?"

"When my grandson is older. That's when."

Earl's phone rang from the study. "If you'll excuse me."

"Dad, please," Darryl huffed. "I'm sure it can wait."

Earl swung his finger into Darryl's chest. "*You* can wait when you want a…a…beef jerky stick in the middle of the night. My job does not afford such luxuries as *waiting*. I am a public servant who neither summers on my yacht nor winters in Belize. And I certainly do not care to wait for my grandson with Asperger's, who I'll add only relates to me, and who is routinely subjected to waiting for his parents to come home from who knows where getting drunk while he cries with that shrewish nanny of his who has no capacity for understanding him or communicating with him."

Earl spun and stormed off into the office and slammed the door.

"Johnson," he answered as he walked to the window blinds and peered out to the street to see if that same car was parked along the curb. While he did so, the Chicago field office's special agent in charge spat a litany of details into his ear. Earl closed the blinds and made a mental note to raise the recent vehicle tail to his counterintelligence staff. "Excuse me. Can you repeat the name again?"

Earl moved to his grandfather's well-worn chair and collapsed. He thumbed through the first edition novel of Robert Louis Stevenson that rested on a small table by his armrest, while the man on the line ranted away. Deputy Director Johnson next scanned the room for the bottle of port he could have sworn he brought into the den. *Curses. I left it by the kitchen cupboard.* "I'm sorry, SAC LaVerne. Theresa Halliday?" He paused. "I'm still not sure who she is. Oh, *Tree-sa* you say. My apologies." He paused again. "Sir, I'm dreadfully sorry, but I know no one by that… Wait. Isn't she the agent who struck her superior and shot a suspect in the back last year?"

Earl crossed the room, opening a lower bookcase cabinet where he had stashed the gift of a fine Macallan 12 Year bottle of scotch. He listened as the special agent in charge briefed him of the situation that was far less troubling than the situation in the kitchen. As he did that, he activated the speakerphone and searched his text messages. Halliday had sent a note stating, "Trouble is coming. But I'm in."

"Excuse me." He opened the box and then the bottle. "Excuse me!" Earl said with raised voice then took a pull straight from the bottle. *God, I may as well be drinking this from a red Solo cup with Darryl.* "It's Saturday evening. Quite late, I might add. If you know me, or anything about me, I direct the Bureau's counterintelligence capacity. From headquarters. Headquarters. Did you hear that?"

Earl only paused for a confirmation of understanding.

"Then, sir, you can understand my confusion as to why you have called me directly regarding a woman in a capacity who you say is NSB. Really?" Earl took another swig, and then another. "The NSB. Since when in my illustrious career at the Bureau did the National Security Branch concern *counterintelligence*, SAC LaVerne?"

Earl swallowed a final long pull during the mumbling of the SAC and then the silence.

"Forgive my impatience, but I am having difficulty understanding how a man has risen to your level of responsibility and attainment of role who lacks a fundamental organizational construct understanding of how a lackluster performer now gone AWOL from a crime scene who evidently works in WMD is my concern, unless of course you are reporting a CI concern, which, my good fellow, has an internal protocol to follow so we don't have agents calling up without a paper trail of allegations on Saturday nights, forcing accusations of field agents when it's *my* night."

Earl eyed the bottle's amber content, which in the last minutes had slipped under the label mark.

"Yes, apology accepted. Please have a good night in Chicago." Earl smiled before hanging up. His free hand tightened into a fist.

Earl's attention shifted to the seven-thousand-dollar first edition novel, and he placed it back between two similarly valued books on the shelf, then slumped into his grandfather's chair with a pouty scowl. His feet hooked around the hand-carved chair legs. "They're not taking Elon to the other side of the world where I can't see him when I want."

He stood and crossed the room to check out the window again for the car that had been following him all week long. Earl thumbed his phone, pressing hard on the numbers, and hit the speaker function. He spoke aloud to himself, "Now what disaster have you created, SA Halliday, that I have to get you out of on *my* Saturday?" As it rang, he heard the garage door open. He expected that it was his wife returning. *Give them hell, Lorraine. They're not taking our grandson away.*

Chapter 72

Earl Johnson's number popped up on Tresa's phone as it buzzed. She held the device with contemplation.

"I'm guessing you're in deep shit," Drake offered. His eyes focused on his own device.

"Yeah. Most definitely." Tresa pocketed the phone. "We're not any closer to finding this bomb or whatever, are we?"

"I've got a name. Two-bags. He runs a gang back in Lawndale. Somehow they're tied into this whole thing."

Sean turned his head for a moment while side-eyeing the road. "Mojo told me a lot of the links were between these Lawndale Legends, Hezbollah, and IRGC. From what I got from Sebastian before leaving, there has been message traffic coming from Tehran that looks like they're trying to stop whatever is going to happen."

"Or cover it up," Drake added.

"There's that possibility for sure."

Tresa remained silent, taking in the conversation, then spoke up for clarity. "So you guys are hunting down terrorists on US soil but getting intel directly from NSA?"

Neither Sean nor Drake said a word.

"This is so fucked up," she said. "And you two are like some dynamic duo, killing anyone who gets in the way or who comes in on your list?"

The two men stared ahead.

Tresa looked out the windows, trying to orient herself. She had been using the building formerly named the Sears Tower as a landmark, but Havens was taking them away from the direction of the Loop, and it sure looked like he was staying clear of the field office area. "Where are you headed?"

Sean looked down at his mobile device screen map. "About two blocks from here."

"Where's here?"

"Next bad guy house," Drake directed, still transfixed on his device.

"We aren't going to get him some rest and talk about all this? He can't go in there and just shoot up another place, and Sean, you sure as hell aren't going to do any good doing stand-up comedy by the car. What are you expecting?"

Havens pulled to the curb, stretching in a number of directions, using all mirrors to ensure they wouldn't have any street guests. He smiled as he turned around. "Listen, Doc."

"Who's Doc?" she asked.

"You. That's your callsign. Doc Halliday. Not perfect but works for me. You good with it, Drake?"

"I'm good." Drake remained in his own world, thumbing his device frantically and fingering red circles on the display.

"Anyway. Our boy here doesn't really care to sleep. He really doesn't like to sit in a small room. His operational tempo over the years could be as many as a half dozen hits in a night. It's what he does. My job is doing the best I can to get him the situational awareness he needs. Your job is to cover his back. As much as I'd like to sit back and analyze what we're dealing with, killing Mena changes how we have to operate. We don't have time to investigate. We've identified at the national intelligence level suspicious activity, and we can't wait. There's a wicked cocktail of crime and war going on in my city, and we're going to take this head-on. And while I hate to think of any innocent casualties, I trust Drake. He shot a cop. One of my few friends who *I* asked to help, and I'm not bitching. It's all we have to work with. Kill as many bad guys as we can and get out of Dodge."

Drake chimed in, still focused on whatever task he was executing with his electronics. "If you take normal people and put them in this situation where their friends get shot or die, innocent lives are caught in the way, enemies get blown to bits, they might feel like you do. They may question what we do." He stopped what he was doing and turned to her. "You're a killer too. We know about you, and I could see it back in there. You just blew the shit out of a chick you were talking to an hour ago. I'd say you're holding up pretty well."

"I—"

Drake held up his hand. "We know you're trying to get close to us. Close to me. But now you have a choice. This is as pure of a counterterrorism mission that there will ever be in your career. Help us and work with us to see this through, or get the fuck out of the car."

"You guys came to me," she spat.

"You can bait a rat or hunt a rat," Sean said. "Keep your enemy close."

Halliday nodded. "I see." She turned to Drake. "I'm in. But this isn't sustainable for you. You're going to get killed. Then what?"

"Doc, let me tell you this about Drake and myself, and then we need to roll. An old bird dog may look like it wants to stay inside and lick its nut sack all day, but once you let him go outside, he starts to sniff and point. You can't take the scent of the hunt from a good dog."

Drake chuckled. "I thought you were going with the Old Yeller one."

Havens engaged the SUV's gears and drove off. He still wasn't sure if Halliday was Old Yeller who could actually save Drake, or if she was the rabid wolf.

Chapter 73

Drake leaned forward from his seat. "Sean, before you stop, just drive up ahead of the building. Slow as we pass by. I've got no signal on my device. None of the guys we've tagged are there. I want to see if I can get any other reading before we go in."

Sean slowed slightly. There were cars on both sides of the narrow residential side street, which seemed like an odd place to put an auto shop, but explained the likely reason why it hadn't blossomed as a business and instead was now a criminal safe house. There were few pedestrians in sight, which was good news. The only way they could really silence sentries would be by killing them, and despite their possible gang involvement, that wasn't enough for a death sentence. He'd have to remind Drake of that as their official position.

"Nada. If it was active, it would be lit up. I've got nothing. Not even security monitoring signal. Just low power Wi-Fi. There could still be someone inside but not with a powered-on device."

"Should we go to any other place then and cross this off the list as a dead end?" Halliday asked, her device vibrating again.

Drake was scanning the area from his window.

Halliday pulled out her device. Earl again.

Havens looked in his rearview mirror. Halliday's face was aglow. He knew she was reading and sending a message. Drake was still looking onward and probably thinking of next moves.

"Kids forget their lunch, Doc? Calling Mom to come to the school?"

She slowly looked up to Sean's eyes in the mirror. "No. Havens, I don't understand half the shit you say. My boss, Earl Johnson, is texting me asking if I can talk and if I've gotten any closer to you guys. I just texted that I'm with you now." Tresa extended her arm to Havens, phone in hand.

"Want to read it?"

"Maybe later. I'm good for now. Thanks."

"I still want to go in and check it out. Let me go alone." The Man from Orange pulled off his raid jacket, checked his weapon, replacing one of the magazines. "Pull up here. Go around the block. There's a back-alley connection. See if there's a bus or anything back there." He turned to Halliday. "It'd be best if you stay here for now in case I need you around back." He patted her leg. "I'll be good. Dome lights."

Havens flipped a couple switches, threw the car in neutral and started swerving the front tires in the darkness of the street to slow the car.

"Okay, fire hydrant and open spot coming," Drake said, his hand on the door.

"I see it. Going left to give you room," Sean confirmed.

"Catch the door so it doesn't make a noise," Drake said to Halliday before jumping out and flinging the door back into her hands before it hit a car.

Halliday watched Drake in the shadows as he never appeared to slow and followed the contours of cars, bushes, walls, and corners.

"He's scary good," Sean admitted, catching Tresa track Woolf's movements.

"He's scary."

"He did years overseas. More tours into hell than guys I've known with almost twice his years." Havens braked only to turn the corner well away from Drake's infiltration point.

"Why does he do it?"

"Didn't have a choice at first. Doesn't know what else to do? Family was pretty much killed in front of him. Brother he looked up to abandoned him. Maybe was involved in the parents' killing. Uncle turned him into a remorseless killer." Sean turned again.

"He has remorse."

"I know. Unfortunately, the guys who often need the most help are the guys we won't get off the ride."

"Were you like him?"

"Not that bad. He has his issues, but just as many came from what he's been subjected to. I have my own stories, I suppose. Lost my family. Wife's gone. Daughter keeps her distance. Lars, the big guy, was my brother-in-law. He was a cop here. Good guy. Loyal to a fault to me and my family."

"I'm sorry."

"Yeah. He tracked you down with the help of our mission support guy." Havens paused to make sure he had her attention before dropping the bomb. "Mafia daughter, huh?"

Tresa breathed out hard from her nostrils. Havens watched from the mirror as she shook her head.

"Guess you don't miss Cicero, but yet, you're still working with the agent who put away your father and then pulled security off your brother. Got him killed in prison. That really sucks."

"How did you—" Tresa stopped. "Never mind."

"Our boss gave us that information. Seems your Earl Grey guy had been using you as a wild card so he could show he was hunting us, but really didn't think you would do it. I'll admit. You did a nice job. We could use you on the team. Although, if you have feelings for him, that could be complicated." Havens braked. "This should be right about the place."

A rear metal door opened to the alley, letting light spill out. The silhouette of Woolf came toward the car. Both Havens and Halliday could see past Drake to the two bodies on the floor before the door slammed shut behind him.

Chapter 74

"I know how they're going to do it," Drake said as he flopped back into the car seat. "I think it's time we let the FBI do what the FBI does best. Call this place in, Tresa. Maybe you can still look like a hero."

"What's going on in there? Do we need to stick around or go to the next?" Havens asked.

"Drive, but she needs to call so they have time to get bomb squads to the parade route by tomorrow. I mean, it looks like the typical jihadi skunkworks bomb shop in there. Ammonium nitrate, gas cans, aluminum boxes. There were wire clippings. Obviously, no one thought we were going to pop this place tonight."

"Are you forgetting anything?" Halliday asked.

"Is it our anniversary?"

"Hey! The zombie made a joke." Havens cheered. "But seriously, who's dead in there?"

"Dunno. Street hoods. Nothing on their bodies. They were laying right there next to each other. Blood smear across the floor to where they lay. If I had to guess, I'd say someone's going to come in and clean up. They weren't killed the quick and easy way. Someone was pissed at them. Fuel stains on the ground haven't fully evaporated, so we may just be an hour or two behind. But no clue where they took the explosives or how."

Halliday called Earl Johnson back but was unsuccessful. She would have no idea that he was passed out in his sitting chair after the family decided it would be best to let him sleep it off. "Jay," she muttered as if an afterthought. She pulled his business card from her rear pocket. "Maybe now he'll believe I'm WMD."

"Oh, does anyone know what that radioactive material was?" Drake asked. "There's some shit on the floor that looks suspiciously like yellow cake."

"Like *cake* cake?" Tresa asked.

Havens chimed in. "Uranium ore concentrate powder. It's what the stuff looks like after it's mined and refined but before enrichment or fuel fabricated."

"Is it really radioactive?" she asked again.

"You're not much of a WMD expert, are you? Better get that fixed before you use that cover again," Sean mocked in fun. "But no, it's radiologically harmless."

"That's a relief," said Drake, "I put it on my finger to smell and taste."

Both Sean and Halliday whipped their heads to Drake.

"What? I didn't know what it was. I figured it was naturally harmless raw uranium. Just pulped ore. We trained on it in…well, places. Although, this I'd say tasted and smelled different."

Tresa had tuned out at this point and was calling Jay's mobile phone. "Jay, Tresa Halliday. Hey, you guys have a real problem on your hands before tomorrow's parade."

Chapter 75

"Hi, Jay. This is Special Agent Halliday. Sorry to bother you." Tresa put her phone on speaker as Havens pulled to the Taylor Street curb with the UIC hospital in sight. It was a safe area with enough police presence that would keep them safe without being scrutinized.

"Uh, hey. This really isn't a good time." There was festive background noise around Jay. It was evident from the party sounds that Jay was at some St. Paddy's Day shindig. "Is this something that can wait?"

"It can't. Can you give me five minutes to explain? There's a major situation at hand."

"Hang on. Let me get to a better place where I can hear."

The team was all turned, staring at Halliday's palmed phone, lifted up to the middle of the SUV like a mini-conference table. In the background Jay must have been explaining to a wife or significant other that he had to step out and wouldn't be long. There wasn't much explanation, which signified someone knew the drill but was not too pleased.

"Okay, sorry," he said. "I've got some major questions for you, but frankly I had to escalate to my boss. I'm guessing one of your guys took our SWAT members' weapons, and from the texts I've been getting all night, you're involved with that mess in Lawndale. You need to come in and deal with it. I'm not getting involved, and I don't want this spilling over to me. I was just helping you out, but you took advantage of that. I'm done with you."

"Jay, I am, and sorry to have gotten you involved in this. You've been so helpful, which is why I'm coming to you now. Showing you my hand."

"I'm not leaving this party to bail anyone out. I can't vouch for people that aren't really military liaisons. I checked with *our* JSOC liaison."

"Look, we believe there's going to be an attack at the parade tomorrow. One of my team members got intel in Lawndale about another site that we raided and found homemade explosive ingredients. We think it's tied to the radioactive material stolen from the university."

"Holy shit." He rocked back and forth as he processed what he was hearing. "You think they're going to do that at the parade?"

"It seems that everything is coming to a head. Tomorrow is the most likely mass public event. It would cause a ton of casualties."

"Casualties are right. It's a drunkfest. Anything could cause a lot of confusion, and the law enforcement working it have been doing double shifts because of all the bar parties and the parade on the south side. Shit. This is bad."

"Can you get a warning out?"

"Yeah, I'll call the teams and the boss. We did a joint special event threat assessment for this with the Crime Prevention Center here in the city and Homeland. Terrorism concerns are usually the top key finding, and I think they mentioned the potential for a dirty bomb or a truck ramming in the threat indicators already. So, we'll already have police presence, SWAT teams, snipers all facing the parade. They use McCormick Place parking lot as emergency response staging and family assistance center," he clarified, "the big event building near the lake right next to Soldier Field. Parade can have over forty thousand people crammed into that little area."

"I know the place. Right."

Drake asked aloud, "Can they just cancel the parade?"

"I'm guessing that's one of your guys?"

"Yeah," she responded.

"Did *he* take our guys' weapons?"

Drake shook his head.

"No, he said he didn't, but Jay, back to canceling. This could be huge."

"Yeah, I mean, they probably won't cancel without more intel. You know how people react when it's just intelligence but nothing going boom beforehand. No one wants to take responsibility to cancel something and then have nothing happen. Do you have more evidence that it's going to be the target for sure or where they'll put the bomb?"

Havens spoke up. "We believe they may be using busses with kids somehow."

"Shit." Jay paused. "Still, they have all these barricades like city trash trucks at the intersections, they close off feeder streets, there's a ton of cops, and no bus is getting within a good few blocks of the place. It'd be pretty tough crashing through or getting anywhere near the event. I'll still raise it up to the JTTF," he said, referring to the local FBI Joint Terrorism Task Force. "They can ping the NCTC, too."

The National Counterterrorism Center, or NCTC, had a local Office of the Director of National Intelligence representative assigned to help coordinate and collaborate items of an intelligence matter that were shared across the community to avoid analysis gaps.

Halliday searched the two operators' facial expressions for any further sense of guidance. Both men shrugged. "Okay, Jay, I'll send you the location of the auto shop where we found the materials. There's a couple dead bodies that were there *before* we arrived."

No one could see Jay, but the silence was indicative of his displeasure of their activities. His cursing before responding further cemented the notion. "Look, we do a pretty good job of keeping things safe in Chicago. And we don't do shit like you guys are doing without being coordinated and collaborating with Chicago blue. Don't go fucking up things here in the city for us. It's taken us a long time to get here. We're a pretty well-oiled machine when it comes to incident response, *joint* raids, and running down special event threats. I'm not cool with this, so, maybe just go on back to DC. This is our field office, and you're really making a mess of things. I've heard about you, and what I heard before I didn't believe when I met you. Now I firmly believe the stories. Go home, Halliday, and make sure you return the weapons you all stole. You violated our trust. You're violating the *law.* Don't call me again, please."

Halliday disconnected the phone. "I'm pretty sure you guys don't plan to go home any time soon, correct?"

"Correct," Havens answered. "Whizzo, you about ready to get high score on a game or what?"

Drake looked up from the distraction of his device again. He closed out of his hacking tools and the device he had been monitoring and downloading content from. "We probably can't do much until daylight. Why don't you guys go get some rest? I need to go somewhere."

"Where could you possibly need to go at this time of night?" Halliday asked.

"Hear that? This is how it's going to be in the future with her, Woolf. Remember she said it here first when we were hunting terrorists. What happens when you want to go out and get a beer with me and the baby's crying?" Havens tossed a Powerbar into Woolf's lap and one at Halliday. "She's locking you down."

Halliday wasn't amused. "Don't be stupid."

"True, Drake would probably say that when *you* wanted to go get a beer with me."

"Damned straight," she muttered, "but I can handle solo just fine."

"I need you to drop me off up north, Sean. Looks like up Lake Shore Drive to Diversey Parkway on Pine Grove, it says."

"Do I want to ask?" inquired Havens, knowing Drake was fixated on something and he probably didn't want the team involved for their own good.

"I just need a ride. I can get back to wherever you are. Best I go it alone. I need to make two stops. Second is close to the first."

"Tell you what," Havens said, ready to make a deal, "we drop you off but stick around out of sight. There's a side road in the park just a block east. We can get some shut-eye but be there if you need to call in backup. You guys already have counts for murder, and I'm an accessory, so let's finish this together." The gallows humor was heavy. "We're the good guys, right?"

Drake nodded and turned to Halliday, who was still staring at him with a look of concern.

"Okay. Lincoln Park we go," Sean said. "Eat that bar and grab a water out of the back if you can reach it. And Drake."

"Yeah."

"When was the last time you had your...antibiotics?"

Drake looked down at his feet to avoid anyone's gaze. He knew Halliday wouldn't buy that Sean Havens carried Drake's wound-related meds.

"Yesterday."

"Yesterday, when?"

"Morning."

Havens didn't respond, but Drake could hear a rattle as his mentor drove and fumbled for something in a small bag on the passenger seat. He handed a bottle back to Woolf. "You don't want that infection to come back."

Tresa turned to her left, appearing to look out the window. Drake knew she wasn't an idiot.

"Hey." He nudged her. "You don't happen to have a Taser on you?"

Chapter 76

The Modarris struggled through the length of the bus aisle, carrying the large weighted duffel bag on his shoulder. He wiped his brow after dismounting the stairs and setting the load down on the gravel surface. Dexter scanned the dark gated lot in the pitch of the late night. There were a number of hoods loitering close by but out of his way as he had requested. Whether they were stoned out of their minds, securing the premises, or keeping an eye on their Islamic business advisor, he did not know.

One of the gang members made a call by the gate once Dexter had appeared. After raising the phone to his ear for a moment, he repocketed the device and signaled another young man, who approached Dex.

"Two-bags be here in twenty minute."

"I need to piss. Can I go back in the lot?"

"Thought you was some A-rab. You don't talk like no A-rab." The kid made a mimicking sound that was a cross between an Asian Indian, African, and Mexican sound but with added English words about blowing himself up. Dex got the point.

"That sounds just about perfect, but do you know the religion of Islam is much more than what you reference?"

"Man, don't you start preachin' to me. I ain't blowin' my shit up on no airplane. Fuck that. You go piss back there and shut the fuck up. Ain't nothin' but old shit that don't work back there an' old broke bricks an' rusty old shit. Prolly been here a hundred years. Just junk wall so five-oh can't see what's in here. Private property. You preach your shit to the skunks and rats that live back there, A-rab."

Dexter headed to the far back, then turned and took a few steps among dark gray heaps in the blackness. He wiped away old spider webs that hung under the tapestry of rusted metal sheets above. And he was careful not to make too much noise when his feet hit old paint cans.

When he returned, he kept to himself while sitting on the large duffel and thumbing his own device, powering it on and dialing.

Once on a secure messaging mobile application with an encrypted and fully obfuscated network pipe, he spoke softly. "It is finished. Everything is enabled. Everything as planned. Our associates are incompetent, so I shall do my best to ensure success while remaining out of sight until after the first event."

Before Dexter powered off and put the device away, he noticed the low battery level and warmth of the device. It had been at nearly seventy-five percent charge when he last powered it down. "Hello, Brother."

General Soleimani, himself, picked up the message alert over six thousand miles away in Tehran. He, however, had no idea that his contact's device had been powned by the Man from Orange's hacking exploits. Drake locked on that, as well.

Chapter 77

"No, I don't have a Taser. Why can't you tell us exactly where you're going? That's ridiculous. You're either going after the bad guys, or you are on some hired assassination that's not involved, which means I can't allow you to do that."

"I'm glad you have your limits, Halliday." Drake mocked the absurdity of her remarks. "The congressional committee that investigates and interviews us will want to know that. If you must know, one of the locations I need to go to shows my target on the first floor of a walk-up. The second is on a high rise. I can't tell if he's within about five floors. That means I need to get answers from either the first guy, which is unlikely, or a doorman."

"I think Halliday is right, Drake. Out with it. We're going after targets. No secrets."

Drake didn't resist any further. "The two Venezuelans that trailed Mena in their SUV."

"Forget it," Halliday rebuked. "They're diplomats."

"They're covered for status and action by the Venezuelan embassy. Venezuelans are selling passports and visas out of their embassies, but many of the Lebanese diaspora with Hezbollah ties got them through the former Venezuelan vice president, Tarik El Aissami. If they're new, they probably came from their foreign minister. Chick named Rodriguez."

"You're not killing someone for bogus passports. They aren't directly tied to the bomb threat."

"I'm going to kill them because they killed a guy who gave me a ride. I got him killed by getting him involved. It was on the news when we got to the field office. It's all part of this triad of partnerships. They may have intel, and at the very least, they're murderers. That's my charter, Halliday. It was sanctioned by the President of the United States, whether he disavows it or not. That's why this unit exists. Shit's happening on our turf, and the law prevents us from stopping it."

"You're saying that if you have proof of a national security threat, you can act on it."

"Yes," Drake confirmed.

"Including drug dealers, murderers, even mafia?"

"All are within the mandate if they pose a clear and present threat to other Americans or our country's infrastructure."

Havens slapped his head at Halliday's mention of mafia. "I know what you're doing Halliday. No way."

"I can get you past the bellman, Drake," she suggested.

"No way." Woolf folded his arms like a stubborn child.

"Like you said, I'm already knee-deep. My career is dead. This is the purest mission I could ever be involved with. Not to mention, I want in because I want your help."

Havens turned. "Drake Woolf, meet Francesca Delaurentis. Well played, Tresa, but you're not getting our task force's cover for family vengeance."

"What are you talking about? Who's Francesca Delaurentis?" Drake turned to Halliday. "Wait. What's going on here?"

"I'd say our little Girl Scout Halliday is looking to get her hands dirty in the near future and is going with you now."

"What's with everyone throwing chicks at me when I just need to do what I do on my own."

"The hell?" Halliday responded, annoyed.

Woolf refocused on his smartphone. "Forget it, Halliday." Drake turned his device outward to Havens and Halliday. He showed three red dots heading south of the city in their general direction. "One vehicle. Two hit-man ambassadors. Thanks for your offer, but they're coming to us."

Chapter 78

Two-bags's car pulled up to the gate. His sentries opened the door and gave a wave to the closed windows. The vehicle rolled up to the Modarris and the three parked busses.

Dexter stood but didn't move from his place when he heard the power windows lower.

After waiting and seeing the white Arab dude wasn't moving, Two-bags exited the car annoyed. "Man, you best show me some respect. You all done fixin' your shit together?"

"I am."

"I tell you, you best not be blowin' up any kids and my homies I'm givin' you to drive."

"If everyone does as they're told, you will be that much closer to controlling this city. I want the children here by nine in the morning to paint the busses with decorations. Have the kids and your men ready to leave for the parade area by eleven in the morning. Have them take three different routes, but have them stop at Michigan Avenue across from the Art Institute. All the children should be dressed in the costumes and ready to go to work. I will be with them. When the commotion starts, I want you to have them come up Roosevelt to Balboa and offer the busses as emergency vehicles to transport people to the crisis area at Soldier Field. I can instruct your men, but I need you to make sure they fully understand so there is no confusion. Timing is everything. I need to ensure you have good drivers with current driver's licenses and clean records in case you are stopped."

"All good on my side," Two-bags assured. "I want my stuff now though." He pointed to the duffel lit by the headlamps.

"Yours is on its way. Your usual partners will be delivering ten kilos of street-ready heroin, as promised."

"Brick or G-packs?"

"You asked for G-packs, you will receive G-packs. We'll deliver them to you, and I will come back tomorrow."

"Nah, man. You workin' tonight. You show my boys tonight how to make your bombs. I ain't taking no chances that you ain't blowin' your shit up before you get back."

"Your men will need to be well rested and in a good mind when working with explosives. I've already made the blends in the container they took in the van from this yard."

"These motherfuckers don't sleep. They my dogs. I need you to show them what they need to do next."

"I sleep. And I need rest so I'm ready. What they need to do is stay away from that mixture until I say so, or you blow your theater sky high."

"Then you sleepin' on the bus. You ain't going nowhere 'til I get my bombs. And your boys ain't coming here. They go where I tell them it's safe to hand off. We goin' to the railroad that we sometimes use. You stayin' here. Tell them to drive inside the gray open garage on 1500 South Blue Island and Throop. They seen it before. They got fifteen minutes to pull in, unload, and get the fuck out."

Chapter 79

Drake kept his eyes on the signals reporting on his map. "Sean, take us south on a street called Cermak."

"I know exactly where that is," the Chicago native confirmed as he accelerated back onto the desolate street. "What makes you think they're headed that way?"

"Trust me."

"Why do I think there's something you're not telling us?"

Drake's tongue began to click. He checked his weapons and rebalanced his magazines.

* * * *

General Soleimani was escorted in to meet with the supreme leader.

Soleimani crossed the room where the supreme leader sat on an immaculate but small white love chair. As the spy master neared, he was instructed by an offering hand to take a seat next to Iran's chief holy man.

"Tea?"

"Thank you." Soleimani strolled back to the opposite side of the room, rolling his eyes for a cup of hot tea. "May I offer you another cup?"

"Please, General, if you wouldn't mind."

The general didn't mind and wasn't surprised, as this was a pattern going back for years.

Carrying both cups back, Soleimani awaited the supreme leader's next move where he moved to the side and then offered his intellectual hit man a seat on the demure sofa.

"Come. Sit. I'm anxious to hear the news."

"I believe you will be pleased. We have done everything we can to assure the Americans that we were not involved with the radiological threat. Similarly, we have cleaned all trails leading back to any *perceived* links of involvement, covered by the blood of our own martyrs."

"But did they succeed in their task?"

"Of sorts. We had a contingency, which worked in our favor. One I had suspected, which also signified to the Americans our commitment to eliminate the threat that was attributed to the regime."

The supreme leader sipped his tea.

"The Hezbollah agent responsible for the theft has been eliminated, our Venezuelan Party counterparts recognize their responsibility in failing to secure the materials as planned initially. We have engaged an American criminal group in Chicago who will be leading the initiative. All responsibility will fall to them. We can then focus on our Mexico connections and let South America's politics be a focus for our investments. My colleagues will then have time to reposition our businesses in the region and vacate Venezuela without losses."

"The aim of terrorism is to sow disorder. Violence for politics to achieve policy goals. The Americans will know this is our resistance to their policy views and actions to the Islamic Republic." The supreme leader gave Soleimani an approving pat on the leg. "And yet, they will be impotent to retaliate, constrained by other foreign powers. You have served your country well. But the strike remains as planned."

"Indeed, but the pieces have been put in place where the world would see a strike or further sanctions against us as unjust."

"And you have something else planned?"

"I do, but that will be their own Americans. It will occur in the weeks to come."

Chapter 80

Drake leaned up to the front seat.

"Still hanging in there?" Sean asked.

"Yeah. Usual, but I'm managing. This thing have emergency lights?"

"I nicked it from DHS when I landed up at the Great Lakes Naval Station. I assume blue and whites." Havens maintained the steering wheel with his club-wrapped hand and reached across his body to the switch.

"Not now. I just want to make sure we have some."

Halliday leaned forward to hear the conversation.

"Mojo gave me an app that allowed me to hack their devices and read communications they were receiving."

"What app?" Halliday challenged. Clearly, as a decent surveillance technician, she thought he was full of shit.

"NSA proprietary," he lied. "They're heading to a train yard storage unit. Dropping some drugs then bugging out. Both guys live in the area they just came from, so I assume they'll head back by the quickest route. We need to position ourselves so we can head them off."

"Won't they just ram us or start shooting? We won't win any firefight if they have automatic weapons."

"They shouldn't. I assume they'll have handguns only. That way they can get them in via diplomatic pouches and claim to be security. They'll know they have diplomatic immunity, so if we approach the car from both sides, I can see what they know."

Halliday was suspicious. "You really think they'll tell you what you want to hear?"

"I'll get everything I need in a matter of minutes."

* * * *

Fadi and Nour bobbed their heads to Chance the Rapper's "I Might Need Security" as they rolled south on Lake Shore Drive in the Venezuelan embassy's SUV complete with consular license plate and the "LC" country designation.

Nour changed the music selection to Teyana Taylor.

"No." Fadi reached over to the AUX tuner on the dash. "We need gangbanger music," he suggested in Lebanese Arabic. "Pull my playlist. DMX or Ice Cube."

Nour scrolled through the old-school hard-core rap artists. "Ludacris?"

"Brother, we are doing drug drop."

"Eminem."

"Yes. Eminem."

As the two drove, they hand-gestured the rap beat, slinging lyrics to the windshield along the way to the turn-off.

Nour switched back to the map, navigating his partner to the destination.

The two men were assigned to the embassy's security office, but their normal duty involved facilitating the thousands of tons of cocaine coming from Venezuela through covered and concealed Hezbollah-affiliated operatives. While the security duo's bosses and supervisors way up the food chain maintained the relationships with Mexican and Colombian cartels, Nour and Fadi were the bag men of facilitated drug deals with locals at the gang and criminal cartel levels. Similarly, for discerning clients in the Chicagoland area, they could provide any number of visas, passports, birth certificates, etcetera, to citizens of the Middle East who were granted temporary travel through the states. And if a hit was required that could be protected by diplomatic provisions if discovered, assassinations also fell into their job description.

The two continued their hip-hop car karaoke, passing the Shedd Aquarium, going over the Dan Ryan Expressway, and turning under a tunnel to the rail yard.

Fadi pointed to the gray abandoned trailer-loading alcove just ahead.

Nour held out his flattened hand, laughing. "I always get a tremble. Oh, wait, no I don't, because I'm a gangster."

Fadi jumped in, and the two sang in chorus, "These triggas we's killas; Sittin' on the porch in between legs; Wit a bitch French braiding my head; Leave 'em—"

"What's a French braid?" Nour asked.

"Those little rolls." He demonstrated on his head while opening the car door.

"Wit a bitch French braiding my head," Nour repeated again, drawing the next lyrics down to a whisper as he continued on to the back hatch.

Each man gave a casual look around, and Nour lifted the trunk mat and pulled a large diplomatic duffel from a locked and concealed compartment in the SUV.

Fadi could see a car idling about fifty meters away. He gave a wave and checked the rear of the open garage. An empty diplomatic pouch was folded, waiting for its return to the bag handlers. Nour set the new bag down, gave a wave, and both men headed back to the truck.

Fadi started the chorus, "The killa, the gangsta—"

"No, the gangsta, the killa, and the dope dealer."

"That's right." And the two sang the refrain repeating four times as they cut a turn and drove down the railroad access road where they rattled over the gravel path until making the next sharp turn onto the road.

From behind a towering stack of China-bound rail boxes, a large SUV pulled out, blocking Fadi and Nour from further forward movement, their back now angled in such a way preventing a reverse. Still, they had no drugs or monies, and their weapons were sanctioned while they drove the diplomatic vehicle.

The SUV's blue-and-white lights turned on, illuminating the narrow industrial corridor. Nour reached back for his weapon.

Fadi reached across his colleague's chest. "There's no need. No gangster today." He laughed. "Passports and Spanish only."

Nour nodded. "No habla, mister policeman." Both Lebanese-born thugs chuckled as two officers approached each side.

"FBI?" Fadi asked Nour, their windows still up.

From the front of the car, Drake instructed Halliday, "I want you to stop at the passenger wheel."

"Better protocol is behind the passenger at the side. I know what I'm doing."

"Please don't go past the wheel."

The FBI agent approached the driver's-side window and tapped on the glass.

Fadi pushed the window button down, lowering the glass halfway.

"Good evening," the agent said. "Sorry to trouble you. We are assisting the Chicago Police with some railroad thefts."

Fadi smiled. In broken English with a Spanish accent, he replied, "We were just leaving the area and got lost. I made a wrong turn. What a maze."

Nour watched as a female officer stood diagonal from his position, the car frame blocking most of her from his view. Nour put his hands on his lap, relaxed that all would be okay.

"Yeah," the FBI agent said. "We got all twisted up too. Hey, you have diplomatic plates. What embassy? I'm guessing from the accent maybe El Salvador?"

"Venezuela."

"Ah." The agent snapped his fingers. "Shucks. Are you sure?" He smiled, then made a slicing gesture to someone in the FBI's SUV. The light-flashing stopped. "Sorry. Don't need all that fanfare. Can I see your passport, then I'll let you guys be on your way. Hope you're enjoying this great city."

What an idiot, Nour thought. There was a reason he and Fadi could get away with everything in this country.

Fadi reached into his leather jacket's front pocket. His fingers felt the outline of his shoulder holster, and he grabbed the passport. He lowered the window all the way, extending his passport.

Before Nour could react, the agent jerked Fadi's arm, lifted a weapon and fired twice. Wetness sprayed on Nour's face with the sound of the pops. Nour heard a clicking sound and then saw another flash.

* * * *

Drake Woolf fired two shots point-blank into the embassy man's head, jerked the arm again and put two more into the passenger's brain.

"What the fuck!" Halliday yelled.

As she stood, hands on her head, Drake opened the driver's door, searching the man top to bottom. Woolf pocketed the weapon and spare magazine, left the passport, and retrieved the man's phone. He paused and pulled the weapon back out. "This is the same Russian-made handgun the Iranians had up on Devon."

While Halliday tried to frame his comment, Drake was around the car and doing the same with the passenger.

"You said you were going to ask them questions."

"I said I needed answers." Drake raised the other man's weapon. "Same. Russian. Russia sells them to Iran, Iran sells them to Venezuela or gives them to Hezbollah."

"You're not getting answers from them now."

Drake held up the mobile device. "I trust phones over people. Technology doesn't lie. The guns gave me answers, too."

"You killed diplomats."

"They killed my driver."

"You used a federal agent's weapon."

"Drug whore's gun." Drake passed Halliday and headed to their own vehicle, patting her on the shoulder. He pulled the weapon from his back waistband and threw it high onto the freight containers. "It was a freebie. Get in."

"Your fingerprints."

Drake cocked his head.

"Right. No fingerprints on record for you."

Chapter 81

Adrenaline coursed through Halliday's veins. It wasn't as much that she was bothered by the killing of two Hezbollah-affiliated drug traffickers sheep-dipped in Venezuelan diplomacy, nor did she have a dopamine rush from fight or flight instincts kicking in. No, it was the fact that she watched Drake Woolf carry on an innocuous conversation, even to the point of being glib with the two men, then in an instant killing them both like they were flies on a window. That. That is what she found to be most bothersome. Now in the vehicle, it was like the event was as routine as a morning conference call.

Havens had seen the whole thing. Instead of saying anything, he reached his arm back in a fist, which Drake bumped in silence.

"Don't either of you have anything to say about what just happened?" she asked.

"No," Drake responded. "But my phone and portable chargers are about dead. I also need to close my eyes."

"And you." She reached and swatted Havens in the arm. "You knew what was going to happen the whole time?"

Havens kept his eyes on the deserted Chicago streets. "I had a pretty good feeling he wasn't going to interview them. But so did you."

Tresa flopped back against her seat. "You're murderers."

"No, Special Agent Halliday," Havens responded, his volume rising. "We're the tip of the spear. You're FBI. You build a case, if you can, and put people in federal prisons. *We* are sent into the world's shitholes for years on end trying to make sure no one crosses the water to fuck with our country. Turns out, we've got an infestation of people on US soil who are looking to exploit our good nature or who are waiting to take their shots at us. If you have any perverse notion in your head that those two guys would ever get arrested here or anything besides a light PNG status and a first-class plane ticket home, you're as dumb as anyone else who isn't in the game. Get it in your head. That's just how it is."

"That's true," replied Drake.

Tresa looked over at Drake's hands, which were manipulating both devices with his own mobile phone on his lap. She saw the device displays both illuminate, asking for a new password reset. He typed the letters T-A-N-G-O on each one, then opened the settings, where he enabled Do Not Disturb and disabled all location settings.

He looked over at Halliday, noticing her watching his activity. "They should have been more careful. They got sloppy." Drake enabled Touch ID with his passcode. He then worked his own phone again, periodically checking the diplomat's phones. The words "Backing up to cloud" appeared on each of the men's devices.

"Where are you dumping their phone information?" she asked, now much more subdued.

"To our analyst. He'll be able to sort it better than I can now. Once he feeds it into the system, it should also correlate other metadata."

"You don't want to see if they may have communications about the bomb threat?"

"They won't."

"How can you be so sure?"

"I know the layers of the organization. Everyone plays a role but sticks to their part. These guys will be replaced in two days. They're commodities. Expendable commodities."

"So why even kill them?"

"You ever get stung by a bee?"

"Sure."

"It dies once it stings you. But we humans still want to punish the little shit and smack it or stomp it when its abdomen is already ruptured." Drake leaned back into the corner and closed his eyes. "It's just payback. One hundred percent personal."

Chapter 82

Thanks to Tresa's Government Purchase Card, or PCard, the crew of herself, Havens, and Woolf secured adjoining suites at the city's Hotel Essex, which overlooked the park area of the parade.

Drake dumped his pockets' contents on a small end table. Weapons, magazines, cash, mobile devices, chargers, cables, his Molar Mic, and more formed a pile as if just a kid emptying a junk drawer. He plugged in devices to devices and chargers to chargers and power sources. "I'm setting an alarm for two hours unless you have a case of Rip Its," he said to Sean as Tresa opened the adjoining door then walked away to use a bathroom. "Meds are fine, but I have no idea what I may say or do at night. Sebastian woke me last. That was a couple days ago now. I didn't sleep the night that Mena stayed at the head shed."

"Go lay down. I'll shut the door and go into her room."

Drake nodded and flopped down on the bed face first.

"She's not stupid, Drake. And regardless of anything between you and her, after this op, we're slowing you down to zero until we all get right."

Woolf didn't respond, so Havens just closed the door and let the man sleep.

When Halliday came out of the washroom, she was surprised to find Havens just looking out the window. He turned to her. "It's hard to believe that something really bad could happen to innocent people tomorrow and there isn't a damned thing we can do about it besides wait."

"You're just crying because there's no one left for you both to kill tonight." Halliday took a pass on the view and inspected the coffee pot and Folgers packets. "It's not like you guys have to save the world. If something's happening, it isn't like the rest of law enforcement, Homeland, the Bureau, and the IC have just stopped working. I've gotta think there's a good reason why we haven't had terror attacks since 9/11 until the past month. Other people are on it, too."

"I know," Sean conceded.

"But does he know that?" She tilted her head to the other room.

"He's always been put out to be the lead dog. I should've put a stop to it, but truth is, we need a guy like that. He just goes until he drops."

"He's not well."

"Trust me. I know."

"Do you know he deeded his house to me and gave me a check for over one hundred thousand dollars? All after I had a cup of coffee with him on his porch then hunted him down?"

Sean smiled. "He'll never hold it against anyone for coming after him. He sees it as their duty. Like a warrior code. That's why he was more fazed by the loss of Mena than the fact that she tried to kill him. Truth is, you're probably the first person he's had around him who did something normal."

"But to just throw away so much money and a house? That's not thinking straight."

Havens moved away from the window and drew closer to Halliday. He lowered his voice. "I drugged him, dragged him back to his living hell, and he also was going to give me the bulk of his assets. Do you really know why?"

She shrugged. "Because he's whacked."

"Yes, but also because he was going to kill himself that night."

"He told you that?"

"Yeah. When he came to my door asking for my daughter's full name and address. He needed it for legal reasons. He's never met her but was giving her his money, too. And Lars. The only thing stopping him was he didn't have that info. Once he got it, he literally turned around, apologized for bothering me and was going to go off and die."

"You stopped him?"

"No. I've been there myself. I grabbed him and I hugged him. I let him cry. I let him know that he had been failed but that we wouldn't fail together, because we were going to keep trying together. He doesn't really want to be dead, he just wants to stop the way he's feeling and what he's doing but doesn't know how to because nothing ever changes."

Halliday's eyes welled. She turned again to the wall of the adjoining room.

"Hey, we're all having a harder time dealing with all this than what shows on the outside. He's not alone. You're not alone. I know you're trying to do your job, Agent Halliday. But like you and like me, we need to find something to believe in."

"What does he believe in? I haven't seen it."

"Right now, he believes in me. I think he believes in you. That's enough to get us all through tomorrow and hopefully help some good innocent people along the way."

"Curse of the sheepdog, huh?"

Sean paused at the remark, his face resisting the term. "In case you haven't noticed, Special Agent Halliday, we're wolves."

Havens pulled out his device and thumbed his screen to his message app, where he texted his only daughter. "Love you, Mags. Thinking of you."

"Woolf?"

"No. My kid. Because as much as I may get caught up in the job, I have to remember my priorities. It's cost me everything." He put the phone away like nothing had happened. "Coffee?"

Chapter 83

Drake awoke in the darkness of the room and fumbled toward the bathroom with only small cracks of light coming from the window curtains to guide his way. He shut the door, found the switch, and after a moment of squinting, he stared at himself in the mirror. The sleep had been without episode. He felt empty but refreshed. He carried a perpetual fatigue, so anything north of that was a plus. His face was pocked with blood. His hands stained again. Yesterday had been hell; today, likely the same.

Drake couldn't shake the thought of Mena. She had a warrior's heart that she hid. He would hold her memory in honor and would do everything he could to make sure that she wasn't exploited in a coverup. Even if it meant exposing himself.

At that moment, Drake identified that lost feeling of his, which was honor. Though his life had been hell and his skills forged by the blood of others, he was what he was. If he went away, someone would just take his place. On the battlefield, he initially worked for his teammates. As they fell away, he fought for pure survival. When he cared no more for his own life, he was only living by instinct, reflexes, and habit.

"Hey, are you taking a shit in there?" Havens asked, jolting Drake from his thoughts. "Halliday and I have some thoughts on how we can still try to pitch in."

Drake heard the sounds but shifted his thoughts to his brother, Dexter.

Chapter 84

For a neighborhood that had been marginalized with the stigma of people not wanting to work, perception was not reality. Oz's Lawndale candy children had arrived bright and early. They were given paintbrushes, paint, and their St. Patrick's Day parade costumes.

"You look funny in your orange beard," said a young girl named Tamiki.

"*You* look funny in your orange beard. *And* your hat," replied Zarielle.

"Zari, where's Mr. Oz?"

"He dead. He got thrown out the window by the po-lice." Zari lifted her sleeve to rub the rope burn. "He *all* dead."

"We still going to the parade?"

"Yeah, we going to the parade."

Dexter Woolf longed to see his own children. They were in a better place now, so he let the past leave his mind. The present was going to set the course for a new future, and of that he was certain. "More shamrocks, kids." He smiled. "And rainbows."

"With a pot of gold."

"That's right. Lots of gold. And you all get to throw golden powder in the sky." Dexter, the Modarris, pulled from his pants pocket stacks of one-hundred-dollar bills. "If you do a good job, I'll give you each two hundred dollars."

The expressions on their orange-bearded faces were priceless.

"More rainbows. Who can give me more rainbows?" he called out as he strolled to a crew of four new middle-aged men standing by the toughs. "Gentlemen. Are you my drivers?"

As if he was asking for their qualifications, each man took a small step forward.

"I drive for our church."

The next informed Dexter that he also drove a church bus and a school bus.

"I drove CTA for twenty years," said the tallest of the men.

"I ran the Chicago Public Schools bus service. Ten years."

"Two-bags clearly found me the best of the best." Dexter was indeed shocked that Two-bags provided actual bus drivers. The gang leader came through.

"Men, I'm going to clean up a bit, and we'll get rolling out."

The men nodded to Dexter. He walked behind one of the junked cars and changed out of his traditional clothes. Dex sported olive cargo pants and tactical boots. On his lap he held a folded navy-blue slicker coat that very much resembled an FBI raid jacket. Especially from a distance with its yellow iron-on FBI lettering.

From a small toiletry bag, he selected a pair of silver scissors and started in on his hair and beard. With a pile of snipped whiskers on the ground, he started lathering his face for a waterless shave. In minutes, he looked like most any other first responder. Most bystanders, however, wouldn't realize just how much he had a striking resemblance to his younger brother, Drake.

Chapter 85

Tresa met Jay just outside the hotel. The first item of business, she handed him a plastic laundry bag from the hotel closet. It was heavy and bulging. Sean Havens limped up to her side as Jay inspected the bag's contents.

The Chicago special agent rocked the bag to check out the contents without reaching in. "I see the guns, I see the IDs. That's a good start. Where are the clothes, and do you have a count on the ammo?"

"No," Halliday answered. Nor had she provided exactly all the guns nor extra magazines that Drake concealed. Her demeanor was convincing, however, and most importantly, Jay never had an exact inventory count.

"I don't know that we've formally met." Sean extended his good hand. "I'm one of those Mr. White guys."

Jay fake-laughed. "I should have known. Spooks."

"I'm afraid so. My colleague was getting frozen from Langley on his pursuit. He's been undercover for over a month in the city. Hunting men he hunted across the Middle East. Bad dudes. He took it upon himself to liberate the weapons and gear. I hold ultimate responsibility."

"But if I call anyone and say a Mr. White from the CIA authorized it, it goes nowhere. Even if you can't operate in the US, we clearly have no say. Chicago field office just needs to suck it up, right?"

"I can send you a coffee mug with a logo." Sean shrugged.

Jay waved it off, pissed.

"Cufflinks?"

Jay's cold glare showed Havens what he wanted to see. The man was in a stalemate.

"Jay, I can say this: we're here to help, or we're here to stay out of the way. I'll go ahead and send cufflinks *and* the mug."

Jay rubbed his face. "No weapons."

"Special Agent Halliday has her issued weapons. I have none. I'm just an advisor."

"And your boy? Where's he?"

"Among the crowd."

"You're telling me you're worried about a WMD and you have a guy in the middle of it?"

"He is the one person in this country who absolutely needs to be in the middle of things."

"Okay." Jay extended a hand. "Thanks for bringing these back. But I want everything before you leave. Even if it's shell casings and my SWAT guys' underwear."

"You got it."

"Anything you need from me?" Jay asked with full collaborative sincerity.

"Three pairs of your best binoculars and access to your snipers."

Jay gave Halliday a sideways glance.

"Give it to him," Halliday said to Sean.

Havens pulled out a thousand dollars cash and handed it to Jay. "You take your wife out as an apology, along with the two SWAT guys and their significant others, to a night at Gibson's on behalf of the Agency."

Jay smirked. "I got a law degree. Been with the Bureau almost twenty years. I ain't takin' your money. I'll let *you* take us all out for steaks. What happens to the bill is none of my business as long as it isn't taxpayer funds."

"I assure you, Havens is good for it," Tresa added.

Jay's head jerked to Sean. "You said Havens?" He gave Sean a hard look. "You used to live here?"

"Did." Sean nodded.

"Beverly?"

"Beverly."

"I remember that situation. Sorry for your loss." Jake initiated another handshake. "Let's get you some binos and linked up with our high eyes."

Chapter 86

The Modarris directed each bus to take a different route but had them converge on Michigan Avenue and roll up to the city's Art Institute museum. Dexter arrived on the final bus, lagging behind the others that weaved through the Loop to the destination. He opened his bus's back door, and as the children were brought around led by their driver, he handed them a large one-gallon Ziploc bag full of the yellow-gold powder. To his right was a large blue container.

"Do not open the bags until you are on the parade street," Dexter instructed. "To make it most colorful, toss the powder high into the air. And if you do a great job, you'll get a bonus."

With smiles and nods, the children were led in a group, according to the bus they were on, either left or right of the museum and toward the parade.

The bus drivers shuffled the kids toward their destination. One, however, continued to look back at Dexter as if he had some misgivings.

* * * *

Halliday raised her binoculars from a ten-story building just off East Balboa Drive. She was aligned to team Charlie on the southernmost end. Havens was on the mid-north end at Randolph, while Drake was atop the Art Institute's southeastern annex school, where he had a view of Jackson Boulevard, Monroe, and the Columbus parade route a few hundred meters away. From Tresa's view, every green shirt that had been on sale at Target, Kohl's, or Amazon was front and center at the parade. She watched as police cut through the crowds, turning away watchers with coolers, open alcohol, and or displays of sloppy intoxication.

* * * *

Havens had a similar view. The SWAT team sniper had a spotter, but both men were more concerned with their coffees. The scene was a complete counterterrorism security nightmare, but despite the threat, he missed going to the Chicago parades with his family and friends. His hand and foot ached. He'd lost so much in the past year. Gained nothing. For no one. Maggie, his daughter, was safe and thriving. But she was without her father and mother. The price he paid to protect strangers was to turn his back and fail to take care of his own. As he watched dozens of orange-bearded kids running toward the parade in leprechaun hats and green shirts, he found some solace in knowing that he was protecting them from the evil that men do. *Oh, to be a kid again.*

* * * *

Drake stayed away from the shooters to his right that Halliday assigned him to, after Jay was clear from seeing Woolf. The shooters had given Drake the up and down hairy eyeball. Fortunately, they weren't the two whose gear and clothes he had swiped. No doubt, they didn't appreciate his wearing an FBI raid jacket when he wasn't an agent. That or they had noticed the blackening blood spatter that Drake gave no mind to. It was okay. He wasn't going to talk to them anyway. Drake had taken another dose of meds and was fully appreciative of the quiet in his head short of the shrieks and groans of bagpipes.

He slung the binoculars over his head, letting them hang as he scanned the signals on his device. Nothing. Nowhere. He flipped through the app features, getting more distracted by the moment with all the capabilities literally at his fingertips. Hacking tools, IMSI catchers, and just as Mojo had said, he could even facilitate a remote, noncooperative penetration of an aircraft through radio-frequency communications, ACARS configurations, and satellite circuit mode supporting voice and data transmission broadcasts. All this he held in his palm. It was astounding, considering the loads of kit he humped around the desert for years.

Still, with all the technology that he had, it was people who made decisions. Hard decisions against other people who were acting on their own decisions and who could mobilize others for action. Yeah, that was why people called him. It wasn't that he didn't feel bad about killing, it was that he felt bad only *after* he had killed. It rarely stopped him beforehand.

Drake lifted his binoculars. *Where are the busses of kids? Where are masses of kids running with bombs?* K-9 units continued to sweep the area. He could see the dog handlers who were instructing people to not touch the dogs.

What had Mena said? Children were the first wave. Hundreds running at the enemy. The enemy was paralyzed to shoot. Then came the next wave. After the children had blown themselves up.

As he pondered, a yellowish puff of smoke rose through the crowd of people. And then another small cloud. The smoke rose slightly, spread, and then hovered. In other sections of the parade spectators, the plumes burst up above the people's heads then morphed into greater clouds, and more yellow poofed up from…from the children.

* * * *

The children were loving every minute of the attention they received crashing the parade. Kids and adults alike were smiling and pointing at their orange beards and green bowler hats. As they tossed Azrael into the air, the crowds reached for the yellow and golden powder swirling the clouds just overhead. Young children jumped to touch the magic golden leprechaun dust.

Then came the pain.

It started with light coughing. Then a tightening of the chest.

Eyes and noses started to water. Wiping them caused burning. The burning wouldn't stop. People were screaming. Shoving. Grabbing, running, trampling.

Chaos ensued.

The police tried to control the mass hysteria. They, too, shortly succumbed to the clouds that hung in the air and moved outward to those who stood idly by not knowing what was happening around them.

Drake watched dumbfounded. This was it. Azrael was spreading his wings. The angel of destruction and renewal. It hadn't come at the hands of a Hezbollah fanatic, a rogue nation state. It came from the hands of children laughing and playing, rejoicing in the euphoria of the freedom they were taking in. He witnessed the presence of evil and stood helplessly.

Chapter 87

The FBI sniper called to Woolf in terror. "What are we supposed to do? It's the WMD?"

The spotter slowly swung his scope. "It's kids. They're moving through the crowd. Luke, we can't shoot them."

The sniper, Luke, drew his weapon in. He peered through the scope. "They're going to take out the whole crowd. No one knows what's happening down the block. We can't let them keep going."

You have to take out the kids. Grab the weapon and do it. They'll kill everyone. Fifty or sixty kids are better than thousands. Go, Drake. Grab the weapon. If you don't, who will?

* * * *

Halliday saw the gradual eruption of yellow smoke emerging from the crowd. "Where's that cloud coming from? Did someone pull smoke?" she called to the FBI sniper.

The shooter was nuzzled to his weapon, the scope reticle trained on the hostile targets. The children. "Holy shit. It's kids. Kids are throwing the dust." He pulled away from the lens, staring helplessly at Halliday. "Are they the terrorists? Holy fuck!"

"Bro," said his spotter, "we gotta stop this."

The shooter peered through his glass. "The kids are smiling. I can't do it. Can't someone flash bang the area or shoot non-lethal bags?"

Halliday lowered her binoculars and could see with her naked eye a contained area of yellow haze that was spreading wide while rolling inward to the city. "We're not prepared for this."

* * * *

Havens, like the others, was stunned by what he was seeing.

The sniper, who had chosen a wind drift reticle, viewed the children through a combination of crosshair lines, dots, and horizontals. He had acquired the moving targets and established the city's wind drift. "The kids are unleashing something that's dropping everyone around them. Permission to engage," he called to his superior. He was as mechanical as his sitrep reports in the minutes prior.

His spotter pulled up from the view. "You can't shoot a kid."

"I'm not shooting a kid, I'm shooting a hostile threat."

The radio called back. "Do not engage. How copy?"

"Copy that. I'll await further, but it's not going to get better. You're wasting time."

"We're monitoring the situation."

"Just give the green."

Havens dialed his preset for Drake's device.

"Yeah, I'm seeing what you're seeing." Drake's voice was cool and deliberate. He offered nothing further.

"The snipers won't shoot. Or aren't authorized to shoot. I can't blame them," said Sean.

"Yeah, it would be a full-out panic if the crowd started seeing kids dropping dead from an active shooter threat, but it's spreading, Sean. People are going to get stampeded."

"Drake, this is weapons-grade material. They'll kill everyone down by the lakefront. Who knows how many more when it reaches the city and dissipates. Once it crosses Michigan Avenue, the buildings will create a vortex of wind and push the clouds high and low and into every HVAC for blocks."

"Windy City needs to blow this out to the lake."

"Well, Drake, that's not going to fucking happen, so try to wrap your head around something else. You're supposed to be the smart guy."

"Yeah. I am." Drake scanned as far as he could see of the crowds, the buildings, the lakefront. The skies. "Let me hang up. I need to call in an airstrike."

Chapter 88

Drake opened the Pitbull app. "C'mon, Mr. Worldwide."

"Dude," the sniper shouted. "Aren't you a counterterror advisor? You going to advise us or send texts? We're paralyzed trying to come up with something. CPD knows it's a chemical weapon or something, and they're only looking to maintain security so no one gets in. Bureau is already starting to set up emergency staging area down by McCormick Place."

"Cool. Now shut the fuck up."

"Cool?" The sniper flipped his head and body over to his spotter. "Did he just say *cool?*"

"And he told you to shut the fuck up. The guy's probably shitting his pants. Worthless, headquarters piece of shit. Probably calling his wife and kids saying he was going to die."

Drake turned to the north, orienting himself as he clicked the display of aircraft flight paths that fit into the thirty-mile-mark legend. Drake scanned the identifiers and outbound course. His fingers tapped on graphs of speed, altitude, and route by latitude, longitude and heading. Drake scanned a digital map warning to pilots, aware of horizontal reference loss at levels below 10,000 feet when hazy or overcast, and tried to factor how that would complicate his idea. The instrument procedures for departures concerning obstacles and vectors would be preset into the aircraft computers. He decided on two aircraft and scanned for their signal emissions and receipt. "Bingo."

Drake sat down as he loaded the scripts to infiltrate the aviation systems. The sniper again called out. "Seriously?"

Drake remained typing on his device, his head bowed over his computer exploits. "Dude, shut the fuck up, or you'll be sucking in a radioactive weapon that will have your insides liquidated in seconds." Whether that was true or not, Drake couldn't gave two shits. He needed to concentrate if he was going to hijack an airplane from scratch.

* * * *

Drake's first hack allowed him access to the communications system, taking full advantage of the commercial off-the-shelf components that he had penetrated in numerous other computer exploits over his legitimate years with JSOC's Intelligence Support Activity. The SQL programming script injection assaulted another computer system's lines of code, bypassing the encryption, and provided the Man from Orange visibility and control of the 747 aircraft.

Drake read the systems as he typed. *Box-IFE-SATCOM...interface Aeronautical Operational Control...fuck me, read only...ACARS system, okay here we go...flight management system...navigation...electronic interface autopilot...good...show me...yes, there you are, you little shit... command line kernel code...connect to IO bus...interface, yes...bypass centralized messaging unit...GIS data and navi...command instrument, you bitch...*

At eleven thousand feet and climbing, the pilot leaned forward. "AOC interface is changing something on the ACARS system."

"Probably data exchange. Didn't you verify it prior to takeoff?" The copilot picked at his finger, then took another little bite, spitting the splintered nail between his legs before attacking another digit.

"Yeah, but…whoa…we're leveling off. Are you doing this?"

The copilot leaned over slightly to give a curious look while chomping another nail. "Autopilot has us decreasing altitude. That's not right. Call control."

Drake rode the feed link into the control tower to feed the plane additional data, dropping altitude further and increasing the aircraft speed. "Okay, buddy, let's call the pilots with some bullshit excuse on why they're buzzing buildings and dropping to under a thousand feet at the lakeshore."

"Vacation Air 452, this is control tower Aurora, flight plan route change. We're changing your headings T six zero right and altitude due to unidentified airspace traffic at prior altitude setting. Switching to setting 0-6-7-2."

The pilot looked over to his mate wide-eyed. "Tower, that's a negative. You're sending us into skyscrapers." He gave a nervous laugh. "Complete violation of visual flight rules." The pilot pointed to the autopilot indicator.

"We're reprogramming coordinates or going manual. We're not seeing anything on collision avoidance system."

"Flight 452, you are on a set path over market given to us by…let's just say…defense authorities. We're trying to keep you out of the fray by descent according to the commo we're receiving."

The copilot's head was looking across the horizon and upward to see if he could glimpse anything out of the ordinary.

"Let the craft fly itself according to settings. System will be increasing speed to forty knots more than current setting. You'll feel like a wild ride, but it's the only way we can clear you of a potentially hostile aircraft above and interceptors who are coming in. Copy?"

"Aurora tower, are you saying what I think you're saying?"

The copilot asked, "How does tower have our system settings? Who's reprogramming?"

"Flight 452, all I can tell you is what I'm telling you. Maintain present heading. I've got you on radar as passing Willis Tower. We've got a few more to clear. Altimeter decreasing. You're going to have a visual of yellow smoke on the ground heading out to the lake. We're dropping you down with increased speed under the hazard area, then giving you a quick rise. There will be no other communications on this frequency."

"Uh, tower, I see the visual. We're not good with this. Trying to take controls. Everything is locked. I need a confirmation code from tower. This is highly irregular."

The pilot muted comms. "Any luck?"

"I'm trying to pull us off, but I can't. We've lost all instrument control. Yoke, flaps, rudders. Locked."

"I'm going to switch channels and declare emergency."

Chapter 89

Zarielle tripped on the street curb and fell to the ground. She dropped her bag of golden powder and looked up at the sea of green people before her. To her rear, in the haze of the yellow air, people were screaming and going crazy, running about in the street.

"You wanna get paid, you better finish." Kayjon reached down to help his eight-year-old friend to her feet. He scooped the bag just as Dantrell ran up and threw a handful of Azrael into their faces. The breeze lifted, but still, Kayjon and Zarielle started fitful coughs. Zarielle fluttered her hands. Her eyes burned so bad. She felt like her asthma had come back. She raised her head trying to open her airway.

"Girl, c'mon," Dantrell yelled, but her eyes couldn't focus. The more she rubbed, the worse they stung.

"Kayjon!" she screamed. "Kayjon!"

Dantrell was on his hands and knees, spitting and vomiting. His eyes were on fire.

Zarielle's screaming cut the air, but with the shouts and the shrill pitch of the bagpipes and Dantrell's own cry of pain and confusion, no one noticed the lone child as the masses rushed her way in a stampede.

Except Drake Woolf.

The Man from Orange panned the crowd and the yellow clouds with binoculars while the airliner sped toward their position.

The high-pitched ring of the jet turbine engines drawing closer caused many pedestrians to look up and scream in anticipation of an impending crash on the parade.

A glimpse of pink in the sea of green meant nothing at first when Drake scanned across. But then something clicked in his mind about the little girl tied to the bed in the Lawndale apartment. He refocused back to the pink and the flopping braids and then to the wave of crowd heading her way. Drake was three stories up. A questionable jump with the concrete below. The staircase was behind him yet had taken minutes to go down and around when he first ascended with the snipers.

Drake looked again to the ground and this time gave more thought to the scaffolding about ten feet under the ledge, but only a few two by fours made the platform, which gave Woolf a small margin of error not to miss or hit the edge and topple the structure over and crushing the construction pickup trucks below. "Fellas, I'm heading out. Cover your ears." He stepped up onto the ledge, readying for his jump.

The jumbo jet flew a mere couple hundred feet overhead, the wingtip vortices and wash blowing Drake over the edge with the short turbulence blast wake.

Chapter 90

Drake fell the thirty feet, missing the scaffolding and hitting the roof of a pickup cab, then falling over into the truck bed laden with construction waste. The truck cushioned some of the fall but still knocked the wind out of him and gave a good smack to the side of the head, but falling over and landing in the debris cut Drake's thigh and arm with a nasty slice from bent sheet metal. Still focused on the young girl, he didn't give a moment of thought to the pain and breathlessness as he rolled out and sprinted to those pink ribbons tying Zarielle's braids.

As Drake had calculated, the weight of the big jet, its airspeed and accelerated lift once it passed the skyscraper wind canyon funnels formed strong vortices of air turbulence that spun the yellow cloud upward in a trail sucked up and out toward the Lake Michigan waters. Still, some of Azrael was pushed down low and outward toward Drake. It clouded his vision and shifted the stampede's direction. The closer he got to the girl, the more people blocked his path. *Stay there, kid, I'm coming.*

Drake, we're going to die. It'll eat us to the bone. Do not go in there, the dark voice warned from nowhere. *Do not fucking go into that death trap. I'll kill you, so help me I will.*

Then let me do it first.

As he ran, shoving people along the way and dropping his shoulders to ram his azimuth trail, he recalled being out of his own body in the hospital. So many years ago, in Tunisia. He couldn't feel pain. He couldn't feel his body, but he had felt cold and alone. His parents were dead. And then he felt the warmth of Tom Mendle's hands wrapping around his. Tom was pleading with Drake to hang on. That everything would be okay. And suddenly, he didn't feel so chilled, nor did he feel the isolation.

Feet away, Woolf watched in horror as a small boy holding a yellow bag was tripped. The kid's plastic green hat rolled for but a second before it was stomped on and crushed. Woolf shifted back to the little girl from the apartment with those pink ribbons. She was gone. Drake hammered himself into the crowd and reached down to grab a fistful of the boy's shirt, yanking him up. The boy was still crying, which was a good sign. How badly he had been injured from being trampled was a question for the doctors if Drake could just get him to someone who could take him to care.

And then he saw the ribbons.

The small girl was scampering on her hands and knees toward an opening of free space. With the young boy tucked into Drake's side, he lowered his center of gravity to resist the flow of the crowd and made a beeline to the girl ten feet away.

* * * *

Special Agent Marcus Collier kept an eye on the crowd through his high-powered rifle scope. There was nothing he could do about the madhouse four hundred yards out from his position. All he could do was look for any UNSUB threat actors who were responsible or making matters worse.

Agent Collier was vaguely aware of the radiological threat but had no real clue about the severity. The yellow haze had to be it. He had given a silent prayer for their souls, and another prayer that the terrorists would come into his sights. When the jet passed overhead sucking the death cloud away, Collier saw another opportunity for a clear shot. He had one kill while on the Bureau's SWAT team. A pathetic drunk loser who had barricaded himself in a house with his fourteen-year-old stepdaughter. Collier had the drunk in his sights just as the FBI negotiator opened the front door to place a bag of food.

In Iraq, when a jihadi had a weapon, they were going to use a weapon. If you had a shot, you took the shot. And so, too, did Marine Corporal Collier, much to the surprise of everyone who had expected a more peaceful outcome before the back of the drunk's head blew apart.

Special Agent Collier received an official reprimand and many unofficial pats on the back, especially from those agents in the field office who had served in the sandbox.

Collier had mouths to feed back home, so when he first saw the yellow FBI letters running to the crowd, he kept his finger far and away from the trigger and gave a mental fist bump into the air for the hero running into the fray, yet when he saw the side of the man's face, his finger moved and he radioed for a request again to take the shot.

Chapter 91

"This is Bravo-3. Charlie-6, do you copy?"

"Good copy, Bravo-3. What's up?"

"CPD's suspect alert that matches our UNSUB is running to the crowd. He has a child in his arms. Looks like he's using the kid as a shield."

"Bravo-3, you're saying the UNSUB is involved in the WMD attack?"

"Can't be a coincidence. He just scooped up another kid, has both of them covering his body. He's looking around. Looks very suspicious."

"Bravo-3, does he have a weapon?"

"I don't have a visual, but from the video and photos CPD is circulating, I've got near certainty it's the guy who killed those people up north and stole my shit. We know he's armed and dangerous. This must be his end game."

"Too many people, Bravo-3. Stand down. We can't take that chance."

Shit.

* * * *

With both children in his arms, Drake tried to scan the area for an ambulance or first responders who were actually responding and not watching from a safe distance. The yellow haze burned his eyes like tear gas and burned his lungs nearly the same.

To his right, four school busses pulled up to the parade blockade. Officers swarmed the busses while the lead driver leaned out the window, pointing to the crowds. Drake saw the series of nods all around, and then the officers moved the barricades and started waving people over. The busses pulled to the sides of the street. CPD all-terrain vehicles sped up to the front of the lead bus and started to clear a path.

Officers directed scores of people carrying their children to get them onto busses where they could be taken to the aid station at McCormack Place a mile away.

Dantrell pulled his head from Drake's chest. His eyes were puffy and bloodshot, but they were open and he was looking around. "Those are our busses." He pointed.

Zarielle lifted her head, too. Her face was a mess of tears, mucus, and yellow stains. "We painted them."

"Who had you paint them, sweetie?"

"Two-bags," she said, "and him." Zarielle pointed.

Drake squinted at the lead driver waving a blue-jacketed arm, heralding people onto the bus. He couldn't make out the other drivers.

The voice of Drake's father entered his consciousness. *First wave. Second wave, Drake.*

Now filled, the lead bus started to move. The driver waved to an officer, looked over the crowd, and in the opening where Drake stood, they made eye contact.

Dexter.

The Modarris, Dexter Woolf, smiled at Drake. His arm out the opening, Dex gave a slow wave below the window.

"Can you walk?" he asked the kids, setting them down. They both nodded. Drake set them down, but Dantrell screamed in pain and collapsed, holding his leg.

An officer jogged toward Drake.

Drake stepped out as the officer neared. "FBI, I need you to help these two kids," Drake shouted to the blue. "His leg may be broken, maybe internal injuries. I have to go after that bus."

"Don't touch the blue barrels," Zarielle warned. "They can blow up."

Drake pulled his weapon.

High above, Special Agent Collier still had Woolf in his sights. "This is Bravo-3, suspect is pulling a weapon at CPD. The kids are out of his reach. I'm clear for a shot."

"Take the shot, Bravo-3."

Chapter 92

Tresa Halliday had just panned to the movement of the lead bus and caught a glimpse of pink and the yellow FBI letters that drew her attention. An agent was putting the children down and talking to an officer. *Drake.* There was some brief discussion; then Drake looked to a bus and withdrew a gun.

The next thing she knew, Drake Woolf's legs were up in the air, arms outstretched as he flew backward.

"Drake!" she shouted.

"What?" the sniper to her right called over.

"Stop it. He's one of us. Don't shoot. Who's shooting?" she screamed.

The sniper called back. "Bravo-1 to Bravo-3. Hold fire. Repeat. Hold fire. Friendly was just shot."

* * * *

Drake gasped for a breath. His whole midsection felt compressed. He waited for those hard-ass punches to continue, but in the moment that he lay there holding himself, they never came.

"Warren!" a voice shouted.

He raised his head to the calls.

Dexter's expression was blank, then he smiled. The Modarris waved his arm. Beckoning Drake to follow. "Let's go. Get in a bus!"

Dazed, Drake looked around again, his breathing becoming easier. He patted his vest, which now had multiple holes. It was toast. The next impact could find promise.

"You're that guy," the cop realized as he took the children and gave Drake a closer look. "You're that fucking guy that shot Detective Daniels."

Drake popped to his feet. "No, man. One of the good guys. And there's a bomb on that bus." Woolf scooped up his weapon and jetted for the busses.

Dexter accelerated and followed the police escort.

Drake waved to the blues on the street. "There's a bomb on the bus. Don't let them go. Stop the busses!"

The officers shouted to other officers within earshot. "Take him down. He shot the detective!"

"Stop the fucking bus!" Drake sprinted to the second bus, pointing his weapon at the driver, who hit the brakes and lifted his hands.

"Get out of the fucking bus!" Drake moved around and directed the nearest officers. "Get them out of the busses." They remained conflicted by what an officer was yelling and what an FBI agent was ordering.

The middle-aged African American bus driver stepped out. "Don't shoot! I'm coming. I don't have a bomb." Woolf yanked him down to the ground.

The other officers just stood around and started gathering and pointing once they pieced things together. "They're saying that's the fucking guy. That's the shooter from up north."

Oh, shit. "Stop those busses. There are blue barrels in back with explosives!" Drake shouted.

As they turned, Drake jumped up and into the driver's seat and floored it to catch Dexter.

From a side mirror he saw some officers boarding the bus, while others withdrew their weapons, eyes trained on him as he drove away. CPD hindered only because of the amount of people behind Drake as he sped off.

Drake floored the bus down Columbus Drive. *He's headed to the emergency staging ground at McCormick Place.* From what Halliday had said, an assistance center would be set up by FBI victim services division immediately, and a number of emergency responders and FBI agents would be congregating to receive casualties and direct family members.

What are you doing, Dex?

He played you, Drake, the dark voice chastised. *Check, check, checkmate to you. You lose. It's been him all along. He killed your parents. He tried to kill you.*

Drake pulled his phone out of a pocket to call Havens.

"Hey, I hoped it was you," Sean answered. "Halliday says you got shot and now you're on a bus?"

"I'm alive. Sean, I think my brother is the operative. He's heading to the victim area. I've got a big blue barrel in the back here, and I can see through the glass, he has one up in front too. I have no idea what the trigger mechanism could be. Probably cellular."

"Can you get in front or stop him?"

"I have a bus full of people. So does he."

"Fuck. You think he's going to ram something or detonate?"

"No clue." Drake turned to the rear. "Is there anything electronic on the blue barrel?" Woolf shouted to the back of the bus. From the back window he saw the red-and-blue lights of a police SUV fast approaching.

"Wires and a cell phone all taped and wrapped," someone from the rear shouted up. "Are we going to blow up?"

"Yeah, Sean. Wires and a receiver. Get Mojo to shut the frequency."

"You can't without shutting off a grid, can you?"

"He should be able to pinpoint the signal emissions around me. Just until we can stop these busses and get them away from more crowds. I'm about five minutes out."

"Drake, we need to take out the driver before he gets close. You need to stop your bus."

"Focus them on taking him out. Get Mojo now. I'm still too close to people along the road. It clears out in another hundred yards."

Drake hung up and tried calling the number he had been surveilling.

"Little brother," the voice answered. "You did great back there, War."

"Dex, what are you doing?"

"What has to be done. But much less than you are assuming."

"Dex, stop the bus."

"I can't. They're watching."

"Who?"

"The world's stage."

"Dex, why are you doing this? You used me. You were the one all along."

"Nothing is as it seems, Warren. You need to make it out. I need you to take care of something for me. You'll find the details on the saved voice memo. I know you have access, and I left it for you. Goodbye, brother."

"Dex!"

* * * *

"We can take them both out as they hit McFetridge Drive," the CPD commander informed Jay by radio.

"Don't shoot our guy," Halliday pushed back. "We'll clear it up after we get this sorted, but our guy has saved thousands of lives. He is not a threat."

"Just tell us what bus and which guy he is," the commander radioed back.

"He's wearing a blue raid jacket."

The commander transmitted the description to his men along the route.

"They're both wearing raid jackets," he informed Jay and Halliday.

"The lead bus is the one to take out," Halliday directed.

"Take out the lead," said Jay.

"The lead bus," the commander called out. He turned to Jay. "We're lining some of the wagons along the sides of the offramp. It should slow the speed and funnel the bus to a stop."

"There is no lead bus. They're side by side. Hard to tell. A CPD unit is in pursuit. Sounds like the busses are jockeying back and forth," the radio squawked.

"They're side by side," Jay relayed to Halliday.

"Let me call." Halliday received a dead signal response. *The phones are killed.*

"Special Agent Halliday, we have to make a decision."

Woolf had body armor on, but they had to take whatever shot they had. It could be a head shot, she rationalized to herself. *Drake, please be wearing your vest.*

"Special Agent Halliday!"

It was an impossible decision. "Can you take them both without a head shot?"

"We're under an attack by terrorists. I'm not askin' if you want a wing or a leg," Jay responded. "We have to stop this now. Commander, have them take the shots."

"You have approval to take them both out," he ordered.

Halliday lifted he binoculars in vain. Just to see him one last time. He'd be clucking away like his own time bomb. "His mouth. Wait. The guy clicking his mouth open in patterns of three. Don't shoot the guy whose mouth is moving. Patterns of three."

Unsure of what he was relaying, Jay ordered, "Don't shoot the guy moving his mouth in patterns of three. The guy moving his mouth in Morse code is not the target."

* * * *

Drake raced parallel to his brother. He couldn't just stop. Dexter wouldn't look over and held his eyes straight ahead.

Woolf could see police lining the street, their vehicles wedging the road to a narrow opening ahead. Their weapons were raised at the busses.

Look over, Dex. Look at me. He's gone, Drake, let him go, the voice of his father encouraged in his mind. *He was already gone.*

Drake looked again to his left. Dexter's hand had dropped. Through the door windows he could see Dex slightly raising his hand goodbye. The fingers suddenly splayed out.

The window was sprayed with red. Again. And again. Dex gyrated but gripped the wheel, intent on driving the bus in control toward the center of the aligned vehicles.

Drake braked as the road narrowed, slowing to a stop as Dex's bus hit and scraped against the paddy wagons slowly coming to a halt, at which time it was swarmed with police.

Drake ran to the back of his own bus, sending people running out the door as he passed their seats. *What's the hurry?* he thought. *The radiation's going to kill us anyway.*

Once at the barrel, Drake inspected the device and wiring.

The phone was powered off. Wires were wrapped around the device, but their connections were free. From a circuitry perspective, the bomb was benign. From the windows, Drake could see FBI agents talking to police and pointing to the bus.

Drake shrugged off his jacket and placed a discarded green hat and beads from a seat on himself and exited with the last passengers. He hurried into the crowd that was directed toward the museum campus along with the other flow of people directed toward the emergency triage area.

Chapter 93

Were it not for the CPD helmet and jacket lying on top of the police four-wheeler, Drake probably wouldn't have considered stealing the quad as he searched for a way out.

The death of his brother was an odd relief, and yet Drake still had questions. Questions, however, could wait. As far as he was concerned, there were no more major threats. And if there were more tangos readying up another wave of attacks, he sure as hell was tapped out on who and where they could be. He'd done more than his fair share as an individual and had little more to give.

It had only happened a few times in his multiple tours that the lost innocence or life of a child hit him hard. That little girl with the pink ribbons got to him. There was nothing more that he could do for her. They were all doomed from the radioactive dust, so if he could do anything at all, it would be to find Two-bags.

Drake slid on the police jacket and helmet, fired up the ATV and its emergency lights, and bolted out through the exit with no nods, waves, or slowing down. It was back into the shit before his face peeled off or he became a pool of Jell-O in the road. A killer he was, nuclear scientist he was not. The Man from Orange focused on what was within his power, and that was dealing more death before he, himself, succumbed to radiological poisoning.

Within minutes of screaming emergency vehicles passing Drake in the opposite direction, he found an area to duck into and assess his target. Between the phone of Oz, the hacked device data from Dexter, and the signals intel from Mojo, Drake was fairly certain that he had captured and tracked the correct signal for Two-bags. Woolf zeroed in on the location transmission depicted on his mapping display and determined that the gang leader was driving only a few miles away. The area, however, looked fairly commercial, which would pose a problem for an outright assassination in broad daylight. Rest assured, most police presence was attending to the parade scene.

Still, Drake knew he needed to divert or follow Two-bags to a more accommodating location. How that would happen, he didn't know. His thoughts moved to the last moments he saw Dexter. How did this all happen and why?

At that moment, he recalled what Dex had said about checking the voice memo. *Nothing is as it seems.* Drake opened the partitioned segment in his device to view Dexter's applications. He selected the Voice Memos with a time-stamped note from the morning. Woolf rotated his head around to ensure he was still in the clear from prying eyes. Fear gripped his insides from what he could hear in the seven-minute message. Drake took a deep breath and pressed play.

Chapter 94

Drake fought the urge to play the message again. He had work to do. A lot of work to do to finish his business in the city and head for Syria. As the tears rolled down his cheeks and pooled in his eyelids, he located Two-bags's position. Drake wiped his eyes and drove off, his wide open-mouthed smile catching the cool air as he sped along.

Dexter had much to say. The priority was Two-bags, then locating the actual radioactive material in the junk area of the parking lot, and finally finishing business in Two-bags's theater where the gang would be preparing for war. After that, he would plan for the Middle East.

Woolf made a series of turns, winding him further into the west side's more economically challenged neighborhoods. Checking his tracker, Two-bags was on the move not far ahead.

The day was cool, and the streets were fairly empty in Lawndale. Those who were out on the corners and storefronts or sitting on sidewalk steps had their eyes to the numerous helicopters flying around the lakefront area. Many of the young thugs, according to Dexter's message, would be at or heading to Two-bags's gang hideaway. All except Two-bags, who was still making his runs before it was time.

Drake watched the target's dot slide from Central Park Avenue to 15th on the map. Looking up and ahead, he saw the white BMW make the turn, ironically making a turn again onto S Drake Avenue.

How poetic, Drake thought as he saw the street sign.

The fact that the driver had just rolled through stop signs gave Woolf an idea and opportunity.

Drake flipped the emergency lights on with his thumb and sped up to the slowing car. He figured that it would be a dangerous approach, but he had few options. Fortunately, he had multiple weapons and spare mags. Woolf slid one of the handguns from the small of his back to his lap before dismounting. He checked the magazine just to make sure and that there was one in the pipe. Drake cocked the weapon, palmed in his hand, as he dismounted and approached the vehicle.

Drake stepped up to the driver's-side passenger door and knocked on the window. The window didn't move.

Drake knocked again.

The driver's side rolled down.

Drake remained in his position along the back-window frame of the door. "License and registration, please," he called out.

"Come up here, officer. I can't hear you so well," the voice called out.

Drake could see the man's face in the side mirror. Woolf had wanted a quiet area off the beaten path, yet realized it benefited the hunted, as well.

Fuck it. "I'm just looking at these holes in the passenger door. Looks like someone shot at you. Are you all right?" Woolf played.

"Huh?" The man stuck his head out and around.

Woolf swung the weapon out and extended it within a foot of the man's head and pulled the trigger, the muzzle lined to the temple. The driver's head bounced, and life sprayed out the forehead to the ground. It dangled out the window, dripping on the asphalt below.

Drake backhanded the weapon into the tinted glass, shattering the window, but the plastic tint coating held it in place. He fired a round into the back seat, unsure of the damage he inflicted on the passenger. The response was a burst of returned fire.

Drake dropped to the ground and replayed the pop, pop, pop then pop, pop, pop in his head to ensure he had the count. He reached up again to the window, which was well-torn but still covering top to bottom, and smashed at it again, trying to draw more undisciplined fire.

Two rounds popped off, then gold.

The passenger's gun came out of the window.

Like a viper, Drake struck at the weapon with his open left hand.

The semiautomatic weapon fired as Drake grabbed the burning hot metal and the slide jerked back, the accessories rail cutting his thumb with the recoil. He lost his grip, but so had the passenger.

Done, motherfucker. Drake sprung up, and an unexpected round smashed into the side of his helmet, knocking him backward into the bloody head of the driver. *FUCK!*

Drake dropped again as two more rounds cracked off. The sound different this time. A revolver. He knew there was just one person in the back, but obviously they had a backup weapon.

Woolf unbuckled his helmet and threw it into the broken passenger-side window.

The pops continued even as the helmet sailed backward and back out the window from the bullet impacts.

And then Woolf heard the music of roundless clicks as the cylinder spun in dry fire impotency.

Drake rose and calmly reached into the passenger side, unlocked and opened the door.

"Yo, yo, yo," Two-bags shouted. "I'm cool. I'm cool."

"Get out of the car," Drake ordered, his tone measured and cool.

Two-bags turned to the door.

"This way," Drake clarified. "Slide out. This way."

"Okay, okay, I'm coming. I surrender. All good, know what I'm sayin'. We all good. I'm cool."

As Two-bags's feet hit the ground, Drake asked, "Are you shot? Bleeding?"

"Yeah, man. On my side, but it's cool. Just get me to the hospital, an' we all good. You just call an ambulance, and I won't give you no troubles, know what I'm saying?"

"I don't give a fuck. I just don't want blood on the outside of the car any more than there is." Drake looked around at the few buildings surrounding him that weren't boarded up. Only a few faces were exposed behind windows. Some stood along the corners of the buildings, a safe distance away. Woolf kept Two-bags in the car; the gun remained pointed at the gangster. "This lot where you kept the busses. Is it guarded?"

"Naw, man. E'rybody's out today."

"Is it locked? Chained?"

"Naw, man, it's our turf. No one gonna come round there and steal no junk. Hey, you need to call me the ambulance so I don't motherfuckin' bleed out an' shit, know what I'm sayin'? You popped me right on my side."

"Get out. Get on the ground. And don't touch the side of the car with your hand."

Two-bags did as he was told. He put his hands behind his head, as if he'd done this before. But he'd never been arrested by the Man from Orange.

"How many people are waiting in your little theater or whatever it is?"

"How you know about that shit?"

Drake kicked the thug in the ribs.

"All of 'em. I told all of 'em."

"How old are they?"

"Fuck, man. How I supposed to know. Niggas be all ages."

Drake kicked him again, cognizant of the growing eyes in windows and slowing cars that chose not to turn down the street where the blue lights were still flashing.

"Kids?"

"Man, there be little Gs. I don't know."

"Well that means I can't blow the place up like my brother intended. Also seems to be against what my new doctor friend Patches would do to wayward kids. But you're not a kid." Drake extended the handgun to Two-bags's head and pulled the trigger, not waiting for a response.

Woolf yanked the dead security chauffer out of the car, flopping him to the ground, and discarded the police jacket over their bodies. Looking at the light spray of blood on the side of the car, he was content enough that spatter was better than smear and headed to the empty lot location.

Chapter 95

Halliday and Havens stood by Jay and another agent at the emergency response staging area, staying clear of the first responders and keeping an eye out for Drake Woolf. It had been an hour and still no word from Drake.

"Still no word from your techie on Drake's position?" Halliday asked. Her arms were crossed, her brow rigid. She looked like a pissed-off mom waiting impatiently for a kid who was late from the playground.

"Nope. No word. Drake disabled the location tracking. He's using a secure channel to mask his signal, too, so we can't even use big brother's eyes and ears. We just need to wait."

"It's not?" the agent with Jay responded on his cell phone to another conversation. "Indian spices and pepper oil?" He rolled the mouthpiece outward and turned to Jay and the others. "It's not radioactive. The WMD powder. They don't have a full report but it's a hoax. It's spice powders and something like a mace pepper oil."

Havens and Halliday looked at each other in disbelief.

"Why?" Havens asked rhetorically.

"Where's the real WMD?" Halliday asked.

The agent was back on the phone. "Jay, they're requesting available resources to head over to the Venezuelan embassy."

Jay shrugged. "What embassy? The Venezuelans have an embassy in Chicago?"

"Civic Opera House." The agent added, "They have a floor in the building. Two containers marked *Radioactive Waste: Store for Decay* stolen from the university were found within the doors of the Venezuelan embassy. Police got a call about that and a bomb in Lawndale at a theater. CPD is responding to a call on a gang and sending over SWAT and EOD.

But they need help making sure the opera house has some help to secure for hazmat and to start an investigation. Power is completely knocked out in the building."

Sean turned to Halliday. "Power's knocked out where WMD mysteriously appears? Still wondering where he is?"

"I think our work's done."

"*Our?*"

She gave a sheepish grin.

"Let's lose the raid jackets and your service pistol in a Bureau truck. I'll have Mojo see if we can get into the FBI system and backdate a lost or stolen report for your weapon.

"And then?"

"We walk across the expressway, and I show you the Weather Mark Tavern. We eat and get drunk. You head back to DC tomorrow, and I go break the news about Lars to my daughter."

"And Drake?"

"I'm sure he'll turn up when we least expect it."

* * * *

Sebastian Haggerty leaned in to his laptop, squinting to read his last line item on the program proposal to justify the budget. His elbows rested on the leather pad, which covered only a third of the large oak desk. He revised the document, adding another capability of the task force that would enhance the domestic program, especially if it reinvigorated the full capacity of the prior Intelligence Support Activity unit, but reestablished under the umbrella of the National Security Agency. And his direction.

Sebastian turned to sip his tea and glance at the continued coverage of the Chicago terror attack. He looked around his home office searching for the television remote control so he could better hear the breaking details of the Venezuelan embassy being involved with the now-recovered radioactive materials. The story was hours old to the intelligence community, and he had already received the intel through a secure National Security Council alert.

Sebastian stretched his legs, swaggering to the overstuffed leather couch where he found the flipper and turned up the sound. *The sweet sound of success,* he thought as he sat back at the desk to proofread his work before sending it to the director.

A small text box had appeared in the middle of Sebastian's laptop screen. It was outlined in a thick red border with the header "Birddog Secure Messaging." It had a beige lock symbol in the corner. A text appeared:

"I have taken back the control of operational funds, which I see you have transferred into personal offshore accounts."

Every few seconds thereafter, the message disappeared and a new one emerged.

"Tsk. Tsk."

"I have made screenshots and will forward to the FBI, DSS and the NSA Inspector General."

"The Task Force will remain. Autonomously. In support of the NSA, CIA, and the FBI."

"$1M still in your accounts. Will add $1M annually for your continued cooperation."

"You WILL ensure that Mena and Dexter receive memorial wall stars at Langley."

"Mojo stays with us but at Fort."

"I'm alive. Stay clear and give top cover and you stay out of jail and alive."

"Now delete the proposal and don't draw attention to yourself."

"D."

Sebastian held his breath throughout the rolling real-time transcript.

After a few moments, when the messages stopped, the screen box disappeared. A Windows prompt emerged, stating, "A fatal error has occurred. Would you like to reboot your system? Press to continue."

Sebastian slowly closed his laptop and walked out of the room while dialing his handler at the British Secret Intelligence Service, affectionately known as MI6.

Chapter 96

St. Patrick's Day didn't stop in the city. Whereas Sean and Tresa were able to belly up and get a seat at the bar while there was still calamity going on outside, five hours later, they remained eating burgers, pretzel bites, and drinking beer like old war buddies.

Halliday slurred her words after the last shot. Havens was outright shitfaced, and waving his bandaged hand like an Irish pirate saying "argh" was only getting old to those around the two but was still hilarious to Tresa and Sean.

"Yer a good-looking guy, Mr. Havens." She pushed on his shoulder and held his gaze with a hunger for what wasn't on the menu.

Sean dropped his foot off the stool to keep from falling off. "I'd do you, too, Halliday, if it wasn't for this." He held up his empty ring finger and pointed to where a band could be.

"You're not married? That's good."

"I still am." His head swayed back and then rolled to the side. "Right here." He thumped at his heart. "I will always be married to her. Christina."

Sean gave Halliday a push with his arm. "And I know you still like our boy."

Tresa laughed and turned her face away. She covered her mouth then reached for the pint of Harp. She pounded the beer then slammed it down on the bar. "Fuck Drake Woolf. He can…just go to hell."

Sean put his arm around her and leaned in. "Don't say that. He's a good man."

Havens struggled to keep his eyes open. "And you'd be good for him, too. If you don't arrest him." Sean burst out laughing. Tresa followed suit.

"And you, Mr. Havens," she added, still bursting with laughter. "Careful or I'll cuff you."

"Me? I'm not a killer, I'm a pirate!"

"Argh!" she yelled, falling into Sean. Seconds later, Halliday remained with her head on his shoulder. "I think he's crazy. I've never seen such rage before. Sometimes he's so connected then the next minute he's like there but not there."

"Marcus Aurelio's said—"

"Aurelio's? Aurelio's is a pizza place. You mean Aurelius?"

"Quiet. As I was saying, Marcus Aurel-ius the guy from *Gladiator* said something like, 'How much worse is the anger than the causes of it.'"

Sean tossed his hands up. "Right? Is he bad? Or, is what caused it bad?"

Tresa took another drink. "I think I love him and I don't even know him."

"You should tell him. Drake. Not Marcus Aurelio's the pizza gladiator," Sean slurred.

"I can't. I don't even know his number. And he hates me." She reached to the bar where her phone was. "Ow. Shit. My phone's burning up. Like on fire."

Sean reached across his body to grab her smartphone with his good hand. "Whoa." He looked at it, pulling it back and forth to focus. "Your battery's almost dead."

"It was just halfway charged a little bit ago." She raised it closer to her face, talking into the screen. "Drake Woolf, where are you?"

A person's phone rang behind Tresa. Then the bartender's. The people to their left and right. Soon, the whole bar was a symphony of bell tones, vibrations, and rings playing over the Irish tunes. Tresa looked at her phone. It went black. Then reappeared with a screen wallpaper selfie of Drake Woolf and their backs and the bar behind him.

"Click, click, click," she heard and turned just as a gentle hand lay on her shoulder and the lights in the bar went out.

Epilogue

Four days later.

At Tanf, Syria

"Haji Qasem." Soleimani's guard jogged up to join him in the walk back to another heavily fortified building within the fence line and auspices of a Syrian construction site. A second armed guard caught up in silence behind them.

"Sometimes a man just enjoys the solitude of the night even when the wolves are just beyond the gate." Soleimani shoved his hands in his loose pant pockets.

Within a matter of steps, Soleimani heard two near-simultaneous suppressed metal movements before his guard fell forward, and a muffled thud from behind told him he was now standing alone in the darkness.

"The Man from Orange," Soleimani said. "It wasn't necessary for you to kill them. They were good men, Warren Woolf. Innocent men, with families."

"That's a pretty great magic trick coming up with my name. And which of your men are you speaking of. I've killed many of them lately," Woolf said in passable Persian and pressed his weapon into the general's back. "Walk over there." The gun moved and hit Soleimani's right shoulder, guiding the man with the press to his left.

"We tried to stop the attack. You killed our messengers."

"I killed illegal Iranian operatives on US soil. You should have sent a message instead."

"It was an unfortunate position. I don't need to explain geopolitics to you."

"You don't need to explain anything."

"I enjoyed my time with your brother. Of course, it wasn't until recently that we discovered the relationship. It was brought to my attention that for years of tracing communications of one of our assets who continuously searched for a Warren Woolf, that it was the Modarris. Right from under our nose. We did not do a good enough job finding out who he truly was. Our Hezbollah resources are very good at capturing their own SIGINT from their networks. It was difficult to make the association since your brother was using a name given to him from the French Foreign Legion. Truly brilliant cover. But when another individual was in the same regions also searching for another man. The pieces came together nicely."

"It doesn't matter now."

"I think it does. Did your brother not speak of our relationship?"

"He said to ask you about North Carolina and then kill you. What are you supposed to tell me about the soldiers you killed at Bragg?"

The IRGC general rose his hands and slowly started to turn around. "I won't resist, but I want to tell you face to face."

"Works for me."

The small man turned and kept his hands up. His features were hollow, almost ghostlike with the deep-set cold predator eyes of a shark, and yet there was a very approachable aspect in his body language and how the general held his head. "There is a new threat in your Fort Bragg area. But it is no threat from our people. Nor is it from the ISOF soldiers and so-called Mohawks. Their actions against the soldiers' children in Fayetteville was inexcusable. But this new finding of ours is a threat from your own."

"My own what?"

"Your own kind, Mr. Woolf. Your own people are your greatest threat. You are a nation divided. A people with evil intentions. People who look for outside assistance to solve their problems in America."

"Lies. I'm supposed to believe the bullshit you're spilling just to keep you alive? I'm in the fucking presence of evil."

"Presence of evil." Soleimani laughed. "No matter your philosophy or belief, the existence of evil cannot be reconciled by the mind or the heart. No, Mr. Woolf. There is no evil in Iran, just as I cannot rationalize you as being spawn of the Satan in America. And yet, if I assess the battle damage in your city of Chicago, it is you, Mr. Woolf, who inflicted the greatest loss of lives and injury. You and you alone. Who is the evil one, Mr. Woolf? Who terrorized Chicago? Who violated the laws of your land and the rules of engagement?" Soleimani cocked his head, ending the Socratic lecture.

Drake found no words with the truthful accusation and reality laid at his feet.

"And I provided my leader with an attack, which appeased his appetite while not inflicting mass casualties, appeasing mine. While we have our own outward Cold War, we will comply with our arrangement and continue to feed your country intelligence as we have done for years. Just as your Israeli counterparts do. It keeps a balance in the Middle East. I had preferred to work through your brother, for obvious reasons. But now, it can be you. I will go through my channels to inform Thomas Mendle. He can work out the details."

Tom Mendle?

"It is well past my bed hour. We will be in touch." Soleimani slowly turned back around, his arms still raised. "And Mr. Woolf, please do not kill any more of my guards. My promise stands of your safe passage. How else could you have gotten in and so close to me?"

"It's my job."

"Just as it is my job to know what rooftop you are on in refugee camps, and what electronic devices you leave behind in homes, and when you are electronically stealing my money from bank accounts your treacherous uncle guided you to. There are costs and prices to war. And someday I will expect your support in return."

Drake raised his pistol toward Qasem and put his finger on the trigger. "Fuck you."

A spotlight burst into the night. Then another. And another.

Woolf fired four shots blindly at the commander. He waited for the thump of a dead man's fall but heard nothing.

Soleimani laughed somewhere off in the distance, but Woolf could see nothing in the blinding white of the high-intensity spotlights. "Safe passage, Birddog. Mr. Man from Orange."

Qasem Soleimani was gone. Drake Woolf was left with only a small nugget about a new terror threat to Pineland and a head full of voices with questions ravaging his mind about the next collision course he would embark upon.

The End

Acknowledgements

I hope my writing is improving. As you know, it takes a ton of time, research, edits, discussions with others, and sacrifices for many. Thanks to my wife and kids who are both encouraging and tolerant of my time at the computer terminal and my random thoughts on using something for a book idea.

The panel of writing and story experts that I lean on, Josh Hood, Mark Greaney, and Joe Goldberg, similarly remain steadfast in their availability for discussions. Thanks for the lengthy chats and spit balling of ideas, guys. My old friend, Cal Pickup, was also a huge help with some of the air traffic vetting and linking me up with some other industry experts to explore the realm of possibilities in flight diversions. "Margarita Ken," the man with his finger on the red button provided some of the radiological insights. He represents the nuclear engineer role in my neighborhood crew, and similarly didn't divulge anything inappropriate but ensured I used correct concepts.

And then there's Bodo, who most thriller writers know as a community power reader and enthusiast. Throwing some draft pages his way are always helpful for mid-writing feedback. Similarly, Kat Herrin, is my ace in the hole for general tone and flow of the story and some great input on Tresa Halliday's character.

Thanks to those guys in Lawndale who came up to my car while I was nosing around their turf doing research. You didn't shoot me, I didn't shoot you, we're good. No more Lawndale settings, I promise.

To the men and women of CPD and Chicago FBI field office thanks for all you do and for allowing me to pull caricatures from some of your personalities, which I hold respectfully and endearing and have taken extreme liberties to fit the narrative. Especially one of you who is my liaison partner.

Within the story is also some fancy gear. Thanks to Michael de Geus with Leatherback Gear who let me bang on a Civilian One bulletproof backpack that Drake used and that Mena should have worn as a hat. Sonitus Technologies was kind enough to let me reference and detail some of the commercial specs of their "Molar Mic" intro-oral sensor platform for real-time wireless commo. Yep. It's real stuff.

To the book people: Thanks to my agent, John Talbot, and to my editor Gary Goldstein at Kensington. I also can't thank Elizabeth May who will still respond to me when I have yet another small manuscript change or question. Lisa Gilliam, thanks for taking some extra time to discuss some of the edits and helping me understand what I can do better the next time. It was a pleasure working on this manuscript with you. And thanks in advance to Renee Rocco and the Lyrical Underground crew for putting the final touches on this work before it reached the hands and hearts of readers.

Finally, thanks to the Publication Review Boards of the Department of Defense, Central Intelligence Agency, and National Security Agency for their time to review the material before any of you could, so it was appropriate to share as entertainment and a small glimpse of what may or may not be in the shadows.

About the Author

J.T. Patten worked for the government and military community in support of national defense and policy. He has a degree in Foreign Languages, a Masters in Strategic Intelligence, graduate studies in Counter Terrorism from the University of St. Andrews, and numerous expertise certifications in intelligence analysis, cyber forensics, mobile device tracing, and financial crime investigations. For more, visit jtpattenbooks.com or find him on Twitter @JTPattenbooks.

Made in the USA
Middletown, DE
18 August 2019